T0300589

MEDUSA

MEDUSA

NATALY GRUENDER

GRAND
CENTRAL

NEW YORK BOSTON

Copyright © 2024 by Nataly Gruender

Cover art and design by Phil Pascuzzo.
Cover copyright © 2024 by Hachette Book Group, Inc.

Grand Central Publishing
Hachette Book Group
1290 Avenue of the Americas, New York, NY 10104
grandcentralpublishing.com
@grandcentralpub

First Edition: August 2024

Grand Central Publishing is a division of Hachette Book Group, Inc. The Grand Central Publishing name and logo is a trademark of Hachette Book Group, Inc.

The publisher is not responsible for websites (or their content) that are not owned by the publisher.

The Hachette Speakers Bureau provides a wide range of authors for speaking events. To find out more, go to hachettespeakersbureau.com or email HachetteSpeakers @hbgusa.com.

Grand Central Publishing books may be purchased in bulk for business, educational, or promotional use. For information, please contact your local bookseller or the Hachette Book Group Special Markets Department at special.markets@hbgusa.com.

Print book interior design by Marie Mundaca

Library of Congress Cataloging-in-Publication Data
Names: Gruender, Nataly, author.
Title: Medusa / Nataly Gruender.
Description: New York, NY : GCP, 2024.
Identifiers: LCCN 2023049612 | ISBN 9781538765340 (hardcover) | ISBN 9781538765364 (ebook)
Subjects: LCSH: Medusa (Gorgon)--Fiction. | LCGFT: Mythological fiction. | Novels.
Classification: LCC PS3607.R716 M43 2024 | DDC 813/.6--dc23/eng/20231031
LC record available at https://lccn.loc.gov/2023049612

ISBNs: 9781538765340 (hardcover), 9781538765364 (ebook)

Printed in Canada

MRQ-T

10   9   8   7   6   5   4   3   2   1

*For the monstrous women
and anyone who has felt severed from the person
they were meant to be,
your story deserves to be told.*

AUTHOR'S NOTE

GREEK MYTHOLOGY HARBORS so many incredible stories of women, monsters, and magic, but these myths also conceal great tragedy and horror. Medusa is an iconic figure of Greek mythology with conflicting origin stories. The origin story represented in this book includes scenes of sexual assault, attempted assault, and victim blaming. In particular, a scene of sexual assault is depicted in the chapter titled "A transformation that sinks to the bone."

I believe that Medusa's story is one that deserves to be told and to be heard, but not to the detriment of the reader. The beauty of mythology is that its purpose is to be told and retold, molded to the current audience, and I thank you for trusting me with this incarnation of Medusa.

MEDUSA

A childhood that bites, stings, and soothes

I WAS BORN THE only mortal daughter of a god of the sea and a goddess of sea dangers. My two sisters reveled in their immortality, holding their arms up to mine to compare the sheens of our skin, claiming their limbs glowed with the gentle golden light of those unburdened by an eventual death. I thought our forearms looked the same. If anything, mine were closer to golden from the days I spent walking the shoreline in the bright rays of Helios's sun.

My sisters did not like it when I tried to point this out.

"It's because you're mortal," Stheno said, drawing near me before dancing away again as if my mortality was contagious. "Your skin is *aging*."

"Ew," Euryale added.

They giggled and pranced away, their dark hair curling in long, handmade ringlets down their backs. There were tiny shells woven in between the strands, and they winked at me as my sisters left me behind, their bare feet making no noise on the stone floor worn smooth by age-old currents.

Our home was balanced on the precipice of space near the sea where the sturdy ground gave way to shifting sands. The ocean was only a few seconds' sprint from the back door. The walls were formed in the shapes of the waves from the sea, gentle curves and sloping ceilings all bleached white by the sun. Against the pale background of our house, Stheno and Euryale stood out like dark, fluttering birds in a clear sky.

They both took after our parents in appearance. I did not. I had been overlooked not only in immortality, but in my looks as well, and my tawny hair announced my displacement amongst my sisters far before word of my mortality could. There were few things my sisters loved to hold over me more than this.

My mother told me that when we had been born, Stheno and Euryale had begun to cry immediately, their eyes squeezed shut in opposition to the bright light of our new world.

But you, Medusa, she had said, *you were quiet. And you had your eyes wide open.*

I was strange, right from the beginning. While some worried that a quiet newborn prefaced a dull child, and an even duller adult, I liked when my mother told me the story of our birth. I liked that while my sisters had cried for the darkness of the womb, I had immediately begun to take in the world around me. Perhaps I had already known I would not live long enough to see it all.

When my mother told this story to my sisters, Stheno

asked our mother if she ever thought of tossing me in the ocean.

After a long pause, Mother had replied, *She does not belong there.*

We did not see our parents very often, since they preferred the wide expanse of the seas over the seashell-colored house on the shore, but when they returned to see three of their children, we were meant to appear in our triplicate. Late in my fourteenth year, our parents came to visit us. One of the quiet, elusive servants who kept the house in order, preparing our meals, and washing our clothes, had laid out the long, white sleeveless dresses my sisters and I wore to be presented as a group. My skin was still damp from the bath and I leaned against my bed, fingering the smooth fabric. A seagull screeched outside my window, the thin linen curtains that hung over the shallow alcove billowing in a faint, salty breeze.

Left on our own, Stheno and Euryale avoided me around our home, barring the times they sought me out to tease and torment me. This was fine with me. I had taken to walking the shoreline when I found that the sound of my sisters scampering up and down the halls of our house, accompanied by their cruel laughter, was soon to drive me insane.

The only time we willingly stood side by side as sisters was when our parents were home. So, on that early morning of their arrival, I stood between my sisters with Stheno on my right and Euryale on my left, our bare shoulders not quite touching. Our hair had been styled similarly, my sisters' straight dark hair twisted into curls and crowned with a delicate wreath of shells and iridescent stones. My own hair needed no aid to curl, but the pale greens, blues, and whites of the wreath did not stand out as sharply against my tawny head as it did with my sisters.

Our mother arrived first, rising elegantly out of the frothy waves in a chariot made of fiery coral, pulled by a sharp-toothed shark and a steely fish with a nose like a serrated sword that thrashed in the shallow water. She dropped the reins and stepped out of the carriage, the pale gray hem of her dress swirling with the tide. The chariot disappeared back into the waves, unmanned.

As my mother strode up the sand, my sisters bowed their heads in turn, first Euryale, then Stheno, and finally I dipped my chin to my chest, tilting my head down just far enough to be respectful. I had no issue with my mother, but she had not tried to harbor any feeling of empathy or motherly affection toward me or my sisters. Child-rearing came as an afterthought for a god.

"Gorgons," my mother greeted us with our shared name. She glided to a stop a few paces away and turned around to face the ocean, crossing her arms and leaning on one leg so that her hip was angled out. The sharp bone of her hip was hidden under the fabric of her skirt, but the attitude in her stance came across all the same. She struck a very un-goddess-like figure when she stood like that, allowing her emotions to project outward through the shape of her body. This was something I had been told only mortals did. I made sure to stand very straight and kept my shoulders back.

Father arrived a few moments later with much more fanfare. The surface of the ocean rippled and bubbled before bursting open as no less than four creatures battled with the waves, their front half made up of a horselike head and legs, the longer tufts of hair around their chin and hooves plastered wetly to their skin, while their flanks transitioned into tightly packed gray and purple scales leading to heavily muscled fish tails. The creatures pulled a dark stone chariot studded with pearls. Father stood straight-backed in the carriage, his bright red, clawed hand resting on the crossbar and his mortal hand holding his spear. The creatures were moving without the guidance of reins. They splashed their way to the edge of the surf and skidded to a halt, spraying frothy white sea-foam and sand.

With far less elegance than Mother, our father leaped out of the carriage and trudged up the slope toward us. The sea creatures whirled away and dove back into the water the moment his feet touched the sand, and the ocean seemed to pull away from them, creating a temporary path for the creatures and the chariot to dive into and disappear.

Unlike my mother, who had emerged from the ocean as dry as desert stone, my father reveled in the drops of water that clung to his reddened skin. He would remain this way, as if he had only just been drenched by a tumbling wave, even when he was on land and away from the water for long periods of time. I thought he began to smell a bit like a washed-up piece of rotting seaweed after a few days.

Father paused next to Mother where she stood with one hip cocked out, high on the beach. I could see a faint smile tempt his mouth at her stance, and he dipped his head to kiss the back of the hand that she had proffered to him to fulfill the expectations of a respectful greeting between husband and wife.

I did not think my parents loved each other. Love was a human fault, a mortal emotion the gods did not have the patience nor the desperation to entertain. My mother and father had probably been paired together for their shared affinity for the dangers that lurked below the ocean's surface. If anything, they had similar tastes in pets.

"Hello, my urchin," my father said. My mother turned her nose up and away from him.

"Phorcys," she greeted tersely.

Turning away from his wife, he brought his gaze to my sisters and me, which commenced another round of the synchronized, delicate bows. I put even less effort to be polite into this one, my chin barely dipping down a finger's length. He did not seem to find this half-assed display of respect as amusing as our mother's thinly veiled irritation.

"And hello, Gorgons. You are well?"

"Yes, Father," Stheno replied, speaking for all three of us. Nothing would come of me saying otherwise, or telling my parents of Stheno and Euryale's treatment of me when we're left on our own. This was a truth I had learned long ago, so I stayed silent.

"We will go to the banquet hall," our father declared, and he swept around us toward the whitewashed house. My sisters and I parted to allow our mother to follow him, and when she stepped between us, she placed her hand on Euryale's cheek and tilted her head up, smiling faintly. I noticed Stheno's jaw tick with annoyance at our mother's obvious favoritism, but she was smart enough to keep her mouth shut. When Mother dropped her hand and continued up the sandy hill, Stheno and Euryale were drawn together once again and they followed our parents toward the house, leaving me to bring up the rear.

The banquet hall was built on the east end of the house, open to the beach and the ocean on one side. The remaining walls had wide windows carved into the sides, flooding the room with light that turned golden and flushed when the sun set over the horizon. In the growing light of the morning the hall looked washed out and dim, tinted a faint blue. Usually the polished stone floor was empty, since my sisters and I had little use for this room on our own, but now there were a few low couches piled high with cream-colored pillows arranged in a semicircle facing the altar at the far end of the hall. The quiet servants in the house always seemed to be aware of my parents' imminent arrival before I was.

My father waved his claw at the couches as he passed them and told us, "Have a seat, girls."

Stheno and Euryale spread out over one of the two middle couches, lounging so that their limbs took up as much room as possible and there would be no room left for me. I sat on the edge of the remaining middle couch. Our mother had followed Father to the base of the altar where two more couches were waiting, and each of my parents took one for their own.

As soon as they sat down, servants carrying trays laden with food filed into the hall. The low tables set in front of our seats became crowded with plates of all kinds of fish and crustaceans, as well as small bowls of the tough fruit that grew on scraggly trees at the edge of the sand. There was also a loaf of bread on each table with some hard cheese and a small knife. A carafe of wine was placed in the middle with small, foggy green glass cups, and my mother immediately reached for a cup when the servant placed the wine in front of her.

My sisters picked at a few of the dishes the moment they were set down, but I kept my hands folded in my lap.

"Father," I said, as he clamped down on the tail of a whole cooked fish with his claw and dug out the meat with his other hand.

"What?" he said around his mouthful of fish. He was peering at me with narrowed eyes, which may have been because I had called him *Father*. I don't think he liked being reminded that he had sired a mortal daughter.

Well, tough for him, I thought, *but I'm the one who must live like this.*

"Why have you and Mother come here?" I asked.

"Ah," he said, wiping his mouth with the back of his human hand. "Right, well—Ceto, would you like to tell them?"

He looked imploringly at our mother, who was idly picking a scallop out of its shell and did not look up at her name. After another beat of silence with our mother refusing to even look up and acknowledge Father, Euryale let out a poorly suppressed giggle.

Father sighed.

"Your siblings will be coming to join us here," he said finally, "to celebrate your sister Echidna's wedding to Typhon. Expect for them to arrive tomorrow afternoon."

I was already sitting precariously on the edge of my couch, my back straight, but as Father spoke, my sisters quit eating and scrambled into an upright position. I looked over at them and, after first sharing a look between each other, they looked over at me.

There were only a few situations in which my sisters and I allowed ourselves to be willingly grouped together; one of those instances was when our parents returned home, and another was in defense against our parents' other children. While we all shared the same parents, the moments of our birth were so widely spaced that we had little in common with our siblings and treated them more like distant cousins when we were forced together. We were far from the most powerful offspring of Phorcys and Ceto, and we had discovered we stood a better chance against our elder relatives as a united front of triplets.

I studied my sisters' faces carefully. Stheno and Euryale would remain connected at the hip with or without me, but I could see they were weighing the benefit of three over two against all our siblings. The last time the entire family had been gathered—when our older brother Ladon and his hundred heads had been assigned by our father to protect the golden apples in the Hesperides' pompous little garden—we'd managed to fend off our relatives long enough to wedge ourselves into the corner of the banquet hall with a plate of oysters. Stheno seemed to be remembering this same moment, as she pressed her lips into a distasteful line and jerked her chin in acquiescence to my unspoken question.

A weight like a heavy cloak seemed to lift off my shoulders. Leaning back on my couch in an ungraceful slump, I realized I had been bracing for my sisters to close ranks against me, and so their decision to let me join them was a stark relief. I turned back toward my parents, who had either not seen our silent truce or not cared enough about our reaction toward the news of our siblings' imminent arrival to show concern.

I pulled the loaf of bread from my table toward me and ripped off a chunk, since the tension I had been holding in my shoulders had transformed into a sharp pinch in my belly. There was a small dish of rosemary and olive oil next to the bread tray, and I dipped a corner of the bread into it before bringing it to my lips.

"Oh," my father said suddenly, raising his attention off his plate, "the gods will be in attendance as well."

Mother looked at him sharply. She must not have been informed of this beforehand. I knew how much our mother despised being the last to know about news and rumors that spread across land and sea.

"Which gods?" she asked.

"Who knows," Father said, spitting out a fish bone. "None of those Olympians can keep a decision in their mind long enough to make it off their high-and-mighty mountain. I suspect that piddly excuse of a sea god will show his face just to spite me."

"Not Zeus?"

Father waved his claw in the air, a move of dismissal that was encumbered by the size and weight of the red exoskeleton. I thought it might have been more imposing when he was underwater. "Zeus would sooner give up his throne than attend a primordial descendant's wedding."

"Is he still angry about the whole devouring thing?" Stheno asked, lazily pulling apart a shrimp.

"Wouldn't you be?" I responded, before Father could. "All of Zeus's brothers and sisters were eaten by Cronus, and he had to cut them out of the Titan's stomach to free them. Would you not be angry, if you had to do the same?"

Stheno wrinkled her nose at me and sniffed, "Mother and Father would never eat us."

"Ew," Euryale added, once again perceptive of Stheno's tone.

"Definitely not, since there are no prophecies that you will ever overtake them in legend, and that seems to be the main reason that parents eat their children," I agreed, and took another bite of bread. "No prophecies yet, anyway."

Father peered at me from over his plate again, and this time Mother turned her gaze on me as well, assessing for something, though I didn't know what.

"Let us hope that none of you ever become worthy of legend, then," she said eventually and lifted a glass of wine in our direction. Stheno and Euryale raised their cups tentatively, sharing a second-long glance, but I picked up my wine and tilted it toward my parents easily before taking a long drink. It was unlikely that I, a mortal, would ever overcome the legend of my godly parents and all the immortal siblings that came before me.

THE WEDDING WAS AT sunset the next day. Stheno, Euryale, and I were dressed to match once again, this time in long, flowing dresses of silver that resembled what our mother often wore. Our hair was pulled away from our faces and braided down our backs in one long plait, tiny shells woven in between the strands, the pale objects standing out starkly against my sisters' hair but lost in the sandy tangle of mine.

Mother had overseen the ceremony. My sisters and I timed our arrival so that we were quickly ushered into our positions beside our parents' other set of triplets, the Graeae, right as the wedding began. With one dingy eye and a single tooth between the three of them, the Graeae had turned toward us with eerie coordination and grinned toothlessly, except for Deino, who had possession of the tooth. Pemphredo had the eye. They whispered to one another as she looked us up and down, and even though Enyo was left sightless and toothless, she sneered at Euryale when my sister stuck out her tongue at them.

I scarcely paid attention to the wedding itself. The moment our mother finished speaking, we had led the way toward the banquet hall, which had been transformed overnight and was now crowded with tables and long benches. My sisters and I positioned ourselves at the back of the room.

"No, no, here," I said as Stheno and Euryale moved to take seats closer to edge of the room. I sat in the middle of the table with the wall at my back. "This way they won't be able to sneak up on us."

"Easier to trap us, though," Stheno said, but she slid into place on my right, and Euryale followed.

As the tables filled with our distant relations and the subjects of our mother and father's oceanic jurisdiction, we kept a wary eye on the guests moving around us. I watched our brother Ladon take up an entire half of a table, his hundred heads and two hundred eyes blinking at every corner of the room. A few of the minor sea gods piled into the table closest to where our parents sat, like their proximity to the god and goddess would increase the odds of Mother or Father acknowledging them. Our parents sat at the front of the room at a long table positioned perpendicular to the others. Father was already digging into whatever fish had been placed in front of him, but Mother was watching the room as carefully as I was. When our gazes overlapped, she raised her eyebrows slightly as if to say *What are you looking for?* I raised my own eyebrows in response, *What are you looking for?* She waved me off and poured herself some wine.

Echidna and her new husband entered the hall to raucous cheers from the minor gods and sea folk, and I clapped as she passed our table. Echidna wove her way to the front of the room on her iridescent, serpentlike tail, the human half of her body almost completely bare save for the white fabric that was wrapped around her chest and crossed over her shoulders, the excess trailing behind her like two extra tails. She had broad shoulders and generous curves, which meant that a lot of dark skin was on display. A dusky green laurel wreath sat on her unbound hair.

Of all the children of Ceto and Phorcys, I liked Echidna the most. This was partly because she had never spoken of my mortality like it was something to be ashamed of, and partly because her hair looked a little like mine. It curled freely over her shoulders in long golden strands, and I felt a little less like an outcast in this family when she was around.

Echidna reached the table where our parents sat and took her place in the middle. Her husband, dark and stormy Typhon who towered over the minor gods with his bulk, his skin covered in long, scraggly cracks flowing with the red-hot magma of his volcanoes, followed right behind her.

With the bride and groom settled, the crowd turned back to their plates. A few people were still wandering around the room, some stepping up to the altar behind the wedding table to make a sacrifice to the gods of marriage or present a gift to the married couple. Suddenly, the steady din of the hall was punctured by a rush of wind and a pressure that made my ears pop. Every head rose up and turned toward the entrance.

A god was standing in the fading light of the sunset, his dark hair tumbling boyishly out from under a crown of coral. He was bare chested and deeply tanned, with a linen wrap around his waist and a trident held loosely in one hand. He held it like a walking staff, as if it were not one of the most feared weapons in all the seas.

"It's Poseidon," Euryale whispered.

"I know," Stheno whispered back.

"Everyone knows," I snapped at them from the corner of my mouth. I didn't take my eyes off the god. As he stepped into the path between two tables and began to walk to the front of the room, I saw his eyes pass over me before skipping back. He looked at me and I felt the weight of his gaze on my face, my shoulders, my chest. I held my breath. Poseidon smiled, a glint of pearly teeth, and looked away.

I wanted to ask my sisters if they had seen the god of the sea look at me, but then Euryale gasped and pointed.

"Look, another one!"

Standing where Poseidon had just stood was indeed another Olympian, a goddess in a cinched white dress with a sword strapped to her hip and a plumed silver helmet resting on her dark hair. She was scanning the room as if searching for an enemy, her steel-gray eyes sweeping over our table with practiced efficiency. When she spotted Poseidon's broad back moving toward my parents and Echidna, she scowled.

"Athena," Euryale whispered unnecessarily.

The goddess of wisdom strode after Poseidon and managed to arrive at the wedding table at the same time he did. They spoke lowly to our parents, but the crowd had begun whispering and murmuring as soon as the gods arrived and so I could not hear what was being said. Eventually, Poseidon and Athena took their seats at the far end of the head table. They seemed to do so a bit unwillingly, though I wasn't sure if they were objecting to have to sit next to the descendants of primordial gods or having to sit next to each other.

Poseidon reached for the wine and a cooked crab as soon as he sat down, looking out across the room. When his gaze turned my way, I quickly averted my eyes, though I didn't know why. A strange feeling beneath my ribs urged me to not check and see if the god was looking at me again, though I could feel that same heaviness from before.

"Why is Athena here?" Stheno asked.

I took a sip of wine to clear my throat, which had gone dry, and said, "She's probably here to represent her father, if Phorcys's suspicion about Zeus is correct and he refused to attend. Athena's wisdom would make her wary of dismissing an affair like this and making our parents angry."

"Oh," Stheno said mildly. "Olympians make everything so complicated."

"Don't say that too loudly with two of them present," I admonished, even though I couldn't help but agree. Stheno rolled her eyes.

When the noise of the hall rose back up to its comfortable volume, I spared a darting look over the wedding table. Poseidon was not looking at me, and I felt both relieved and disappointed. As I glanced over the hall one more time, my gaze snagged on a set of three heads moving in our direction with unnerving coordination. I straightened my spine and set my shoulders back.

"Be ready," I said out of the corner of my mouth, and Stheno and Euryale both dropped the bites of food they had been preparing to eat and copied my posture.

The Graeae glided to a stop in front of us. They'd traded the tooth sometime after the ceremony, and so now it was Enyo who looked sightlessly down at us with a single-toothed grin as she began to speak.

"Word of the Gorgons has yet to cross our path," she said, her voice thin and terrible. "Are our triplet sisters fated to remain on this lonely beach, unheard and unseen, their entire lives?"

"If I recall correctly, you three had yet to step one foot out of whatever cave you called home, hiding your faces, at our age," I shot back. Experience had taught me that remaining silent under the Graeae's attention did not encourage them to leave any quicker, but perhaps if I gave them the satisfaction of a response, I had a better chance to control the conversation.

"Indeed," Enyo hissed, "but time does not matter for those who are not weighed down by it, little mortal Medusa.

How long can you afford to waste away on this beach before you realize that your sisters will live long past your death, and longer after your bones have mixed with the sands?"

Stheno and Euryale shifted uncomfortably on either side of me. I had figured part of the reason they had allowed me back into their fold was that I was always the easiest target amongst our other siblings, but their connection to me meant that they could never avoid these attacks completely. This had been terrible to bear at first, but after years of practice trading blows with the Graeae and our older siblings, I now had the sharpest wits between the three of us.

I tilted my chin up. "Perhaps you would allow me to borrow that eye, so that I may see just how much longer I have to waste."

Pemphredo reflexively cupped a hand protectively over their dingy eye, as if I was going to reach forward and rip it out of the socket.

"We would not let you taint it with your grimy mortal hands," Enyo spat.

I was surprised when Stheno leaned forward and asked, "Could I hold it, then?"

Euryale made a face, crinkling the smooth skin between her brows in disgust, though I couldn't tell if it was exaggerated or genuine.

"You would touch that nasty thing?" She sounded as if she was going to retch from the thought of it.

Probably genuine, then, I thought.

The Graeae scowled down at us, their thin limbs trembling in divine anger that would have made any other mortal quake in fear.

"Maybe if I had a bit of cloth or something to hold it with, so that it wouldn't touch my hand," Stheno amended thoughtfully.

"Our eye is a divine blessing that was gifted to us to protect," Enyo said hotly. "You are not worthy enough to bear it."

"It's a blessing to only be born with one eye between the three of you?" I asked. "Are you quite sure?"

Stheno grinned like one of our mother's sharp-toothed sharks, a look which I knew prefaced something cruel coming from her mouth. "I guess you are blessed that with only one eye you cannot see how truly hideous you all are."

"Foolish children," Enyo wailed, drawing the attention of the nearby guests. The vile power in her voice made my sisters and I lean back and away from the Graeae, who seemed to have grown in size in the last few seconds, and now loomed over us. Enyo's voice was different, shaking and layered as if each of the sisters were speaking through her mouth. Now the Graeae had the attention of the entire hall and I could see the two Olympian gods watching us from the wedding table. "Listen well, for we have indeed looked beyond your current years, Gorgons, and we have seen the terrifying future that awaits you. Beware your looks." Pemphredo turned their yellowed eye on me as Enyo continued, "Especially you, Medusa, only mortal of divine lineage, for you have a truly horrifying monster that awaits you."

Their prophecy hanging in the air, the Graeae shrank back to their normal size and turned away from our table, moving once again in their eerie coordination as they left the hall. A tense silence followed their departure, and I felt every eye in the room turn to me. At the front of the room, Athena tilted her head, a move greatly exaggerated by the plume of her helmet, which she had yet to remove, and the weight of her gaze blanketed me. I tried to breathe but found that the air was stuck in my throat.

"So," Stheno said to Euryale quietly, "that went well."

Euryale didn't respond. She was staring at me with a look on her face I had never seen before. She leaned forward, as if to ask me something.

I stood, jerking to my feet in a move that surprised my sisters and they flinched away from me as I clambered over the bench and fled the room.

The sun had set over the horizon a few hours ago and the sea was dark as the night sky. I sat just above the reach of the waves, each crashing tide rushing up the sand as if to seize hold of me and drag me back into the water. I let the sound of the waves breaking on the shore wash out the ringing in my ears.

The Graeae always knew what nerve to pinch on both immortals and mortals alike, though they always seemed particularly cruel with their siblings.

"Gray-skinned freaks," I muttered. I wrapped my arms around my bent legs and rested my chin in the divot between my knees.

"You are not wrong about that."

I lifted my head and looked over my shoulder, ready to snap at whoever was behind me, but closed my mouth when

I saw Echidna making her slow, curving way toward me. She left a long, winding trail in the sand behind her.

"Why are you here?" I asked, and then grimaced at my harsh tone. I was not angry at Echidna. "Should you not be inside, celebrating with your new husband?"

Echidna scoffed and folded her arms across her chest.

"Typhon was prearranged to be my husband since before I was your age," she said. "I have the rest of my life to be stuck in his sullen company."

I was momentarily glad for my mortal status, as it discouraged my parents from trying to pair me off with an immortal being. Though, they may still try to do so just to be rid of me.

"Marriage is stupid," I said. Around my sisters or my parents, that statement would have earned me a disapproving look and an admonishment. But Echidna laughed.

"Right again, little queen," Echidna said with a tight grin. This was her nickname for me, taken from the meaning behind my name. In our language, Medusa could be translated as "queen" or "ruler." I did not know what came over my mother when she named me so, as my mortality had been apparent from the very moment I was born. Perhaps she had given me a regal name in hopes of drawing me incrementally closer to divinity.

I returned my chin to my knees and stared out at the black night. The pinpricks of starry constellations in the sky were reflected on the ocean, though they were bent and distorted as they rode the waves.

"I thought you were smarter," Echidna said eventually. She did not mean it cruelly, but I tucked my shoulders up near my ears in shame anyway. "You should know better by now than to provoke the Graeae. They are much older than you and do not take lightly to insults."

"They started it," I muttered into my dress.

Echidna laughed again. "You are so young, aren't you? Perhaps too young still to find a sense of self-preservation." She curled her tail under her, folding the smooth, green-scaled muscle into a tight coil, and settled down on the sand beside me. She removed the dusky laurel from her head and handed it to me. I sat up and took it, the leaves soft and waxy underneath my fingertips, still a little warm from where they had been resting on her head.

"Do you think what they said was true?" I asked softly. When I had all but run out of the hall earlier, I had hoped to avoid meeting anyone's gaze so that they would not see the rising fear on my face. While I had always known that I would most likely live an uneventful mortal life, fated to die in nameless oblivion, I did not know what to do with the idea that my future may be anything but painlessly ordinary. With only Echidna and the crashing waves here to hear me, I allowed a bit of that fear to seep into the question.

I was glad Echidna did not respond right away. She thought on the question as if she did not already know the answer, even though we both knew what it was. She was probably trying to think of the least upsetting response that was still in line with the truth.

"From what I can remember," she said evenly, "the Graeae's predictions have never been wrong before."

I pinched a laurel leaf between my thumb and first finger, crushing the delicate structure of the leaf under the pressure.

"Although, when the Graeae were still young, before you

and your sisters had even been conceived, they used to think I was the most terrifying thing they'd ever seen." She flicked the tip of her tail at me. "Do you think I am terrifying?"

"No," I said immediately. I looked at Echidna's gold hair, her deep brown skin set in sharp contrast against the white of her tightly wrapped tunic, the bulky coils of powerful muscle folded neatly underneath her. "You are beautiful."

Echidna reached over and plucked the laurel crown out of my hands and placed it on my head. She adjusted a few leaves to set it in line with the curls that had escaped from my braid.

"Well, then," she said as she leaned back and appraised me with my new crown. "The future that is awaiting you may not be so terrible after all."

I let my head tip back, becoming acquainted with the light but reassuring weight of the laurels, and allowed a vague hum of acknowledgment to rise from my throat. The stars blinked down at me from the inky sky and I let my eyes go unfocused until the minuscule dots began to blur together.

"I should go back inside," Echidna said eventually, though it sounded like she would very much rather do any-thing else.

"Back to your husband," I added. She made a dismissive noise.

I lolled my head to the side and raised my brow at her, teasing, "What? You do not enjoy his sullen, stormy com-pany? Do not tell me that he is not a riveting conversational partner."

Echidna rolled her eyes as she unfurled her tail and rose out of the sand.

"Just wait until you get married, little queen, then we will see who is still laughing," she warned. "You think Mother and Father will pick out a handsome hero for you? Or maybe they'll find another sullen sea deity just waiting to weasel his way into our family."

I did not say that I doubted Mother and Father would ever try to marry me off to anything other than another mortal. I did not say that I thought I would rather come to the terrible future the Graeae had predicted for me than be married off for my family's gain, though that was the only way I could ever be useful to them.

"Maybe," I said instead.

Echidna bid me farewell and carved a path back up to the brightly lit hall. I looked over my shoulder to watch her retreat, wondering if I should return to the hall to try and save face in front of Mother and Father, or escape to my quiet room at the other end of the house. But then a figure appeared in the entrance to the hall, and I stopped thinking of retreat. Echidna bowed her head respectfully as she passed the backlit figure, whose tall plumed helmet bobbed indiscriminately in response.

Athena stepped out and strode down the beach. I scrambled to my feet and whacked the sand off my dress, trying to make myself presentable for a goddess. She may have just seen me humiliated in front of the entire wedding, but at least I could pretend to keep a grasp on my dignity, which was nearly as formless as the sand on the beach.

As she got closer, I began to make out the details of her dress. It was surprisingly plain and functional for a divine being, especially in comparison to the richly decorated and embossed metal of her helmet. The silver gleamed in the moonlight and shone brightly against her pale skin. Dark hair curled out from under the edge of the helmet to frame her face and twisted down her back in a thick braid.

It was her eyes that struck me the most. Gray, as all the legends had said, and fiercely calculating like she could see every possible outcome the future contained laid down at her feet. I felt small under her gaze.

I copied Echidna's bow when Athena was close enough.

"Goddess of wisdom," I greeted.

"You are Ceto and Phorcys's mortal child," she said, her voice rough and loud as the crashing ocean behind me. It did not sound like an accusation, as I had heard so many times before, nor was it a question. Just a statement.

"Yes," I said.

Athena peered down at me. She was nearly a head and a half taller than I was and I would barely come up to her chest standing on the tips of my toes. I felt my shoulders strain as I straightened them under her scrutiny.

"The Graeae gave you a prediction." Another statement.

"Yes," I said again, and couldn't help but add, "Though they were likely to create it out of nothing just to frighten me."

"You think it to be false?"

She watched me from her great height, her gaze focused, like the goddess was actually invested in the thoughts of a mortal. This question felt like a test, like my answer would inform Athena of everything she needed to know about me. I thought about it, considering what Echidna had told me just moments before.

"The Graeae tend to err on the side of the truth," I said slowly, "but what is true for them may not necessarily become the truth of my own life."

"So you do not fear the future they have predicted for you?"

"I hope I will be strong enough to evade any fear toward my future life," I said. "Though I would be a fool if I was not at least wary of it."

Athena made a sound of approval. I forced myself to refrain from displaying any outward signs of relief.

"You have a strong heart and a steady head for a mortal," Athena said, the sawed-off edges of her voice softening. "I will give you some advice. You must begin to use your appearance, lest others use it against you. If you ever find yourself in Athens, visit my temple. We shall see what kind of future is waiting for you."

I could only nod in agreement. Athena stepped past me and I bowed my head once more in farewell, and when I looked up the goddess was gone. Only a few indentations in the sand from her steps indicated that she had been here at all.

"It is strange," said a deep voice, "for Athena to take such interest in a mortal girl."

I turned and took a sharp breath. Poseidon was standing close behind me. After a brief moment when I stood blankly looking at the god, I quickly dropped into another formal curtsy. I was tired of being surrounded by so many gods, as it meant I had to bow quite a bit more than I liked. It felt like I had spent nearly half of the past day with my head bent down.

"Yes," I agreed blindly to Poseidon's observation, and hastily tacked on, "lord of the sea."

"You best be careful, girl," Poseidon said with a conspiring grin. "Gods have a habit of using the mortals they like for their own personal gain."

He tracked his eyes up and down my figure, and I felt that I would be swallowed up under his gaze. His eyes were a dark, stormy blue, like the deepest ocean during a hurricane. Even though he had to be about the same height as his niece, I felt minuscule next to him in a way that I had not felt when I stood before Athena. His broad shoulders were carved with muscle that twisted down over his arms. He held his trident in one hand, and the metal looked rusty and corroded by the salt water, though I had no doubt that it was still a fearsome weapon in his possession.

I folded my hands together and nodded again. I did not know how to respond to his blatant jab at his own divine relatives.

When he finished his observation of me, he grinned once more and stepped past me. I turned to the side so that he would not brush against me.

"Just something to think about," he called over his shoulder. He waded into the water and the surf threw itself at him in excitement like a loyal dog. Trident in hand, he dove headfirst into an approaching wave and disappeared just as Athena had.

When I was sure he was gone, and with a quick glance around the beach to make sure no other divine beings were going to sneak up behind me, I dropped to a seat in the sand with a huff. Although both of my parents were gods, I had not realized just how impressive and overwhelming the presence of the Olympians could be. I felt drained from upholding my polite and calm appearance.

The celebration continued in the hall behind me, but I decided that I had had enough interaction with my family, and anyone else, for the day. When the next few people began to file out of the brightly lit hall, I dragged myself back to my feet and returned to my room in the dark.

I tore my hair out of its braid and left my dress in a trail on the floor before I buried myself under the blankets on my bed. Sleep wouldn't come easily.

IT WAS SO LATE in the evening that it was early morning when I heard footsteps outside my room. Tucked under the covers, I couldn't tell who it was until she spoke.

"Medusa," Euryale whispered.

It sounded like she was alone. There were only a few times I had ever seen Euryale without Stheno by her side in our whole lives.

She crept closer to my bed. I held still, barely breathing. I didn't know what she wanted. To tease me about the fate the Graeae had predicted? To tell me to stay away from her and Stheno? I had already planned on doing that.

"Medusa," Euryale said again, louder this time. Her voice was gentle. I realized I rarely heard her speak without her taking cues from Stheno. "I just wanted to tell you that you can talk to me about—about what the Graeae said, if you wanted. I know you're probably scared. But you do not have to be scared alone."

I didn't move. Was this a trick? She sounded genuine, but I was wary of accepting any sort of help, even when I wanted it desperately.

"Just," Euryale said, her voice moving away, "know that I'm here, too."

I waited until her steps faded down the hallway before flipping off the covers and sitting up. The weak light of the moon lit up my shadowy room.

I didn't know what to think about Euryale's offer. Of course, I knew that Stheno took the reins in teasing me and compelled Euryale to follow along, but the few moments Euryale and I had just between us had always been stilted. Neither of us knew how to act around the other. Why had the Graeae's prophecy drawn her closer to me, rather than pushed her further away?

I blew a lock of hair, tousled from the blankets, away from my face. Even if Euryale did mean well, I knew that the best way for me to handle my uncertain future was to approach it like I did everything else. Alone.

Ceto

THERE WERE A FEW pleasant things about being the wife of a sea god. One was the space, as the ocean had plenty of it, and Ceto rarely crossed paths with her husband when she wished to avoid him. There were many, many islands she had discovered amongst the waves that were nearly impossible to find, unless you knew exactly what you were looking for. She also liked her status, but she had already had that in her own right before marrying Phorcys. Their marriage had been one of inevitability and convenience. And now, having been married long enough to sire multiple lines of squabbling children, Ceto filled her days with her sea creatures, traveling the waters and terrorizing a few mortals when she felt like doing so.

There were many things Ceto disliked about being the wife of a sea god. The largest and most cumbersome was handling Phorcys's ego, which was fragile as dead coral.

"Ceto," Phorcys demanded, and she slowly tracked her gaze from where it had been lingering over the sea back to his pinched face. They were sitting in the empty banquet hall, the tables and chairs cleared off so that the floor gleamed like an empty pool below their lounging thrones.

Phorcys had called her here, back to the home their youngest daughters shared, and she had agreed to come largely because it meant she would get to see Euryale again. Of all her many children, Euryale was the sweetest. Many of her children were monsters, according to the cowering mortals on land, but Euryale and the Gorgons were different. With their smooth skin and mortal faces, Ceto knew that many of her children resented the Gorgons for their sheer youth and ignorance of the world outside.

The Gorgons' distance from their monstrous siblings also frightened Ceto. They didn't quite fit within the family, which was why she had insisted that the sisters have their own home on this secluded beach, but in doing so she had also sheltered them from the world. They were untested and vulnerable.

"Are you listening to me?"

Ceto blinked at Phorcys, and said, "Tell me again."

With a huff, Phorcys repeated, "I want to marry one of the Gorgons to Atlas."

Ceto stilled. She waited for Phorcys to laugh, to tease her for ignoring him, but her husband was deadly serious.

"You want to marry one of our youngest daughters," Ceto asked slowly, "to a son of Poseidon?"

He nodded, gesturing broadly, and said, "They have to be of some use rather than hiding away in this big house. They will be of age soon. Perhaps Euryale." Phorcys scratched at his large, clawed hand with the ragged fingernails of his other. "She would put up the least resistance. Or maybe

Medusa, as she has no other use. I can show Poseidon that his slimy offspring are no better than mine. Should he be daft enough to turn down this offer, then I will finally have reason to challenge him."

"Why?" Ceto asked, and realized that her question applied to many things that Phorcys just told her. "Why the Gorgons? Why would you even wish to give one of our family away to a son of Olympus? Why are you so intent on war with Poseidon?"

Phorcys slammed his claw down on the arm of his throne, the sound echoing flatly against the empty room. He did not address the questions about the Gorgons, but jumped straight to the prod at his ego. "Because I will not settle for this false peace! He has no claim to the ocean that was once all mine. It is far time that he cede his false rule back to me."

"But must you involve our daughters in this feud?" Ceto snapped.

Phorcys looked bewildered. "What else are daughters good for?"

Ceto stood abruptly. The sound of waves hurling themselves against a stubborn cliff was crashing in her ears. She wanted to hurl her throne at her husband, to try and hammer some decency into his thick skull or at least knock the thought from his head, but she reined in her anger with practiced restraint. She took a breath. The air above the sea was visceral, like a flood in her lungs, and she let it fill her until she could speak calmly.

"My children will not be traded like some piece in a game that men play." She turned sharply on Phorcys, and he leaned away from the movement. "And I will not stand by while you throw those girls in the path of a god who does not care if they live or die in his shadow."

She descended the stairs and was crossing the echoing hall before Phorcys could respond, the hem of her seawater-gray dress snapping at her heels.

"Ceto," he called from behind her. He did not bother to rise from his throne. "Ceto, darling, please, you misunderstand."

"No," she said without slowing. "I understand you quite well."

Echidna had been married to Typhon as part of a plot for Phorcys to gain some powerful grandchildren, Ceto knew. But Echidna was not as vulnerable as the Gorgons. When her snake-tailed daughter had found out about her father's plan for her engagement, she had simply asked Ceto, "How soon?"

The Gorgons would not be so blasé. Even without knowing which of her daughters Phorcys had wanted to tie to Poseidon's son like an anchor on a shipwrecked boat, Ceto could not allow the triplets to be separated by a doomed marriage. Together, the Gorgons could hold their own against their siblings, which was the first step in being able to face the mortal world beyond this strip of beach. But if the sisters were apart, Ceto worried that they would crumble.

This concern was partly her own fault. For so long, she had demanded that the Gorgons act as three parts of the same body, hoping that they would become strong like the Graeae. Ceto's prophesizing triplets had nurtured their power together, letting it grow within each other until it would only work when all three were present. However, the Gorgons had not yet achieved that unity. They were fractured, and Ceto wasn't certain if Medusa had caused the cracks or if she was endlessly attempting to fit the broken pieces together.

Ceto couldn't let her Gorgons break further, before they even had the chance to see the huge, terrible, incredible world beyond the beach. Especially since Medusa had so little time compared to her sisters.

She would have to send the Gorgons away from this isolated house. Phorcys had too easy access to the sisters in their sandy home. But where could they go that he could not reach? The ocean was wide and vast, and Phorcys knew every corner of it.

As Ceto emerged into the bright sun of the afternoon, amplified by the glinting ocean, she let her gaze fall over the horizon. Far across the water, there were cities full of mortals where Phorcys did not care to venture. The humans found him unsettling, a relic of past gods. He preferred to keep to the company of the sea gods that revered him, and he especially avoided cities with ties to the Olympic gods. There were plenty of those crowding mortal shores now.

The wind whisked sand across Ceto's feet as she approached the edge of the surf. She spared a glance back at the house, but as she turned, she spotted the figure of Medusa far down the beach.

Her mortal daughter was standing in the ankle-high surf, a loose shift pulled up and tied around her knees, arms crossed across her tanned chest as she stared out into the water. Medusa's hair was loose and curling wildly in the wind, the sun glinting off the tangles like flashing bronze blades. With her feet trapped in the tide and her eyes trained on the horizon, Medusa looked stuck in time. If Ceto hadn't known better, she would have thought that her daughter could have stayed in that spot for the next millennia. But Medusa barely had that.

Ceto loved her children. They were monstrous, and sometimes wicked, but they were beautiful to her like marvelous sea creatures, incredible in their design. She wanted them all to figure out what made them happy and spend their lives, no matter how short, seeking it out.

With her mind made up, Ceto slipped into the water, which welcomed her like an old friend. Medusa, caught up in a far-off horizon, scarcely noticed her mother disappear beneath the waves.

Athens, city of rivalries

FOUR YEARS PASSED BEFORE my sisters and I left the white house on the beach. Out of the blue one slow afternoon, we received word from our mother that we were to travel to a large mortal city and live amongst the humans.

"Any city?" Euryale asked as she smoothed her thumb over the words Mother had scratched into the smooth side of a shell. Most of her messages came like this, either etched into the grain of a shell that washed up on our beach or even scrawled into the sand itself, appearing at the feet of whichever sister was nearest to the water at the time.

"Any *large* city," Stheno replied, and leaned back on the couch with her arms crossed, although she still managed to look elegant. All three of us had grown in height, but Stheno seemed to carry it best, and she knew how to arrange her long limbs so that they draped over any surface *just so*. She was elegantly stretched out across her couch in the high-ceilinged sitting room with the columned windows and opaque curtains gently fluttering behind her. Euryale, sitting on the couch to her left, had her legs folded under her and was fiddling with the shell in her lap.

I leaned over and plucked the shell from Euryale's fingers. Our mother's handwriting was slanted, like she had written the message in a hurry.

"It might be nice to go to Argos," Euryale said. "Or Corinth. Or—oh! What about Delphi?"

"Not Delphi," Stheno snapped. Euryale frowned, but I had to agree with Stheno. The Graeae, with their skill in prophecy, were likely to lurk around the location of the divine oracle. We had been able to avoid the triplets since our last encounter with them at Echidna's wedding, and I hoped to keep it that way. I had not forgotten the prophecy they had spat at me the last time we met.

Euryale and Stheno began to bicker back and forth, tossing out the names of cities that we had heard about from our siblings and read about in the scrolls that Ladon, our sibling with a hundred heads, had brought us for our fifteenth birthday.

I flipped the shell over in my hands, tracing over the white grooves and sloping curve of the back. In my brown hands, the shell seemed to become an even brighter white, or perhaps the pearly white of the shell was making my hands look darker than they were. I turned the shell over again and felt the smooth, iridescent inside, my finger sliding over the engraved message. When I turned the shell so that the sun reflected against the inside, it flashed like silver.

"We are going to Athens," I said.

Stheno and Euryale, who had still been arguing over whether Naxos was big enough to be considered a large city, stopped and looked at me.

"What?" Stheno said flatly.

"That is such a large city, though," Euryale said. "Like, the biggest."

"We will go to Athens," I said again.

I waited for Stheno to disagree with me. In the past few years my sisters had grown out of their childish rebellion against my relation to them, but they still treated me as the lesser, mortal sister whose opinion they could take or leave. Stheno especially. But I would fight them on this if I had to.

"What would we benefit from going to Athens?" Stheno asked eventually, and I knew that the *we* she was referring to was Euryale and herself. "You will probably find your rightful place amongst all those mortals, but what do we get out of going to this city?"

"Other than the fact that Mother has ordered us to go?" I said, but continued quickly as I knew that Mother had not told us to go to Athens specifically. "Think of it this way—the only mortal you have known your entire life is me. But the mortals in this city worship gods, they build entire temples for them, and they would probably bow at your feet if they knew the lineage from which you descend."

Stheno made a small noise of interest, but I could see the light that sparked in her eye. One of the frustrations of living on a lonely beach with only other godly siblings as visitors is that none of us have had real experience with the mortal world, though we had heard of it. The Graeae had been so fond of taunting us when we were younger, and they had often dangled their own interactions with humans in front of us. I always figured they were exaggerating the extent to which the mortals worshipped a set of toothless, blind women, but Stheno had always been the most snappish after the Graeae spoke of their followers.

I laid it on as thick as I could. "You would be a divine being amongst the common people. Perhaps if we draw in just enough attention, they would build an altar for the Gorgons."

The likelihood of this was quite slim, but if Stheno had to believe that an altar would be built in her name for her to travel to Athens, then I would let her believe it. Stheno looked at Euryale, who was chewing on her lower lip thoughtfully.

"Will they make sacrifices on the altar?" Euryale asked.

"Most likely," I said slowly.

She smiled. "That's nice of them."

"It is, isn't it?" I grinned back at her and returned the shell to her fingers.

IT WAS WARM IN Athens. There were so many people packed into such a small stretch of land, and it was hard to walk down any of the wide streets without brushing against an Athenian or knocking into one of the stalls that crowded the edges. Stheno and Euryale had linked arms behind me, but as I walked ahead the crowd seemed to flow around me.

I had traded the traditional long gown my sisters and I were accustomed to wearing in our house for a common mortal woman's cropped tunic, the hem of the material brushing my calves. Stheno and Euryale had acquiesced to the change after a bit of convincing, and I had reasoned that we should try to walk, unknown, amongst the mortals to see their daily lives before we revealed our lineage to them. Our dresses were a faded, sandy color that washed out my sisters' skin but stood out against mine. Stheno had braided her dark hair back and away from her face to accentuate the sharp angle of her cheeks, and Euryale had pinned back half of her hair, though the softened edges of her face were not as prominent as Stheno's. I let my hair curl long and free over my shoulders.

I led us toward the middle of the city, which was easy to find as I kept track of the tall hill that surged up out of the flat horizon of buildings. We were headed to the Acropolis, the hilltop that held many of Athens's sacred temples and altars. I knew that Athena, who was the patron goddess of this mortal city, would have a temple there.

While we walked down the streets, I noticed that some of the mortals were watching us. The women were leaning close together and whispering behind raised hands. The men tracked our movements like dogs on a hunt. I glanced back at my sisters to see if they had noticed that we were being observed, and although there was a tightness in Stheno's shoulders, I did not think she was bothered by the looks of the Athenians.

"They don't know who we are, do they?" Euryale asked quietly.

"How would they?" Stheno replied. "This is the first time we've walked amongst mortals like this."

"Perhaps they like the way you look," I told them. The farther we walked into the city, however, the more crowded it became. When we came to a street that was walled in by buildings so high that I was unable to see the central hill, I approached a stall.

"Excuse me," I said in the common tongue, "could you point us in the direction of the Acropolis?"

The man running the stall, which was full of small wooden tools and trinkets, looked up from the bowl he had been carving. He looked older, and quite a few wrinkles appeared around his eyes and mouth when he smiled at me.

"For a beautiful woman like you, I could do much more."

I blinked down at him. "Just the directions would be fine, thank you."

The man eventually pointed us down the street with a few vague markers to follow, though he finished by saying, "Come back whenever you like. These old eyes have not seen anything as fine as you in many years."

I bowed my head in thanks and ushered my sisters away.

"Why was he speaking to you like that?" Stheno whispered fiercely.

"Like what?" I asked.

"He called you beautiful," Euryale said, appraising me from the side with her wide eyes.

"Yes, well," I said, and then found that I had no answer for them. I had been smothered under the divine beauty of my two immortal sisters for as long as I had had enough awareness to notice the differences between us. I had never considered what other mortals, other people like me, would think of my appearance.

"This is a strange place," Stheno decided, and dragged Euryale forward by the elbow.

Many of the buildings we passed were of similar coloring,

dusty whites and faded marble dotted by bronze ornaments. When we came to a break in the crowded buildings, I saw that we had climbed part of the hill that rose in the center of the city and a sea of red terra-cotta rooftops stretched out in front of us. Scattered cypresses rose above the buildings like stalks of seaweed blooming up from the ocean floor. The hard-packed dirt and stone streets amplified the echo of scuffing feet and the clatter of wagons pulled by stout donkeys.

As we continued our approach toward the center of the city, the crowds finally began to disperse. The road grew narrower, more dirt than stone, and the street-side vendors disappeared, until finally there was only a narrow path, unlined by stone walls, that led up toward the Acropolis. The collection of buildings sat on top of steep, rocky cliffs that looked over the entire city. From where my sisters and I were standing at the base, I could see a few mortals making the trek up to the temples, and those who had nearly reached the top looked minuscule.

"More walking," Euryale said glumly.

A brusque breeze sliding off the ocean and over the city pushed its fingers through my hair, swirling around the hem of my dress and tugging me forward. I took a breath, and the familiar scent of sea salt on the wind flooded my lungs.

I took another step forward, and though I did not check behind me to see if they were following, I could hear my sisters' tentative steps start up again.

When we crested the top of the hill there was a series of white stone steps that levered us even higher above the city, until we finally stood in the Acropolis itself.

The huge Parthenon towered over the humans that

gathered around and under it, the thick columns and fresco all shining in a carefully polished marble. My sisters were drawn toward this temple, either by its grandness or the godly power that emanated from within. I let them go. The Parthenon was not the reason I had forced my sisters to choose Athens as the mortal city we would visit, and instead I focused on the smaller temple next to the massive building.

Athena's temple was hushed when I stepped inside for the first time. My footsteps echoed lowly against the brushed marble floors, and I kept my hands clasped carefully behind my back, feeling a bit like a child in a forbidden room. The heat of the midday sun was lessened under the temple's roof.

Women in draping white dresses walked in twos or threes through the columned halls. Many of them had their hair bound back, but I could see a few whose hair ran loose and wild down their backs.

Priestesses, I thought, *or virgins. Or both.*

"Hello."

I turned and saw that one of the women with bound hair had approached me. She had dark, unlined skin, though her eyes were wiser than that of the old man who I had asked for directions.

"Hello," I said back, unsure how to explain myself. I had walked into the temple only knowing that I needed to be there, not what I would do once I had arrived.

"Are you here to make a sacrifice?" the woman asked me, and I shook my head.

"Athena told me to come here."

The woman's eyebrows rose, though the composure of her face remained the same. It had been years since I had seen and spoken to the goddess, but this woman reminded me quite a bit of Athena's commanding, no-nonsense presence.

"Did she now," she said doubtfully. "When did this happen?"

"When I was a girl."

Eyeing me up and down, the woman said, "It seems to me that you are still a girl, are you not? You must be no more than eighteen."

"You have keen eyes," I said, attempting to keep the sarcasm from my voice. I wore the dress of a woman near marrying age, and my unbound hair gave away my youth.

Either I did a poor job of concealing my derision, or the woman was a mind reader, because her composed face shifted into a look of unimpressed neutrality.

"The goddess of wisdom does not have time to indulge in every little girl that visits her temple," she said. "So, unless you have an extraordinary reason for calling on Athena today, I would suggest that you make a customary sacrifice and then take your leave." I felt my cheeks heat with a slight flush as the priestess watched me, waiting for my response.

It was like she had struck a nerve in me with a hot iron.

I was accustomed to being spoken down to. My sisters had looked down on my mortal body and my mortal emotions and my mortal existence for my entire life. There was no doubt in my mind that my mother and father had deep shame in siring a mortal daughter, if my father's expressive face told me anything.

But my family was made up of gods and divinities. I was

able to handle being spoken to as small and weak and dumb from them because I knew where I stood in the hierarchy.

And while this woman was a priestess of Athena, she was still mortal. She did not come from a divine lineage. She did not have traces of gods in her veins as I did, faint as they may be. The warmth on my face did not fade, though the cause for the flush changed from humiliation to anger faster than I could track. I opened my mouth, and the words just darted out.

"I will not go. Athena herself told me to visit her temple and I will not leave until I have spoken with her and figured out why she has instructed me to come here." I had been standing straight while bearing her interrogation, but now I shifted my hip to the side, mimicking the pose that my mother often took with my father. "And I do not think that a mortal such as yourself, even one tolerated by Athena, should speak for the goddess of wisdom. Do you think you know more than the wisest being in this world, enough to assume what that same being wants, even if it means going directly against the words that came from her own mouth?"

The priestess's mouth was agape. The look did not suit her regal face, and I was savagely pleased with myself that I had cracked her composure.

After a moment while the priestess was trying to piece together a response, I noticed the heavy silence in the rest of the temple. I glanced around and saw that the other priestesses and temple visitors were watching us and whispering to one another. I did not know how long they had been listening, and I wanted to be glad that someone else had witnessed my barbed defense, but the longer they looked at me, the more my anger began to fade and give way to wariness.

Then I noticed that the mortals were not looking at the priestess, or at the two of us as a pair. They were all looking at me. More specifically, many of them were looking at a spot just behind me. Even the priestess who still stood in front of me was now looking over my head.

I turned and looked up. And then looked up some more. I wondered if I had not felt the shift in the atmosphere because the divine presence in the temple of a god was already overwhelming, or if I had just been blind to the change during my raging.

The goddess Athena stood behind me. She looked the same as she had four years previously when we first met, with her thick hair curling out from under her polished helmet that shone spectacularly against the sunlit marble. Athena was looking down at me with her carefully controlled face, and I was immediately worried I had overstepped by reprimanding one of her priestesses.

The women of the temple had begun to drop into respectful bows and curtsies, murmuring greetings to their goddess. I felt the priestess behind me move to do the same after a heartbeat.

Athena did not look away from me to acknowledge them.

"Well," Athena said eventually, when it became clear that I could not speak around the catch in my throat. "It appears that I must come speak for myself."

"Goddess," the priestess behind me began, her voice entreating, "I tried to tell this girl—"

"Hush, Desma," Athena said, and the priestess fell silent. Athena addressed me, "You have come."

"As you instructed me to," I agreed, finally finding my voice. "Though you never gave me a reason."

"You did not need me to give you a reason. I simply gave you an option. Did you want to stay in that house on the lonely beach?"

I thought about it for only a moment before saying, "No."

Athena observed me, searching for an answer on my face. I had forgotten what it felt like to be so closely examined by her, and it seemed like the walls I had built to protect myself from my sisters turned to glass under her gaze. She looked away, and I wondered if she had found her answer.

"I did tell this woman to come to my temple," Athena told Desma, though she was also addressing the whole room. "And I did not provide her a reason, but she has followed my commands despite this oversight. She is welcome here." She turned back to me. "I do have cause for telling you to come to me when you found yourself away from that beach. You have shown great promise in your wits and wisdom, which you know I value. I will ask you to stay here in Athens and become a priestess at my temple."

I felt my jaw loosen and was worried my face reflected the same shock that had appeared on Desma's face after I spoke against her. Athena tilted her head, considering.

"Lest you wish to return home with your immortal sisters?"

"No." I did not have to think about that for a second.

"Goddess," Desma began behind me, having regained

some of her composure, "may I ask why you have chosen this...woman?"

I could tell she really wanted to say *child*. But I was also curious about why Athena wanted me to stay here in Athens, in her temple, when we had only spoken once before in my youth. I hoped Athena would not mention this with Desma so insistent that my age was an issue.

"She has shown me that she will not cower under the mental strain of an opponent. That strength of mind," Athena explained, "is not something that can be taught. Each of my priestesses has portrayed some level of this strength, but this woman here has displayed great promise, provided she is given the guidance and room to grow. I intend to offer this to her. Do you disagree?"

This last question was directed at Desma. I had been focused on the goddess since the moment I realized she was there, but I finally turned back to look at the priestess. Desma was looking me over again, as well. I was impressed that she had not immediately cowed under Athena's pointed question, and instead she was carefully considering her answer. This slow progression to her decision was probably why she was made a priestess of Athena.

"No, goddess," Desma answered, finally. I was a little shocked that this mortal woman had stowed away her anger so quickly. I wondered if she was satisfied with what the goddess had said about me or if she had decided that siding with the goddess on this was the safest option. Perhaps it didn't matter.

From the sharp glint in her eye that scraped over me as

she stepped back, I did not think I had heard the last from Desma, especially if I intended to remain in the temple.

"You have not given me an answer," Athena said to me.

I turned back to the goddess. "I—"

"What are you doing?" Stheno's sharp voice cut right through the airy hall of the temple, and I just managed to suppress a flinch.

In the entryway behind Athena's towering figure, I could see my sisters standing shoulder to shoulder a good two arms' lengths away from any mortal. The people around them had turned to look when Stheno spoke and then continued to stare when they noticed the otherworldliness of my sisters. In this close proximity, I could see that my sisters were taller than all the women around them, and some of the men as well, and while the glow around them could be attributed to a trick of the sun slanting into the room, they were brighter than everyone else. It was like I was seeing them in sharper focus, as if all the mortals were farther away.

Athena turned partly, enough to look over her shoulder and down at the interruption.

"Ah," she said, her raspy voice stretching like a cat in the sun, "perhaps this will speed things along."

Stheno and Euryale seemed to realize right then that it was the goddess of wisdom who stood in front of me, and they dropped into hurried bows before rising again.

"I apologize on behalf of my sister, goddess," Stheno said.

Athena waited a moment, then asked, "Why?"

Stheno blinked, and said with a bit of hesitation, "I simply figured that she had disturbed your temple."

"She has not," Athena said firmly. "In fact, I myself have

disturbed the temple in coming to greet your sister. She has come here upon my request. From the looks on your faces, I am right to assume that she did not tell you of this before your coming to Athens." Athena glanced back at me. I shook my head. "Nonetheless, your sister is welcome here. I have just invited her to become one of the priestesses of my temple, and to remain here in Athens for as long as she wishes."

Now it was Stheno and Euryale's turn to look like gaping fish. Stheno, as always, recovered first.

"You...her?" she stuttered. Maybe she had not entirely recovered yet.

Athena frowned and turned back to me.

"Why is everyone intent on questioning my decisions today?" she demanded.

I shook my head. The idea of staying and living in Athens, leaving that white house on the beach, still seemed like a trick. Like Athena was just waiting for me to agree before laughing in my face, teasing me for my mortal naivete. What she had said about the strength of my mind had sent me reeling, as I had never thought of my willpower as a skill, just a tool that I used to defend myself against those who tried to hurt me.

Athena looked down at me from her great height, but for seemingly the first time in my life, I was not being looked down on. I was being viewed as someone worthy of recognition, just the way I was.

"I want to stay," I told her.

Athena's cool face split into a fierce grin, and a breeze whipped its way through the hall like the first volley of arrows fired on a battlefront.

"Then welcome, Medusa," she said, her voice raised so that the whole hall and even the heavens could hear, "priestess of Athena. The ceremony for her induction will be held tonight."

Once she finished her declaration, the goddess nodded to me once and then disappeared. The manner of her departure was not very clear, since it seemed as if she was standing right in front of me one moment, and then in the same second she was gone, though I wasn't sure if I hadn't blinked and missed it. If I tried to focus on figuring out the exact moment Athena was no longer in front of me, my head began to ache. Without the presence of a divine god the temple felt much bigger, as if the ceilings had risen and the walls had moved farther away. Athena's presence had not been suffocating, though. It had simply felt like the temple had fit itself to her dimensions, and now that she was gone it snapped back into its original form.

I sucked in a breath, feeling my lungs expand just as the room had, finally free of Athena's overwhelming attention.

With a soft trample of footsteps, my sisters hurried up to me and cut through the crowd of mortals that had remained stock-still after being witness to Athena's brief arrival and departure. Stheno was dragging Euryale with her on a hooked elbow. She looked ready to accuse me of something, though there was also a wary look in her eye that caused her to hesitate.

"So, your name is Medusa, then," Desma said before Stheno could speak, and I turned to face her instead of my sisters. I felt them rock to a stop right behind me.

"Yes," I said, and then hurriedly tacked on, "priestess."

It may have been too late for formalities with Desma. Judging by the unimpressed tilt to her mouth, I was probably right. She eyed me up and down once more, as if she could find something incriminating that Athena had missed in her evaluation of me, and then did that same for my sisters.

"And they are?"

"These are my sisters, Stheno and Euryale," I said, and thought on how I should introduce them. "They are immortal daughters of the sea gods Phorcys and Ceto. Amongst the gods, we are known as the Gorgons."

Stheno tilted her chin up at the introduction, as if daring Desma to look down on them as she had done to me, but Euryale just smiled.

Desma looked between us and asked, "You are not immortal?"

"No," I said, and did not give her an explanation.

Her mouth twisted, as if she was about to ask, but then she smoothed out her expression.

"Very well," she said. "You will come with me to prepare for your ceremony. Your sisters are not permitted to attend."

Stheno bristled. "Why not?"

"Only priestesses of this temple are allowed to witness the induction of a new member," Desma explained promptly. "If you so desire, you may attend the announcement ceremony that will take place later in the month, which will present new priestesses to the public."

I wanted to laugh at the look of disgust on Stheno's face as she considered standing amongst mortals to see me being recognized as someone of worth.

"I will not ask you to stay," I told them. "You may continue without me."

Euryale, still lagging on the uptake, asked in her sweet voice, "You are not going to keep traveling with us?"

I gave her a small smile and shook my head.

"You will be fine without me," I told her. "All you two ever needed was each other, after all."

I had not stopped to think of what Stheno and Euryale had thought when they discovered they were meant to travel the mortal cities with me, back when we first received Mother's message. Surely Stheno had been annoyed that she would be stuck with me, forced to accept my presence amongst them for so long. When I thought back on our travels to Athens, though, I could not recall any time that the two of them had complained about me. At least, not to my face.

Now that they were given the opportunity to go on without me, however, they both looked taken aback. I was surprised that Stheno had not jumped on the chance to leave me in this dusty city full of mortals.

Stheno pressed her lips together in a thin line.

"Fine," she said, snappish, "we will go."

She spun away, her tight braid whipping around behind her, and began to stride out of the temple. Euryale slipped out of Stheno's grip before she could be dragged along with her, and she stepped closer to me. While the plain mortal garments looked insufficient on Stheno, paired with Euryale's kind countenance the dress made her appear more approachable. It suited her.

"Will we see you again?" she asked.

I opened my mouth and then shut it again. I had spent so

long wishing to be away from the white house on the beach that I had had no time to think that I would want to come back to visit. I could see Desma waiting impatiently out of the corner of my eye, so I answered vaguely. "Perhaps."

Perhaps priestesses were not allowed to leave the city unless they were on official duty.

Perhaps my parents would not allow me to come home, now that I was about to dedicate myself to an Olympian goddess.

Perhaps I would never even be able to find my way back again.

Euryale just nodded and said, "Be well. And be careful."

"And you," I told her with a split-second glance to see that Stheno had paused only a few steps away and was still listening. "My best to you both," I said and dared to smile. "Avoid the Graeae if you can."

Euryale dipped her head with a grin, and then skipped to catch up with Stheno, who had begun striding away. The mortals parted like a stream around a boulder to let them pass, and my sisters did not look back as they left me in the temple.

DESMA LEFT ME IN the care of another young priestess with straight dark hair and a widow's peak who didn't speak a word to me as she beckoned me farther into the temple. She led me through a series of halls that branched off the main room until we arrived at a small chamber. It was dimly lit, with only one thin slit in the wall near the ceiling, which allowed in some of the afternoon sun. I could see a shallow washbasin, a rough bar of soap, and a large metal pitcher of water placed on a table in the corner of the room. At the chamber's center there was a square sunken pit in the marble floor. I stepped forward to peer into the pit and saw that another, smaller hole had been carved into the bottom, like a drain.

"You will bathe before the ceremony," the priestess told me. Her voice was soft and a little breathy, but somehow it still commanded the same authority as Desma's. "Remove your clothes and leave them outside. You may use the pitcher and soap, but be sparing—you won't be given any more water."

Abruptly, she turned on her heel and left the chamber, pulling a heavy curtain across the entrance as she did. I watched the fabric sway in the entryway for a moment more. I wondered if bluntness was also a trait that Athena looked for when she was selecting priestesses.

Concerned that the priestess would return before I was finished and chide me for my sluggishness, I quickly stripped off my dusty dress and folded it carefully. I placed it on the floor right outside the chamber, reaching out from behind the edge of the curtain quickly before retreating.

I tested the water in the pitcher with one finger. It wasn't as hot as the water the servants at the house on the beach had always prepared for my baths, but at least it was not freezing. I hauled the whole pitcher into the pit with me, stepping down onto the narrow ledge and then all the way to the floor. I tipped the pitcher over my shoulders first, shivering at the tepid water despite knowing what to expect.

I was glad to wash away the dust of travel, but I had to set the pitcher down and climb out of the pit to retrieve the soap from the table. The bar had very little scent, even when I brought it to my nose, but it frothed up like the edge of the ocean's surf when I rubbed it into my skin.

Having saved about half of the water, once I had rubbed the soap over all the creases of my body, I dumped a good amount of what remained over my head. Water streamed from my hair, and I tugged my fingers through the damp strands to untangle them. I used the last of the water to wash away the remaining streaks of soap.

I climbed carefully out of the pit, empty pitcher in one hand and the slippery soap bar clutched in the other. The priestess must have been waiting outside and heard me place the pitcher back on the table, because she called from behind the curtain, "I have a towel to dry off with, and your new dress."

"All right," I said. When she didn't immediately enter the chamber, I approached the curtain. At the sound of my footsteps, she parted the side of the curtain wide enough to hand me a folded stack of cloth.

"Thank you," I told her. She simply made a sound of acknowledgment and her hands retreated behind the curtain.

Drying off quickly, I unfolded the dress from the pile and held it in front of me. The priestess had given me a plain, white shift, which cinched at the waist and then flowed to my feet, my arms left bare. When I stepped out from behind the curtain, I noticed she had taken my common clothes away, and I did not think I would get them back.

My sisters and I had not brought anything with us when we had left the house on the beach. We had very little possessions, anyway, and I had never felt the need to hold on to material objects. But when the priestess took the commoner dress from me, I felt like I had lost something. It had been the only connection I had left to my life before I came to this temple.

Once I had donned my new outfit and exited the bathing room, the young priestess returned and led me back through the dim halls.

I was used to the silence that came with isolating myself at the beach house, avoiding my sisters' shrill laughs and taunting jeers when I could, but I found myself bothered by the unending quiet of the back of the temple and the young woman who led me through it. The hum of the main hall faded as we left the mortals behind, and then all I could hear was our soft footsteps.

"Where are you taking me?" I asked finally, genuinely curious, but also desperate to fill the noiseless halls.

The priestess, who had been walking steadily a few feet in front of me, slowed and glanced over her shoulder at me. She searched my face with wide brown eyes.

"You will wait in the priestesses' antechamber until nightfall, when the ceremony will begin. The ceremony cannot start until all the visitors have left the Acropolis." She slowed her pace until she was walking beside me, instead of in front of me. A conflicted look passed over her face, and then she flicked her gaze to both ends of the long, torchlit hall, as if she was worried of being overheard. In a lowered voice, she asked, "Is it true that you reprimanded Desma?"

I blinked. My sisters were incorrigible gossips, which may have been developed due to our secluded home and lives, and I had always considered it to be one of their most mortal qualities. I don't know why I was surprised to find that the priestesses, who had some divine-adjacent influences, also participated in this mortal interest in other people's business.

"I was merely defending myself," I started, and she waved her hand at my guarded tone.

"Oh, maybe *reprimanded* is too strong a word," she said airily, "but you did not back down, right?"

"Right," I said. She smiled at me. The pull of her lips poked a dimple into each of her full cheeks, making her look very young. She couldn't have been much older than me, but I wondered if Athena allowed for priestesses to be younger than eighteen.

"All of the priestesses here are terrified of Desma, and yet you come in your very first day and stand up to her." She sounded impressed. However, knowing that all the other women who served at this temple were also scared of Desma made me feel very stupid.

"Perhaps I should not have said anything," I muttered.

"Perhaps," she agreed in that same airy voice, "but you have already made a name for yourself amongst the temple, and the goddess seems to approve of you. I would not worry so much."

"Am I that obvious?"

She stopped walking, and so I stopped too.

"We were all nervous on our first day, I think," she considered me, "you have already faced the worst of it."

I highly doubt that, I thought, remembering the look on Desma's face after Athena had left.

"And you are not alone," the young priestess finished. "Not anymore."

Though I had never really been alone, always in some sort of proximity to my sisters, her words comforted me in a way that their presence never had.

"Thank you..." I said, trailing off when I realized I did not know the priestess's name.

She seemed to realize this at the same time. "My name is Pollina. Most everyone here calls me Polli."

"I am Medusa."

"Yes," she said with a laugh, "I know. I think all of Athens will soon know who you are."

THE ROOM POLLI LEFT me in was comfortable, if modestly furnished. There were low couches lining the walls and the woody smell of lit torches, which illuminated the room in the place of the fading rays of the evening sun shining through the thin windows.

The sun had only dropped a few fingers' lengths, from where I could see it in the window, when another woman came into the antechamber carrying a tray. She wore the same dress as Desma and Polli, the same one I wore now, so there was no doubt she was another priestess. She placed the tray next to the couch I had been sitting on, even though I had stood up when she entered.

"Eat," she said simply. "You will be retrieved when the ceremony is about to begin."

On the tray was a bowl carved out of wood and smoothed to a polish, filled with a thick soup that smelled of the earthy herbs the servants at the beach house had often rubbed into the skin of large white fish. There was no meat in the soup, only roughly chopped vegetables. There was also a half of a small loaf of bread, ripped down the middle. The priestess who had brought the tray left the room only to return moments later with a cup and a pitcher of water.

When I was alone once again, I poured myself some water and sipped at it. I took a small bite of soup off the spoon that matched the polished wooden bowl and, suddenly finding myself ravenous, quickly ripped off a piece of the bread to dip in the broth. In all the craze and impossibility that had occurred since I first stepped into Athens, I had not once thought of how hungry I was. Now with food offered to me, I could not think of anything else.

The bowl emptied quickly, and I sopped up the last dregs of broth with the rest of the bread and tried to savor it in my mouth. I poured myself some more water and sat back on the couch, pulling my legs up under me.

With the comforting weight of a full stomach, I began to think about my sisters and how they had left so readily. But hadn't I told them to go? Hadn't I told myself I would be fine without them, and that they would be better off without me?

I wondered where they would go now that they were on their own. They had used me as a buffer while we were amongst the mortals, since Stheno deemed speaking to any mortal, besides me, beneath her, and Euryale had always been too nervous. Would they try to find the nearest temple that sacrificed to our parents and demand hospitality? Or would they leave Athens behind altogether?

The last option seemed the most likely, since Stheno would not want to remain around a population that accepted me so easily. I hoped she was smart and steered clear of the cities that boasted great prophets and oracles, or else they could stumble upon the Graeae. I shook my head and drank more water. Stheno was not a helpless lamb, and neither was Euryale. Though they were immortal, they grew up in the same house that I had. They would be just fine.

When the last of the sunlight faded from the room, Polli came back for me. She beckoned me silently and I stood from the couch and followed her out of the room. I had thought it strange that she was so silent, since it seemed that she had warmed up to me during our walk down the dim halls, but as I stepped out of the chamber I understood.

There were two other priestesses, older women, waiting in the hallway. Polli began to walk quickly down the left hall that branched off into the many rooms, and when I noticed the older priestesses were waiting for me, I followed her. The women flanked me, reminding me of when a shepherd's dog would herd a sheep to slaughter.

I mimicked Polli's quick pace, and we reached the main hall of the temple in no time.

I faltered a step when I came out of the shadowy hallway, because the long columned corridor where my sisters had left me behind seemed to have transformed. Instead of the sun's harsh light flooding through the spaces between the pillars and illuminating every nook and cranny, the cool light of the moon washed over the marble. The lingering darkness in the corners of the temple did not feel constricting, however. The long, slanting shadows of the pillars were thrown across the floor and the angled roof seemed to stretch high into the heavens. There were no torches lit. I thought the lack of orange-tinted light, of manmade light, was what made me miss my footing.

Polli had proceeded to the far back end of the temple where a huge figure loomed. She passed by the sacrificial altar and I hurried to catch up.

I realized too late what else waited for me at the end of the temple. More priestesses were arranged in a half moon facing the large figure, whose face was shadowed in the back-light. I kept my wits about me this time and walked carefully, following the path Polli had taken until I reached the curved line of priestesses. I did a quick count of the women around me, recognizing the priestess who had brought me the tray of food at one end of the line.

Eleven. There were eleven priestesses here, excluding me.

The two priestesses with their backs to me moved, breaking the line and swinging out in opposite directions like two double doors, creating a path toward the empty space under the figure. I didn't need any instruction to know that I was meant to go to the middle of the half circle.

As I stepped through, I met a few gazes. Only when I was passing right by her did I realize Desma was one of the women who had stepped aside to let me enter the circle. The look on her face was carefully controlled, and so I kept my face still to keep it from revealing the hammering of my heart in my chest.

The women closed the gap in the line behind me once I was through. I walked until I was right under the shadow of the great looming figure and then I looked up.

I had to stifle a gasp. I had been expecting Athena, as I

had recognized the silhouette of her plumed helmet and the pommel of the massive sword at her hip, as well as the broad line of her shoulders and the wide stance of her feet. A fighting stance.

But it was not the goddess who stood above me on a raised platform, but rather a huge marble statue in her exact likeness. The hard lines of her face were carved expertly out of the stone, and the delicate paint work made it look like her steely gray eyes were watching me from above.

I spared a glance over my shoulder and searched the line of women until I found Polli. I hope she understood the question in my eyes, *What do I do?*

She remained as still as the priestesses beside her, but I saw her gaze flick quickly from me to the statue and back again, just a split-second motion.

I turned back and looked up at the statue, assessing for some sort of clue or signal as to what I was supposed to be waiting for. The marble Athena continued to gaze down at me, eyes unblinking and focused. This reminded me of a moment during my first interaction with Athena, all those years ago on the beach after Echidna's wedding. Athena had asked me a question and then watched me, waiting for a response. Waiting for a mortal to give her goddess an answer.

I realized what I could do, though I was not sure if it was what I should do. I squared my shoulders. *You have come too far to let a statue stand in your way*, I scolded myself.

"Athena," I said, forcing all my intention into my voice and willing it to be steady, "goddess of wisdom and patron of Athens, my name is Medusa. I have come to be a priestess of your temple and serve a divine purpose. You once asked me if I feared for my mortal future." I paused and sucked in a breath. "I would like to begin on the path toward a future where that fear does not control me. Allow me to join your temple, so that I may serve you and learn what wisdom you would grant me."

The wind that tore through the hall after I spoke would have snuffed out the torches, had they been lit, but it tugged incessantly at the loose fabric of my dress and whistled over my ears. I felt the pressure of the room change and I closed my eyes so that they wouldn't pop out of my skull. When it was quiet once again, I opened them.

Athena, the real Athena with her faintly glowing skin and a fierce grin on her face, stepped off the pedestal and placed her hand on the top of my head. The weight of it pressed my curls flat to my crown.

"I accept you as one of my own, and from this day forward, you will be one of my trusted attendants. Welcome, Medusa," Athena said in a voice that sang like a sword being drawn from its sheath, "to the priestesses of Athena."

A sisterhood of a different sort

THE DUTIES OF A priestess in the temple of Athena were not what I expected. Or at least, many of the tasks were not what I thought a priestess would be doing.

For the first few days, I followed Polli around the temple like a stray dog as she did her chores: lighting torches, sweeping the busy front hall that always seemed to have a fine layer of dust from the sandals of visitors, collecting the offerings from the altars at the end of the day, and even going outside to tend to the olive trees that grew around the Acropolis. Polli chatted brightly to me through all these tasks, not deterred by the fact that I often went long stretches without replying. She seemed happy to have someone new to talk to. I was not familiar with this kind of unending conversation, since any conversation I'd had with my sisters was often as brief and terse as possible, especially when our family was around. But Polli told me about the kinds of ritual sacrifices she'd witnessed while we scrubbed the marble altars, and described some of the weirder offerings that visitors had brought for Athena as we shook olives from the trees outside the temple to send to the olive oil–makers.

I had never done manual labor before. The white house on the beach had been well staffed and so I had never had to sweep out the sand from the entranceway or make my own food. At the temple, I spent an entire afternoon in a small, hot kitchen kneading dough to make the tough bread that was served with every meal. My arms ached from the repetitive movement of pushing at the tacky dough with the heel of my palm, copying Polli's efficient movements.

After a week of chores, I collapsed on my thin bed one evening after the final prayer to Athena and let out a great sigh. Polli, who slept in the bed next to mine, laughed.

"It is hard work to be a priestess," she said, "though no one really knows quite how hard it actually is." She shuffled under her blankets and pulled them up to her chin, a childish way of sleeping that made her seem even younger than she was.

"I thought that priestesses..." I trailed off for a moment, trying to think back at what I thought priestesses did before I became one. "I thought they were much more revered, praised by the citizens as conduits to the gods and all that. I suppose I had expected to be spending more time cutting the throats of goats and heifers, rather than scraping up the oil from under torches and cleaning the floor," I said, describing how we had spent the last few hours after dinner.

A priestess a few beds away, I thought her name was Ariana, chuckled from under her blankets. The lone remaining torch that illuminated the sleeping quarters flickered over her thick, curly black hair, the only part of her I could see from my bed.

"I think we all thought that when we first joined, too," Polli said. "But only the most experienced priestesses get to perform those huge public sacrifices. Desma has done the most, as she's been here the longest."

I had been able to avoid Desma for the most part during my first week in the temple, other than when the priestesses took meals together or gathered for morning and evening prayers to the goddess. I had noticed that Desma acted the most like a leader out of all the women, and everyone deferred to her when it came to distributing tasks or controlling the large crowds of visitors that would flood through the temple. I would have to face Desma again eventually, but I'd hoped to prolong that meeting for as long as I could. I had only just gotten to the temple, and I was not looking to get thrown out of it straightaway.

Desma herself came into the room as I thought about how I would need to remain at the temple for a long, long time before I would be allowed to perform any kind of ritual. While I was sure I had the patience to wait for my time to be an active role in these rites, I worried the sudden flare of my temper that had reared its head my first day here would end my journey before it had even begun.

Desma said, "May Athena grant you all pleasant dreams," and then got into her bed right beside the door. Someone blew out the torch, and the room was thrown into darkness.

I WAS STANDING AT the front entrance of the Acropolis greeting visitors, a task I had only recently been allowed to do on my own, when Polli came running up behind me.

"We get to go out!" she said excitedly, seizing me by the arm and giving it a little shake.

I smiled politely at the people who were passing through the entrance before I turned to Polli, offering them a basket of plucked laurel branches to bring to Athena's altar if they had come empty-handed.

"Go out where?" I asked her, once the group had passed.

"Out! Out into the city!"

I felt my brows draw together over my eyes. "What would we do out there?"

"Medusa," Polli said with a gasp, "do not tell me that you have not wanted to explore Athens since you arrived here?"

"I saw Athens," I replied. "I saw the streets that I took to get to this temple, and the tops of the buildings from the side of the cliff that led to this temple. That is Athens."

"For shame," Polli said, shaking her head slowly, though she was still smiling. "Desma has assigned us to travel to the sector of Athens where the richest citizens live and offer them simple prayers and dedications to Athena. She said it's a good idea to remind the rich that even they are not above paying their dues to the patron goddess."

"Desma thinks I am ready for that?" I asked, taken aback that Desma would see me fit to do anything at all, other than keeping the floors clean.

Polli thought for a moment. "Desma did seem a bit... tight, when she told me that we would be going out."

"Tight?"

"Yes, you know, like," Polli clenched her jaw and set her shoulders and gave me what was probably meant to be a stern look, similar to how Desma stood anytime she spoke to me.

I couldn't help but laugh at Polli's impression of the high priestess, and she broke her pose to smile at me. "You think she is starting to trust you?"

"Definitely not," I said, "but I wonder if she was not given any choice in the matter."

"What do you mean?"

"Well, who would Desma have to listen to and obey, even if it meant that it would somehow benefit me?"

Polli tapped a finger to her lips, and I quickly tilted my head in the direction of the large statue at the back of the hall. She gasped, "Athena!"

"That would make the most sense," I agreed. While I had kept my thoughts to myself about the work I performed at the goddess's temple, each night during final prayer I asked Athena why I was there, why she had called me to her, and why I spent so much time kneading dough. Perhaps she was finally sending me to find the answer.

"Well, then," Polli said with confidence, "if wise Athena wants you to explore Athens, then you have no choice but to do so."

"I suppose you are right," I mumbled, but Polli had already begun talking about all the places she wanted to take me while we were out in the city. It had been almost a year since she had been down off the Acropolis hill, since priestesses left their temples so rarely, and she was excited to see what had changed.

I only half listened to Polli, smiling absentmindedly at

the visitors who streamed in and out of the entrance. Why would Athena want me to travel through the city? What could I see or hear or learn there that would be more beneficial than my life at the temple?

I did not share the same level of excitement as Polli at the thought of getting to descend from the Acropolis, but the more I thought about it, the more I realized how little of the world I had seen. Other than the few weeks of travel it took me and my sisters to get to Athens and then to the Acropolis, I had never experienced the life of a mortal woman.

I turned to Polli and interrupted her mid-sentence. "When do we leave?"

WE WOULD REMAIN IN our plain dresses when we traveled down from the temple, Polli had told me, but we would need to be adorned just enough to be recognized as acolytes of Athena. I had no belongings that would suffice, as I had given up everything I had worn on my first day, but I soon realized that nothing I had previously owned would have identified me as one of Athena's priestesses.

Desma was waiting for Polli and me by a towering column that flanked the entrance to the temple. It was too early in the morning for any visitors to be coming up the steps, and we had the temple to ourselves. Desma's face was calm, but I could see the way she was holding her shoulders stiffly, like her spine had been replaced with a shepherd's crook. She was, as Polli put it, *tight*. In her hands Desma held a small wooden box, simply carved from a piece of oak but polished to a shine. She held it out to me when we stood before her.

I reached to open the lid, but Desma jerked the box back out of my grip and hissed at me.

"No," she spat, "you are not permitted to open it. Hold it for me."

Pressing my lips into a thin line, I reached out for the box again, this time cupping the bottom edges in the palms of my hands as Desma carefully let go. She lifted the edge of the lid closest to her. I tried peering over the lip of the box but Desma quickly tucked her hands inside and pulled out what looked like a thin silver necklace. There was a pendant swinging on the bottom of the chain, but I could not make out its shape until Desma turned and placed the chain over Polli's head. It was not a necklace, but rather a circlet with a delicate silver owl that rested on Polli's forehead right underneath the point of her dark widow's peak.

When I peered closer, I saw that the owl was resting on a crescent-shaped olive branch. Athena's bird, resting on the symbol of Athens's patron goddess.

Desma turned back to the box and pulled out another circlet. Desma and I were nearly of the same height, so I had to dip my head a bit for her to place the chain around my crown. My hair was loose and curled over my shoulders and down my back, marking me as young and unmarried, and I could feel the silver chain catching in the curls. The owl pendant weighed barely anything at all, and the cool metal quickly warmed against the skin of my forehead.

I lifted my head and saw Desma watching me carefully.

"This will mark you as one of Athena's claimed

priestesses," she said importantly. "Do not make a show of yourself whilst you are wearing it."

Polli made a face like she would rather sleep in the pig-pen than draw any dishonor to Athena's name, but I held Desma's gaze as she gave us the warning. I knew her words were meant for me. Desma shut the lid of the box with a snap and took it out of my hands.

She said, "May Athena watch over you," and then strode away, back into the temple to assign morning chores.

Polli and I descended the steps and made our way toward the edge of the Acropolis's plateau where the dirt-packed road would lead down into the city. Our sandals scuffed against loose stones and kicked up dust that clung to the hems of our dresses. Tilting my head back, I squinted toward the steadily rising sun as it burned away the lingering coolness from dawn.

"Has a priestess ever done anything," I asked Polli slowly as we walked, "*shameful* enough to have been removed from the temple?"

Polli, who had been swinging her hands by her sides, quickly clasped them in front of her and assumed a more ladylike posture. From the way her neck was angled, it did not look too comfortable.

"Well," she said, "not that I've seen, though I have not been here for very long. I heard from one of the older priestesses that there was a girl who was caught having some sort of relations with a man in the temple." She said *relations* like other people said *infection*. "And she was asked to leave."

"Really? They just asked her to leave, and that was it?" I

had a hard time believing anyone could get away with bringing disgrace on Athena without consequence.

"I think so," Polli said, but she didn't sound sure. "She
was never seen or heard from again, in any case."

We had reached the edge of the Acropolis and began
down the dirt road, which felt much wider than the last time
I had traveled on it since there were no other people travers-
ing up or down from the hill. Huge cypress trees lined the
cliff edge of the road, and as we descended, the trees seemed
to stretch high over our heads to try and brush the heavens
with their pointed branches.

"Hey," Polli said suddenly, bouncing on her toes. Any
thoughts she'd had about the priestess who had disappeared
were far behind her. "I'll race you to the bottom!"

"Desma said we were not to make fools of ourselves," I
said, but I was smiling.

She scoffed, "No one can see us here! But I suppose if
you're so worried about Desma finding out you had a bit of
fun when no one was looking," she drawled, "then you've
already lost!"

Polli suddenly burst into a run, the bottoms of her sandals flashing as she flew down the hill, her arms pumping
and her dark hair streaming behind her.

I didn't think. I just took off after her.

I caught up to Polli quickly, the skirts of my dress whipping around my legs. I could feel the grit of the dirt we were
kicking up getting stuck between the bottom of my sandals
and my toes, but I didn't care. My hair was bouncing with the
rhythm of my strides and it skimmed lightly over my shoulders, soft as a breeze. The last time I had run so freely was

at the white beach house when I was much, much younger. When my head had been free of trouble.

Polli laughed, clear and bright, as we hurtled down the hill, and I joined her.

All too soon the road flattened out and we slowed to a stop, our steps loud and thumping on the ground as we lost momentum.

My chest was rising and falling rapidly, and I could hear my heart beating like waves crashing on a cliffside. There was dirt caked on my feet and calves, and I could feel beads of sweat dripping from my hairline. But I was smiling.

Polli had her hands on her hips as she tried to catch her breath.

"Okay, that was a draw," she panted.

Once our breathing had calmed down, we smacked the dirt from each other's dresses and dabbed at our foreheads to get rid of the sweat. We deemed each other presentable, and then Polli linked her arm through mine.

"Do not be nervous," she told me. "I grew up in this city as a young girl, so I know all the best ways to get around."

I had not thought to be nervous, but now as she spoke, I wondered if the other mortals living in Athens would notice that I didn't quite belong. The customs of gods and demi-gods were not so different from that of mortals, but I knew there must have been some things about living with mortals that I had never gotten the chance to learn.

Noticing my hesitation, Polli smiled soothingly at me and then pulled us forward and into the waking streets of Athens. A few early risers were out already. There were produce sellers who had journeyed into the city from their farms, and a few fishermen hauling in baskets of the catches they had made before dawn had climbed into the sky. A small group of servant women trying to get the washing done in the communal tubs before the heat of the day set in were chatting loudly at a corner.

As we walked through the orderly roads, Polli turning us down the right streets, I noticed the mortals were watching us from their places on the threshold of houses or in stalls on the side of the road. An old man with thinning white hair was stringing up fish to dry on a line, but when we passed, he lost his grip on the string and it slithered out of his hands, sending the fish flopping to the floor. He was gaping at Polli and me like one of his own wide-mouthed fish.

A younger man appeared from behind the stall. When he saw the fish on the floor he began to complain, loudly, about the older man's clumsiness. But when he noticed where the old fisherman was looking, the young man looked up at us and blinked. Then blinked again. A slow, creeping grin stretched from one side of his mouth to the other, which I thought made him look like he had been caught on a hook.

"Beautiful lady," he called out, "would you bless me with good fortune?"

The old fisherman smacked him on the arm, and the young man flinched.

"Fool!" the old man said in a whisper that carried across the road. "Are you blind? Do you not see the circlet that she wears?"

The young man squinted at us, moving his gaze from head to toe and back again in a long, slow sweep that made me want to cross my arms over my chest. I could tell the exact moment he saw Athena's pendant sitting square in the middle of our foreheads, flashing silver in the morning light, because the healthy glow to the man's face flushed away and he mumbled an apology.

I turned to Polli with a question in my eyes.

She shrugged daintily. "The citizens of Athens know to respect Athena's priestesses. That has never happened when I've been out with any of the others before, though."

We continued walking and I could hear the two men whispering back and forth behind us, forcing their voices low enough that I could not hear.

"What, specifically, has not happened before?" I asked Polli.

"Oh, men have not called out to us like that," she said, grinning at me, "though I quite understand why that one was not able to resist."

"How do you mean?"

"Come now, Medusa," Polli chided, as she patted my arm. "You must know how captivating you are. Have you not seen how everyone on the street has stared at you while you walk by?"

"I thought they were looking at us because we are two of Athena's priestesses," I admitted.

Polli shook her head and laughed. "They are looking at *you*, you and your godly beauty."

I nearly missed a step. "Godly?"

She nodded. "I'm sure that is how everyone else who stares at you would describe it. Your golden hair, those dark eyes." She had tilted her head to observe me as we walked, and I felt a spot of warmth spread over my cheekbones. "And sometimes it seems like your skin glows, like the beauty is coming from within you and has no choice but to reflect on the outside."

The warmth on my cheeks was like the sun on a hot summer afternoon. Trying to not let the tangle of emotions I was feeling—confusion, embarrassment, and, oddly, pleasure—show on my face, I just clutched Polli's arm tighter to my side.

"Thank you," I said quietly. "No one has ever—" I stopped.

"No one has ever...what?"

"I have never gotten a compliment on my appearance," I admitted.

Polli looked shocked. "Surely this isn't true? Well then, the people who have known you before did you a great disservice."

I didn't tell her that where I came from, the mortal blood within me was more appalling than anything on the outside.

"What about when you left your home?" Polli pressed on. "I find it difficult to believe that any man or woman with eyes and a beating heart who passed you on the street would not end up with their jaw hanging open, like that man back there."

Thinking back on my first day in Athens, when my sisters and I had traveled to the temple, I remembered the man selling the wooden tools.

"Actually," I said, "yes, there was one person, a man. I was asking for directions to the temple and he called me beautiful."

I remembered the confusion I had felt, and the bewildered looks on Stheno's and Euryale's faces. It was that same feeling I had felt just now when Polli was talking about my skin, and my eyes, and my hair. I reached up with my free hand and tugged at one of the golden curls, wrapping it around my finger. For so long I had hated how this hair mocked the difference between my sisters and me and marked me as an outsider in my own family. Letting the strands slip from my fingers, I carefully tucked the lock behind my ear and flicked the rest over my shoulder so that the great mass of curls glinted golden in the light.

The men and women on the street around us looked toward that flash of gold, and then continued to stare. I met their eyes. And I smiled.

ONCE WE REACHED THE richer neighborhoods, with their sprawling, sun-drenched villas and high boundary walls, I stayed a half step back from Polli and let her do all the speaking. She would introduce us at the gates, or at doorways, and servants would glance nervously at the silver pendants on our foreheads before hurrying off to report to their masters. Most of the homes we visited agreed to the in-house prayers and dedications to Athena. Those who welcomed us farther into the villas brought us to miniature altars for Athena that were built into the sides of courtyards, where Polli would press the tips of her fingers to the small statue of the patron goddess and chant a simple prayer for goodwill and wisdom.

At a few houses, Polli would ask the family to join in the prayer. I studied the people that Polli drew into the chant and compared them to those that she simply smiled at and finished the prayer on her own.

There was a smiling older couple, the man with thinning white hair wisping over the top of his head, and the woman with trembling hands tucked through her husband's arm. They welcomed us in and offered refreshments, which we gratefully accepted. Polli did not ask this couple to join the prayer. Out of the corner of my eye, I saw how they bowed their heads as Polli spoke, and the woman's mouth was moving voicelessly.

The couple had looked at me with kind eyes. The wife reached up with a shaking hand as if to take ahold of one of my curls, but she drew back before she touched it.

"It has been many years since I have seen such golden hair," she said, her voice soft and brittle as a blade of grass. "Only the gods themselves have hair as fine as yours."

"I am not a god," I told her.

She kept smiling at me. "Nonetheless, your looks could rival a fair few of them." She winked at me, conspiratorially. "Though, I am not senile enough to say *which* few. I would like to avoid any outright conflict with a god at my age, if I can."

One of the largest villas was owned by a severe-looking man who did not come to meet us in his courtyard. Instead, a nervous servant brought us to an open study where the man lounged with a few scrolls of parchment open on a low table in front of him. He agreed to the prayers with some annoyance and led us back through the house to his altar, which was half hidden behind an elaborate tapestry. The master of the house stepped back and crossed his arms, ordering us to proceed.

This time, before Polli began, she turned to the man and waved her hand in a summoning gesture.

"More than my voice is necessary to bring a blessing on this house," she said. Somewhat cryptically, I thought.

The man sighed out through his nose, but he stepped forward and recited the chant. Once the prayer was done the man instructed the nervous servant to see us out and strode away.

"Why did he need to perform the prayer?" I asked Polli when we were out on the street again. The sun had trekked its way across the arch in the sky while we had been visiting these homes, and it now rested to the west. My feet ached from traveling up and down rough stone streets. Polli still looked as cheerful as she had been when we'd departed from the temple this morning, but I could tell that she would seize the earliest chance to take a seat, just as I would.

"There are citizens in Athens," she said, "who are well enough off to afford great dedications to Athena to show their thanks for any blessings or aid they might have received. There are also citizens who know what they can afford, and yet choose to do less than they should. We find it is often easier to give them a nudge in the right direction with, say, a house call from a priestess, rather than having Athena herself thunder in and disrupt their lives until she has been satisfied."

"Has Athena done this before?"

"Oh, sure," Polli said, steering us back toward the Acropolis. "You have heard of Athena's wrath over mortals who have wronged her, have you not?"

I nodded. There were countless tales of Athena and every other god bearing down on mortals who offended them, from reasons trivial to dire. Once I thought it over, I could see why Athena would keep the citizens of her city under sharp supervision, like a commander observing the soldiers in her infantry. I had never witnessed a divine punishment or curse before, only heard about them from the rabble in my father's feasting hall or through the gossiping mouths of my siblings. Perhaps now that I was surrounded by mortals, I would finally see what it was like for divine justice to be delivered.

The ascent to the Acropolis that evening took much longer than our frenzied run down it had in the morning. By the time we crested the rise and the temple came into view, my legs were burning and I wanted to push past all the lingering visitors to reach the cool marble, but I remembered Desma's warning from this morning and managed to keep myself composed. People tilted their heads to us as we passed, our pendants glinting over their faces in the setting sun, and I felt their eyes linger on me as I swept past them. I felt my lips tug up into a grin, unbidden.

Athena's temple was almost entirely empty when we stepped into the shaded hall, and I let out a deep sigh that Polli echoed. She giggled.

"What I would not give," I said lowly, plucking at the skirts of my dress, "for a bath right now."

"We will have to wait until after dinner," Polli said.

"There is a fountain outside," I replied, raising my brow.

Polli gasped. "Medusa, you would not."

"Not so different from a bathing pool, is it?" I wondered aloud and smiled at Polli's noise of distress.

"It is much appreciated," a sharp voice said to our left, "that you refrain from misusing the temple's outer features." Desma was striding toward us with the box from this morning in her hands.

The mirth disappeared from Polli's face, but I did not shrink under Desma's scathing look. I took the box from her when she thrust it at me and bent my neck so that she could lift the chain from my head. The fine links caught in a few strands of my hair. Desma *tch*ed and pulled at the chain, yanking my hair, but when I hissed in pain Polli hurried forward and quickly picked the hairs free of the links. Polli's pendant came off with no issue, and Desma placed both chains back into the box and snapped it shut.

"Medusa," she said as she lifted the box from my hands, "you will clear the altar of this evening's sacrifices. Pollina, kitchen duty."

She marched away, Polli sending me a *what can you do?* look over her shoulder as she followed the head priestess out of the great hall.

The altar where visitors could deliver small sacrifices and make offerings to Athena stood a few lengths in front of the towering statue of the patron goddess. The most common offering was silver—in the form of coins, engraved cups filled with wine, and even a few pieces of armor. But there were also stacks of laurel wreaths from victors of war games and battles, left for Athena to thank her for her wisdom in warfare. The great sacrifices of animals did not take place in the temple, save for the rites that the priestesses performed on special holidays, but there were still many food offerings piled on and around the altar: plates of finely spiced meats, piles of flat breads, and soft fruits and figs from the outlying farms.

The food, wine, and crowns of laurels would be burned in the wide, iron bowls behind the statue of Athena that blazed with fire day and night so the smoke could rise to the heavens. As for the silver, I had to remove each piece from the altar and carry it to a side room off the main hall where all of Athena's more expensive donations were kept.

What a goddess who did not eat or drink in the mortal realm needed with fifty sets of silver cutlery, I had no idea. However, I knew Athena highly preferred the armor left at her altars. She would reuse the sacrificed armor and bestow it upon the next mortal she decided to favor in battle, now with her divinity infused into the metal.

It was slow work, hefting all the silver into the storeroom, and by the time I had dumped the last polished helmet onto a rack full of silver helmets, night had fallen outside.

Taking up the broom that sat just inside the door of the storeroom, I swept around the bottom of the altar to clear away any debris from the offerings and provide a clear place for the next morning's sacrifices. As I was finishing up, the air around me trembled and the torches lining the room fizzed and crackled, spurred on by a salty breeze. My ears popped as the air pressure changed.

"So, this is what happens to pretty girls who catch Athena's eye," came a deep, rumbling voice from the back of the hall. I looked up, and in the bright light of the moon I recognized the sturdy outline of Poseidon's bare shoulders and head of curly black hair. Like Athena, four years had not changed anything about the sea god's appearance.

Poseidon was leaning casually against the base of Athena's statue, his arms and ankles crossed, looking right at home in the temple of the goddess who he, supposedly, had an era's worth of conflict with.

My fingers tightened around the smooth wooden handle of the broom as Poseidon's gaze slid over me. I could feel every speck of dirt that coated my feet and clung to the hem of my dress, and I wondered if this was how every mortal felt under the gaze of a god—small and dirty. But as he continued to watch me, the unblinking moon filling the space between us with light, I remembered how I had felt this afternoon when every citizen I passed could not take their eyes off me. I remembered that Athena had requested me to join her temple, and that she had instructed the high priestess to send me out amongst the Athenians. Athena saw something more than plain mortal when she looked at me.

As he was a god and I was no fool, I performed a quick bow. When I glanced up once more, Poseidon's gaze was still intent on my face.

Pretty girl, he had called me.

Conscious of every move, I shifted my body into the haughtily slanted stance my mother had taken so often. I tilted my chin up at the god and lowered my lashes just so. I was new to the feeling of being wanted, but I could recognize it. My mother was able to turn the desire of others into tools for her own gain—I had seen her do it to countless sea gods, including my father. This was the pose she took when she wanted something and knew how to get it.

I didn't know exactly what I wanted, but I hoped that mimicking my mother's confidence would give me some of my own.

"Lord of the sea," I said, greeting him, "these are the duties of a priestess for Athena."

He laughed at that, and I frowned.

"No," he said, "those are the duties of a servant."

"What are priestesses and priests but servants to their gods?" I asked.

He shrugged. "Servants with high opinions of themselves."

That smarted a bit. I turned back to my work, even though the altar was spotless, and began to sweep around the edges, watching Poseidon out of the corner of my eye.

Another salty breeze blew through the temple, shifting my hair across my bare shoulders and curling around my legs. When he spoke again, Poseidon's voice was much closer this time. I had not seen him move.

"I mean no offense, of course," he said. "It just seems a shame that one such as you, who has grown into such a beautiful young woman, should be left to clean the floors."

Looking over my shoulder, I saw that he was now standing on the other side of the altar, a devilish grin parting his handsome face.

"Your words are too kind," I said. A brief flash of something—frustration?—flickered over his face but disappeared just as quickly. Perhaps it had just been a trick of the torchlight.

"That they may be," he said lowly, "but there is still truth to them." He leaned over the altar, bracing himself with one hand splayed on the pale marble, and tucked his fingers into a handful of my curls.

I opened my mouth, but no words came out as he let the strands glide from his grasp.

"So fine," he said. "And golden. The color is nearly the same as the ichor that runs in my veins."

I scrambled for a response, but I felt as though my head had emptied out. The only feeling I had was a heat on my cheekbones and a gentle prickle along the top of my head. It was not something I had experienced very often, I thought, and I did not think it was altogether pleasant.

A sound echoed out from one of the hallways that branched out from the main temple, caused by a footstep or an approaching voice. Poseidon drew his hand away and leaned back.

I blinked, and then turned to see a shadow moving toward us from the hallway that led to the kitchens. Probably Polli, come to see what had been taking me so long.

Poseidon had returned to the statue's side when I looked back to him, half hidden in the shade that Athena's massive figure threw across the floor. His teeth flashed white in the dim moonlight.

"Be well, priestess," he said. And then a final briny breeze swept through the temple and disappeared into the dark.

"Medusa?" Polli called from the threshold of the hallway.

I did not turn to her, as I was still looking at the statue, the face half concealed with shadow. Athena had come to greet me my first day at the temple by bringing this statue to life, the cold stone giving way to solid flesh and bone and metal.

As I met the gaze of the one gray eye, I wondered how much Athena had seen of Poseidon's visit.

Stheno

MORTAL CITIES WERE UNBEARABLY warm. Stheno disliked feeling as though the air clung to her skin, hot and ragged. There was no respite in a cool ocean breeze like the house on the beach. Even with her hair pulled high off her neck and the lightest fabric draped over her reclined form, Stheno grew more and more irritated by the heat.

"This is awful," she said. Euryale, who was sitting on the floor in front of Stheno's chair reading a scroll spread out on a low table that kept trying to roll back in on itself, didn't seem to hear her. Stheno repeated, louder, "This is awful!"

"Hmm? What is?" Euryale asked, not taking her eyes off the scroll.

"This place! This stupid trip, everything that we're doing. It's been nearly two years already and we've nothing to show for it. We should just go home; I don't even know what Mother was thinking by sending us here. What did she hope we could learn from these stupid mortals?" Stheno dropped her head onto the back of the armchair and stared up at the ceiling. She and Euryale had found a temple in a small coastal town during the first year of their journey that still worshipped some of the non-Olympian gods, and they were welcomed in with wide eyes and bowed heads.

At first, Stheno had felt that they had finally found some mortals with an ounce of sense, unlike the people that littered Athens. The priestesses at this temple were demure around Stheno and her sister, fulfilling their every wish at the slightest question and nearly falling over themselves to make offerings. But after a few months of this treatment, Stheno felt ready to crawl out of her skin.

She was unfamiliar with praise. Growing up around her older siblings had better prepared her to face down a mob of angry mortals than stand on an altar while they bowed to her.

Euryale, on the other hand, had taken to life in the temple and the little town easily. She was kind to the priestesses, generous to the mortals who came up to her with tentative questions, and eager to learn about what mortal knowledge had to offer her. It seemed like she had a new scroll to read every day. The scroll keeper of the temple was becoming increasingly friendly with Euryale, instead of just polite.

In many ways, this was not unlike their life at home on the beach. They were waited on by drifting servants and spent most of their days amusing themselves. But if they were meant to keep living as they had been, why had their mother bothered to send them so far away?

They were sitting in a large atrium in the temple, which was filled with comfortable chairs and couches for guests. Huge skylights allowed sunlight to filter into the room, illuminating lush plants and a shallow fountain set into the floor.

Stheno and Euryale preferred this room, and the priestesses had given them free rein of it ever since they arrived.

Faint footsteps echoed down the hall, growing louder as they approached the sisters' room. Stheno turned her head as one of the temple priestesses stepped into the doorway with her eyes downcast.

"Gorgons," she said, "I have news for you of other temples, as you requested."

"Oh yes," Euryale replied brightly, reaching back to tug Stheno into a sitting position on the couch so she could move off the floor and take a seat next to her. "Please do come in."

The priestess bowed and approached. She risked a flickering glance up at them, her eyes widening when she met Stheno's gaze, before dropping back down to the floor.

"Sit." Euryale gestured to the couch across from them.

"That won't be necessary," the priestess said. "There are only a few things to report. A traveler arrived in the temple this afternoon, having moved down along the coast to us from Athens. I believe you instructed us specifically to ask about the temples from Athena's city?"

Stheno swayed forward in her seat, exchanging a curious look with Euryale. "Yes."

The priestess continued, "The traveler says that he had visited the Acropolis while there, but there was unrest in the city. Apparently, there are rising tensions between the city's patron Athena and Poseidon."

"What kind of tensions?" Stheno asked. She remembered the night at Echidna's wedding, when the two Olympians had appeared. How they had bristled against each other. She also remembered watching Medusa run out of the banquet hall after the Graeae had laid out a terrible fate for her, and how the two gods had taken their leave soon after. Had Medusa spoken to them that night? If she had somehow become entangled in the gods' feud, Stheno worried what the consequences would be. "What are the people saying?"

"The city was founded on their feud, as you know," the priestess replied, and Euryale nodded. "There are rumors that the sea god intends to seek revenge for his loss against Athena. The city's citizens all seem to have their theories about what that revenge will look like, but most of it is idle gossip."

"But he lost fairly, did he not?" Euryale asked, her tone genuine. "The people chose who they wished to have as patron."

"Euryale," Stheno said before the priestess could respond, "you and I both know that gods care nothing for fairness, when their pride is involved."

Euryale's mouth thinned, but she nodded, likely remembering every interaction they had ever had with their prideful father. While Euryale asked for a more detailed account of the traveler's story, Stheno stood and walked to the thin windows of the temple.

When they had left Medusa in that cavernous temple in Athens, Stheno had thought that her sister had finally found the refuge she had been searching for. Athena was a goddess revered by mortals of all kinds. Any priestess that served her would have the protection of the wisest Olympian. But Athena was still a god, and Stheno understood the fickleness and self-serving vices of gods quite well.

Stheno hoped her sister had not let down her guard after

being away from their family. Medusa had found a place to belong, but now she was trapped in the middle of a feud that could bring the wrath of two Olympians down on her golden head.

The priestess finished her report and bowed out of the room. Euryale stood and joined Stheno at the window.

"You're worried about her," Stheno said.

"Yes," Euryale agreed. "And try as you might to conceal it, I can tell you are too."

Crossing her arms, Stheno tapped her fingers against her elbow in an annoyed rhythm. "Why should we be worried? She was the one who left us, remember?"

Euryale's tone was strained. "Perhaps she was right to leave us. We were never very kind to her."

"And why should have we been kind to her?" Stheno drawled, even as the thread of guilt tugged at her. The strand had been steadily building ever since she was a child, when teasing Medusa had been nothing more than a game, but now it threatened to strangle her. "She was mortal. She made us outcasts in the family. She was destined to become a monster anyway—"

"Stheno."

The absolute coldness in Euryale's tone stopped Stheno in her tracks. She had never heard her sister sound so angry, and she had especially never heard it directed at herself. When Stheno looked at her sister, Euryale's face was torn with emotion.

"Do not," Euryale said slowly, her voice trembling, "talk of Medusa's prophecy as a death sentence. We were terrible to her before we had even heard it. If being called a monster is the worst thing you can imagine—worth being cut off from your only family—then," Euryale took a breath to steady herself, "then you will have to cast me off as well."

"What are you talking about?" Stheno asked, her arms falling open as she stepped closer to Euryale.

Her sister tilted her head back, blinking away the wetness in her eyes.

"I never told you," she started, "because I saw how you—how we—treated Medusa. She was only human. And yet, you made me believe she was less than us. And I did believe it. But before Medusa got her prophecy, I realized something. About myself."

Now Euryale crossed her arms, hugging her sides. "I was arguing with one of the servants one day, you had already left the house. Medusa was gone, too. I can't even remember what I was upset about, but I just felt like there was something roiling in my chest, like a heat storm, that grew and grew as I got more frustrated. Eventually, I just screamed."

In bits and pieces, Euryale described how her scream had struck out like lightning. The servant, confused and not at all prepared, had pressed their hands to their ears against the noise, but it was no use. They had collapsed, a thin stream of blood leaking from their ears. Dead.

"I had no idea what I had just done," Euryale whispered. "I had no idea what was inside of me. But I had killed someone."

Stheno stared at her. She did remember how Euryale had closed herself off suddenly when they were younger. She had still followed Stheno around, but she rarely spoke, often only venturing to talk once Stheno had set a tone for her to copy.

Dumbly, she asked, "What did you do with the body?"

She immediately wished she could take the question back. The bleak, hiccuping laugh that burst out of Euryale echoed through the room. "I dragged it out to the water and let the tide take it. It took me all night. I was so worried you or Medusa would notice the marks in the sand in the morning, but by the time the sun rose they were gone. Mother probably helped me, even though I didn't realize it at the time."

Their mother had always favored Euryale, so this did not surprise Stheno. What did surprise her was how her sister had been able to hide this from her for so long. She couldn't imagine young, sweet-faced Euryale struggling with a corpse that she had made.

"Medusa won't be the first one of us to become a monster," Euryale told her. "Because I already am one."

"You aren't—" Stheno began, but Euryale cut her off.

"I am. Whatever you need to think of me, there is no doubt that there is something in me that has taken after our family. My scream scared me then, and my fear of it turned me into something even worse. It turned me against my own sister." Euryale blinked as thin trails of tears began to run down her fine cheeks. "It turned me against the one person who might have understood."

Stung by the idea that Euryale would have trusted Medusa with a piece of herself, and left Stheno by the wayside, Stheno stepped closer.

"You never gave me a chance to understand," she argued. "What, it was either you told Medusa, or no one?"

They were no longer children, squabbling over meaningless slights, but Stheno couldn't let go of the idea that it would always be her and Euryale against the world. She had been the focal point for Euryale to orbit around. Stheno thought that Euryale had always looked to her for direction, for guidance through the years. Stheno thought that Euryale had need of her. She had thought, tied up in her threads of guilt, that she was the stronger sister.

Euryale's confession had Stheno's illusion crumbling around her. In their family, monstrosity was a given. But amongst the Gorgons, it was an abnormality, because Stheno had decided it was so.

However, if Medusa's fate was laid out on a path of monstrosity, and Euryale had already discovered hers, that meant that Stheno was the odd one out. She had no power. She had no prophecy. These years in limbo, ruminating over the mistakes of her childhood, solidified the fact that she had nothing to offer. Once Medusa's fate came to be, she would be the only Gorgon with nothing to her name. What would her sisters need her for? What had she done, except tear them apart?

"Did you want to tell Medusa and…and what?" Stheno asked, her bruised heart leaking guilt all over her words. "Have a reason to leave me behind?"

"No!"

"Then why couldn't you tell me?"

"Because I was even more terrified by the thought of losing you forever!" Euryale shouted. The sound echoed sharply against the smooth marble of the room, multiplying Euryale's voice like the frenzied cry of an animal caught in a trap. Euryale gasped and clapped her hands over her mouth.

Stheno had stiffened when Euryale's raised voice clawed through the room, but she steadied her heart. She knew that even with a deafening wail lurking in her throat, her sister would never hurt her. Stheno was not the strongest sister. She might have been wrong about that their entire lives, but she knew she had one thing right. Euryale needed her. Not to be strong for her, but to simply be there, as her sister. Stheno took another step closer so that she could grasp Euryale's wrists.

"You will never lose me," Stheno promised. She tugged at Euryale's wrists until her sister dropped her hands from her mouth. Stheno told her, voice cracking, "I am sorry that you have had to carry this on your own. I am sorry that I made you think that your power could scare me away from you."

Stheno brought one of Euryale's hands up, pressing it against the column of Euryale's throat. She could feel her sister's pulse fluttering quickly, but steadily, beneath their fingertips. "This power is a part of you. Don't let it take your voice from you." She tightened her grip on Euryale's hands. "And don't let me rob you of your voice, either."

Euryale dashed the tears from her cheeks, their hands moving in unison.

"You didn't!" Euryale told her. "I was only able to keep going, to come all the way here, because I knew you'd be with me. It hasn't happened again since the time we were children, but I was always so worried that if I wasn't able to control it, you would be the first one to suffer. I was selfish," she said. "I knew I could have hurt you. But I didn't want to give you up."

"Then I'm glad you were selfish," Stheno said. "And...

and I'm glad Medusa got to be selfish. She got to choose her path, even if every fork in the road leads to the same fate."

"We can't leave her to face it alone," Euryale said, determined. "We messed up when we were younger, but it isn't too late."

"Do you think her prophecy has come for her yet?"

"If it has, then she'll need us more than ever," Euryale said, her eyes shining with resolve and leftover tears. "But I hope she has more time."

Stheno nodded slowly but doubt still pulled at her. "What if she doesn't take us back? You said it yourself, we were awful to her. How could we go back now?"

"Because I need to tell her that she was never alone. I can't have her believing that we're better off without her. We're not," Euryale said. "If she is a monster, then I am a monster, too. And the Gorgons wouldn't be the Gorgons without her. I need to tell her I'm sorry, for failing to see that for so long."

She gave Stheno a pointed look. Stheno took a deep breath, feeling the threads around her heart pull tight once more, before she released it and let them loosen. "And I need to apologize, too," Stheno agreed. "I would be nothing without the two of you. It's true," she said, louder, when Euryale started to protest. "And even if I didn't want to admit it, that scared me when I was younger. I let it rip us apart, and I've only hurt you, Medusa, and myself in the process. I have to mend that wound before it destroys us."

"Then we need to get to Medusa before the gods destroy that whole city," Euryale said. "Which, by the way, I can't believe they're still fighting about that. You remember when they came to Echidna's wedding, right? And just glared at each other the whole time? I always thought that was weird." Stheno released Euryale's hands as her sister rambled on. Euryale wiped the last of the tears from her face and walked back to the table, still talking. Her shoulders loosened with every sentence. "They're supposed to be these all-powerful Olympians, and yet they're stuck on one rocky little city? I don't think Father was even that bad. But if Medusa's caught up in it, we need to get to her as soon as possible. When should we leave? Should we leave now?"

Stheno glanced around the room that they had claimed, in the temple where the mortals had treated them with such kindness and reverence. She had done nothing to deserve it. Stheno decided that she would earn it, whatever it took. She would earn her place in the Gorgons.

"Yes," she said, looking out the window to the sea, as if she could see Medusa somewhere in the horizon. "We can't leave Medusa waiting for us to catch up any longer."

A transformation that sinks to the bone

TWO YEARS PASSED WHILE I served in Athena's temple. Many
of my chores remained the same: plucking olives, welcom-
ing visitors, and kneading endless amounts of dough. But the
longer I stayed at the temple, the more involved I became
with the duties I had envisioned the work of a priestess to be
when I arrived. Desma, as the high priestess, was in charge
of teaching me the words to the more complicated rituals we
held for the public. She took pleasure in my mistakes, berat-
ing me for wrong pronunciations or mixing up the order of
words, but this only made me learn the correct presentation
that much quicker.

The first time I flawlessly performed the ritual for sacri-
ficing a hecatomb of cattle to Athena for luck and guidance
in battle—without actually killing any animals, of course, as
it was only practice—Desma had pressed her lips into a thin
line and nodded her head once.

"Acceptable."

Just over a year into my service as a priestess I aided the
other priestesses in a large public event, held in the city

center, where the archons of Athens requested for Athena's priestesses to make a demonstration of the city's lasting loyalty and gratitude toward the patron goddess. Hundreds of animals were slaughtered, and their bones and meat were wrapped and tied tightly together to be scorched over blazing fires. Amongst the smoke, all twelve of the priestesses were positioned in a half-moon shape facing the crowd of citizens who had come to watch the spectacle.

I stood at the end of the line, closest to the edge of the stage, speaking my part in the ritual script when prompted by Desma. During a pause, I looked out over the crowd of citizens, and their faces shifting amongst one another made me think of a field of golden wheat ready for harvest.

Near the front of the crowd was a group of fine-looking young men, all in the prime stage of life just past youth, their limbs hardened with training for military service, with expensive cloth draped over their shoulders and around their waists as a marker of their upper-class status. A few of them were already looking back at me.

I lowered my lashes at them, moving my body as much as I could without making it obvious what I was doing, until the oiled shimmer of my shoulder and calf, revealed by the slits in my ceremonial dress, caught the sun just right. I knew how to make my limbs place themselves to seem natural, even though I was very aware of each movement. The first few times I had attempted this, I recalled Stheno's ability to situate her body just how she pleased and tried to mimic her calm movements. For the better part of a year I had been practicing how I could use my appearance to attract the attention of men and women and test just how far they would go to earn my consideration.

Just before Desma began the final chant, I tossed my curls over my shoulder and sent the silver pendant on my forehead glittering in the midday sun. Out of the corner of my eye, I saw that group of men look away from the main event to gaze distractedly at me.

Raising my arms simultaneously with the eleven other priestesses, I completed the final lines of the ritual, my voice ringing out over a breathless crowd.

After that large public event, I had been a part of many more, most of them smaller events sponsored by one or two families and hosted at the temple. My days became repetitive.

The only thing that broke up the days was when Poseidon visited me.

The visits from the sea god were unpredictable, but each time my ears popped and the hair on my neck stood on end as the pressure in the air changed, I felt a secret smile grow wider and wider across my face. He always visited at night, when there were no visitors in the temple and most of the priestesses had turned in for the evening. This meant I could at least expect him on nights when I was tasked with clearing the altar or minding the temple while the others slept.

We talked about many things, and yet we also talked about nothing.

I would ask him about his domain in the sea and try to compare it to what I remembered of my parents. He spoke about the ocean, tales of the mortals he had aided or hindered during their long journeys across vast seas, or the fearsome monsters that lurked at the edges of his realm. As much as I was enthralled by the stories he was able to tell me, I was not naïve enough to ignore that he never gave away anything conclusive about himself. So I did the same.

"Why do you continue to serve her?" he asked one night, when the winter chill rolling in off the Athens coast bit at my toes and fingers as I swept the marble. He was fiddling with a bit of seaweed.

"I am a priestess," I said. "It is my duty to serve."

"Yes, but why do you continue to serve Athena, of all gods?"

"Could you recommend another god to whom I could swear loyalty?"

He smirked and flicked the seaweed on the ground in front of me, right where I had just finished tidying up a heap of wilting perennials. I kicked it into the pile and cleared it away without comment, turning my back on the god as I did so.

"You should not let your body be wasted under the jurisdiction of chaste Athena," he said, voice dropping low and sweet like honey in wine.

"I have many years before my body will waste away," I snapped back.

"But the day will come, will it not? Mortal bodies can only take advantage of the pleasures of this earth for so long before they are too withered and brittle to even walk on the rough ground."

This was another of Poseidon's favorite topics: my mortality. All the scathing remarks I had received from my sisters in childhood blunted the edge of any tone of disgust in his voice, but more often his tone was that of pity. He spoke of my mortal heart and life span like that of a flickering candle drawing nearer and nearer to the end of the wick: burning bright and beautiful to its death.

Standing with the broom in one hand, I gazed out at the city before me, lit with small stars of torchlight along the streets like a cluttered sky. There was still so much of this city I had never seen, so much of the world that was a mystery to me.

"There is still time," I said quietly, talking to both Poseidon and myself.

The scent of salt water curled around me like a wave as Poseidon drew himself right behind me until our shoulders were only a finger's length apart, and the breadth of his chest dwarfed me entirely. When he spoke, his breath rustled the hair behind my ear.

"What is that time worth?"

That was an unfair question, coming from a god. He had as much time as there were drops of water in the oceans.

"We will have to see what I make of it," I told him. He paused behind me for a moment, going still, but then he hummed noncommittally and brushed a hand down my arm. One intake of breath later and he was gone.

Although I knew Athena must have been aware of these meetings, she never warned me against them or tried to put an end to her rival sneaking into her temple at night to flirt with a sworn priestess. I highly doubted this meant I had her permission, and I was curious as to why she let it continue, but I did not have the will to bring it up with Polli or one of the other priestesses. That would mean explaining Poseidon's presence in the first place.

And so, Poseidon's visits to me remained a secret. At least, as secret as one could be under the all-seeing gaze of the heavens, where countless divine eyes peered down into the mortal world to watch the lives of humans unfold.

ATHENA'S TEMPLE WAS RARELY quiet. Oil-soaked torches crackled softly from their posts on the smooth marble walls, occasionally sputtering and flaring in the breath of a breeze. During ritual sacrifices the ceiling echoed with murmured prayers. When Desma dragged a finely sharpened blade across the throat of a heifer, the sound of the blood splattering on the stone altar was nearly as sharp as the smell. Even when the temple was empty, save for Athena's sworn attendants, the polished floors amplified every shuffled footstep, every rasp of draped fabric over skin, every inhale and exhale I took.

Tonight, the temple was silent as a battlefield after the last soldier had fallen, lost amongst the scattered bodies of his allies and enemies both.

I had welcomed him earlier, briefly, as I had done so many times before. I had no other choice. He was a god, and while my status as priestess could now send mortals to their knees with one word from my lips, I was still nothing in the face of true divinity. He'd appeared at the top of the steps and approached me where I sat at the foot of Athena's gilded statue, watching over the temple through the night. A flickering oil lamp sat by my side. Athena's sharp, stony gray eyes seemed to track his approach from above. I greeted him, tilting my head demurely so that one of my burnished gold curls would slip over my shoulder. I remembered one of the first things Athena had told me.

"I will give you some advice," she had said, her voice like the sound of two swords clashing and scraping against each other. "You must begin to use your appearance, lest others use it against you."

I looked up at the god when he stood before me. He did not spare a glance at the towering figure of the goddess that the Athenians had chosen over him. The statue stared as he reached for me.

At first, I simply watched as his fingers easily circled my arm, his grip pressing indents into my skin. But as he leaned in, drawing me toward him till his breath washed over my forehead, my nose, my mouth, I tried to pull away. This only made him tighten his hold. He dragged me away from the statue.

I did not go without a struggle, but I was like a glimmering fish trapped in a shark's teeth.

I'd said, "No."

I'd cried, "Lord of the sea."

I'd screamed, "Stop."

He brought the scent of salty brine and seaweed crumbling in the heat of the sun with him, the dark tendrils of his hair still dripping as if he'd only just emerged from the waves. With his lips and teeth caught on the juncture between my neck and shoulder, the smell was nearly suffocating.

I knew that the other priestesses would be gathered in their beds, in a room that was only a few halls away, but felt as if an ocean separated us. My throat strained to call out to them, but my tongue was a leaden brick pressing against my teeth. I feared I would bite it as the god moved above me.

His body, immortally heavy, crushed me into the marble. My hands were pinned above my head between his thumb and index finger, as one of his hands was nearly twice the length and width of mine, and my wrist bones dug into the unforgiving stone. Before he had trapped my hands to the floor, I had gouged long scratches down his bare chest and face with my nails, though they faded to nothing almost immediately.

Cursed divine healing, I thought. He smiled as he trapped my hands, his teeth overly bright and unnatural against his sun-bronzed skin, and I wanted to claw that off his face, too. Each movement I made felt like a monumental effort, as if I were trying to haul a boulder off me. I felt myself growing tired, even as the blood thrummed through my veins, heated with panic and desperation. But every time my thrashing and kicking and screaming had no effect, I felt a piece of myself breaking away.

I turned my head and stared up at the ceiling, the angles and shadows on the roof flickering sharply in the torch-light, as he pushed and tore at my dress until the fabric was bunched around my waist. His breath was hot and damp and it made my skin crawl. I did not think gods relied on air as mortals did, but his ragged panting was the loudest sound in the temple. He reached for my neck with the hand that wasn't holding my wrists and wrapped his fingers around my jaw, forcing my head back even farther as he dug his thumb into the delicate skin under my chin.

With my head tilted back I could meet the eyes of

Athena's statue, the motionless marble face glaring down at us from on high.

Help me, I prayed to her, *save me from this monster.*

I received no response. I waited and waited for the statue to come to life with my goddess's presence, but the marble face remained still and cold. The feeling of being ignored was one that I had grown unaccustomed to, after leaving the whitewashed house on the beach. With every prayer that went unanswered, I felt a cold hand reach up and squeeze my heart tighter and tighter.

Finally, I went limp. I tried imagining myself anywhere but where I was.

Either it did not last very long, or I had simply turned my mind so far away from this horrible moment that I did not realize it was nearly over until it was already done. He hadn't spoken a single word the entire time.

My hair was fanned out above me on the marble floor, and he took his hand away from my throat to tease out a few of the strands, still holding me down with his body weight as his breathing slowed. I kept my eyes locked on a space above his head, though I could no longer bear to look at the statue of my goddess.

He finally released my hands, and I lunged forward to rake my nails over his face once more. I felt the meat of his cheeks catch and split under my claws, my fingers curled and rigid like a harpy's.

He jerked back and swore, the temple trembled with his rage, and I thought, *Earthshaker.* Maybe the earth would crack below us and bring the entire temple down on both of our heads. I should only be so lucky.

He touched the tip of his finger to his lip and drew back to see the shimmering drop of golden ichor, turning his hand to follow the path of the drop as it slipped between his fingers. His lip and cheek had healed by the time he turned his gaze back to me.

"Give your goddess my greetings, won't you?" he said. I wished I could pry my lips open to tell him just where he could shove his greetings, but I feared my voice would fail me. My body trembled, and I scarcely trusted it to try and sit up.

He left in the same manner as he'd arrived. One moment he stood at the top of the steps and by the next he was gone, leaving only the scent of rotting seaweed in his wake. The presence of a divine being was incomparable to that of a mortal; a god or goddess took up more space, even if they were the same stature as a human, and whatever room they inhabit seemed to reorganize its composition to fit itself around the god. I could feel the room settle back into its original shape the second he disappeared. I wished I could go back to my original shape now that he was gone, but I could still feel phantom fingers around my wrists and the delicate skin on the inside of my thighs felt scraped raw. Each breath I took was weighted, the air heavy in my chest and a burden on my lungs.

I hadn't noticed that the temple had filled with sound, the torches crackling in their posts and the distant sound of the ocean hitting the shore, until it began to disappear again. The light of the torches blinked out one by one like an invisible hand was pinching them between finger and thumb. When the last light went out at the far end of the main hall, a brisk, harsh wind flooded across the marble, sweeping my hair into a tangle that would leave it in furious knots, and making the torn edges of my dress tremble around my hips.

Between one of my shuddering breaths and the next, the temple rearranged itself once more. I recognized this presence; I'd devoted my life to this presence for the last few years.

"Where were you?" I asked, my tongue finally unsticking from the roof of my mouth, though my voice cracked halfway through the demand as I had feared it would. I kept my eyes trained on the ceiling of the temple; the shadows were more pronounced in the faint moonlight that now illuminated the pillared hall. I didn't think I could move my limbs, even if I wanted to.

The towering statue stepped gracefully off the raised altar, the smooth marble transforming into tan skin, shifting as easy as silk. Athena knelt near my head, as I was still lying flat on the floor, and reached up to remove her plumed helmet. When she had embodied the statue, the helmet had turned to silver and the metal clinked against the stone as she set it down next to her.

"I have been here," she said, and I repressed the urge to flinch against the force of divine power in her voice. "I have been here for everything."

"You were not," I said. I moved my gaze slowly, my head remaining still, until I could look upon my goddess's face. I used to avoid looking directly at Athena's face out of learned respect, as the other priestesses did, but I pushed past the urge to avert my eyes. Athena was watching me thoughtfully like I was a complex battle strategy that she had yet to solve. There was no pity in her eyes.

I said, "I called for you and you did not answer. I have seen you answer the prayers of greedy beggars, of men who would use your power and call it their own, and yet you did not answer me. You did not respond to one you have claimed."

Athena's hands had been folded in her lap, but she reached forward and smoothed her thumb over my forehead. At her touch, the ache between my legs disappeared and the thin skin around my wrists, which had been sure to bruise, cleared of pain.

"I could not answer," she said, and I hated her for it. I felt the anger bubble up in my chest and simmer behind my eyes. She continued, though I knew she could feel the fury in my fractured spirit, "Had I intervened and forced him to turn away, the fragile state of our rivalry would have sparked a division amongst the gods." Athena's eyes were now pitying. "My uncle was looking for a way to anger me after the Athenians rejected him, and he knew the simplest way was to go through one of you, as mortals are easy to manipulate. I could not stop him."

The gods used humans for their own entertainment, putting us through misery and torment for their own purpose like pieces on a war map. I knew this. I had heard the tales of mortals forever remembered for the legends of when they crossed paths with a god or two. In the vast majority of those legends, the human perished.

I studied Athena's face.

"What are you going to do now?" I asked. I expected that

she had already thought through how she would react to an assault on her temple, and then thought through two alternative plans, but I was once again deceived by a goddess I thought I understood. In all the time I had been in Athena's presence I had never seen her falter. Her face was always serene and collected; she was an optimal war general in the face of conflict, and I had always wondered what, if any, emotions she was working through behind that vigilantly maintained shield. Now, I watched her draw back her hand and saw, impossibly, her features waver with a flash of regret.

"Poseidon cannot be punished. For me to call for his atonement for this crime would be to instigate the same war I have been trying to avoid. Many more mortals would suffer in the skirmish—"

"I do not care," I snapped, interrupting the goddess as I had never done before, the cold fury that had been building in my chest lashing out in a savage strike. "I do not give a damn about other mortals. *I* am the one who was raped at the foot of your altar and *you* are the one who allowed it to happen. Don't I deserve justice?"

"There will be punishment," she said, "but not for Poseidon."

Athena was not a coward. She did not shy away from my gaze as I worked through her meaning. When I realized the intent of her words, thinking of the momentary flash of regret that broke through her calm facade, I felt as if Poseidon's hands were holding me down once more.

"You are not serious."

"Others must see that an offense against me, in my own sacred temple, will not avoid vengeance." Her words were measured, almost practiced, and I wanted to reach out and rip them from her mouth. "A god cannot be punished, but a mortal can."

I wrenched myself off the ground, my muscles and joints screaming in protest. My head felt like it was filled with sand. I stumbled away from where Athena remained kneeling on the ground and shivered. The marble where I lay had been warmed by my skin, leeching the heat from my body, and now that I was standing on unsteady legs I felt as if all the warmth had left the temple. This place I had, foolishly, called my home had turned its back against me.

"You cannot," I gasped, trying to back away but stumbling over my own feet, my hair falling like a snarled curtain over my shoulders. "You cannot mean to punish me for what has been done. It is not fair," I cried. "It was not my *fault!*"

Athena rose to her feet and the temple seemed to hold its breath. I took another step back but did not dare look away. I'd managed to build a bit of distance between us, but in the blink of an eye she crossed it to stand before me, the divine stature of her body looming over me like a rising tide.

"I know you are not to blame," she said soothingly, but I bristled. She reached forward and took hold of the end of one of my twisted curls, like Poseidon had done when he had finished with me, and gave it a tug as she said, "But you will face the consequences all the same. You invited him here, encouraged him to seek you out on my own doorstep. He will talk of you as a victory against me. The mortals need to see that their goddess will not be made a fool."

I felt my scalp tingle with revulsion as she pulled the strand of hair, and I wanted to tear myself away from her, but before I could move, a searing pain ripped its way around the crown of my head. I screamed, thrusting my hands into my hair and clutching at the roots as I fell to my knees. The skin under my fingers was *moving*, as if things were crawling right beneath the surface.

The pain spread, like a poison or a red-hot spike from the fire forcing its way through my skull, and my eyes burned. I squeezed them shut and cried out once more.

A bright, piercing noise flooded my ears, but I could still hear Athena as she spoke, though the words sounded as if she were speaking to me from under water.

"You must see it as I do, Medusa. What would the people of Athens think if their goddess was so dishonored, and she did nothing to avenge herself?" She pressed a large, cool finger to my overheated forehead, but instead of soothing me, it felt like she was pressing down on a bruise. "They cannot think of me as weak. I cannot have them lose their faith in me, and in my ability as a goddess."

She pulled her hand away from me, and I released a strangled gasp.

"The people will take one look at you and know that their goddess is still one to be feared. I once warned you of the beauty that you hold," she said. "You have experienced it as a blessing; now you will know the curse in all its terrifying glory."

Athena did not sound angry. Even while my head seemed to be splitting open at the seams, I could hear the note of remorse in her voice.

She said, "I will tell you as I have told you before—learn to use your appearance to your advantage, as you have used your beauty, for this curse can work in both directions. I can help you no longer. You must learn to help yourself."

I moved my hands from my head and covered my ears, a childish gesture that did nothing to drown out the noise that seemed to be coming from inside my own skull. My eyes were burning behind my eyelids, and I barely suppressed the desire to claw them out with my own fingers. I opened my mouth and let another scream rip out. Something smooth brushed against the back of my hands, rasping gently against the skin, but I could not focus long enough to figure out what it was.

Then, as quickly as it had started, the pain vanished. I gasped and panted, hunched over on the floor with my chin tucked against my chest. The cold marble bit into my bare knees. I kept my eyes shut as a few burning tears slipped down my cheeks in damp, fiery tracks, but moved my hands away from my ears.

"You will not be weighed down with the burden of his children," Athena said, an attempt at kindness, like a soothing caress after being slapped, and I flinched. "You may at least be eased by that."

Her voice had its usual grating nature, though it seemed the piercing noise was lingering as something hissed in my ears. Then I felt a soft rasp against my cheek, like the touch on the back of my hand I had felt moments ago, and my eyes flew open.

Out of the corner of my eye I saw an iridescent green snake raise its head away from my cheek. I tried to jerk back, but the snake moved with me. "What—"

The snake flicked a bright red tongue in my direction. Its

body disappeared up out of my sight and I reached up to trail my fingers along its side until I touched my scalp. I bit back another scream.

Where my golden hair used to flow in long, soft strands, there was now a writhing tangle of snakes; their thin, muscled bodies, about the width of two of my fingers, were weaving in and out of one another like a living imitation of my curls. They pressed against my palm as I felt over them.

"What have you done to me?" I asked Athena, breathless. I lifted my head to look at her but found that she had turned her face away. I tried to meet her gaze but was shocked to see she had her eyes pressed shut. "Look at me," I demanded.

"I cannot."

I felt my fury spike and the hissing rose in volume. She couldn't even spare the decency to look at what she'd done to me?

"Why not?" I pressed.

"The curse," she explained slowly, like I was a child, "it comes from your eyes. You may never look upon another being without punishment being dealt. And another being may not look upon you without fear of turning to stone."

I blinked and touched the delicate skin above my cheek. Compared to the firm scales of the snakes now encircling my head, the skin under my eyes felt as smooth as it always had.

"My eyes," I said slowly, "can turn humans to stone?"

Athena had pulled up the shield to conceal the emotions on her face once more, but I swore I could see the edge of her mouth tick up just slightly. She motioned to her own eyes, tightly closed.

"Not just humans."

Athena

AFTER CENTURIES OF WATCHING mortals crumble in her path, like weary flowers underfoot, Athena thought she had grown impervious to their cries. What did it matter if a few humans lost themselves within the plans she had laid out, so long as she got the outcome she desired?

Medusa stood before her on legs as unsteady as a newborn foal. Athena kept her eyes trained down, away from the girl's face. She had caught a glimpse in the moments before Medusa had opened her eyes, and she had seen the vivid green snakes circling her head. They were unlike any serpent Athena had ever seen. Unique, just as Medusa had become.

Even after explaining why she had not been able to punish Poseidon, Athena knew that Medusa would not see her reasoning. The girl had grown up mortal and could not comprehend the sort of foresight Athena needed to use in every moment, every action, to ensure the rule of the gods continued. Medusa could only see what was directly in front of her. Athena could not spare such shortsighted emotions.

Still. When Medusa felt her snakes for the first time, screamed when her fingers felt the scales fused to her own body, Athena gritted her teeth at the song of rage she could hear buried beneath Medusa's fear. She had heard that scream before, from countless heroes.

That sound was the siren call of death.

"Medusa," Athena said softly, speaking as she would to a cornered animal. "You cannot stay here anymore. This place is no longer safe."

Medusa had braced herself against a pillar, palms pressed into the marble as her legs trembled beneath her weight. Her ragged breathing was accompanied by the soft hissing of the snakes. In the quiet, echoing hall, it sounded as if the snakes had already doubled in number.

"No longer safe," Medusa spat. "For who? For me? Your warning has come too late. Or," she paused to take a desperate breath, "is it no longer safe for *you* to have me here? Where do you expect me to go?"

Athena spoke resolutely. "You must go away from here, though where you go is still your choice. As long as you remain here, you are a danger to everyone, including yourself. Anyone who crosses your path has reason to fear you now."

"Because of what you did to me!"

"Yes," Athena agreed. Medusa may have been lost to her horror and anger, but she was no fool. Athena could not lie to her. If she thought the girl would understand, Athena would have told her that this curse was also a blessing. Medusa had no power of her own, no way to protect herself against someone like Poseidon, until now.

She knew that Medusa would not see it that way. In her eyes, this was nothing more than a cruel punishment.

Athena could feel Medusa's stone-making gaze on her, accompanied by dozens of eyes as Medusa's snakes turned their attention toward her. She had been on countless battlefields in her life, for wars both mortal and divine, and she knew what it felt like to have someone look at her with the intent to kill.

Subtly, Athena braced her feet. But just as quickly as it had come, Medusa's bloodlust disappeared. Athena heard her gasp, scrambling away from the pillar she had been leaning against, increasing the distance between them. The snakes' hissing increased.

"Medusa?"

Athena turned to see Pollina, one of her youngest priestesses, standing in the archway. She was holding a small candle in her delicate hands, illuminating her face and surrounding her in a halo of light against the dark hallway. She asked Medusa, "Are you all right?"

Athena knew what would happen next. She could see each moment pass before her like scenes depicted in painstaking detail on the hull of a shield. Every moment of this night was playing through her mind like moves on a battlefield. She had already lost one pawn in Medusa, but she knew that some battles must be sacrificed to win the war.

Medusa needed to leave her temple. Athena couldn't have her remain there as a symbol of Poseidon's insult, nor could she let her roam through the city Athena worked so hard to build. The Athenians would only see her as a monster. Athena needed to give Medusa a reason to run.

She saw the moment play out. She could have stopped it. Instead, she let Medusa look up.

Medusa gasped, "Pollina, don't!"

But their eyes had already met over the flickering candle. Athena turned her head away from the bright red flash coming from Medusa's direction. Under the cacophony of hissing snakes and Medusa's cries, she heard Polli let out a small noise.

It was over in a single moment. She heard Medusa collapse onto the ground with a thump, her breathing ragged.

"What have I done?" Medusa whispered. "What have I done?"

"Are your eyes closed, child?" Athena asked.

"Yes."

Athena opened her eyes. Medusa was crumpled on the floor, her face in her hands and her head bowed over her knees. The snakes were tentatively touching their noses to her hands, her neck, any bit of her they could reach. They didn't look up when Athena moved. Her sandals made soft scuffing noises against the floor as she approached Pollina.

Athena studied Medusa's handiwork. Pollina's face was the color of a winter tempest blowing in off the sea: a deep, troubled gray that lacked any warmth of life. The rest of her body was the same, from the loose strands of her hair to the hands that still held the candle. The candle, too, had been turned to stone, and the little flame was now just a speck of rock.

She reached out and brushed her thumb over Pollina's stiff cheek. The girl had been a faithful priestess, loyal and kind to everyone who stepped foot in the temple. In the end, it was her trusting nature that led to her end. Athena allowed herself one moment to mourn her. She would ensure that Pollina's spirit found peace in the Underworld.

"Medusa," she called, stepping back from the statue, "you may look. There is nothing more you can do to harm her now."

She waited for Medusa to uncurl, but she remained crouched on the ground with her eyes tucked away. Like a child hiding their face and expecting all their fears to disappear.

"Medusa," Athena said again, sharper. "Look."

Medusa flinched at her voice, but she finally obeyed. Athena closed her eyes as Medusa lifted her head, and she heard when Medusa saw what she had done. Her cries grew closer as she began to crawl toward Pollina.

"No," she whispered. "No, no, *Polli*."

Medusa stopped at Pollina's feet and clutched at the hard, gray hem of her unmoving nightdress. Athena stepped back and circled around until she was behind Medusa. She opened her eyes slowly, to ensure that Medusa hadn't turned around.

But Medusa was consumed by grief, using Pollina's stiff limbs to lift herself to her feet. She traced Pollina's gray cheek with her fingers. The priestess was frozen with a wide-eyed look of confusion, and Medusa tapped her thumb against the corner of her eye.

"I'm sorry," she told the statue, as if Pollina could still hear her. "I'm so sorry."

"Do you understand now, why you must leave?" Athena asked. The snakes stirred at her voice, but they didn't turn to look at her. "Your power cannot discriminate between your friends and your enemies. It will not spare anyone. You must leave my city before any more mortals fall prey to your power."

Medusa sniffed. She took her fingers from Pollina's cheek and touched her own face, and her fingertips came away wet with tears.

"And I am no longer mortal," Medusa said slowly, "am I?"

"You are not a human," Athena said carefully, "and I do not think you will have a mortal life span, but whether or not you lose the entirety of your mortality is up to you."

The power Athena had given her would trigger anytime she made eye contact with another living being, but it was not uncontrollable. Medusa would be able to choose when to use her stone-making ability. How she used the power from now on was up to her. Athena had seen many mortals lose themselves to lesser powers than this, consumed by greed and pride, but Medusa still had a chance to live as her mortal self never could.

Athena started when Medusa began to laugh. It was a wild, terrible sort of laugh, closer to a scream.

"*Whether I lose my mortality*," Medusa mocked and spun around. Athena quickly closed her eyes and folded her hands in front of her. Medusa was spitting her words like arrows. "If I am no longer mortal because of the monster you turned me into, then the loss of my mortality rests on your shoulders as well."

"Perhaps it does," Athena said. She had expected this anger. "But from here on, Medusa, you are on your own. I hope you can face your future without fear, as you once told me you would."

She felt Medusa studying her face. Athena thought about telling Medusa that she did not mean this as a punishment. Doubtless, Poseidon would spread word of what he had done, framing it as if one of Athena's own priestesses had turned against her for him. Boasting that he had been able to desecrate Athena's temple right under her nose. Threatening that if he could lure in one of Athena's loyal attendants, he could take the whole city.

She thought about explaining to Medusa that the people of her city would want to see someone take the fall for the slight to her reputation, and how she couldn't let them see her as weak. But she knew Medusa would only hear excuses, and she wouldn't be completely wrong.

However, Athena reminded herself, she was a goddess. She did not need to explain herself to anyone, either mortal or monster.

Athena drew herself up. She felt Medusa preparing another barrage of questions, but before she could speak, Athena released her hold on this consciousness. In a blink, the statue she had assumed was back on the altar, shining helmet turned back to stone and placed on her head. Athena remained loosely present, hovering behind the stone eyes of the statue to watch as Medusa looked from where she had been just standing to the shadowed altar.

Medusa stood as still as Pollina for a few moments. A thousand thoughts seemed to cross her face. Athena knew she had just ripped Medusa's home from her and told her to leave with nowhere to go. But while Medusa may have been mortal before this night, she was still the daughter of gods.

The shadows of the hall were changing as the first dim

light of dawn crept up over the horizon. The early morning noises of the temple and the city below grew louder as mortals rose from their beds. Before long, the streets would be filled with Athenians, and it would be nearly impossible for Medusa to escape from the city without crossing the paths of hundreds of mortals.

Medusa stared out across the temple toward the edge of the Acropolis, where the dirt path would take her into the city and then out into the country. Athena could tell that, for Medusa, this distance seemed never-ending.

A new noise came from deep in the branching hallways of the temple as Medusa stood there desperately thinking about what to do, and it wasn't until the footsteps were quite close to the doorway that Medusa flinched from the noise. Athena's high priestess Desma was always the first to come into the hall every morning.

Medusa lurched toward Pollina, as if she wanted to bring the poor girl's statue with her, but Desma's shadow was rounding the corner. Athena saw Medusa's face drop, and she fled.

"Medusa?" Desma's voice followed her out of the temple. The high priestess called out Pollina's name, as well, just a few feet from Athena's statue. A moment later, Desma released a horrified gasp, but Medusa had already reached the temple's entrance. Her voice broke as she screamed, "Medusa, what have you done!"

Medusa didn't look back, and the last Athena saw was a flash of sparkling green as the sun hit Medusa's snakes.

After the poison sets in

KEEPING MY GAZE AIMED low, I dashed through the streets of Athens. Whenever I saw the edge of a tanned foot in a sandal or the hem of a dress, I turned and ran a different direction, my eyes on my own feet. The ripped pieces of my dress flapped around my legs.

Horrified gasps followed me everywhere I went, and even though I was not looking at the people who saw me, I could feel the snakes looking back at the mortals. Their bodies jostled with the rhythm of my feet hitting the ground. When someone shouted at me, they hissed back.

"Shut up," I snapped at the snakes, and they did.

My head felt as heavy as stone, a thought that startled another terrible laugh out of me.

Without Polli's guidance, and with as many twists and turns I had to take while avoiding the mortals who were early to rise, by the time I finally reached the edge of the city the sun had fully breached the sky. I stumbled to a stop where the paved roads gave way to dirt. I remembered how the buildings and streets of Athens had risen quite suddenly when my sisters and I first traveled to the city, and how there were only a few outlying farms around the city boundaries. The edges of the wheat fields were ragged and there were weeds sprouting up closer to the road, and these were the only things I could see of the farms as I walked with my head down.

Breathing heavily, I limped slowly along the road, hoping that any farmers I passed would be too focused on their crops or too far into their fields to notice me. The adrenaline that had pushed me so quickly through the city was nearly drained, and I didn't think I could run any more, even if I had to. My feet ached.

By the grace of some god, I did not see another soul on the road. The dirt path became steadily less smooth, less straight, and then eventually, it mixed with sand.

I heard the crash of waves and the sound nearly brought me to my knees. I risked a look up and saw the shore stretched out before me in a long, unbroken line of blue. The sand was still cool from the night and I walked right up to the edge of the water before sitting down, the skirt of my dress instantly soaked by the damp sand.

The sound of waves crashing in on themselves and then tumbling up onto the shore reminded me of the whitewashed house on the lonely beach. My childhood home seemed to have existed a lifetime ago.

I wondered if my parents could see me now, so close to their beloved ocean.

But then the smell of the water hit my nose as the wind shifted, and I recoiled. It was the salty, briny smell that had clung to Poseidon's skin and stuck to mine when he touched me. I scrambled back from the water and turned onto my hands and knees as I retched into the sand. The snakes, sensing my revulsion, switched back and forth between hissing defensively against an unseen threat and sliding soothingly against my forehead, my temple.

Now with a sour taste in my mouth, I wiped the back of my hand over my lips and panted, trying to get my breathing under control.

I was too close to the sea, where Poseidon lived and ruled.

All at once I felt like crying again. The ocean had been a place of solace for me in the past, the only friend I had been able to turn to when I lived in the white house on the beach, and now I could scarcely stand the smell of it. There was a unique kind of cruelty in that. I had already lost so much today, but this proved I could still be brought lower by the gods. My only friend, the place where I had felt I had finally found somewhere to belong, and now one of the only good memories I had from my childhood had been ripped away from me, ruined by the actions of two gods who would go on as if nothing had changed.

My eyes stung from the threat of more tears and the smell of brine, and I knew I had to move away from the beach.

Judging it worth the risk, I slowly looked up. I told myself that if I saw someone's feet or legs I would just look away, but I was able to raise my gaze without seeing anyone.

I had wandered all the way out of Athens's farthest boundaries, where cultivated land gave way to a wild and scrubby forest. Sitting back on my heels in the sand, I turned my head slowly to look left, and then right. I saw no one and nothing in both directions. Dusty pine trees rose above the patchwork of bushes that covered the forest floor beyond the sandy beach, and the trees' branches offered sparse shade to those on the ground below.

With the sun rising ever higher behind me, I struggled to my feet and went into the forest.

The rips in my dress kept getting caught on the thin bushes, and the tears only widened as I tried to tug them free. I stared down at the ravaged hem of the dress Polli had given me on that very first day in the temple. This dress was made only for the use of Athena's priestesses, and I was certainly no longer a priestess for the mortals of Athens to depend on.

But Polli had given me this dress. As painful of a reminder as it was, I tied up the pieces of the hem so that it left my legs bare from my knees down, to try and preserve what was left of it.

While I walked, the sounds of the forest dipped and rose as birds called out to one another to give warnings, and then waited silently to see if I was really a threat. Their melodies picked up again after a few moments when all I did was keep walking. The leaves on the trees rustled together in the breeze like the chattering, gossipy mortals that I would see gathered around Athens's public squares.

I could also hear the snakes. They never seemed to be silent, at least one of them was always hissing and flicking its tongue in every direction, but the sounds were also coming from in my head. They didn't use words, exactly, or at least they didn't have a language I could discern, but now that I was not focused on fleeing the city, I could hear that the snakes were speaking to me constantly. My head cleared the farther I got from Athens, and their voices got louder.

Rabbit over there, said a not-voice. I just knew, suddenly, that there was a rabbit hiding in the bushes to my right. A snake on the right side of my head lifted its own face closer to mine as I thought this, and I realized that this snake had tasted the rabbit on the air and then made me aware of it. But for what?

"What do you want me to do?" I asked, and then immediately felt foolish for speaking to the snake.

Food, the not-voice told me, *eat*. Then, *Hungry?*

I was shocked enough to stop walking, and I said loudly, "I'm not going to kill a rabbit!"

The loud noise sent the little animal in the bushes running, and a few birds in the trees above me were startled off their perches. The fluttering of their wings caught the snakes' attention and a few of them hissed at the sky.

"Shut up!" I told them and left the birds and the rabbit behind. The snakes, seeming to sense my distress, fell silent.

As I walked, the details of the morning's events came back to me piece by piece. While I still wasn't sure just how the cursed powers worked, I did know that the red haze I had seen out of the corner of my eye when I turned Polli to stone had come from the snakes. I wondered if the ability to petrify mortals came from them, since I could think of no other reason that Athena would transform my golden curls into a mess of green snakes if they did not have something to do with this wretched power.

"I do not need your help," I told them, when the not-voice tried to direct me to another rabbit.

But as much as I didn't want to admit it, the snakes were correct. I was hungry. My stomach grumbled hollowly as I thought about the tough bread the priestesses and I made at the temple. Even more pressing than the hunger was the dryness in my throat. Between the screaming and the crying and the running, I felt as though my body had been pressed dry, like an olive.

The forest had begun to rise in a gentle incline. My legs felt heavy as rocks as I climbed, but I didn't stop. I feared that if I paused to sit and rest for a moment, I wouldn't be able to get up again.

The plants on the forest floor changed the higher I hiked up the hill, but I didn't recognize many of them. I had seen the plants that Athena's citizens occasionally brought in for tribute, plants that had medicinal properties or special something-or-others, but I had never bothered to learn any of their names or what they were good for. They had just been another crumbling sacrifice for me to sweep away.

That way.

I stopped as a sudden awareness of a nearby stream of water trickled into my head. I crossed my arms and glared at nothing, like a petulant child refusing to move after being given a command, but the snakes who were pointing the way with their blunted snouts and wiggling heads did not shrink away from my frustration. I had told them to leave me alone. Then again, they were a part of this body, too, so they may have also been feeling the effects of my thirst, and they weren't willing to let me die of dehydration just because I was angry with them.

One of the snakes flicked its tongue in the direction of the stream and pulled its body taut until I felt a slight tug on the side of my head.

With my dry mouth and rising irritation, the temptation was just too much.

"Fine," I gave in, throwing my arms open in defeat, "lead the way."

With their red tongues flashing, the snakes led me to the left of where I had been walking, up a steeper part of the hill. I had to climb around a few boulders, but their insistent encouragement in my head kept me going as they promised the relief of cool water in my throat. I couldn't experience smells on the air the way they could with their sensitive tongues, but the snakes shared the idea of what the *smell* of water tasted like to them the best they could; it was sweet and clean like the first breath of wind after a storm.

"This is just making me thirstier," I grumbled to them.

Finally, once I had passed the last crop of boulders, I stepped into a relatively clear patch of forest with a glittering stream carving its way around the edge and down the hill. With a noise of relief stuck in my throat, I hurried toward the water.

Coming to my knees just a scarce finger's length away from the shore, I leaned forward to dip my whole face in the stream. But before I could come close enough to see my face in the rippling reflection of the water, I felt my head being yanked back. The snakes, all the snakes around my head, were pulling frantically in the other direction, away from the stream.

"What?" I said, bewildered and desperate for a drink. "You brought me here!"

Don't look, the snakes told me, the voice that wasn't a voice urgent in my head, *can't look, don't look, don't, don't.*

"Look at what? At myself?"

The stream was not moving very fast, and though there were breaks and tiny undulations in the water, there was a decently clear reflection of the trees and the sky above.

"I can't look at my reflection?" I asked them.

The snakes loosened their bodies so that they no longer felt like they were trying to remove my head from my neck, and their affirmation rattled through my mind.

Can't look, they said. *Danger.*

Athena had told me this power that now lay behind my eyes worked on mortals and gods alike. If I looked into my own eyes through a reflection…would the petrifying gaze work on me as well? How did the snakes know this?

When I had just begun to use my appearance to cultivate the attention of mortals who visited Athena's temple and, I thought with a harsh twist in my gut, to draw Poseidon's gaze, I had practiced the most alluring ways to hold my body and let my hair fall. I had also studied my own face in the reflection of the silver shields given to Athena, watched as I lowered my lashes or turned the corner of my full lips up in a coy smile. That vanity, for it had been vanity even when I did not recognize it, had not felt self-indulgent at the time. Now that I was unable to even catch a glimpse of what I looked like with snakes where my golden curls had been, I felt tears prick in the corner of my eyes.

I swiped them away angrily, but they just kept falling.

"This isn't fair." The complaint sounded weak even to my own ears.

To be afraid of one's own reflection. That was truly

a curse that only a god could think of and bestow upon a mortal.

As the tears dried in salty, tacky trails down my cheeks, I couldn't wait any longer. I pressed my eyes shut and leaned forward again, feeling in front of me with one hand until I could splash some water into my face. I cupped a handful and brought it to my mouth to test it, and when I didn't taste anything wrong with it, I dipped all the way down and took long pulls straight from the stream itself. I thought I could hear the small sounds of the snakes touching their own tongues to the water for a drink.

When my throat ceased its complaining, I leaned back, eyes still closed, and took up a double handful of water to splash over my face. I rubbed away the tear tracks and pressed my fingers to my eyelids. The skin felt the same as it had before and so did my eyes beneath it, even though I knew that everything had changed. How could something be so entirely different, and yet feel as it always had?

Once I had leaned back from the water, I let my hands drop and blinked my eyes open, the bright midmorning sun glittering and refracting off the surface of the stream. When I tipped my head back and sighed, the snakes swayed with the movement. Beads of water slipped down their scaly bodies and dropped onto my shoulders, and I reached up to catch one of the drops on my finger before it slid off the snake's torso. My finger brushed against the snake's vivid green scales. I pulled my hand back quickly enough to jostle both myself and them, but of course, they followed wherever I went.

The snake I had touched just eyed me lazily. I moved,

slowly, to bring my hand back up and let my fingers touch the scales, following the tightly knit pattern that ended at my scalp. Other snakes rubbed themselves over my hand. All I had seen of the snakes was what I could catch in my peripherals or when one of them moved far enough forward.

"Can I look at you?" I asked the snake that I had touched. "I mean, without looking at myself. If I don't look into my own eyes, should I be able to see what you—what I—look like now?"

I could feel the snakes move a bit more restlessly around my head, but then the not-voice said, *Careful, careful.*

"I'll be careful," I promised.

Breathing out through my nose, I pressed my palms to the ground right next to the stream and inched forward until I could see just the tip of one of the snakes reflected in the water. Stretching my neck out as much as I could, I kept going until the crown of my head was visible and I caught a glimpse of my forehead. I didn't go any farther.

Close to two dozen vibrant green snakes curled and twisted around my head, their bodies wavering in the movement of the stream, but the sight was mesmerizing. The snakes never ceased moving, and they reminded me of the way my hair would move independently when I was underwater, caught in a current. I followed the line of one snake, from the base of its torso all the way out to its tapered neck and diamond-shaped head. Seeing the brown of my skin next to the green was a bit startling, but then the snake curled around my hand and rested its head in my palm. Pulling back from the stream, I lowered my hand, and the snake extended its body to its full length as I brought its head down to my eye level.

Warmed by the heat of the sun, the snake's skin was hot against mine, and I could feel the thrum of life under its scales. The snake flicked its tongue out to taste my skin. The recognition from what it found echoed in my head, and I knew the snake was thinking, *We are one and the same.*

They were alive because of a curse, but it was clear they did not mean me any harm. How could I hate them for being a part of me?

I sighed. "What now?"

None of the snakes seemed to have an answer for me, which I should have expected. They may have been able to taste water and animals on the air and point me in the right direction to reach them, but if these snakes and I were really part of one body now, they wouldn't have any answers I couldn't think of myself.

I tilted my head back again and closed my eyes. The gentle burbling of the stream and rustling of wind through the trees was soothing, and very different from mortal noises, like footsteps on marble floors and synchronized whispered chants with tripping melodies, which I had become used to at the temple. I tried to focus on the feeling of the gritty forest floor pressing into my knees and shins, the cool air blowing off the stream fighting against the unrelenting heat of the sun. When I lived in the white house on the lonely beach, I had practiced this quiet focus often, drawing my attention to the sand or the birds above me instead of whatever my sisters had taunted me with that day. I hadn't tried to meditate like this in a while, and I felt out of practice. The easy silence in my head was just out of reach.

I could feel a little wrinkle form in between my brows as I tried to clear my mind.

I was so intent on emptying my head that I didn't notice the warning calls of the birds above, the same call they had chirped when I entered the forest. Then a dog barked behind me and my eyes flew open.

Startled, I turned around on instinct to find the threat and was met with the dark brown gaze of a panting mutt, his red tongue lolling out of his mouth in happiness. I felt the same sharp heat behind my eyes as I looked at this dog that had occurred when I turned Polli to stone. In the next moment, after a flash of red haze, the dog was frozen rock solid with his tongue, now gray and dry, still hanging out from between his teeth.

Gaping at what I had just done, I did not react quick enough as two people stepped out of the forest and into the clearing.

"Deka?" one of the travelers called, a man with a walking stick and a large sack over his shoulder. When he spotted his dog standing like a statue with his nose pointed straight at me, the man looked up. My eyes were still wide with horror, and I couldn't close them fast enough. I saw him register the snakes coiling and curving around my head and his mouth twisted in horror.

Another red flash and the man, his walking stick, and even his pack hardened to gray stone. The look now permanently formed on his face was fearful and confused.

I squeezed my eyes shut and scrambled to my feet. The

second traveler, another man, though this one sounded younger, shouted after me. I didn't bother to slow down and listen, but I caught the word he screamed repeatedly as I splashed blindly across the shallow stream and disappeared into the forest.

"Monster! Monster!"

In the clutch of the woods

I DID NOT WANT to take another chance and accidentally turn another innocent person, or dog, to stone, so I ripped a strip of fabric from the already torn hem of my dress. It smelled faintly of dirt and sweat, but I tied it over my eyes anyway. I had to work the knot around the snakes' bodies to make sure I didn't pin any of them down, but they seemed intent on getting in the way as they wound around my fingers and tried to wrap themselves around my hands. When I succeeded in pushing them out of the way long enough to pull the knot tight, they relented.

During my hurried flight away from the surviving man and the two living creatures that I had turned to stone, the low bushes of the forest had cut numerous little scratches into my bare legs, and I had stubbed my toes on more than one rock in my blind rush.

The snakes had been willing enough to help steer me away from running face-first into any trees or off a cliff, but they were not empathetic to the guilt that was seeping into my heart.

"I don't want to hurt anyone else," I told them, adjusting the strip of fabric so that it lay flat over the bridge of my nose.

They hurt no more, the snakes argued back. *Stone has no feeling.*

"That's not who I meant," I snapped, sure the snakes were being obtuse on purpose. "I can't turn anyone else to stone. You heard what the man called me."

Monster, the snakes said, but when they said it, I could tell they did not consider it an insult.

"I'm dangerous to everyone," I said, wrapping my arms around myself. I had stopped running somewhere in the forest, higher up the mountain than the stream had been, and the trees grew closer together at this altitude. They pressed in from all sides, and even though I couldn't see the tops of them I knew they must have towered high above my head like great giants. I felt small underneath them. Like they could swallow me whole.

Dangerous, the snakes repeated my word, and again, the word did not sound like a reprimand in their not-voice. When they said *dangerous*, it sounded like they wanted to say *powerful*.

I squeezed my arms tighter around my middle and frowned. "I don't want this power. All I've done so far is destroy the lives of innocent people."

Polli had been so young, younger even than me, but because of me she would never be able to grow up and become...whatever it was she had wanted to be. My heart sank as I realized I had never asked her what she wanted to do with her life, if she wanted to become like Desma and take over as high priestess for Athena's temple, or if she had wanted to travel and visit the shrines and dedications to Athena that were scattered across the mainland.

She would never get to make that decision, because of me. Because of what I had done to her.

But was I really to blame? I had not asked for this power. Athena had decided that I would take the fall, and had made sure that I would have no one on my side.

I felt anger bubbling up in my chest again, a dormant volcano disrupted from an uneasy sleep. Hadn't Athena said that this power worked on gods, too? There had been a moment in the temple when I had wanted to take advantage of that, wanted to force Athena to look me in the eyes and fall victim to the monster she created. I could go back into her precious city and wreak havoc. Make her feel the pain and guilt that she had cast on me.

Could I take on a god? Athena had created me, but it seemed like even she was not immune to what she had made me into. My anger was buoyed by images of her regal face, at last cracking to show true emotion, turning to stone.

But if I did let my anger overcome me, let it drag me back into Athena's city and become the monster that loomed beneath the surface, what then? The thought of descending into anger and not being able to climb back out terrified me.

I took a few breaths, letting the anger run its course. I wouldn't go back. I couldn't let myself succumb to this punishment so quickly. I needed to find a way forward. Athena had said I could learn to use this power, and if I could learn to control it, I could learn to suppress it.

I tightened the knot of my blindfold.

"Don't let me trip," I told the snakes, and began walking, trying to leave my thoughts behind. I was slower than before, now that I couldn't even see where I was putting my feet, but I did not want to stay still for too long if it meant some unlucky traveler could cross my path by accident. The snakes nudged me to and fro as I picked my way through the undergrowth. Sometimes they told me *low branch on the right* or *big rock in the way* or *turn left, too many trees here,* but the thoughts they shared with me were clipped and lacked any of the sensations they made me feel when they had shown me to the stream.

Since all the snakes' directions were delivered soundlessly, my journey was quiet. I still stumbled over fallen branches or raised patches of earth from time to time, and I swore quietly to myself when I hit a particularly sensitive toe against a hard surface for the third time.

"Hello?"

I froze in place. The snakes went still, as well, but they all seemed to be focused on one point a few paces in front of me. If a mortal was close enough to have heard me swear, they must have been close enough to see me. I may have hidden the world from my eyes, but there was no hiding myself or the bright green snakes that sprouted from my head.

The same voice spoke again, and it sounded feminine and weathered with age. "If you think you can sneak up on a blind old woman, you should think again. My sight may be worse than a bat's in a dark cave, but I reckon I can hear better than anyone. Then again, if you are so desperate that stealing from a blind old woman is your only option, perhaps you deserve whatever you find in my pockets. I'll have you know there's nothing there, though!"

I opened my mouth and closed it again, bewildered by the woman, and still recovering from the fear that had seized my body when I heard her voice so close. The air seemed charged with the silence that followed, and I felt the weight of it prickle over my skin like a scratchy blanket. From what the snakes could show me, I knew that the part of the woods I was in had trees that were set wide apart from one another, and the woman was at least a few steps away, so I did not understand why it felt as though there was something pressing in on me. I forced myself to take a deep breath.

The woman waited for my reply for a few moments longer, and then she seemed to get impatient. "Well, if there's anything I hate more than a thief it's a thief who makes their victim wait for the blow."

"I'm not a thief," I said cautiously.

The woman's voice had the teasing tone that often accompanied a grin. "Then what are you, girl?"

A priestess of Athena, is what I almost said, until I remembered that I wasn't. Not anymore.

"I'm—"

I had no answer for her. What could I say? *I'm a monster that can turn people to stone if they look at me, and just so you know, I've got a nest of snakes instead of hair, but don't be alarmed.* Even from the glimpse I had seen in the reflection of the stream, I knew that the sight of me and the snakes was almost unbelievable, even when you were looking right at it. Describing it aloud sounded even worse.

When my silence stretched longer and longer, the woman snorted.

"Don't know what you are, hmm? You sound young, so I suppose that's all right."

I heard the woman shuffle toward me, and along with her steps came the gentle *tap* of a stick on hard dirt, like a cane or a staff that I had seen older mortals use when their legs alone would not support them.

"Why are you out here, then? Can you answer that?"

I could. "I needed to leave Athens."

"For what purpose?"

I took a shuddering breath and wrapped my arms around my middle, gripping my sides. "I'm no longer welcome there. I did something...bad, to a friend of mine. I've got a power I can't control, and I don't want to hurt someone else."

The *tap, tap, tap* sound moved closer, and then the woman laid her warm hand on my arm. I flinched. Her touch was not cruel, but for some reason my body was alarmed at the feeling of her skin on mine. I thought, absurdly, that it felt like when Athena had touched my forehead, but that was probably because the goddess had been the last one to put a hand on me.

The woman didn't immediately move away at my reaction, and instead she squeezed my arm once, then patted me before taking her hand back. When she spoke, her voice came from around the height of my shoulders, and so I looked down, even though I couldn't see her face.

"Why didn't you hurt me?" she asked. Taken aback by the question, I struggled for an answer.

"You cannot see me," I said, "and I cannot see you. That means you are safe from me."

"Oh," the woman said happily, as if she had not just questioned why I had not caused her any bodily harm like she was asking after the weather. "Have I finally happened across another who is sightless like me?"

I felt the air near my face shift and, even as the snakes warned *Too close*, the woman brushed her fingers over my cheekbone, feeling up toward my eyes. When she met the fabric of my blindfold, she made an inquisitive noise.

"What's this for?" the old woman asked, and her inane fearlessness confused me just as much as it impressed me.

"I am sightless by choice," I told her.

The snakes were thrumming their concern through my head, but I silently told them to stay still and keep quiet. I didn't want her to brush up against one of their scaly bodies by accident. They would be much more difficult to explain than a blindfold.

"An odd choice for a woman wandering in the woods," the old woman said. "Tell me, how many trees have you walked into so far?"

Technically none, thanks to the guidance of the snakes, but I couldn't tell her that I had a dozen pairs of eyes seeing for me and steering me away from collisions.

"Not too many," I said instead. "I've been careful."

"Bet you're still scratched up, though, hmm?"

"Yes," I admitted, and breathed out a subtle sigh of relief when the woman moved her fingers away from my face to run her hands over my arms. She was feeling for scars or injuries, I realized after a few moments of her gentle patting.

"You need to get yourself a staff, like mine." She thumped the end of her staff against the ground. "Helps me avoid walking into trees. It also helps when I do come across someone who wants to harm me."

Without warning, she gave me a sharp whack against the side of my calf, and I jumped back with a shout. The sharp lance of pain was a bright point to focus on, and I felt the tension fade from my shoulders as I reached down to rub the sore spot. The snakes were conflicted, furious at the injury they had not seen coming, and slightly amused that this old woman had gotten the better of us.

"What did you do that for?" I asked, wincing as my fingers pressed against tender skin.

"Just in case you were reconsidering whether you were going to hurt me or not!" the woman cackled.

"But I just told you that I wouldn't!"

"People say things they don't mean every day of their lives," the old woman said. "I find that the best way to protect myself, as a blind old woman, is to cut off the danger at its knees," she tapped her staff against my other calf, and I jumped in the other direction at the touch, "sometimes quite literally."

She was laughing, but my lips had pulled into a frown.

"So, you hurt people before they hurt you," I said, "even if they didn't mean to hurt you at all?"

The old woman's laughter faded. "Not always. But tell me, girl, if you were me, blind not by choice, but by fate, old enough to hear the creak in your bones, and a lone woman left to walk the earth, would you be inclined to trust every traveler you came across?" The tone of voice she used was

one that made me think she was accustomed to being listened to, and again, I was suddenly reminded of Athena.
"Now tell me, if you had a staff as I do, would you choose not
to use it to defend yourself? I carry this staff because it makes
traveling easier, yes, but since I have it and can use it to protect myself, why shouldn't I do so?"

A beat of silence passed, but I thought that she was not
actually waiting for an answer to her questions. And indeed,
after another moment, she spoke again.

"This staff is my power and my protection, and I will use
it as I please."

She was right, I supposed. With so much uncertainty
around her, I shouldn't be surprised she was inclined to
strike first in defense of her safety, especially since her staff
was so effective. I did wonder how many people she had
hit who had not even thought about causing her harm, and
whether they now acted upon the same idea. How much
more violence had come to be through this strategy? But
even if I had my reservations, the fact that she was standing
before me, whole and unharmed, proved that her methods
worked.

"We are alike," I said, reaching for the description she
had given of herself and attempting to find something in
common, "as women traveling alone."

"But I've been able to defend my lonely self for years," the
old woman said vehemently. "And you seem to have only just
begun. Do you have something to protect yourself?"

The snakes moved restlessly, sweeping across my forehead and nudging at the blindfold, though they kept quiet
as I had asked them to. They were worried for me, I realized.

"I think I do," I said honestly, "but I don't know how to control it."

"You are speaking of that danger you pose to others that you first warned me of, yes? That power you spoke of, which, conveniently for both of us, cannot harm me? You think of that power as a danger," the woman said. "Well then, my advice to you is to learn to control that power. Don't allow it to just be a crutch that helps you hobble along your path, or worse, an obstacle that keeps you from your path entirely. Use it for yourself."

We were miles from Athena's temple and the air felt loose and untampered, but I could not shake the feeling of being in Athena's presence as the woman spoke. This advice sounded familiar, and it tugged at my mind as I tried to remember what Athena had told me before I'd left. Had she recommended I learn to use my power before it used me, too?

The old woman let me sit with what she had said for another few moments and then she let out a great sigh. "At least think on what I've told you, girl. But while you're here, could you tell me how far I am from Athens?"

"Not far," I said automatically, my mind still reeling. "About half a day's walk from here."

I couldn't be too sure about the timing of how long it had taken me to get this far *away* from Athens, since I had been sprinting in a terror-ridden frenzy for a good part of the journey.

"Then I will leave you with one last bit of advice," the old woman said, "which I can give to you because I am old and wise from all the years I've lived. You needn't be afraid of using the power that resides in you. It was placed there for a reason. While I can lay blame on the Fates for my blindness and the events that have led me to be alone, I have not let those three immortal meddlers finish me off just yet because of the power I chose to use for myself." She laughed again and patted me on the cheek, her aim unerring. "I hope you'll listen to an old woman's ramblings."

I bowed my head, even though she would not be able to see it, and said, "Thank you."

I had to admit that it had been a bit of a relief to speak to someone other than the snakes, but I was anxious to get away from the woman. The snakes, too, seemed eager to move on.

"Oh, don't thank me yet!" she said. "Wait and see if you can actually get your power to work for you, first, and then you can show your appreciation once we meet again," she said with a laugh, and I could hear the grin that must have been stretching across her face.

Her last words were odd, I thought, as it was very unlikely we would run into each other again after we parted, but before I could ask her about it, I heard the tapping of her staff on the ground as she began to walk in the direction I had come.

"Farewell, girl!" she called, and then there was only the sound of the forest filling the air once more.

I CONTINUED TO TRAVEL away from Athens. As the days passed, I became very good at noticing when other travelers were coming close to me, and with the help of the snakes I was able to avoid coming face-to-face with any more people.

Either I would hear the louder mortals stomping through the undergrowth of the forest and just angle away from the noise, or the snakes would catch a scent in the air and give me the best approximation of where the smell was coming from. We worked well together, at least for this purpose.

I removed the blindfold only for a few moments at a time each day, to wash my face with cool water from a stream or river, and sometimes in the very early mornings I would leave the blindfold off to watch the sun climb into the sky. If I was high on a hill, I could see how the blue of the ocean and the blue of the sky would split apart at the seam of the horizon when the dawn appeared, and the mornings were so quiet. The sea and the sky made no sound as they were parted, and the birds and animals in the forest were silent when the night gave way to the day.

Finding food was difficult. I had enough water to drink, since the snakes could find me a stream easily enough, but I did not know how to hunt, nor did I have the tools to do so. Instead, when the snakes scented a rabbit and occasionally a large animal like a deer, I would inch my blindfold up and study what the animal was eating from a distance. I made certain to look away or cover my eyes with the blindfold if the animal turned to face me.

The animals chewed on the varying green, leafy plants that were scattered across the forest floor. After watching a small rabbit stuff its cheeks with one plant that had green and purple leaves, I plucked the rest of the leaves for myself. They were bitter and tasted more like dirt than anything else, but it was something. Most of the plants I was eating were bitter in flavor, but I thought I recognized some of them from the salads we would mix in olive oil and eat alongside our bread at the temple.

At one point around the third or fourth day, the snakes had smelled something on the breeze and pulled me toward the scent without even trying to tell me what it was. We arrived at the base of a fruiting fig tree, and when I removed my blindfold to see where they had brought me, I was speechless with joy. I took as many figs as I could carry, eating many of them right then and there, and holding the rest in a makeshift basket I had made from holding up the edge of my dress to make a pocket. The soft give of the fig under my teeth as I bit into it and the sweet taste on my tongue were divine.

When I slept, I would have the snakes lead me to a copse of trees or a rocky overhang where I could have a solid wall at my back. I kept the blindfold on, even while I was sleeping, and the snakes seemed intent on keeping watch over me throughout the night.

One evening, when I had already settled down with a large oak behind me, I heard people moving around the forest in the dim remains of the setting sun. My shoulders stiffened, and I listened hard and waited for the snakes to flick their tongues out to taste the air. They would let me know if they sensed danger.

Suddenly, I felt the snakes recoil and I jerked up, braced on my hands, as a low male voice spoke, "What do we have here?"

A hand closed around my ankle.

I kicked my leg out, the feel of the man's rough palm against my skin reminding me of how Poseidon's hands had felt around my wrists, my neck.

"Let go!" I shouted.

"A *woman*," said another voice, also male.

"All alone out in the woods," said the first man, and his tone was oily as fish guts. "Why don't you come with us?"

He tightened his hold on my leg and pulled with enough force that I slid out of the spot I had curled up to sleep in, which was shadowed under the great oak. He laid his other hand higher up my leg where the edge of my ragged dress had bunched up.

The blindfold I was wearing meant that I had not been able to see the clouded night sky, or how the forest had become a smudgy, dark place, but as these men reached for me a small section of clouds peeled away from the moon and let the light through.

"Gods above," the second man exclaimed, "that's no woman! What the hell is it?"

My snakes were writhing and hissing, released from their temporary shock, and I could feel their fear. That same fear was crawling over my skin.

"It's got the body of a woman," the first man said, though his voice was now tinged with revulsion as well. I felt a cold chill wash over my body. "That's good enough."

Unlike Poseidon, this man was so focused on gripping my legs hard enough to bruise that he paid no attention to my hands. I reached up and ripped off the blindfold.

Do you have protection, girl? the old woman had asked.

It's your power. Use it for yourself.

I opened my eyes, glad it was night so that the dim light was not so different from the darkness under the blindfold.

The man holding me was large, with a wide face and

unkempt hair. He was looking down at my body, but as the second man behind him made a noise, he raised his head.

My eyes did not flare in pain this time. When the flash of red came, I felt a sensation like relief pulse through me from head to toe. The man's hands turned cold and I winced as I pulled my legs from his grasp, the heavy stone scraping across my skin.

I caught my weight on my hands as I hit the ground and scrambled backward away from the statue.

The snakes were still hissing in my ears, *The other, quick, get the other.*

I looked up wildly and found the second man, who was able to take just one step back, his hands raised in surrender, before my gaze found his and the red haze flashed as he was turned to stone. The rock seemed to come from inside of his body, the granite spreading across his skin like a rash as each limb stiffened and halted in its final position.

The look petrified on his face was one of horror.

I kicked my feet against the ground to push myself farther away from the two statues. My back hit the tree I had been sleeping under, and I used my legs to push myself up the bark until I was standing.

The snakes were writhing wildly around my head, their mouths wide open as they tasted the air for any more enemies lurking out in the wood. I could feel their irritation, upset that they had not been able to warn me in time and allowed those men to cause me pain. Threaded through their anger was my own desperation. Hadn't I said that I would not hurt another mortal? Hadn't I told myself, and the snakes, and that blind old woman, that I didn't want to hurt another being? Was I really so weak that I had to use it again, despite my reservations?

I dug my fingers into the bark of the tree and felt splinters press into the soft skin under my nails. The pain of it was sharp and clear. It helped me focus my thoughts.

The old woman had told me to use my power to protect myself. Athena had told me to use it for myself before others used it against me. But what did they know of this power, truly? Only I understood the full consequences of what this power would do to people, and what it would do to me.

No more, the snakes told me as they finished searching the area for more people, though they did not cease their wriggling. I loosened my grip on the tree and levered myself off the trunk. My legs pulsed dully, weary from adrenaline and throbbing under the skin where the man had held me.

The familiar feeling reminded me of Poseidon, again, and the memory that the feeling dredged up soon made every sound, every movement, feel like a hot spike through my forehead. Even the snakes' concerned motions made me feel nauseous.

"Stop," I bit out, and the snakes stilled at my harsh tone.

My head was blessedly silent for a moment, and then the not-voice asked, tentatively, *Hurt?*

"Be *quiet,*" I snapped. And then, once I felt the snakes' dismay, I added, "No."

I wouldn't be getting any more sleep that night, so once I felt that my legs were strong enough to support me, I left the two statues behind and began making my slow, trudging way through the forest once more. The blindfold hung loosely around my throat. The starry sky and shadowy trees were quiet, and so my thoughts were the loudest of all.

I could not keep traveling like this. Every time I came across another living thing, I ran the risk of either killing them if I left the blindfold off or endangering myself if I left it on. There was no way to predict when I would happen across someone else. And when I did come across a human, how could I trust them long enough to see if they meant to harm me? With my appearance being what it was, any mortal was more likely to come at me with their weapons drawn rather than their hands outstretched. That meant going anywhere near a city or town was out of the question.

I needed to go somewhere where mortals could never get to. Where mortals would never be able to stumble across me in the night. I knew these places existed, since I had grown up in one. The white house on the beach had only been accessible to those with divine blood in their veins, or someone like me, who had been born there. But I had never learned the location of another place like that. I needed someone to tell me where to find a place where no mortal could go, and how to get there.

A bird trilled in the branches above me. It was still early, hours before the sun would reach the eastern horizon. The bird may have been calling a warning, or perhaps trying to find its nest after getting lost in the dark by calling out to another. We both listened for an answer.

As the silence stretched out in the darkness, I thought of who I could call out to, like that bird. Who could guide me to safety? If there was anyone who could tell me what lay on the path before me, I knew there was only one being I could rely on to tell me the untampered truth. Three beings, to be more specific, though they comprised one entity.

I asked the snakes to tell me how to get to Delphi.

They answered easily, and as I turned northwest, I heard another bird call out in the darkness, responding to the lost one to guide it home.

Another gods forsaken prophecy

I HAD SEEN A few maps of the mortal lands before. One sketched onto an old scroll in the library at the white house on the beach, the paper yellowing and soft to the touch. Another map I had seen was left at Athena's altar, carefully rolled and sealed with wax until another priestess had broken the seal to see what it was. Astounded by the craftsmanship and detail, the priestesses in the temple had surrounded the map and studied the careful inking of names near noted cities and landmarks. A few priestesses had been able to point out the towns they had been born in. The old white house on the beach would not appear on any mortal map, as it was a place made only for divinities, but I had enjoyed tracing my finger along the coast of the mortal country.

Recalling that map, I knew that Delphi was a fair distance from Athens, located at the base of the large peninsula, whereas Athens was situated near the tip. In my past week or so of wandering I had moved north of Athens and now I just needed to trek westward, and though I knew there were dirt roads that wound their way through the forests and cut across great hilly ranges, I couldn't risk traveling on such populated routes. I would need to travel alone through the country, where I was less likely to see mortals.

Avoiding the roads meant that what might have been a two-day journey became a four-day hike. The snakes had an incredible sense of direction that made certain I did not stray away from the westward angle they had laid out for me, even when the sun was concealed by clouds.

Each night I unlaced my sandals to rub at my aching feet, brushing off flecks of dust and dirt from that day's journey. I had abandoned the blindfold entirely, and so I stumbled over fewer rocks and did not have to put up with low-hanging branches whipping across my face, but the trek was still difficult. I was used to remaining in one place. In the past few days, I had traveled farther than I had ever gone in my entire life.

But once I thought about that, I wondered how I had ever been content to stay in one city, in one house, for so many years. During the past week alone, I had seen dozens of sunrises and sunsets, and each one was as sweet as the last as I moved up and down hills, in and out of the forest so that the view was always changing. The few small towns I had spotted from afar were often bustling with mortals, children running in and out of the streets, and adults moving between houses with familiar noises of greeting. I made sure to stay out of sight when I passed these towns, but I ached to run into the markets I saw with stalls of fruit and baked goods and eat as much as I could.

That ache of hunger, however, seemed like a superficial itch that only grew more persistent the more I thought about it. When I was traveling and was able to push the thought of food to the back of my mind, I was not hungry. It seemed like the act of seeing food was what reminded me that I should feel hungry. My stomach did not pinch as it used to when it was empty, though, and even after two and a half days with no food I did not feel weakened.

With no one to speak to, I had all the time in the world to think, and I began to ask the snakes questions about whether they needed to eat or if they felt hunger only when I did.

But are you hungry? the not-voice asked in response.

"No," I said immediately and was surprised to find that it was the truth. "I have not eaten in three days, but I'm not hungry."

Either I was more exhausted than I thought, too tired to even feel hunger, and my body was about to give out on me with no warning, or I no longer needed to eat to live.

"How can this be?"

We are not mortal, the snakes said, and their tone suggested that I should have already figured this out. *We do not succumb to mortal needs.*

"This body was mortal for many years," I said, but even if I remembered what it felt like to be in a mortal body, I knew that was not who I was now. Whatever Athena had done to me beyond these snakes and my eyes, I was no longer the Medusa who needed to eat to stay alive.

In the early days of my wandering, I had only eaten the plants and fruit I found because I thought I should. But had I really been hungry then, or had I just thought I should be?

The answer was right in front of me, of course. I just didn't want to pick it up and examine it. I remembered how my parents and two sisters had treated food, as a luxurious, but unnecessary, action to take part in. I ate the fish and bread the servants prepared because I had to; my sisters ate it for fun. The immortals I had grown up with did not rely on food to keep their bodies healthy and working—their inherent divinity made sure that nothing would kill them except for what the Fates had in store.

If I no longer relied on food to live, it was because this new, monstrous, immortal body did not need to be coddled like a frail human.

Good, the snakes thought smugly.

"Stop listening to my thoughts," I bit back and then frowned. If these snakes were truly just another part of this body now, I was only arguing with myself. But that thought made my head ache, so I pushed it away.

The last bit of land I had to cover before I came to Delphi crossed right over a small mountain range. As I rose in elevation, I could see a larger mountain loom up to the north of my path. Recalling the map that I had seen in Athena's temple, I knew it to be the mountain of Parnassus and, recalling the gossip of the priestesses, I knew it to be a mountain favored by the god Dionysus. I knew only a little about the god of wine and ritual madness, but it was enough for me to want to steer clear of that mountain. Once I was over the hill, I turned my back to it.

The problem with Delphi, I soon discovered, was that there were many lesser oracles that flocked to the cliffside town to be closer to the god-blessed oracle of Apollo. Sifting through all these oracles to figure out where the Graeae had sequestered themselves was going to be difficult. Especially since I could not speak to anyone.

"Can you help me find them?" I asked the snakes after I had been sitting on a rock up in the dwindling trees and staring down at the rooftops of Delphi for nearly an hour.

Need something to look for, the not-voice explained, *need a smell, something to track.*

I thought back to the last time I had seen the Graeae, at Echidna's wedding. Their empty sockets boring holes into me and their skin, wrinkled and gray like a dried-out sea creature, closer to the color of a corpse than a living body. I didn't know if divine beings, real divinities, not the fanatic devotees like the ones flooding this town, had a specific smell. I would have to go with something that I had been able to pick up on while I was still human.

"Decay," I said slowly, "see if you can catch the scent of three women who smell as though they're halfway in the grave."

The snakes complied immediately, some of them flicking their tongues in the quick pink flashes that I had become accustomed to seeing, and the others dropping their jaws in a wide smile that revealed the twin fangs in each of their mouths. I stood and turned in a circle for them before I realized what I was doing. A part of me had thought that it would be easier for them to pick up a scent trail if they were able to face multiple directions, and though the snakes could swivel their heads to look around, the rest of my body had reacted and made it easier for them without thinking. I wanted to be frustrated that the remaining human limbs I had were responding to the needs of my monstrosity, but I just couldn't find a reason to be angry at myself.

One of the snakes above my left ear suddenly snapped its jaw closed and began flicking its tongue in quick movements. The snakes surrounding it turned in the same direction and copied the movement.

There, the not-voice told me, *death, up there.*

The snakes were looking higher up the cliffs, even higher than I already was above the town, and I could see the columns of a temple and shrine peeking out above rocky outcroppings.

"They're near Apollo's temple?" I asked with disbelief. I could hardly imagine the Graeae releasing their death grip on their pride long enough to recognize another divine being with similar, or superior, abilities.

No, the snakes said, their bodies now tense and coiled with anticipation, *higher.*

Above the temple were more cliffs. Once I climbed up, careful to skirt around the flattened areas where stone paths created a network around the temples and the smaller shrines to Apollo and the oracle, I was able to see that there were caves carved into the cliffside. The first few caves I passed were too small to even crouch in, and I began to wonder if the Graeae were further into their graves than I originally thought. But, once I was at a height where I could glance down and see the temples and the large half circle of a theater like small toys in the distance, I felt a change in air pressure pass over my skin.

The feeling was nothing like I had felt when I was in the presence of Athena. When a god entered the room, I felt it like a shock, and everyone and everything became accustomed to a tighter pressure. This time, it felt like stepping through a torrential waterfall. I could feel the weight of it, but it only lasted for a moment before it faded away.

"What—" I began to ask, but felt the confusion of the snakes wash over my mind and knew they didn't have a clue about what had just happened, either.

I looked back, but there was nothing behind me, just the same rocky trail and scrubby brush I had been picking through for the last thirty minutes. I reached out, stretching my arm until I brushed up against a faint resistance. It was like there was a curtain of air that was heavier than the surrounding atmosphere.

"It's like a gate," I thought aloud. "Or a wall."

Either way, I had been allowed to pass through.

I continued up the cliff, moving much more slowly as the incline had taken a sharp turn from steep to nearly vertical, and I had to use my hands to pull myself up in some places. Edging around a large boulder, I suddenly found myself on a small, flat stretch of the cliff, with a straight drop on one side and a dark cave entrance on the other. The cave was about a head taller than I was at its opening, and even though the bright midday sun was beating down on the cliffside, the interior was shadowy and cool.

In there, the snakes told me, though I had already figured that out for myself. The feeling emanating from the cave reminded me of being backed into a corner as the Graeae loomed over me. But there was no wall at my back, now.

I paused to consider whether I should cover my eyes before going in, but I had been traveling with the blindfold off for so long that putting it back on would have felt like defeat. I left the scrap of cloth where it was, tied around my wrist.

My steps echoed off the rough stone of the cave. The snakes curled in protectively, their bodies folding into S-shaped curves that were filled with tense energy, but I was not nearly as nervous as they were. The snakes were seeing my memories of how the Graeae had treated me as a child, experiencing those emotions for the first time, and they responded with a sharpened defense, but I couldn't call back the fear I used to feel when facing down the Graeae. Perhaps it was because their great prophecy about my fate, about the terrible monstrosity that was waiting for me, had already passed, but I did not think the Graeae could tell me anything that could hurt me further.

Still, the snakes coiled protectively around my head, their scaly bodies sliding against one another and making soft scraping sounds. I tried to soothe them with a few silent thoughts, but they didn't let up.

The cave sloped down gently as I walked, like I was descending into the belly of the cliffs, and the echo of my steps amplified when I came to the end of the tunnel.

A small fire burned in the center of the floor, the wood blackened and crumbling, and it cast dancing shadows across the rocky walls and the three figures crouched around the edge of the flames. Pemphredo, Enyo, and Deino had not changed at all in nearly a decade, but I had not expected them to, since gods and divinities did not age.

I realized, suddenly, that I would no longer age, too.

"Who has come to the Graeae?" Pemphredo, who was

sitting between her sisters, asked, her scratchy voice seeming to come from every direction in the cramped space.

While they must have heard me coming from the moment I entered the cave, I looked closer and noticed that none of the three sisters was using the eye, so they had not seen who I was. Instead, Pemphredo held the eye clutched in her sickly gray hand. When I remained silent for a moment too long, she began to lift the eye to her empty socket.

"Wait," I said, "do not put it in. I am Medusa."

Even though Enyo and Deino did not even have possession of the eye, they reacted instantly, each of them letting out a sharp screech and fumbling for Pemphredo's hand to make sure she did not try to use it. Pemphredo twisted out of their grip, but I could see how tightly she was squeezing the eye now. I thought it would pop if she tightened her grasp on it too much more. She put her hand, and the eye, behind her back before I could find out.

"Snake-haired Gorgon," Pemphredo said nastily. "How many mortals have you turned to stone since Athena cursed you to take this form?"

I frowned.

"How much did you know when you gave me that prophecy at Echidna's wedding?" I countered.

"Enough to know that you have taken the appearance of a monster, even though we cannot look upon you," Pemphredo snapped. She opened her mouth to say more, but Enyo whipped her hand out and snatched the tooth from her sister. Pemphredo reached out to try and take it back, but Enyo was already shoving the tooth into her dirty pink gums.

"We knew that you would become something so horrible

that it would be fatal for humans to look at you," she said, "though Athena is certainly wise, to have cursed the only positive aspect of your mortality."

"And what was that?" I asked, surprised that the three of them could have found anything positive about mortality, especially my own.

"Why, your appearance, of course. You were a very beautiful child," Enyo said, like this was an obvious statement, "and your beauty only grew as you did. We know you became vain while serving at Athena's temple once you were surrounded by mortals who would value your looks. Mortal beauty is precious because it fades. Athena took yours from you before you could fully savor it, and she turned your own face against you."

Pemphredo and Deino grinned at me toothlessly, savagely pleased with my predicament. I realized this was the first time I had been able to look at another being's face since I had been cursed, and I did not need to fear that I would turn the Graeae to stone. They couldn't see me. Even though their faces were mottled gray and carved with deep wrinkles, I looked at them with wonder. Their empty eye sockets were dark as the entrance to the cave. I reached up and touched the soft skin beneath my own eyes, where the curse sat waiting to strike, and was relieved that it felt normal. The heat that accompanied the stone-making power was not there.

The Graeae, of course, could not see this realization come over me, and so they took my silence for frustration.

"Yes, what a beautiful curse for you to suffer," Enyo continued. "Though we do wonder what has brought the stone-making Gorgon to our threshold. Are you angry that our prophecy came true?"

"No," I said honestly, for I knew that being angry at the Graeae for a curse caused by two gods would get me nowhere, even if they were the ones who had been a part of the events that led to my monstrosity. It was because of my squabble with these three at Echidna's wedding that Athena and Poseidon had taken an interest in me. But I had more pressing concerns than avenging events from my childhood. "You speak the truth when it becomes available to you, and though you had malicious intent, your warning was rightfully given. I come to you now to ask for your help."

"Us help a Gorgon?" Enyo laughed scratchily. "Nothing we could tell you would get rid of that nasty curse of yours."

I opened my mouth and then closed it again. Having been so preoccupied with not letting any other mortals fall prey to my eyes, I had only thought of separating myself from society, and I had never even considered trying to rid myself of the curse. Perhaps I had known that there would be no way to undo a curse laid upon me by a goddess like Athena.

While I thought about how it would feel to relieve myself of the curse, the snakes began to hiss worriedly and brushed themselves against my temples and forehead. I could feel their flash of terror at the thought I would get rid of them, and I felt shame bubble up in my chest. The snakes had done nothing but try to take care of me since they had become a part of my body. They may have been a part of the curse, but if anything, they were the only good part of it.

"Shh," I soothed them under my breath. "You are not going anywhere."

The snakes seemed mollified, and they settled back into their wary positions.

"Talking to yourself now, are you?" Enyo asked. "Or are you talking to those serpents that have taken over your head and rid you of your beauty?"

She and her sisters laughed again. I ignored her question, even as the snakes bristled.

"I want you to tell me where I can find a place away from mortals," I said firmly, "somewhere for me to live without hurting anyone else."

Enyo did not have an eye to roll, but I still felt as though the gesture was apparent when she said, "The only places where mortals are not allowed to go are places that belong to the gods. A horrible monster like you would never be welcome."

"But I do have godly blood in my veins," I pressed, "and now that I am immortal because of divine intervention, I will be recognized as such."

Deino, who had been laughing and sneering alongside her sisters the whole time I had been there, suddenly straightened from her hunched posture. She reached blindly over Pemphredo, hitting the middle sister in the side of the head with a stray hand, and grappled for Enyo's mouth. The sisters squawked and scuffled with one another for a moment before Deino leaned back, the single tooth gripped in her fingers. She fit it into her mouth.

"You were able to find this cave," she said, like an accusation. "You passed through our protective gate."

I blinked at her. "You mean that heavy wall of air outside? Yes, I felt that."

"Only beings with some level of divinity can pass through that wall, unless we will a mortal in," Deino said, and now Pemphredo and Enyo were gaping in my direction. "You are indeed no longer mortal, but you are also much more than just some simple monster." She tapped her chin, her fingernail dirty and cracked.

"We do know where you will go," she continued and bulled on even as Pemphredo and Enyo whipped their heads toward her and made noises that were all breath and smacking gums, trying to shush her. "We have seen a vision of an island, away from the cities of mortals and where no ship skims the shores, where you will settle and turn men to stone no more. You will find peace there."

I opened my mouth to ask where this island was, as it sounded like exactly what I was looking for.

"But you will not be alone," Deino said, and I stopped short. "Your sisters Euryale and Stheno will be with you as well."

"What?" I blurted out.

"Your sisters," Deino repeated, speaking slowly and loudly like I was a daft dog. "They will find you and join you on the island to live together as you used to. Triplets of divine lineage cannot be away from one another for too long, you see. We Graeae are a testament to that. The Gorgons will be together again."

My mind reeled from this information. I had not seen or heard anything of my sisters since we parted. Why would they come in search of me, especially now, when I had become a monster? I couldn't understand it.

"This is not all that we have seen."

Deino's voice took a sudden turn, and it became dark and echoed around the cave as her words took on the tripled nature I had experienced the last time the Graeae gave me a prediction of my future.

"This peace comes with a cost, as all things do. You will suffer much in your journey to this island and many will suffer because of you, and there is nothing you can do to avoid this. The damage you inflict will anger a king and make him tremble with fear of your power, and he will send a boy to your island, and he will order this boy to bring him your head.

"The boy is named Perseus. He will find your sisters' island with the aid of Hermes and the goddess Athena herself, and he will come prepared as if to fight a ferocious battle clad in shining armor with winged sandals on his feet. He will carry a shield from the goddess of wisdom, clear of any marking or engraving that would warp the glinting reflection he can use to misdirect your gaze.

"However, he will have no need of these tools of war, for he will come to you while you are in the likes of sleep, as helpless as a lamb under the suckling teat of its mother, blind to the surrounding danger. Perseus will not wait for you to wake or risk another moment before your fatal eyes open again. The boy will cut off your head with the sword Athena gave him and take it back in a sack as proof to the king who sent him. This is what we see waiting for you beyond the veil of the present."

The cave was too quiet when Deino finished speaking. The snakes, which had been seized by a flurry of action at the beginning of the prophecy, fell still and limp like weighted stones at the end of a string. I felt a ringing in my ears, like Deino's words were still echoing around the cave and rebounding through my head. The Graeae were considering me sightlessly, waiting for my reaction.

I did not give them that satisfaction.

I ran from the cave. My footsteps echoed wildly against the stone walls as I sprinted up and out of the darkness until they were muffled against the dirt of the cliffside. I stumbled to a halt right at the edge of the flat landing and collapsed on my knees.

The sun was shining brightly down on the cliffs and thin forests surrounding Delphi. The smell of hot dirt and dry brush filled the air, and I could hear birds calling out from the cliffs below me. It was all too normal.

A terrible scream clawed its way up and out of my throat, and I was too frustrated and angry to try and stop it. I let it shred my lungs of air and spill out into the too calm afternoon.

When my throat was raw and I didn't have any strength left in me to scream, I got to my feet and left the cave behind. Hot tears were streaking down my face. I hiccuped and rubbed the heels of my palms into my eyes, pressing a bit too hard. The blackness under my eyelids fluttered under the pressure.

Knowing that I would live in this monstrous body for the rest of my life had been something I was slowly growing to accept. I had thought that if I was able to avoid all contact with mortals, I would be able to find some sort of peace in which to shelter myself from the rest of the world. I didn't know how long I would live, but maybe I could have been content.

Now I knew that that had been a foolish dream. I had already hurt too many people, and I had no way to ensure that my curse wouldn't turn anyone else to stone. I would petrify and kill more mortals. The Graeae had said there was no way to avoid this. And, on top of that, my curse would bring about my own death since a monster like me would not be allowed to live in the mortal world. If I ever did find myself content and settled with my life, I would know that my demise was drawing near.

As I left Delphi, eager to leave the Graeae's dark cave behind, and headed into thicker forest, my mind wandered, unbidden. The Graeae had said that Athena would be the one to arm the boy who would kill me. They had said that Athena would give him a shield with which he could divert my killing eyes. Would it be one of the shields I had found on the altar at Athena's temple? One of the shields I had stored and polished with my own two hands?

And how could this shield protect the boy from me? I was not surprised that Athena knew more about my curse than I did, but I burned to think that there had been a way to stop mortals from dying from one look at me, and she had not even mentioned it.

However, I struggled to hold on to the idea that I didn't want to hurt mortals anymore. If so much destruction and death was already fated for me, who was I to try and avoid it? Why should I waste the effort?

I had to stop walking then, surprised by the resigned tone of my thoughts. Would I really be willing to give up on trying to protect others from my own monstrosity, just because I couldn't see a way out?

"This is just shit," I said aloud, fresh tears spilling from my eyes. My snakes hissed in agreement. I cursed the gods, too, but kept that to myself so that I would not anger the god it was directed at, in case she was listening.

I wandered deeper into the forest for the rest of the afternoon and into the evening. The snakes were oddly quiet compared to the previous times I had been traveling like this, with my head full of tremulous thoughts, and they simply hung around my head like they, too, had a lot on their minds. I wondered if they were thinking about their own role in the curse, and the death that was coming for us both.

Just as the sun was setting a few hours later, and I had shaken myself out of my rapidly descending train of thought long enough to look for a place to sleep, I heard shouts ahead of me. Even though the forest was tightly packed with towering pines, it sounded as though there was a great procession of people stamping their way through the undergrowth. This far from Delphi or any other town, I wondered what so many people could be doing in the middle of a forest at twilight.

The snakes raised their heads as I crept toward the noise. Either they, too, were intrigued, or my sudden interest and focus had encouraged them to go on the alert. I moved quietly through the trees, though I really needn't worry about being stealthy. The noise of the procession grew more boisterous and bawdier as I neared, and perhaps nothing but a volcano erupting would be loud enough to distract them. When I drew close enough, I saw figures moving, their shadows thrown sharply across the forest floor by bright torches held aloft, and I realized they were dancing. When I came even closer, I realized they were all women.

Hair loose and eyes wild, the women leaped around the small clearing in bare feet. They all wore the common dresses I had seen many women wearing both in Athens and the small towns I had passed, but a few of them had torn the hems of their dresses so short I could see the long stretch of their thighs. Others had done the reverse and ripped the sleeves of their tunics so the fabric hung uselessly below their bare breasts. All the women gleamed with sweat.

The women were moving in one direction, though their rhythmic flailing kept them at a very slow pace, and so I turned and looked in the direction they were headed.

Mountain, said the not-voice.

It had been a while since the snakes had spoken directly to me, I realized, and I couldn't help but feel relieved that they were talking to me again. But that relief faded away rather quickly when I realized their meaning. I had wandered right to the base of Parnassus, without realizing it.

Which meant that these women were likely followers of Dionysus, caught in his madness. I backed away from the clearing. I had had enough of gods and divinities for one day, and I did not want to fall under the spell of another.

"Well, that's a pity," said a voice from behind me. "Are you not going to join us?"

Soaked in wine and blood

I WAS NEARLY STARTLED enough to turn around. In fact, I had begun to twist my head to look over my shoulder, but before I could get a glimpse of who was behind me, the snakes raised their bodies to my eye level and hissed. Their attention was split between me and the speaker. The snakes closest to my face were turned toward me and flicked their tongues emphatically, making sure I did not petrify whoever this was.

The rest of the snakes were baring their fangs at the speaker.

"Is that a very unique case of bedhead," they asked, "or am I right to guess that you are under some sort of curse?"

"Who are you?" I shot back, indignant on behalf of the snakes as they fumed at being called a *bedhead*.

The speaker laughed. "A fair question, though I wonder why you won't turn and see for yourself."

"I cannot," I said tersely. "Unless you have a death wish."

"Indeed, I do not," they said good-naturedly. "Let me see, if you cannot look at me, perhaps this will help you figure out who I am."

As if I had been suddenly plunged into the ocean, I felt the pressure of the air around me increase and make me want to pop my ears. My stomach twisted.

"You are a god," I whispered. I briefly wondered how he was able to control the weight of his presence so fluidly, but I didn't have the chance to ask.

"Correct! Now, guessing which god may be difficult, since there are a fair few, but I'll allow you three questions to—"

"You're Dionysus."

"Oh," said the god of winemaking and revelry and pleasure, sounding dejected. "You got that very fast."

"I'm at the base of your mountain," I reasoned, "and that crowd of women who just passed was acting very odd. Are they under the influence of your madness? Your maenads?"

Dionysus was quiet for a moment before he answered, in a tone that conveyed more sorrow than I thought was possible for a god.

"Yes, they are. And I suppose I should not be surprised you were able to put that together." His tone brightened, like sunlight breaking through a part in the clouds. "Well, then, you know who I am, so by right I should know who you are. I'm not acquainted with many people who have snakes for hair."

My snakes hissed at him again. I shushed them mentally, not wanting to offend this god. I had already been cursed by a divine being, and I did not want to invite another to add on to it. Though, I had a power Dionysus should fear in turn. If he tried anything, would I be able to use this stone-making ability? The snakes quieted, but they remained coiled in a defensive position and the tension in their bodies made it feel as though I was drawn tight, like a pulled string.

"I believe," I said carefully, "it would be better that you don't meet me."

"Why is that?"

The firelight from the procession of women had nearly disappeared beyond the trees, but the light of the moon filtering down through the treetops was still enough for me to see by. The vague shapes of the trees were eerie, but I addressed one of them as I refused to turn to face Dionysus.

"I cannot look at you," I explained again, "or else I could kill you."

"You don't have to look at me," Dionysus said simply. "I just want to know your name."

I pressed my lips together in a thin line. "Medusa."

"Hmm," he said, "*queen*. I have certainly never seen a queen like you."

"My mother did not know I would look like this one day," I said, frowning as I recalled that my mother had named me Medusa in the hopes of aligning me with a position of power. If she could see me now, I'm sure her reasoning behind my name would seem all that more ridiculous. I paused, considering how much I should say, but figured that coming right out with the truth was the best option. "Nor did she know that I would be cursed with eyes that would turn anyone who dared look at me to stone."

Behind me, Dionysus clapped his hands together. "Oh, is that how your curse works? Well then, there's a simple solution, isn't there. I'll just close my eyes." He paused. "All right, closed!"

I was speechless for a moment. "You want me to look at you?"

"Consider it a trade," he said. "You look at me, and I'll get to look at you. Few get to see me as I am, but I think you will be able to see the truth of me."

The god's thoughts seemed to be moving at twice the pace of mine, and even though we were in the same conversation I was struggling to keep up. He spoke quickly and openly, which was very unlike Athena's measured commands and it skewed the regal image of gods I had always been able to picture in my head. Although I had only spoken to a handful of gods in my life, Dionysus was the strangest by far. I wondered what he meant about the truth of himself, and that curiosity was enough for me to finally turn around.

He was unlike any god I had seen before. A young man stood a length away, his pale skin shining under the moonlight and thrown in sharp contrast to his dark brown curls that were woven through with a crown of bruised purple and green grape leaves. When I looked closer, I saw that there were still clusters of grapes clinging to the vines. Dionysus was wearing a loose tunic draped casually over one shoulder, leaving the other arm and most of his toned chest bare. His eyes were closed under thick but elegantly arched eyebrows, and his full lips were tilted up just slightly in a smile.

He was incredibly handsome. I knew that being attractive was something of a given for most gods, but Dionysus's appearance lacked the severe beauty I had come to expect with most divine beings. Instead, Dionysus was flaunting the gentle loveliness of a boy who had just come into his prime, and that struck me as distinctly human.

"Why do you look so young?" I asked without thinking.

Dionysus's small smile split into a grin. "I felt like it!"

"You mean, you changed your appearance to this at will?"

"Oh sure," Dionysus said, waving his hand in a dismissing gesture. "Most of my counterparts use that ability to disguise themselves so they can interfere with the lives of mortals. You know, they turn themselves into little boys with news that only a god would know, or old women who know more about you than you do, right? Sure they do. I decided to use that power to please myself."

"What do you usually look like?" I asked, thinking back to what Dionysus had said about his truthful self.

Dionysus just smiled again and shook his head, the fluttering leaves of his crown throwing shadows over his closed eyes. "Maybe you'll get to see it some other time."

He clapped his hands together again. "My turn! Shut those dangerous eyes of yours."

I opened my mouth to refuse, but quickly reconsidered and did as the god said. Nothing good would come from refusing him. As my eyes shut, the snakes coiled tighter around my head.

We waited in silence for a moment, and then two, until Dionysus asked impatiently, "Well? Are they closed yet?"

"Oh," I said, startled that he had waited for me, "yes."

Dionysus made no noise as he opened his eyes. I wished I could see what shape his face was taking. The snakes, at least, did not seem alarmed.

"Interesting," he said finally. "A mortal woman with a divine curse that has taken over her body. You seem to be struggling quite a bit, dear, with what you consider the two sides of yourself."

"What?"

"Ah, you're right," Dionysus said gently, though I thought the grin would be back on his handsome face. "This is a conversation that cannot happen until after we've had a cup or two of my best wine. Here, I'm going to walk past you and face away. Turn around and follow me, if you please. Which you should."

"I should what?"

"You should be pleased to follow me!"

Now he spoke with the commanding tone I associated with gods like Athena, like he was accustomed to telling others what he wanted and then used to getting it. There was something slightly off about him, though, since he also spoke like a spoiled child. I had only just met him, and yet he had a complete disregard for the power I had, and he seemed determined to plow through any warning I could give him like it was a shield of grass. However, there was no possible way for me to deny him. He was still a god.

I felt him edge around and behind me, the dirt and rocks crunching under his steps. When I was sure he had enough time to put some distance between us, I opened my eyes, and with a calming breath, looked over my shoulder.

Dionysus was facing away from me like he said, and I could see the back of his curly hair and grape leaf crown as well as a great swath of his bare shoulder.

"Are you ready?" he asked. He began walking away before I answered him, heading in the same direction as the procession of dancing, half-naked women. Hurrying after him and maintaining a good length between us, I silently asked the snakes to keep a lookout for anything suspicious. I was worried about an attack from the crazed followers. While Dionysus may have been determined to ruin my idea of what a god should be, and he was very dissimilar to the Olympian gods I had met before, that didn't mean he wasn't dangerous.

I continued to follow him despite the danger, however, because he had not looked at me and reacted with disgust, but rather he had looked beyond the exterior and dug up what lay beneath. Hadn't I been thinking that my body and I were two separate things just days ago? I wanted to know how he had picked me apart to easily.

While the moon and stars shone brightly against the inky sky, their light was too feeble to breach the treetops as the forest became thicker and wilder. I began to see vines curling around the trunks of trees, their broad leaves forming a thick coat around the bark, and I tried to think back on all the plants I had seen thus far in my journey. I couldn't remember seeing vines like these anywhere.

Either my steps had slowed as I studied the vines, or perhaps Dionysus could in fact tell what I was thinking, because he called out from in front of me to explain, "Grapevines. They tend to sprout up of their own accord in the places that I spend a lot of time in. Determined little things."

He brushed his hand lovingly over the leaves of the next vine we passed, and it shivered at his touch like a dog wagging its tail after receiving its master's approval, and then shot out a handful of new leaves along the main stem.

Soon enough, I could hear the noise of the dancing women again. Whatever music they were dancing to, something from a stringed instrument combined with the stamping of feet, grew louder and the noise reached us far before the light did. After a few more minutes walking uphill I finally saw the flickering of torches through the gaps in the trees. Dionysus led me into a clearing where the women had gathered, spinning in a giant circle and kicking up leaves and small flowers as they danced. My steps slowed, and my stomach turned as I saw how many people there were. I had not been in a crowd like this since I had left Athens. There were too many eyes.

Through a gap in the dancers, Dionysus darted into the middle of the circle and spun his hands in the air with his eyes closed. The women cheered at his arrival, joyous shouts and wordless cries piling up on top of the music.

I stayed outside the circle, closer to the edge of the forest. Dionysus had said he wouldn't look at me, but these women had made no such promise, and I didn't think they were all too concerned with any danger, at the moment.

"My friends," Dionysus said, and the music quieted just a bit, enough for his voice to be heard, "welcome to my mountain. I hope you dance and drink to your heart's content. I do have one request, however. I have a special guest with me tonight, and she is very worried about hurting you."

"Let her try!" one of the women called out tauntingly, and the others laughed. I was surprised. I had thought their minds were lost to whatever wildness was driving them here, but the woman who had shouted seemed of sound enough mind, enough to make a joke.

"Yes, yes," Dionysus said with a grin, "you can fend for yourselves; you've shown me that. But, please, do as I ask for your sake, and mine, and for the sake of my guest: *Do not look in her eyes.*"

The god's voice changed at this command, and it sounded similar to how the Graeae spoke when they delivered a prophecy, like his voice was being amplified through many throats. Dionysus was looking more serious than he had thus far. Once his words had settled over the clearing and he received a few confirming nods from the women, his face split into a smile again.

"Find your pleasure," he told the women, and they cheered back in response. The music struck up again even louder, the women launching into a fast, quick-footed dance that sent their hair flying like ribbons behind them.

Dionysus waved to catch my attention, continuing to look away, and then beckoned me forward. I glanced around carefully and saw that the women closest to me were indeed following Dionysus's command; their eyes slid away from where I was standing like water flowing around a rock in a stream. Still, I kept my gaze down as I followed Dionysus through the middle of the circle, dodging the errant limbs of dancing women.

On the other side of the clearing was a cove of trees. The trees' drooping canopy combined with the flourishing grapevines that stretched up the trunks gave the cove a distinct cave-like feeling. Spread out on the floor under the trees was a collection of cushions, congregating around a low, rough-hewn table that was piled high with all kinds of fruits. There was also a large carafe of dark red wine and a few cups.

Dionysus waved me past him. "You may sit at the back

and I will sit in front, looking away from you, so that you can keep an eye on me, yes?"

"Mm," I replied, stepping past him and sitting on the cushion closest to the back of the cove. Though it was not really a cave, the feeling of a thick wall of foliage behind me felt comforting. Since I had been sleeping with my back to a tree or a boulder for the past few weeks, and those were often the only moments of calm I had, the feeling of having a solid wall behind me allowed me to find a bit of ease around the god.

Collapsing across three cushions with his back to me, Dionysus plucked a string of purple grapes out of the pile of food on the table and began picking them off the stem and popping them in his mouth one by one. He was looking out over the clearing, watching as the women danced.

"How did you know?" I asked. I didn't think he would need me to explain what I meant, since he had come to some understanding of my inner thoughts with just one look at me.

"Are you referring to the fact that I thought a lone woman who has been cursed by a goddess and subjected to a life on the run would prefer to have her back protected and all possible dangers in her line of sight," Dionysus asked easily, "or that I knew you prefer red wine?"

"I—" I looked down at the carafe of wine, which was a dark burgundy color, and then back up at Dionysus. "The first, mostly, but also the second now that you mention it."

He was correct, I did prefer red wine.

Dionysus laughed merrily and reached back, fumbling around the table until he found the jug of wine and two cups. He filled the cups nearly to the brim, without looking at them, and handed one back to me.

"Well, the second has an easier answer. As the god of wine, of course, I know what each person I meet prefers in terms of drink. Makes it much simpler to please them." Dionysus took a long draft and smacked his lips. "As for the first, I can also recognize someone so highly strung and defensive such as you," he said, and then quickly continued like he could feel me bristle, "because I have been where you are now."

The snakes flicked their tongues at Dionysus, trying to catch a scent of lies in the heady night air, and it made me feel better when they did not react with alarm. A few of them were leaning toward my cup and trying to catch a drop of wine on their tongues. I pulled the cup out of their reach absentmindedly, still staring at the back of Dionysus's head.

"I find it difficult to believe," I said slowly, "that any god could feel as I do now."

Dionysus laughed again. "We are not all born with the powers we currently wield. I am not like many of the gods you may meet. I am completely unlike my sister Athena, for example."

At the mention of her name, the snakes hissed and coiled near my ears defensively. I narrowed my eyes at Dionysus.

"Your sister?"

"Indeed," Dionysus said. Having finished his grapes, he sifted through the fruit on the table and picked out a pomegranate. He pressed his thumbs into the hard outer skin until it cracked and split under the pressure, spilling juice and seeds over his fingers. "Did you know that Athena was born from Zeus's head?"

I nodded, and then remembered that Dionysus wasn't looking at me. "Yes."

"How?" he asked. He sounded surprised.

"I learned the story at her temple in Athens," I said quickly, which was the truth, if a bit watered down. "The legend of her birth is carved on the walls."

"She would be proud of that," Dionysus said, though his tone made me think that this was nothing to be proud of. He licked some of the dark pomegranate juice off his fingers. "Born from the mind of the king of all gods, right? Well, I too was born from Zeus, but I did not come from any place as high or mighty as his head. I," Dionysus said with a flourish, "was born from his thigh!"

Dionysus lifted his right leg and gestured grandly to it with his pomegranate, the rich material of his tunic sliding up his leg and revealing toned muscle. He tapped a place in the middle of his thigh, presumably the same spot where he had emerged from Zeus, and left a sticky mark behind.

"You see," he continued, lowering his leg, "my mother died while still pregnant with me. Or perhaps *died* is too kind a word. My mother, Semele, was kind and beautiful, but she was also a bit of an idiot." Dionysus's voice took a tricky turn, hard and fond at the same time. "Hera hated her for sleeping with Zeus, of course, and she convinced my mother that Zeus needed to prove his love for her by revealing his true form. My father cared for her and had promised to grant her every wish when she became pregnant, and so he had no choice. He showed Semele his true form, and it killed her."

Dionysus flicked some of the stringy pit of the pomegranate off his hand. The set of his shoulders was still loose, but I wondered whether his relaxed posture was due to his forced lack of feeling toward the story he was telling, or if it was something born from decades of time to come to terms with the events of his birth.

"My father took me from my mother's womb and sewed me into his thigh until I was ready to be born, fully formed. Much like Athena, no?"

"Yes," I agreed reluctantly. I'd had to recite the story of Athena coming out of Zeus's head fully formed so many times for visitors at the temple that I had it memorized, and I could see the similarities. Athena's mother, Metis, was also destroyed by Zeus before giving birth to her child, but it was due to Zeus's fear of a prophecy that he ate Metis and gave birth to Athena himself.

"But of course, my story is not as interesting, since I just came out of his leg, and Athena had the glory of coming from his head," Dionysus said airily. He took a sip of his wine, and then snorted. "We both came from his other head, though, didn't we."

I choked on the sip of wine I was taking, surprised by such a crude joke coming from a god's mouth. Glaring at Dionysus as I wiped my chin, I said, "Still not something to be proud of, I think."

"Perhaps not," Dionysus agreed. "Father does not have the best reputation. Neither do his children, it seems." He drained his cup and poured another one.

"Not that this history lesson hasn't been interesting," I said, "but could you get to the part about how you and I are similar? Or were similar at one point?"

"Yes, yes. But first, tell me how your curse works."

"What, don't you already know?" I asked, exasperated. I scarcely cared that I was snapping at a god who could destroy me. He felt more like one of my immortal siblings, full of too much power and too little sense. "You seem to know everything else about me."

"Only a few educated guesses, dear," Dionysus said.

I blew air out of my nose and the snakes flicked their tongues in sympathy, but they didn't seem as frustrated with the god as I was. I took a breath.

"No being, mortal or immortal, can look upon my eyes or else they will be turned to stone, and petrified."

A moment of silence passed, and then Dionysus asked, "Is that all? What about the snakes?"

"What about them?"

"You did not explain what they have to do with the curse. Are they merely for decoration?"

"No," I snapped. The snakes shifted uneasily as I tried to explain. "The snakes are a part of the petrification, I think. My eyes are the cause of petrification, but I've seen a red flash of light come from the snakes when the curse is working."

"Hmm. I was able to look at your snakes, and they looked back at me, and yet I am not petrified. So the curse is contained only to your eyes, yes. Why, then, are the snakes now a part of you?"

"I don't have a clue," I said.

"Liar," Dionysus said genially, and I could see just the slightest corner of his mouth kicking up in a grin along with the accusation. "You must know what they're for. I think you must have been a very beautiful mortal woman, were you not?"

"I," then I closed my mouth. All the times I had flaunted my golden hair and tried to dazzle the mortals with my appearance flashed through my mind, and my stomach pinched in shame at my useless vanity. "I was...pretty."

"Understatement of an era, I think," Dionysus replied. "That curse of yours has been crafted to torture you in two parts. First, no one can ever safely look upon you again, and so they may not appreciate you like they have in the past. Second, the looks you prized so highly were stripped from you. So, I ask again, why snakes?"

I reached up and offered my palm to the snakes and one of them fit its body into the curve of my hand, nudging my fingers with its rounded snout. Even though the snakes were as far from the soft, golden curls as I could get, I had begun to care for them these past few weeks, just as they cared for me. Had Athena intended for this to happen? Surely, I was not supposed to learn to love a part of the curse that had destroyed my life.

The silence in the cove stretched out, but Dionysus did not seem to want to break it this time. He reclined back, propped his head up on one hand, and watched the dancing women. His foot bounced up and down with the beat of the music.

"Why are we similar?" I asked again, knowing that I was changing the subject.

With a deep sigh, Dionysus put his empty cup back on the table and flopped onto his back. The movement was distinctly juvenile, but it did not look out of place on his young body, even though I knew he was centuries older than I was. His eyes were closed again.

"Hera, in her all-encompassing jealousy, could not settle with just having my mother destroyed by Zeus. And so I, as a symbol of my father's never-ending infidelity, needed to be punished as well. When she found where Zeus had hidden me after my birth, she laid a curse on me, very similar to yours."

I looked him up and down, doubtfully.

"My curse cannot be seen externally," he said, answering my silent judgment. "But I, like you, am a danger to all mortals who come near me." He flapped his hand at the circle of dancers. "Why do you think those women are acting that way?"

"I thought they were under your spell," I said honestly.

"That is partially true," Dionysus said. "Their wildness and madness are because of me, but not because of something I've said or done. Mortals who come close to me are simply driven out of their minds. Hera cursed me with the gift of madness that has seeped into every pore of my being, and the closer a mortal is to me, the more insane they become. Many have no control over what they do."

"You mean, those women are here against their will?" I asked, outrage readily boiling up in my chest.

"Oh no," he said quickly. He covered his eyes with one hand. "The mortals around this mountain know of my power. These women knew what would happen if they sought me out. They are here because they *want* to be out of their minds for a night or two."

I sat back from the braced position I had taken, ready to rip Dionysus's hand off his face and petrify him to free the women. I didn't care if he was a god. I did not want anyone else to be helpless and at the mercy of a careless god. My snakes were tasting for the scent of deceit, the tang of lies in the air, but they came up with nothing. Dionysus was telling the truth.

"Of course," he went on, "there were many who did come against their will, during those first few years while I struggled under Hera's curse. Many died, including people close to me." He gave a hollow laugh. "It's hard to control the madness when you yourself feel as if it is going to consume you. I tried to separate myself from society, to put as much distance between any mortals who could fall under the spell and myself." He pointed at me and then back at himself. "Birds of a feather, hmm?"

Swallowing the last of my wine, I chucked the cup on the table and lay down like Dionysus. His loose manner, in opposition to everything I knew about gods, had put me at ease. The overhang of tree branches was stirring softly, swaying in the wind, and it helped disrupt the cave-like feeling. It looked as though the copse itself were breathing.

Dionysus seemed to take my silence as agreement and pressed on. "Hera's curse would not be ignored. I had to run into mortals eventually, and when I did, the madness ruined them. It was awful watching the people around me go insane, knowing that I was the cause, simply for existing as I was. Mortals are much too gullible."

Coming from a god, this should have sounded like a cruel accusation against humans. But Dionysus did not sound as though he thought the inherent trust that humans could have in another being was something to be ashamed of. He sounded like he pitied the mortals.

"You said you lost people who were close to you. Were they human?" I asked, thinking of Polli, and how her eyes had been frozen in a look of such confusion the last time I had seen her. Had her kindness toward me been a part of her gullibility? I hated to think that it was her easy affection of me that had led to her death. The snakes shifted, feeling my discomfort, and I turned her out of my mind.

Dionysus blew out a stream of air between his parted lips. "Yes."

The music in the clearing had slowed, and now only one musician was plucking out a mournful tune on the lute's strings. A few of the women had paused at different points in the trampled circle of grass and were swaying side to side. Others were spinning on the spot, their hands held aloft and fluttering above their heads like trapped birds. The lute cried out another few notes, and then the women joined in, their untrained voices rising in a melody I had never heard before.

Dionysus had turned his face toward the singing women, eyes still closed.

"You can try to run from the curse," he said quietly, "but there is no escaping yourself."

I reached my arms up above my head like the dancing women, flipped my hands a few times, and then dropped them onto the plush grass and pillows.

"That's shit," I told him.

Dionysus barked out a laugh.

"That is life," he replied, "for mortals and immortals alike."

He sat up and poured us both another cup of wine.

Slow rivers can become raging rapids, wearing stone to nothing

I STAYED WITH DIONYSUS for many days, though I had a hard time separating one day from another. The only real indicator of time passing was that the mortals who flooded the clearing would change, still mostly women, with only the occasional few young men. With each new batch of mortals, Dionysus would repeat the same command he had delivered my first night with him, telling the humans that they were not to look at me.

I was comforted by his continued attempt to protect his followers from me, and vice versa. Sometimes, when the wine flowed a bit too freely from the jug to his cup, I was worried he would forget his promise and take a look at me himself, but he never did. No matter how drunk the god became, he always had enough sense left to keep his eyes, and the eyes of his followers, away from my face.

Even though the god appeared like a careless boy of twenty years, his actions often gave away his true nature.

I saw his fierce dedication in protecting the mortals who sought him out, and the way he protected me.

I was reminded of Dionysus's real power about a week after he found me at the base of his mountain. It was midday, and the mortals from the night before had finally trickled out of the clearing to return home, or at least to sleep off the madness before coming back again when night fell. Dionysus had disappeared sometime during the early hours, allowing the mortals to come to their senses.

I was lying in a patch of thick grass, letting my snakes nose around in the dirt. I was so used to the clearing being full of music, full of noise, that the silence of the afternoon felt otherworldly. The wind rustled the trees above me.

My snakes stopped poking around in the grass and tensed. Alerted by their sudden stillness, I sat up. The breeze passing through the clearing was gentle, hardly more than a gust of air, and yet the trees were rattling like a gale was shaking their branches.

"It's a message," Dionysus said, appearing silently behind me. "There are mortals coming this way. Men." He pointed to the copse of trees at the edge of the meadow and told me that he would make sure no one could see me, and that no one would be able to look in that direction.

"Will you be all right?" I asked. I turned my face toward his, looking up at him while he stared in the direction of the approaching men.

Dionysus smiled, and I was glad when the furrow between his brows disappeared, if only for a moment. His face was one that was made for smiling.

He said, "I am a god, Medusa. These mortals will not

harm me." And then he waved me away and said, "But thank you, for your concern."

As he walked to the center of the clearing to wait for the hunters, I followed his suggestion and retreated to the shaded copse of trees. He had said no one would be able to see me, but I crouched near the edge of the trees, pressing my shoulder into the thick foliage and bark to try and conceal myself even further. My snakes had been testing the air ever since Dionysus had gone on alert. The mortals were close.

In the few moments it took for me to hide in the trees, Dionysus had planted himself in the middle of the clearing and stood facing south. I blinked a few times, wondering if the light was playing tricks on me.

I knew that Dionysus was the only one in the clearing, but the man standing there now looked nothing like the Dionysus I had met or the one I had just spoken to moments before. This Dionysus was as tall as Athena, with broad, tanned shoulders draped in a leopard skin, and a thick torso like a tree. His arms were nearly as big around as one of my thighs, and in a hand as large as a dining plate he held a staff—a thyrsus. A thick grapevine wrapped around the staff like a snake.

From the back, with his dark, curling hair and brown shoulders, he could have passed as Poseidon. My heart tripped in my chest for a beat, the snakes curling in distaste at the thought. I was reminded that while I had grown a small sapling of trust with Dionysus, he was still an Olympian god. His blood flowed gold just like Poseidon's. In what other ways were they similar?

But then Dionysus turned, slightly, as if to glance back at

me, and I saw that his face was still kind. He had a rounded belly like a well-fed nobleman. The strength and power that emanated from this form were unmistakable. Was this the true version of himself that Dionysus had wanted me to see that first day we met? Or was the kind-faced boy with a mischievous smile who Dionysus truly was?

Dionysus was tilting his head, like he was listening for a distant call. I didn't hear anything other than the sound of the wind through the leaves.

Then my snakes gave me a phantom tug and warned, *There.*

I stared at the spot across the clearing that the snakes had picked out, and sure enough, I saw a shadow moving through the trees. The hunters moved through the forest quietly. There were a dozen of them, and they all stepped into the clearing together as if to make sure no one man could be singled out. Each of them held a weapon, either a short sword or a spear.

Dionysus waited until they stopped a few lengths away from him and then spoke. His voice had changed, too, with this new form. It was deeper, and more commanding.

"What business do you have with me?" he asked. He was holding his thyrsus out away from his body, the end braced on the ground. Even though this pose left him completely open to attack, the men were smart enough to be hesitant.

A man in the middle of the group spoke up.

"We've come to free our women from your spell," he said. "You may be a god, but it is not right for you to take our wives and daughters from our homes. Release them from your corruption."

Dionysus twisted the thyrsus. "Was that a command?" he asked airily.

One of the hunters, a younger man, nudged the speaker with his elbow and whispered something.

"No, my lord," the speaker said, though it was through gritted teeth. "A request." He paused, and when Dionysus did not immediately respond, he continued, "But we will use force, if necessary."

"Have you ever thought," Dionysus asked, crossing one foot over his ankle in a casual pose, "that perhaps these women don't want to be at home with you?"

The speaker took an angry step forward, and when the man who had nudged him tried to grab his arm, the speaker shook him off. "Don't be ridiculous. They leave us because they are under your disgusting spell. If you won't release them, we will take them back by force."

I scanned the line of faces. While many of the hunters were frowning and glaring at Dionysus like the speaker was, a few of the men looked worried. They held their weapons loosely, as if they were afraid to even raise them against Dionysus. When the speaker threatened him, a few of the hunters glanced at each other nervously.

Dionysus tilted his head to the side, like he was considering a tricky question, and let out a sigh.

He gestured to the empty field around them. "As you can see, the women are not here."

"If they are under your command, you can bring them here," the man spat.

"That may not be a good idea," Dionysus said. "They will still be winding down from the revelry last night. If

I bring them back too soon, I won't be able to control them."

"You're speaking nonsense. They will no longer have to listen to you. We will be there to protect them." He raised his sword, pointing the tip at Dionysus. "Call our women back here. Then they can watch as we free them from your spell by taking your head."

Pressing myself deeper into the foliage, I wondered how a mortal could be so stupid as to threaten a god. My snakes were tense around my head as they flicked their tongues toward the humans. The air was laced with fear, even though the speaker didn't show it. Perhaps he himself had been caught up in the madness that surrounded Dionysus, and it was allowing him to speak with no inhibitions.

While I could not see his face, Dionysus shrugged his shoulders and said, "As you will it."

He tapped his thyrsus against the ground. After days spent at Dionysus's side, I was familiar with the feeling of his aura, the inherent magic that seemed to drip off him. The moment his staff struck the earth, his power rolled over the meadow and into the forest like a ripple spreading across a water's surface. A beat passed, and then two, and then I heard a wild call go up within the forest. It was the discordant call of all the voices that had chanted and sung the dancing songs the night before, but now they sounded like a pack of wild animals on the hunt.

"You said you would protect your women," Dionysus drawled, lazily scraping a small pattern in the dirt with the tip of the staff, "but who will protect you from them?"

When the women emerged from the tree line and

stepped into the light, a few of the hunters flinched. The women were mud-stained. Their dresses and tunics were still ripped along the neckline and hem, but it was their faces that terrified the men. Their eyes were bright and clear, and there was a simmering heat to them I recognized at once: pure hatred.

Coming down from a god-induced high would incite a huge drop in emotions, and these women were like raw nerves, called back into the fray before they could recover. They wore their emotions plainly on their faces. These women were still flayed open by madness.

"What have you done to them?" the hunter accused. He had turned his sword toward the closest woman, a dark-haired girl who had danced with so much spirit the night before. Her dirt-stained hands were curled into fists. The hunter said, "Celena?"

The woman took a step forward, and the hunters who had traded nervous looks took a step back. "You should not have come here," Celena said. My snakes hissed at her voice, and even I could feel the hatred and resentment that dripped from her every word.

"Lord," the hunter called to Dionysus, "what is wrong with them? Release her from your spell!"

"I cannot," Dionysus said. He was leaning on his thyrsus again. "You told me to call them here. You are the reason they have become this way. I told you it was a bad idea."

"Dionysus!" the hunter pleaded, frantic now, as Celena took another step forward. The entire field was blanketed with the women's power, fueled by untethered emotions.

I thought the men were right to be scared. These mortal women seemed to have the power of the gods within them.

"I told you," Dionysus said again. And then something snapped. All the women who had entered the clearing moved as one, and the hunters fell under their bare hands. The hunters' weapons seemed useless against the half-bare women, and I covered my mouth with one hand as I watched the field turn into a bloodbath. My snakes curled in close to my head.

Dionysus was a calm, solid pillar in the middle of the madness. The women, young and old, tore apart the hunters one by one. A few of the men were calling out the women's names, but their cries quickly turned to screams, and then to silence. I did not dare close my eyes.

In the end, there were a few men still left alive, lying in the grass. They were splattered with the blood of their companions, and they were staring wide-eyed at the blood-soaked women who stood above them. The women were breathing hard. Slowly, their hands uncurled, and they wiped the blood from their faces with the backs of their palms.

Celena looked at Dionysus from where she stood above the remnants of the hunter who had spoken. The hatred had faded from her gaze, but she was still clear-eyed. Dionysus nodded at her, and she tilted her head in return. Without one glance at the bodies in the field, the women left.

Dionysus addressed the remaining men, three of the boys who had shared nervous looks when their leader threatened the god.

"Beware a woman," Dionysus said, "and furthermore,

beware a woman who gives power to her emotions. She can tear the world apart with her bare hands." He stepped forward, around the bodies, and crouched near the boys. "You will go home. You will tell others what has happened here. You will advise them to not make the same mistake."

One boy nodded, his eyes wide as a deer with its leg caught in a trap. Dionysus made a shooing motion with his hand and the three men scrambled to their feet, slipping on blood-slick grass, and fled into the forest.

Dionysus stood. Once again, the only sound in the clearing was the rustle of the wind through the leaves. I had not moved.

"You can come out, now," Dionysus said.

My legs were stiff when I stood up, sore from staying crouched for so long. I walked to Dionysus carefully, my eyes on the ground so I could avoid stepping in blood or other bits I didn't want to look too closely at.

By the time I reached his side, Dionysus had transformed back into the young, slim form I had met him in. He was looking into the forest where the women and the three boys had retreated, and so I spent a moment studying the god's face. What I saw was completely opposite of Athena; Dionysus's face was an open book of emotion. His eyebrows were pinched with worry and his full mouth was pressed into a thin line.

"Don't hold it against them," he said. "The women."

"I can't," I said. "I understand them."

Finally, Dionysus smiled. It was faint, and small, but it was there. "I thought you might. I'm sorry you do, but I think your ability to understand them is the reason you and I get along so well." Then he nudged me with his elbow. "You shouldn't hold it against yourself, either."

"What do you mean?"

Dionysus jerked his chin toward the forest. "Whatever you did, whatever you had to do before you got here, don't hold it against yourself. You don't have to be ashamed of the actions that allowed you to escape a bad situation. If you can forgive those women for using their power to free them-selves," he said softly, "you can forgive yourself."

I hated Dionysus in that moment, for picking apart my thoughts so easily once again. But I knew he was right. If I had been one of those women, I knew I would have done exactly what they had done. I had felt that desire to rip apart the people who caused me pain with my bare hands. I couldn't fault them for giving in. And I wanted that same consideration for myself.

I cleared my throat and asked, "What did you draw in the dirt earlier? With your staff."

"Oh, this," Dionysus said, stepping back so that I could see the symbol under his feet. I couldn't understand what it said; it wasn't written in the common text. "It was to protect those three boys. This mark allowed the women to know that they were okay to leave alive. I've found," Dionysus explained as he rubbed the mark back into the dirt, "that fear flies faster than rumor. It is a powerful thing, when manipulated in just the right way."

"Yes," I agreed. "It is." I reached up and allowed my snakes to twirl around my fingers. The smell of the blood in the air was dulling their senses, and they sought comfort in my touch. I tightened my hold on them. As I did so, I noticed that Dionysus was clutching his thyrsus, holding on to it like a lifeline, like I was doing with my snakes.

"Can I ask," I started, "that form you took, when the hunters arrived, is that your true form? The one you mentioned when we first met? Or is this," I motioned to his current form, "who you really are? Or just who you want to be?"

Dionysus twisted the thyrsus in his hand, digging a small indent into the earth. "When you saw that form," he asked in return, "did you think I looked more like the other gods you have met? More like Athena?"

"I did," I told him, though I did not tell him that he had reminded me of Poseidon most of all. I did not think he would want to hear that from me.

Dionysus nodded. "That form is the one people expect of me. When men like those hunters seek me out, expecting some malicious, all-powerful god who has stolen and bewitched their women, they expect to find *him*." Dionysus gestured broadly with one hand, indicating the huge stature of his other form. "They don't expect me." He laid his hand over his chest, now thinner and softer, though still toned with underlying muscle.

"So you give them what they expect of you?" I asked. "Why bother?"

"I can see why you would think of it like that," Dionysus said. He slid his hand up to cup his own throat. "But that is not how I see it. I do not take that form because I think it will satisfy the expectations of mortal men. I take that form because I wish to protect this one. This body," he explained softly, "is for me. It is who I wish I could be, all the time. I am still a god in either form, but this is the one that makes me feel like myself."

He smiled. I was glad he seemed content to stare off into space, because I could not look away from him.

"This is your true form," I said slowly, piecing through what Dionysus had told me. "And the other is—a front?"

"I suppose that's a word for it," he agreed. "Perhaps it is like this mountain, which most mortals fear to climb because they know I live here, and yet those who make it to this meadow find that it is different than the rumors."

"And that form protects your true self, and the people you care about," I said. "Like a shield."

Dionysus's smiled widened, and he nodded. "Yes. That's it. Just like a shield."

A few nights later, after a sudden storm had washed the blood from the grass and the remains of the hunting party had disappeared, I was sitting just outside the circle of dancers and watching as the young-faced Dionysus joined in the quick-stepped dance. I wondered if the god could become drunk the way the mortals did. He certainly swallowed more than enough undiluted wine to kill a human, and he could be careless with his movements and his touch, but the way he threw his arms around a woman's shoulders or brought a man's hand to his lips seemed all too aware. Perhaps he did it for the sake of the people around him. Being the only clear-headed one in a crowd of drunks was not an enjoyable experience, and Dionysus was in a crowd of drunks nearly every night.

Or, I thought as I watched Dionysus smile lazily up at a tall, finely muscled man with shining dark skin and a wide grin who had been keeping close to the god all evening, Dionysus desperately wanted to be drunk like the mortals around him. But the closest he could get was this false performance.

I had noticed that the wine did not have the same effect that it had had on me when only mortal blood ran through my veins, just like how my desire for food had waned. Swirling the remnants of my red wine in my cup, I leaned back on one hand and looked away from Dionysus and the man and studied the other mortals near the god.

Dionysus had told me, when I questioned him about why I did not go out of my mind when I was close to him, that his effect on immortals was stunted, like a surging river reduced to a trickle through a rocky dam. But mortals received the full force.

I tipped my cup against my lips to finish the wine, and when I set it down in the grass a woman appeared at my side. Ever since the day the hunters had come, I had tried searching the mortals for any familiar faces of the women who had left the clearing stained in blood with their eyes wide and clear. I had not seen any of the women since then. From the corner of my eye, I could see that the woman standing near me was barefoot, and her tunic was hiked up high on her thighs, revealing the long stretch of her legs. She had shallow scratches along her calves and smudges on her knees from traipsing through the forest, as all the followers of Dionysus had to do to reach this clearing.

"Do you dance?" she asked me.

I startled. She was the first person to speak to me besides Dionysus, and it shocked an answer out of me. "No."

"Too good to dance with us, but not too good to drink with us," she teased, and I looked up at her. Because of Dionysus's command, anytime I drew close to someone's gaze they immediately found somewhere else to look. She may have been staring at me right up until I raised my head, but when I looked at her, she was looking out over the other dancers, tracing their movement with her eyes. I did not recognize her. Long black hair fell past her shoulders, and she had a smile that flashed like a star against the dark sky, lighting up her heart-shaped face.

"Drinking is easy," I told her as a few of my snakes picked up their heads and flicked their tongues. "I can do it without being watched."

"No one can watch you anyway," she protested, "we're not allowed to look at you."

I couldn't protest that, and she preened a little at shutting down my argument. This woman was speaking to me like I was no different from anyone else in the clearing.

"So, since no one will be looking at you," she continued, holding one hand in front of my face and wiggling her fingers, "are you going to join me?"

"Why are you asking me?" I shot back, eyeing her hand. The snakes flicked their tongues at the woman's fingers curiously. "There are others more willing, and much easier to talk to than me."

The woman didn't lower her hand. "This is true, but none of them are quite as interesting as you."

"By interesting, do you mean dangerous?"

"Maybe," she said with a laugh. Shifting her weight from one foot to the other, she wiggled her fingers at me again, and with the movement she caught one of my snake's tongues against her skin. She tasted like sweat and a little bit like earth, but also like the sharp tang of madness that wafted off Dionysus's followers. It was oddly muted, like it had been watered down.

I knew that only someone half out of their mind would be brave enough to approach me, but I had been on Dionysus's mountain for long enough, and so perhaps a few of the mortals who had been loitering near the god had become used to my presence. Like how one became used to the smell of sea rot after living near the ocean.

I looked up at the woman again, and her eyes flitted away a second before they could meet mine. If I was being honest with myself, I was relieved she had come to speak with me. Sometimes it felt like I was invisible, or like I didn't exist at all, since no one in this clearing could look at me, and only Dionysus spoke to me. But she had sought me out.

"Fine," I said, and then said it again to get myself moving. "Fine."

Abandoning my cup in the grass, I got to my feet and took the woman's hand only when I was standing. Her skin was warm.

"Let's go!" she shouted gleefully and dragged me into the circle.

My feet were clumsy, but I tried to copy her movements as best I could. The snakes swayed with the momentum of my head, but they seemed obliged to let it happen and didn't resist. The music was not as fast-paced as I had heard it before, although the dance was still quick, and any time I focused too much on where my feet were going, I ended up stumbling.

"Don't look at your feet," the woman told me, her hand still wrapped tightly around mine as she tugged me along in the path of the circle. "They don't know any more about what you're doing than you do. Just listen and follow me. The rest will sort itself out."

I did as she told me, looking away from my feet and focusing on her, careful to keep my gaze just to the side of her face. Her black hair was tumbling wildly around her eyes and mouth as she moved, but she didn't bother to push it away. A few strands were stuck to her neck with sweat.

The music rose in volume. Because I wasn't staring at the ground, I began to see the pattern in the other dancers' steps, how they shuffled quickly from one foot to another, and balanced their weight while spinning. I mimicked the sway of the woman's body, and my feet fell naturally into the rhythm that I had been stumbling over just moments before.

"Good, good!" the woman cheered, her cinched skirt fluttering around her thighs as she spun us both in celebration. I started to trip when coming out of the spin, but she pulled me back into the rhythm easily.

I smiled as I fell back into the pattern, and when the dancers accompanied the music with their own stomping feet, I joined them.

The woman and I danced until my dress stuck to my back with sweat, and I began to feel dizzy from spinning. When I felt as though my legs were going to give out from under me, I tugged on the woman's fingers and leaned forward so that my mouth was closer to her ear and she might hear me better over the music.

"I need to sit down or else I'll fall over."

The woman laughed but nodded, and, still bouncing, she led us out of the circle of dancers and toward the edge of the clearing. Somehow, she found a table cluttered with food and pitchers of wine in the midst of the throng and picked out a string of grapes with her free hand.

She led me past the edge of the forest, where it was significantly cooler and quieter under the pine canopy. She walked in front of me so that I could only see the back of her head, and I realized with a start that I had never asked her name.

"What should I call you?" I asked.

The woman tried to flick a gaze over her shoulder, but Dionysus's command prevented her from looking all the way behind her, and so she just ended up tilting her head to the side like an inquisitive bird.

I added, in a quieter voice as we left the din of the clearing behind us, "Sorry for not asking earlier."

"Oh, that's all right," she replied airily. "You can call me Naidah."

"Naidah," I repeated.

We walked until the clearing was just a faint light and muffled sound behind us, almost completely obscured by the trees and leafy vines. Naidah's hand was warm in mine. She finally paused by a shallow stream and sat down with her back to a thin, willowy tree trunk, tugging me down with her. I sat with my legs crossed under me, but Naidah made an impatient noise and slid her hand up my arm to keep me moving down until my head was resting on her leg, just above her knee.

I jerked when I felt the skin of her thigh touch the scaly bodies of the snakes and tried to sit up again. The snakes, too, seemed startled by the feeling.

"It's all right," Naidah said soothingly. "I do not mind them."

"But," I started, and she shushed me again.

"As long as they don't bite me, they're fine."

All of this she said with her eyes mostly closed, the lids lowered and her long black eyelashes creating small shadows on her cheeks. She tightened her grip on my arm until I put my head back down. The snakes arranged themselves so that none of them were crushed between my head and her thigh, but even as they tried to hold themselves as still as possible so as not to startle her, a few snakes flickered their tongues against Naidah's skin.

"Hmm," she said with a laugh, "that tickles a bit."

I silently snapped at the snakes to stop at once, and then said aloud, "Sorry."

"Oh really, it's fine!" Naidah leaned back against the tree and rested the bunch of grapes on her stomach with one hand curled around them to hold them up, picking at the fruit with the other and bringing one piece to her lips at a time. "You need to learn how to relax."

I hadn't had a moment to relax since I ran from the temple. I couldn't explain to her that I had probably forgotten how to relax after the countless days traveling on high alert for the faintest sounds of mortals, or because I blinded myself, or because of the terrible fate that waited for me beyond an unknown but finite amount of time.

"Hmm," I mumbled instead.

"When was the last time you slept through the night, with no worries?"

"Ages ago."

Naidah popped another grape into her mouth and then offered one to me, her fingers bumping clumsily against my chin before finding my mouth. She pressed the fruit to my lips and I parted them to take it. The taut skin of the grape broke under my teeth and the juice that spilled out was sweet and fresh. Naidah tapped a finger against my closed mouth.

"You can sleep now, if you want," she said, and her voice was steadier than it had been in the clearing, like the fog of Dionysus's madness was parting from her mind. "I can keep watch for you."

"Why?" With the stream burbling softly and the pale light of the stars barely filtering down through the trees, I could not deny that this place felt as safe as I could get. Especially with Naidah looking out above me. Even if I had only met her earlier this evening, I felt connected to the women who flocked to Dionysus's mountain. I had seen what they were capable of with simple, mortal hands. They were capable of great acts of rage, just as I was. Perhaps I felt that Naidah could understand me, more than even Dionysus could. But I didn't understand why she was offering me such a kindness.

The finger that had tapped my mouth patted its way gently up my face and to my eyes, where it paused and waited for me to close them, before stroking lightly over the thin skin there.

"Because I want to," she said simply.

A few reasons why she should *not* want to care for me like this bubbled up on my tongue, but I let them dissipate before they became words in the air. Naidah was now gently stroking my temple where my skin gave way to the tough green scales of the snakes, and both the snakes and I were getting lost in the sensation of this touch.

I fell asleep. Not by choice, but because my body had not been so loosened from anxiety in so long, and the sudden exhaustion of letting go had swept over me like a rip current.

When I woke, it was still night. The sky beyond the leaves was dark, although the stars had disappeared in deference to the sun that was sure to climb over the horizon soon. I blinked the sleep out of my eyes, my lids heavy from such a deep rest, and looked up at Naidah. She, too, had fallen asleep against the tree trunk, her eyes closed and head tilted sideways onto her shoulder. A bare grape stem rested on her stomach, plucked clean of fruit.

Beyond the stream, I heard a fallen branch snap under the step of a heavy foot.

I sat up quickly and the snakes, still groggy with sleep, swayed loosely with the movement.

There were men emerging from the trees on the other side of the stream. They wore light armor with a crest on the shoulder and short leather skirts, and they carried the long spears of foot soldiers. Their plumed helmets obscured most of their faces. There were five of them in total.

"Hey," one of them shouted. He sounded so young. "Look there!"

I was frozen in place, my limbs weighed down by exhaustion and sudden fear.

I had been so careful, had been so persistent on my own about wearing the blindfold, but living amongst Dionysus and his followers meant I had grown accustomed to mortals who were unable to meet my eyes. These men had no such restriction.

The first man, the one who had spoken, turned to stone in a mere moment and I felt nothing as the snakes' eyes flashed red around me. The next two men were startled as their companion was petrified, and then they were angry, and they did not know to avoid my eyes. When the red flash came for them, it was like I could feel their spiked hatred behind my eyes as their snarling mouths froze in place. Their anger was what finally unfroze my limbs. I scrambled back on my hands away from the stream and flipped over, thinking that if I could just get to Dionysus's clearing, I could end this. Dionysus could make the men stop.

Behind me, I heard feet splashing through the stream, and then Naidah gave a sharp cry.

That sound brought my mad dash to a halt. I recognized that sound. It was the helpless cry of someone who couldn't fight back. I knew that sound because I had made a sound just like it when Poseidon grabbed me in the temple.

There had been no one to help me when Poseidon seized me. Even Athena had refused to help me, for fear of her cursed reputation. I remembered how I had felt when I realized no one was coming to save me—how I had wished the whole world would crumble under my rage. I had been helpless then. How could I leave Naidah in the same place? With

Dionysus's influence waning, she was not prepared to fight back. She didn't have the strength.

But I was no longer helpless.

"Use it," I muttered to myself. My snakes were moving wildly around my head, enraged at being snuck up on once again, but they stilled at my words. "Use it for yourself."

I pushed myself to my feet and whirled around in one fast movement, and when I saw the fourth man yanking Naidah up by the arm I felt my own spike of rage flare up. The man was yelling something, and his face twisted unpleasantly as Naidah shook her head frantically, but then she began to slip out of his grip. I thought perhaps that the man may have loosened his hold on her, but he also looked confused. I blinked and realized that Naidah was literally slipping out of his hands, her wrist sliding out from the grasp of his fingers and her skin shimmering like the light of the sun glancing off a still pool. Naidah's arm, and then the rest of her body, clothes and all, turned into nothing but a few handfuls of water that flowed quickly into the stream and disappeared.

Naidah, I thought stupidly, shocked that I had not realized what she was before. In our language, her name could mean "river." She was a water nymph, and that was her stream we had been sleeping next to.

The man who had been holding her looked from his empty hand to the stream and made a noise of confusion. He looked up at me.

"How" was all he was able to say before I turned him into rock. His stiff fingers were still curled around a phantom wrist.

The fifth man—

When I looked back at the edge of the trees, the fifth man had disappeared. I was tempted to go after him, the rage I felt toward the man who had tried to hurt Naidah still pulsing through my veins. I could have caught him if I wanted to, I was sure; my anger could have fueled a mad dash after the man with no issue. He would not stand a chance. I felt my blood pumping through my legs, making me strong. I was no longer the helpless victim.

But I did not follow him. The snakes were eager to pursue the last man and turn him into stone as I had done to his four companions, but when my gaze caught on the first gray figure, and then his stony companions, my anger twisted into shame, and then weariness.

Their deaths were my fault. I had grown too comfortable. I had become lazy in my attempt to protect other people, and these four men had suffered for it. While one of the men had tried to harm Naidah, and most likely would have harmed me if given the chance, that first boy I had petrified had done nothing to me. His only fault was to have stumbled into the wrong clearing. I took a breath and the angry beat of my heart faded.

Pressing trembling knuckles against my mouth, I tore my eyes away from the four statues and hurried back into the forest, following the path Naidah had led me down.

The clearing was still flush with sound when I finally found it again, and even though I knew that these mortals were not able to meet my gaze, I kept my eyes moving around the field like a flitting bird. Dionysus was standing just off to the side of the circle of dancers, and he had his head tilted down to listen as a woman with long black hair spoke quickly in his ear. It was Naidah.

From the way Dionysus's face was washed of merriment and his full lips thinned and pulled down at the corners, I knew that the naiad was telling him everything that had just happened. She finished her report, glancing over her shoulder, and when her shifting eyes found the place she could not look, a pinched expression crossed her face and she disappeared into the crowd.

I considered leaving right in that moment, just turning back into the forest and leaving Dionysus and his mountain behind before the god could make a scene of throwing me out. At least when Athena had punished me, we had been alone in the temple. Knowing how Dionysus adored his theatrics, I would not put it past him to stir up a huge ruckus in confronting me just for the fun of it. I turned away from the clearing.

"Medusa," Dionysus said, now just a pace behind me, his voice low and measured. I silently cursed the gods and all their abilities.

"I'm leaving," I said sharply.

"Okay," he said. "Why?"

"I can't stay here, I can't—I won't hurt anyone else. Let me leave."

"I won't stop you, if leaving is what you desire," Dionysus told me, and he spoke just loud enough for me to hear. The mortals around us were not watching us. "But please, would you let me escort you out, so that I may speak with you one last time?"

My shoulders tightened. "If you are going to punish me for what I've done, then yes, I would prefer it if we did not have an audience."

Dionysus sighed. "My dear," he said with exasperation. "I am not going to punish you for defending yourself. Those mortals meant nothing to me. I only wish to warn you about what they, and their surviving companion, might mean to you and your future."

He placed a tentative hand on my elbow. I flinched, at first, but he did not draw away or tighten his grip.

"I wish to help you, if you would only let me," he said softly. I wanted to see his face, but I could not bear for him to see mine, in that moment.

The mortals continued their frantic chanting and stomping behind us, and it seemed as though the air around us was the only still space in the clearing. Dionysus's presence did not bring me any feeling of bedlam. I felt calmer at his touch. The snakes, who had been tense and alert since the five men had appeared by the stream, loosened their muscles and I could feel how they were soothed by a familiar presence. The fact that Dionysus had become a familiar and calming presence in the short time I had been with him should have been troubling, but I desperately wanted to have someone I could trust. And he had only ever acted in my good interest.

"Why?" I asked. This seemed like the question we were constantly throwing at each other, *Why you, why now, why me?*

Dionysus's answer nearly knocked the breath from my lungs.

"Because I am your friend," he said. "Even if you are not mine."

His fingers were still resting lightly on my arm. He was waiting for me to give him permission, respecting my space as he had respected my power by removing my fear of hurting him or his mortals.

My shoulders dropped as I made my choice. I bent my arm just slightly, and he stepped forward and slid his hand into the loop I had made so we were linked at the elbows. When I took a step into the forest, he matched me pace for pace.

It was now almost dawn, and the pale blue of the sky disappeared and reappeared in the breaks between the treetops. As the music faded behind us, I could hear the first few chirps of waking birds calling out to one another. I led us down the mountain, the snakes giving me gentle nudges in the right direction from time to time, and Dionysus walked amiably beside me. Only when we reached a part of the forest where the grapevines ceased to sprout up on the tree trunks did he speak.

"Have you heard of a man called Polydectes?"

I looked at Dionysus and saw him gazing up at the trees, a small crinkle folding the normally smooth skin between his brows as he thought.

"No."

Though he was not even looking at the ground, Dionysus steered us around a tangle of bushes and rocks before continuing.

"I am not surprised," he said. "He is a king, on an island far to the south of here. Like most men, he is unhappy with the hand the gods have given him, so he sends his soldiers out to other islands, and even to the mainland, in search of places he might take for his own." Dionysus huffed out a breath. "Polydectes's men have been tramping around my mountain for weeks now. The sprites of the forest, and the naiads from the rivers and streams, have been tracking their whereabouts and warning me if they get too close." I remembered how Dionysus had listened to the leaves rustling in the trees, the day the hunters came, and realized that it must have been a message from a dryad. He continued, "Today, I did not get the warning fast enough. Those five men you and Naidah crossed paths with belonged to that king. Naidah told me that one of the men got away before you could petrify him, yes?"

I nodded, and Dionysus caught the movement out of the corner of his eye.

"Right, well, that may bring you trouble in the future. I do not think Polydectes will take kindly to you killing his men." Dionysus gave my arm a few pats with his free hand when he felt me tense up and prepare to argue. "Accident though it may have been, I do not think that is how this surviving man will tell it once he returns to his king. I simply wish to warn you against the fragile pride of mortal men—especially kings."

"You think he will send more men after me?" I hated to think that after all my careful work of avoiding crowded cities and towns, avoiding being hunted as a monster, I had finally slipped up when I decided not to chase that man down. And now he and his kin would bring their fear and anger down on my head.

"I believe that surviving man will tell anyone he meets about the snake-haired woman he met in the mountains, and how she brought down four young soldiers in a matter of seconds," Dionysus said. "And then once he finally reaches his homeland to tell his king how his men were so easily conquered, that king will be scared," Dionysus was speaking disdainfully now, "and that king will turn that fear into a reason to paint you as a monster in the eyes of all who live under his reign."

Monster. That was the word the Graeae had used to describe my future all those years ago when they had predicted what I would look like, what I would become. When I had first felt the snakes in the place where golden curls should have been, I had thought that this body was monstrous, but perhaps if I did not use the power that came with it, I would not become the monster itself. Surely the part of me that remembered being human would not disappear so easily. I had thought I was simply trapped in a body that looked like a monster, but if I kept a tight hold of what made me human, I would be able to separate myself from the fate the Graeae had prophesized.

But this had never been the truth. While I had been denying my power, I had petrified Polli, and the traveler and his dog in the forest outside of Athens, and then terrified myself into covering my eyes so that I would not hurt any more innocent mortals. But when those men had tried to attack me in the night before I found Dionysus, I had used the power, really used it with an intent to harm, for the first time. Ever since then, there was no doubt that the power was a part of me, and so the body I thought of as monstrous was a part of me, too.

And hadn't it felt good to petrify those men who had come after me in the dark? I had stopped the man who dared grab me by my leg, killed him before he could go any further. Hadn't I felt relief at the idea that I could kill any man who put a hand on me, any man who felt my body was something he could claim, and I could do it with just one look? Could I outweigh the cost of innocent lives, like Pol-li's, in exchange for the power to protect myself? Even think-ing about my actions like that made me feel unsettled. The small, vindictive part of me that was glad I had killed those men was growing harder and harder to ignore.

However, now with the escaped man running to spread word of my ability across the entire land and beyond, what could I do? The mortals who heard the man's horrifying description of how I turned his companions to stone would undoubtedly believe I was a monster. Would any of the women who heard the tale wonder how a lone woman, as monstrous as she may have been, was able to take down four soldiers on her own? Would they wish they had the same power, even just for a moment? I remembered how helpless I had felt on the floor of Athena's temple, and how I would have given anything to feel in control of myself again, to feel like I could have shown the rage simmering inside of me.

As the forest brightened, the sloping path Dionysus and I were winding through slowly cleared, the trees growing farther apart. Dionysus had been quiet as I worked through these thoughts. Something about the way his chin was tilted showed me that he had something else to say, though.

I asked a question first. "There are people who think you are a little like a monster, aren't there? Like those hunters?"

This was an impertinent question to ask a god, but Dionysus just laughed, his young face full of genuine mirth as his dark curls bounced against his forehead when he threw back his head.

"Oh, sure," he replied, "the mothers and fathers of mortals who seek me out or get swept up amongst my other followers, they curse me behind closed doors for stealing their children away. Even some of the braver sons who have lost mothers to me will try to challenge me, and the names they hurl at me are just rude." He tutted and shook his head. "And indeed, *monster* is often tossed in at one point or another. It's never the most creative one."

Dionysus did not seem bothered by recalling the insults against him, but I supposed that after centuries of dealing with angry mortals the sting of their words dulled quite a bit. Either his skin had toughened to their flimsy abuse, or the blade of their words was worn down by years of attacks. I did not have centuries of time to dull the sting.

"Do you think that being a monster is a bad thing?" I asked softly. This was the question that had been pressing against my teeth, the one I was so anxious to have an answer to.

Dionysus waved a lazy hand in the direction of the southern lands and the sea that held the many islands clustered around the tip. "That king will think you a monster, as will the mortals who have not met you but have already made up their minds about you from the word of one scared man. Let me revise your question first: Do I think that their fear makes you a monster?" He answered his own question. "No. They may call you what they like, but that does not make you who you are. Do I think it is monstrous that you protected your-self? Absolutely not. But if using the power forced on you by a goddess makes you a monster, then I say that a monster is not a bad thing to be." I could see the glint of his smile from the corner of my eye. "Speaking as one monster to another."

I sighed and closed my eyes, slowing to a stop before tilting my head back to listen to the wind stirring in the branches and the rough scrape of stone and dirt under Dionysus's feet as he stopped, too. Our arms were still linked, and I felt him draw me in tighter to his side.

"You are not a bad thing," Dionysus said, quietly, even though we were alone amongst the trees.

"Neither are you," I said.

He laughed again, and I smiled. I admired how he was so full of laughter, even after everything he had faced.

"Right, well," Dionysus said, and we began walking again after I opened my eyes, "just know that I will always be on your side, monster or not. My divine senses tell me you will have to face that internal conflict you've been harboring many more times."

"Can your divine senses be any more specific, by chance?"

"Nope," he said with a snort.

"Of course not," I said, resigned, knowing that no god or divinity ever wanted to, or even could, give a straight answer.

"Even without my divine senses," Dionysus said as we finally neared the base of the mountain and the thin dirt trail that would lead me away, "I know that Polydectes will bring you much trouble. Be careful, snake-haired girl. Not every-one is as understanding as I am."

"Thank you," I told him, and I meant it not only for the advice, but also for the moments of peace he had afforded me, and for the kindness of his friendship. "You are a very peculiar god, but I think I would prefer no one else to be my friend."

We still could not look at each other, but I saw the smile that spread over his face, and I desperately wanted to know what his eyes looked like. Wanted to know if that smile reached them.

"We cursed beings have to stick together," he said. He unlinked our arms and took up my hand instead. "May I ask where you intend to go from here?"

I had scarcely thought about it. The snakes, who had been sitting quietly through our conversation, flicked their tongues in every direction, trying to find a nearby town or place for me to head toward. Reaching up with my free hand, I traced my fingers along a thin, scaly body near my ear, and the taut muscle coiling under the iridescent green pattern reminded me, with memories so sudden and vivid that it made my stomach flip, of Echidna.

"I will go see my sibling," I said, deciding immediately and surprised that I had not thought of going to her before. "She may be able to…" But I had no words for what I wanted from Echidna. The conversation we had on the beach the night of her wedding, with her laurel crown on my head and her snakelike tail curled up underneath her, was tucked in my memories like a pressed flower between the pages of a book.

Do you think I am terrifying? she had asked me.

And I had replied, *No. You are beautiful.*

"I will go see Echidna," I said firmly.

"Very well," Dionysus said, giving my hand one last pat. "Let me give you a parting gift."

With a flourish, he pulled a long piece of fabric out from nowhere. It was a dress, I realized as he held it up, made of a fine-looking, pale green linen. I looked down at the ragged remains of the temple dress, plucking at the torn hem, and decided that it was time for me to let it go. Dionysus placed the dress in my hands and then spun around, facing away from me just like he had done on the day we met, so that I could quickly change.

The new dress was light and soft, and I felt as though a weight had been lifted off my shoulders when I removed the stained dress from the temple. I had no more use for this dress, other than the memories it held, but I needed to leave them behind. I crouched by the base of a tall tree and buried the dress in the dirt. At the very least, I thought, a part of me that had been mortal would remain here.

I finally told Dionysus he could look, as I could tell he wanted to, and his wordless gasp of appreciation made me smile.

He picked up my hand again and kissed the back of my palm. "Beautiful," he said. "Now be careful on your journey. Try not to dirty it up."

When he let go of my hand, I felt a flash of overwhelming loneliness. Then the snakes, who had been quiet while we walked down the mountain, brushed their torsos gently against my temple to get my attention.

That way, the not-voice told me, directing my feet south, *that way to Echidna.*

There was a gentle popping sound behind me, and when I looked back, Dionysus had gone. His departure did not feel as though the surrounding air needed to remold itself into its original shape, as I had felt with Athena or Poseidon. Rather, he simply slipped between the folds of air like he was walking between two curtains, and it fluttered briefly before falling still once more.

A simple, sweet dawn

MANY ROADS LED SOUTH. I skirted alongside a few of them on the days I woke before the sun rose, traveling in the half-light of dawn when no mortals were around. Most of the time, I picked my way through forests and across mountainsides, the snakes acting as the inner compass that steered me toward the lower western edge of the mainland.

We did not talk much, the snakes and I, partly because there was no need to use words to convey the directions they gave me, and partly because they knew everything that I thought, anyway.

I did not put a blindfold back on. The scrap of fabric I had torn from my old dress and used to cover my eyes before I had met Dionysus was lost, dropped or forgotten someplace on Mount Parnassus. After so long without wearing one, the thought of concealing the rest of the world from myself seemed utterly foolish. Who had I been trying to protect with that strip of linen? Neither I, nor the mortals I had come across, had been protected by it, in the end.

After a few days of walking, leaving Parnassus far behind me, I came to the edge of the sparse forest I had been navigating through all morning and found myself on a sheer cliffside that dropped into the ocean. The sudden, overwhelming smell of salt water, unfiltered by the scent of the pine trees and decaying forest litter, shocked me into a standstill. It was brine and seaweed and hot sand, and I could feel it, thick and cloying, clinging to the inside of my throat.

I had not smelled the ocean since I had fled Athens, when I had been sick on that windy beach outside of the city because the smell of the salt water had reminded me so viciously of Poseidon's hands on my neck, on my thighs. The streams and rivers I had come across in the forests were fresh-water runoff from the mountains, and they often smelled of wet stones and mud. Pressing the back of my hand under my nose, I backed away from the cliffside and caught myself against a tree. I turned my face into the trunk and leaned my forehead against the rough bark to feel the rough edges press indents into my skin.

Even though they had not yet existed when Poseidon had assaulted me on the temple floor, the snakes were squirming with discomfort as they remembered that night along with me. Their reaction was visceral. It made me wonder if they were upset at my suffering, or did they not want to confront the event that had led to their creation?

The sound of waves crashing against the rocky base of the cliff seemed to echo the rushing panic that was slowly consuming me. I coughed, trying to get the taste of salt water out of my mouth. The snakes flicked their tongues, and the scent of the ocean grew sharper, but when I gagged and pleaded, silently, for them to stop, they did. Keeping their mouths shut tight, the snakes tried to convey their regret at causing me more harm by smoothing their bodies across my temples. One of the snakes drew away from me and tugged, trying to lead me back into the forest.

Water, the not-voice said, *fresh water, there.*

With great relief I let go of the tree and retreated into the forest, leaving the cliff and the tumbling ocean behind me. I kept my hand pressed to my nose and gasped in strangled breaths as I hurried through the undergrowth.

A wide but shallow stream appeared between the pine trees. I came right up to the water's edge and finally dropped my hand, but even though the ocean was far behind me I felt as though I could still smell it on my clothes and my skin. My breath was coming too quickly and it only grew worse as I began to tug at my dress. I wrestled it over my head and the snakes hissed as a few of them were caught in the fabric, but they did not try and stop me. Once the snakes and I were free of the cloth, I dropped it behind me and waded into the stream. The straps of my worn sandals got tangled in the river rocks, and with a frustrated grunt, I bent to tear them off my feet and flung them, one after the other, back onto the shore near my crumpled clothes.

Don't look, the snakes reminded me, a quiet but firm nudge that kept my eyes trained away from where my reflection waited in the water.

"I know," I gasped back. The water was moving too quickly for there to be a smooth surface. When the snakes continued to lean on my mind with their caution, I pressed my lips together tightly and kept my eyes trained on a point across the water, near the opposite bank.

The stream was cool and clear, and when I waded into

the middle with splashing steps the deepest part of the river only came up to my waist. I stirred up the silt at the bottom, and streaks of pale brown mud appeared. I hardly minded, too focused on bringing up handfuls of water to douse my shoulders and throat to try and rid the smell of sea salt from my skin. I dropped to my knees and felt the rough, rounded edge of the river stones press against my legs.

I closed my eyes and cupped my hands together, bringing the water to my face and rubbing it into my skin. I stopped before I could rub my face raw and sat back on my heels to finally take a breath through my nose. All I could smell was the earthy trace of the muddy streambed and the pine trees around me. I took several more breaths until my chest no longer felt like it was being held in a vise grip.

I stayed in the water for a long time, dousing myself repeatedly as my shoulders dried under the sun's warmth. Eventually, when my heartbeat had finally slowed, I maneuvered to the shore and lay down on my back with my head resting on the piled fabric of my dress. I kept my legs and hips in the water, just to feel it lap gently at my skin. Current-smoothed stones dug into my back. The places on my body that I had drenched with stream water were cool, but they were heating quickly in the sun.

With no prior thought or reasoning, I had kept the snakes out of the water. When I realized that I had done this, I asked them, "Do you not like to get wet?"

You have a warm-blooded body, the not-voice told me, *we do not. Snakes do not like getting wet; getting wet for snakes means cold.*

"How did I know to keep you out of the water?" I asked.

227

"I didn't know why it would make you uncomfortable, but I avoided it anyway."

We may have different bodies, but you have learned to care for us as we care for you. The not-voice of the snakes was fond as they explained this.

I felt a warmth in my chest as I considered how the snakes and I had begun to take care of one another, consciously or not, but then I began to think about the first part of what the snakes had said. *Different bodies*: physically, the snakes and I were incompatible, and yet we were still one being. Was my unconscious act of keeping the snakes out of the water due to my inherent understanding of their needs, since their needs were also mine? We protected one another because we were one and the same.

"Hmm," I hummed as I thought, and reached up to stroke one of the snakes. Drops of water that had been clinging to my skin fell onto the snake's scales as I pet it, but the snake only hissed in mock displeasure and nudged my hand away with its head.

Perhaps another hour passed as I lay half in and half out of the stream before a small splash from higher up the current broke the peaceful quiet of the forest. I sat bolt upright, but before I could look at the source of the noise, the snakes spoke up, *Careful!*

"Wait, wait!" a familiar voice called. "Don't look, it's me, it is Naidah!"

I shut my eyes. Dionysus's command, though it surely could stretch across the range of his mountain, might not have such strength this far away from its speaker. I did not want to risk it.

"What do you want?" I called back to her, wary. While Dionysus had seen me off with some good advice and a new dress, I wasn't sure how Naidah had reacted to my power. She had told Dionysus what had happened, but she had not stuck around to see what became of me. I couldn't understand why she was here now.

"Can I come closer?" she asked.

"Why?"

"Because I wish to speak to you without shouting."

Even though I was on edge, I couldn't help but smile, because that was not really the answer I wanted, but I had to expect that a naiad would be able to slip through a conversation like she had slipped through that man's fingers. I curled my legs up to my chest and wrapped my arms around them, the rocks now digging uncomfortably into my bare backside. I was aware of my nudity, but I did not want to move any further or open my eyes to put my clothes back on. I felt no shame in my nakedness, especially since I had become accustomed to having live snakes as a part of my body. There was no concealing them for the sake of modesty.

In any case, Naidah had already seen my snakes up close. The rest of my body would be all too conventional compared to them.

"Fine," I said, to let her know she could move closer, but I did not hear the water splash with her movements.

After a moment, she asked, "Can I open my eyes? It'll be hard for me to come over to you with them closed like this."

We had been sitting with both of our eyes closed against the other, unaware that the other was doing the same thing, and the absurdity of the image was not lost on me. I laughed, once, before smothering the rest with my hand against my lips. Naidah, like Dionysus, waited for my consent before moving. When I told her she could open her eyes, I only heard a faint rippling of the water.

"May I ask first," I said as she drew closer, "how you found me?"

She must have been only an arm's length from me now, and the gentle waves created by her movement lapped around my shins and waist.

"This stream belongs to one of my sisters," she said. "And we are all connected. I sent out a message asking if anyone had seen you, and I was able to travel through the streams and rivers to find you here."

"A water nymph," I said, more to remind myself than to accuse her of something. "You did not tell me."

Naidah must have shrugged, because the water moved a bit, and then she said, "You did not ask. Does it bother you?"

"Hardly," I told her, with a faint smile. "How can it, when I look like this? I should be asking if I bother you."

"You don't!" she said emphatically. She set her hand tentatively on my upper arm, and when I did not pull away, she curled her fingers around my arm and settled close enough so that our shoulders and hips brushed. Her touch was warm against my cool skin. "You saved me from those men. You could never bother me. I came here to thank you."

"But you could have escaped those men without me," I said quietly. "You had already slipped out of that man's hands when I—"

"Doesn't matter!" Naidah spoke over me. "You helped me, and so for that I am grateful."

"It was," I said slowly, "no problem."

Those men would be forever frozen in Naidah's stream, their stone bodies scattered from one bank to the other. Perhaps the water would slowly erode the rock until there was nothing left. But with Naidah sitting next to me, her fingers warm on my skin, and her kindness extending so far beyond Dionysus's mountain, I soon forgot any worry I had for the stone men.

"Where are you headed?" she asked. "I mean, I'm assuming you've got a destination in mind since you've come so far in very little time, with your human legs." Naidah tapped my knee with one finger.

"I'm going to see my sibling."

"And where are they?"

I paused, trying to find the words to explain how I knew where Echidna was. The snakes and I had never had to discuss it.

"Echidna—that is her name—lives to the south of here, out to sea and just to the left of the point where the sun will set on the horizon." I spoke slowly as the snakes' thoughts flashed through my head, showing me the way. "She lives on an island that is not accessible to mortal ships."

"Then how were you planning on getting there?" Her voice held the shape of a grin. "How far can you swim?"

This was something I had not stopped to consider. How would I cross the ocean—besides the point that I could barely stand the smell of it—when I had no vessel to bear me across the waves? I could not board a ship full of mortals. And, as Echidna lived on an island that would be protected by the same barrier that surrounded the Graeae's cave and the beach with the white house that I had grown up in, no mortal ship would be able to take me there anyway. I had to navigate to Echidna's home by my own hand.

I ducked my head into the space between my knees and blew out a long sigh.

Naidah, her voice serious for once, asked, "Do you need help crossing the ocean?"

I shook my head, still facing down, and said, "I wish that was my only issue. It is—the smell—" My dry throat clicked as I struggled for the words. "The smell of sea salt is paralyzing to me. I have terrible memories associated with it. When I breathed it in for just a moment it was like something was choking me. That's why I came here, to try and get rid of the smell."

Moving slowly, as though to avoid startling me, Naidah curled her arm around my bare shoulders and squeezed softly. The snakes, torn between comforting me and inspecting the water nymph who was now so close, flicked their tongues at her questioningly.

"These memories," Naidah began, "do they have anything to do with why you have your little friends here? Why you have your power?"

I nodded, the skin of my forehead catching on my knees. The snakes had perked up at being called my friends.

Naidah was rubbing her thumb against my shoulder as she spoke. "I am not sure if there is a way for you to forget these memories, but perhaps you can make new ones with the smell of the ocean. It wasn't the ocean that harmed you, was it?" Another shake of my head. "Was it someone who smelled of the ocean?" A nod. "Well, then, it is not the ocean you should be afraid of after all, as it has done nothing wrong. The person who hurt you does not deserve to keep the ocean hostage in your memories."

Naidah took up my hand with her free one and twined our fingers together. I focused on the cool press of her palm against mine.

"Do you have other memories, before that one, with the sound or smell or sight of the ocean?"

As my eyes were already closed, it was easy to picture the fleeting images of my life in the white house on the beach. How I had walked the shore for hours with only the crashing waves for company. How my parents had emerged from the sea-foam, their steps digging divots in the sand each time they came to visit. How the water had reflected the stars at night when I sat with Echidna after the wedding. I held on to that memory in particular: Echidna and I sitting on the sand with the dark sea pushing and pulling at the shore in front of us, the smell of salt mixed with the oil from the laurel leaves in my hair and Echidna's voice over the sound of water tumbling over wet sand.

"Yes," I answered finally. "I have a memory."

"Good," Naidah said. "Can you use that to counter the other memory? It will not be easy."

"No shit." I laughed dryly.

I lifted my head off my knees, wiping at my hot cheeks with the heel of my palm.

"Here, just…" Naidah pulled away, sliding through the water effortlessly. "Hold on one moment. And you can open your eyes if you want. I won't look."

Blinking my eyes open, I saw Naidah rise up and search

through the weeds and undergrowth on the opposite bank. She was still wearing the dress with the tied-up hem, and water streamed from the soaked fabric down her legs and into the dirt.

After a few more moments of searching, Naidah made a victorious sound.

She turned back and waded across the stream, a clump of green, twiggy plants held in her fist. Keeping her eyes trained down, Naidah returned to her seat next to me and crossed her legs underneath her. She held the plant out for me to inspect.

"Rosmarinus," she explained, "or 'dew of the sea,' as my sister would call it. She taught me about this plant. It should help with the smell. Hold it for me, for a moment."

Dropping the plant into my hand, Naidah began to dig around in the river rocks until she found a wide, flat stone, as well as a smaller, rounded one. She placed the flat stone between her legs, braced against her bent knees. Taking the rosemary back from me, she placed it on the large stone and began to grind up the plant with the round rock. As the thin leaves broke down, a sweet, earthy smell rose up from the oils and grainy remains of the stem, reminding me, unbiddenly, of the kitchen at Athena's temple where Polli taught me to knead bread.

Naidah ground the rosmarinus until only the oil and a loose paste remained. She scraped the paste to one side, pressing down on it while tilting the rock just enough so that the remaining oil was squeezed out. Then, making sure not to spill her oil into the stream, she dipped her fingers into the water and brought them over the stone, mixing in a few drops with the oil to dilute it.

She smeared her index finger through the watered-down oil and brought it to my lips.

"I'll need to look at your face while I do this," she warned me, and so I closed my eyes, my face still tilted toward her.

She gently patted her finger on the skin between my upper lip and nose. The oil clung to my skin, and it was soon all I could smell. I took a deep breath in through my nose. The scent was thick, but it concealed anything else that may have been lingering.

"Better?"

I sighed. "Much."

Naidah ran the pad of her thumb, which was clean of the oil, along the thin skin under my eye in a gentle sweeping motion. I couldn't tell if the perfume of rosmarinus that followed the motion was from my own skin, or from her hand.

"I'll soak the rest into a cloth for you," she said, "and when you need to reapply the oil you will just need to wet the cloth and dab it on your skin." I heard the sound of fabric tearing. I opened my eyes, certain that she was not looking at me, and saw her tearing a small strip from her own hem. She pressed the strip into the remaining oil, and then dragged it along the flat stone to soak up all the liquid. Once she had gotten all she could from the stone, she folded the cloth, oil-soaked side in, and held it out to me.

"Thank you," I said as I took it.

"It's no problem," she said, and grinned at the echo of my

earlier statement. "Well, that's one issue resolved, for now. You still need a way to cross the ocean."

"I can swim," I told her, twisting to place the cloth on top of my dress.

"Not as far as you will need to go," Naidah argued, and I frowned, even though she was right. "You need a boat."

"I can make one."

"Have you ever made a boat before?"

"No," I said, glancing around the edges of the stream for any loose branches that may have fallen from the surrounding trees. "But I think I can get by with the general idea."

"Then let me help," Naidah demanded, getting to her feet.

"You've helped enough already," I protested, rising to my feet as well, running my hands down my sides and over my legs to slick most of the water away. I turned and shook out the dirt from my dress before pulling it back over my head, navigating around the snakes, and then pawed at the folds until I found an inner pocket to tuck the folded rosemary cloth into.

"Right," Naidah agreed. She was standing in the middle of the stream, bent at the waist to press her palm flat against the surface of the water. "So you will allow me to finish out the last of my assistance, as my thanks to you."

"I already told you that there is no need—"

"And yet, I want to do it anyway." Naidah stood, brushing her hands together like she had just finished a hard job and wanted to knock the dirt from her palms. Her hair was now mostly dry, and it shined under the sun's light, falling in a thick curtain down her back. She turned, and I quickly looked down. "Right," she said, splashing her way back to me, "it should be here soon. You should put your shoes back on."

I frowned at her feet, which were bare, but then reached for my abandoned sandals. I had just finished tying off the last strap when Naidah made a satisfied sound. She was looking upstream, and I leaned to the side to peer around her and see what she was so excited about.

A small but sturdy-looking wooden raft was floating down the stream toward us. Four thick pine tree trunks were strapped together with hardened ropes, and a fifth, thinner trunk sat in a carved hole, perpendicular to the others with a loose-hanging canvas sail tied to it—the mast. Another vertical piece of wood that was narrow at the top and gradually widened to a flat paddle at the bottom was attached to the back of the raft as a rudder. With no weight pressing down on it, the raft floated high out of the water. There was just enough space for one body, and there were two objects huddled around the base of the mast.

Naidah hurried back through the stream and caught hold of the raft before it could float past us, and I waded out to help her push it to shore when the current almost pulled it from her hands. Together, we beached the raft so that it was lodged on the rocky edge of the stream. The two objects, which had actually been tied to the mast with string, turned out to be a skin of water and a small cloth bag full of leafy green plants and a few handfuls of nuts, which I recognized as something I used to scrounge from the forest floor when I still felt the need to eat.

"Oh, I should have told them you didn't need food," Naidah said.

"Told who?" I asked, bewildered, looking between the food and water in my hands and the raft that had just appeared out of nowhere. "Who sent this?"

"The other naiads!" Naidah said happily. "I asked if any of them had a boat caught on their waters. I think this came from Corycia; she lives near Delphi."

"Did she take this from someone else?"

Naidah waved her hand dismissively. "I'm sure it was abandoned or something. Or maybe the previous owner did something bad to Corycia's spring and drowned. Well, either way, it's yours now!"

Retying the skin of water and bag of food to the mast, I ran a hand along the wood and tugged at the rigging. It held firm.

"Thank you," I said quietly, and then, "Naidah, close your eyes for a moment."

"All right."

When I turned to her, Naidah's face was relaxed, a small, smug grin on her lips. I put one hand on her shoulder and leaned forward to press my mouth to her forehead, just below her hairline. As I began to pull back, she caught my elbow. When I didn't pull away, she leaned in, and I froze.

"It's okay," she whispered, and it was. She pressed her lips against mine, warm and firm, and it was like the first bright pink light of dawn as the sun burst over the horizon, there and gone. She pulled back. Her eyes were still closed, which I was thankful for, as I could not stop staring at her. The snakes, too, were focused entirely on Naidah's face. One of them flicked a tongue at her, licking her forehead. She laughed.

The sun felt too hot, and I had to blink against how bright the stream, the forest, and even the air around us had become. The sleeve of Naidah's dress was scrunched under my fingers where I gripped her, and I forced myself to let go and straighten out the fabric.

"I—" I stuttered, and licked my lips. "Thank you."

She laughed again, and the sweet sound echoed across the stream. "Now *you* need to stop saying thank you. That was for me as much as it was for you."

"I won't forget," I told her. And I meant the kiss, and the kindness, and even the way she looked when she danced with a wild smile on her face. I hoped she would understand.

"Good!" she cheered and reeled me in to wrap her arms around my waist in a tight squeeze. I had barely brought my arms up to hug her back when she drew away. "Whenever you see a stream or a river, or even the wide ocean, just know that a friend is nearby."

I nodded, even though she could not see it.

"Till we meet again," I told her, slightly dazed, hoping beyond hope that we would meet again someday. I turned to shove the raft back into the water. When it was floating freely again, I stepped onto the wood and pushed off the rocky bottom with the other foot. The raft sailed toward the middle of the stream where the current was the strongest, but before I could get too far away, I looked back.

Worried that she may have opened her eyes to watch me leave, I kept my eyes down, and saw that in the wake of the raft there was a flat arrow on the surface of the water that reflected Naidah's face.

I was too shaken from the kiss. I wasn't paying attention,

and that was what ruined it. I met her eyes in the stream. Even through the distortion of the water, I could see that Naidah's eyes were a saccharine, golden brown.

I was seized by overwhelming panic. Stumbling back on the raft, my back hit the mast and I slapped my hand over my eyes. The snakes were in a riot, too, and hot tears pricked the corners of my eyes.

"No," I sobbed, sure that I had once again ruined the life of someone who had been foolish enough to be kind to me, but then I heard a call from the shore.

"No, no, Medusa, look!" I did not want to remove my hand, but Naidah's plea finally made me tear it away from my face. "Please!"

I looked. Naidah was still standing on the shore, bare feet in the water, eyes closed, and she was waving her arms in a faint reminiscence of the fluttering motions from the dances she did on Dionysus's mountain. She was not petrified. I had seen her eyes, and yet she was not petrified.

"What color," I started softly, the question bubbling forward without warning as relief crashed down around me, and then I shouted to her, "What color are my eyes?"

The stream was carrying me away much quicker than I had expected, perhaps aided by the naiad who it belonged to. Naidah had to shout back for me to hear her.

"Green!" she said, something like relief in her voice. "Green, just the same green as your snakes."

Danae

THE KING'S RECEPTION HALL was dark. There were fires burning in braziers on every other column lining the room, and yet Danae had to squint to see who was kneeling before the king from her seat to the left of the throne. Danae did not like dark spaces, a leftover fear cultivated from a life spent in a locked tower, and then the traumatizing journey of being trapped inside of a chest floating at sea. When she had brought this up to Polydectes, however, he had just smiled at her and told her, *The darkness cannot hurt you, silly woman.*

When she told Perseus what the king had said, her son had begged her to let him confront Polydectes, but Danae refused. Perseus was hotheaded and proud by nature. Danae knew that patience was the virtue that yielded change, more than any other.

She also knew that Polydectes lusted after her, as many men, and even a god, had. So long as Danae had a place in the king's court, she could live comfortably, beyond the dim moments in the reception hall.

The man kneeling before Polydectes was trembling with exhaustion. He was one of Polydectes's soldiers, sent to scout out possible lands that could be taken in the name of the king of Seriphos. His face was shadowed, as everything was shadowed in this room, but Danae could still see the whites of the man's eyes in the orange firelight as he quickly reported of his encounter with—

"A monster, majesty," the man panted. "It had snakes where hair should have been, and it turned four men into stone statues just by looking at them."

Polydectes leaned forward in his throne, hand curled possessively around the armrest. He was unfailingly regular, as men go, and even more unremarkable as kings go. His small, dark eyes were fixed on the soldier, but Danae could see the thoughts of disbelief change to realization and then fear as the man continued to talk about the monster he had scarcely escaped near Mount Parnassus.

Polydectes dismissed the man once his story was finished. Danae could see that not only he but the remaining soldiers who stood guard around the reception hall were alarmed by the description of the snake-haired monster. The men shuffled their feet as they glanced at one another, silently asking: *Do you believe it? Are you more the fool to ignore it?*

The soldier had called the monster an *it*, but from the way the man spoke, Danae guessed that the monster was female. Men had no problem identifying male monsters and calling them what they were, but when it came to female monsters, they were more likely to get rid of any association with sex altogether, as if they had to erase any trace of femininity in order to convey the terror the monster posed.

"You are not cowed by this creature, are you?" a voice

called from the side of the room, and Danae sighed as Perseus stepped out of the shadowed side hall and into the light of the fires. She'd told him to keep his nose out of the king's business, but he had his father's sense of tact. "Surely a king like you, Polydectes, would not let a slight against your men go unpunished."

"Hush, boy," Polydectes barked.

Danae tried to catch her son's eye, but Perseus was keen on the king.

Even though he was scarcely out of boyhood, Perseus had a sense of strength and control about him that he had inherited from his father. Zeus might not have been looking down on his son at the moment, but there was no denying his divine lineage in the straight line of his shoulders and the muscles wrapping around his arms and legs. Polydectes, no doubt, would have noticed how his men came to attention when Perseus was around.

Her son approached slowly, passing the point where the soldier had been kneeling to brace his foot against the first stair of the raised throne. Clasping his hands behind him, Perseus met the king's gaze through the gloom.

"You seek more land, but your men come running back to you with their tails between their legs after crossing one monster," Perseus scoffed. "How can you lay claim on what is not already yours, if you would not fight for it?"

"Silence!" Polydectes growled. "Where is your respect, boy?"

"You would find it more apparent," Perseus said lazily, "if you stood up to this monster."

Polydectes's throne creaked as he leaned forward. Danae

could see that his knuckles were white from his grip on the armrest, and she braced for the explosion.

But after a tense moment, Polydectes settled back into his throne.

"Why would I need to?" Polydectes shot back, faux casual. "This monster is not threatening my borders, and I can afford to spare four men. Why should I divert my attention from my own land, especially when my wedding is so close?"

Polydectes turned and smiled down at the woman sitting to his right. Concealed by a long veil with only her folded hands left bare in her lap, Hippodamia sat silently by her fiancé's side.

Hippodamia had arrived quietly at Polydectes's door nearly a month ago. Danae and Perseus had listened, startled, to Polydectes explain that she was to be his wife. Hippodamia was the daughter of another king, he had told them, and he considered it a great honor to be able to claim such a beautiful woman as his betrothed. As he explained, Polydectes did not look at Danae once. He barely glanced at Hippodamia. He spoke, with a self-satisfied smile, entirely to Perseus.

Later that evening, Polydectes had come to Danae's bedroom door. She listened as he paced back and forth, explaining how he had brilliantly devised for a sham marriage to be proposed between himself and Hippodamia, which would convince Perseus he had nothing to worry about concerning Danae.

"What of Hippodamia?" Danae had asked.

Polydectes paused. "What of her?"

"Does she believe this marriage will happen?" Danae pressed, hoping to come off as if she was worried about a threat to their own marriage. And in a way, she was. She was worried about losing the security that being Polydectes's wife and queen would provide. With a fickle thought, Polydectes could replace her. If she had to grit her teeth and smile in order to ensure her safety and comfort, she could.

Polydectes barked out a single laugh and waved her question away. "It matters not. She is a king's daughter. She will be married soon enough to another king, after we have been wed."

Danae leaned forward in her stiff chair in the throne room to peer around Polydectes and try to get a sense of how Hippodamia felt about her approaching wedding, as she had been trying and failing to do every day since the woman had arrived. Polydectes kept them separated. The veil, which Polydectes insisted on, kept her face hidden from Danae. She wondered if the poor woman had figured out that her eventual marriage was a ruse.

At the same time, Danae thought that Hippodamia may have been enjoying her position. She had all the title without the burden of Polydectes's attention.

The smile seemed plastered to Polydectes's face as he looked down at Hippodamia, and when he turned back to Perseus, Danae thought that he had been seized by some sudden, cruel glee. She did not like the predatory way he was looking at her son.

"Speaking of my wedding," Polydectes said, "I will be expecting a gift from all of my attendants. As you and your mother are included on that list, Perseus," Polydectes' voice was sickly sweet as a rotten apple, "what do you intend to bring me?"

Perseus frowned. The king knew that he and Danae, as his wards, had no gold or possessions to their name that did not first belong to Polydectes. This was a sore spot on Perseus's pride, one that Polydectes knew how to irritate.

"What would the king like?" Perseus asked rigidly.

"Well, since you are so passionate about how this monster is a threat to my kingdom and my pride, why don't you do me the favor of bringing me the monster's head?" Polydectes smiled, all teeth. "I think that would be a wonderful gift. Do you agree, Danae?"

Polydectes did not look to her even when he spoke her name. The king had been attempting to drive a wedge between Danae and Perseus for years, but he clearly thought that Danae would choose him over her own son, no matter what.

Danae looked to Perseus. Her son had kept his head held high as Polydectes neatly trapped him with his own words, but Danae wished that just once, Perseus would back down from a fight.

"Yes, your majesty," Danae said slowly, "Perseus and I would be honored to give you the head of this monster as a gift for your wedding. My son will not fail you."

Perseus finally flicked a look at Danae. His blue eyes, once so bright and dear to her, were hard. But he gave her a slight nod, glad to have his mother's approval.

"Excellent," said the king. "You should begin your hunt in Delphi, boy, for my men tell me that there are foreseeing oracles there who may help you track down the creature." He waved his hand. "You are dismissed."

The dismissal wasn't necessary, as Perseus had come of his own accord, but Polydectes seemed glad to have seized control of his hall once again. With a grim look on his face, Perseus spun on his heel and left the room. He didn't look back. Danae closed her eyes and sent up a silent prayer to the gods to protect her foolish son. If Zeus did not hear her, perhaps another god would.

A chain in one hand and a key in the other

I BARELY SLEPT ON the raft. The rudder needed to be held constantly in the correct position to keep me moving in the right direction. I kept a piece of the rope tied to the boom in my other hand so that I could pull it into the wind when it threatened to go slack. I was no sailor, but I managed. The raft rode the waves like a leaf bobbing along the surface of the water, and though the wooden trunks kept me from sinking into the ocean, I was soaked from the sea spray.

I couldn't avoid the smell of sea salt. It surrounded me on all sides. But I was able to keep the paralyzing memory I associated with it at bay, thinking about Echidna, and the night she and I sat on the beach. The rosmarinus oil that Naidah made me helped, since every time a breeze brushed my face the scent flooded my nose. I remembered Polli's small but sure hands forming a lump of dough into a ball, or the feeling of Naidah's fingers on my skin, or, better yet, the feeling of her lips on mine. The waves surrounded me, but I had made myself the eye of the storm.

There was no way for me to keep the snakes dry, and I could feel how uncomfortable they were as they were splashed and left dripping, but they made no complaint other than a few half-hearted hisses. They kept the direction of Echidna's island clear in my head.

As temperamental as my father, the ocean switched between high, choppy waves and smooth, flat sailing from one everlasting moment to the next. I wondered if my father could feel me on the water. I knew he and my mother always had a general idea of what was going on in the ocean, and they could pinpoint the exact location of a creature or being in the sea if they concentrated hard enough. However, there was no reason for them to be looking for me. They may not have been able to recognize me if they did, anyway.

If my parents knew what went on in their oceans, I thought, then of course Poseidon would have been able to tell, too. I was surprised that the thought of Poseidon recognizing me in his waters did not scare me, when the memory of him had nearly caused me to give up altogether.

The snakes hissed at even the slightest thought of the memory, and I realized why I was not scared of Poseidon knowing where I was. If he appeared before me, I would only need one second, one glance, to turn him to stone. While I had never petrified anything beyond a mortal yet, Athena had been afraid of what my eyes could do to her before I left the temple. I could think of no better subject to test that theory than the god who had been the cause of it all.

This thought buoyed me through the long nights I spent awake, navigating across an endless horizon. Small islands appeared in my peripheries, but I knew that they were not the one I was looking for.

When the third island I had come across finally faded into the sea and sky behind me, I lodged the rudder against the mast and stretched out of the tense sitting position I had taken up to steer. I untied the skin of water from the base of the mast and took a few sips from it, mostly just to wash the taste of salt out of my mouth.

During my first day at sea, I replayed what had happened when I left Naidah by the stream in my mind. She and I had met eyes, through the reflection of the water, and yet Naidah had not turned to stone. Did my power not work because I had not looked directly into her eyes? The snakes had been looking right at her, even while I had been looking down, and yet she was still flesh and bone. I wondered if Naidah was special, because of what she had come to mean to me. But then, hadn't Polli meant a lot to me, too?

I had to believe the reason my power did not work was because Naidah and I had not looked directly at each other. And if that was true, then there was a loophole in my seemingly inexorable power. Had Athena intended this, or was this simply something she had never foreseen when she had crafted this curse and put this power behind my eyes? Back in the first few days after I had fled Athens, when I had rushed to the first body of water I could find to slake my thirst, the snakes had warned me against looking at my own reflection. Why would they have been nervous for me to see my own eyes if a reflection could not turn me to stone?

As I thought this, the snakes shifted uncomfortably. They

seemed to know something I did not, and they did not want
to tell me what it was.

"You can't keep a secret from me," I told them, even as
they grew more and more uneasy.

Not secret, said the not-voice, sounding slightly ashamed,
a truth you have not realized yet.

"But you know what it is?"

They paused. *Yes.*

"And you won't tell me?"

Yes.

"Then it is a secret," I snapped. A wave pushed the raft
off course, and I yanked the rudder back into position.

The snakes writhed with displeasure. I knew that they
did not want to keep anything from me, but they were torn
between the desire to let me in on the truth and the desperation to protect me from the pain the truth could cause.

We did not speak again for a while, but I still thought
about what the snakes were trying to shield from me. It had
to do with my reflection, and specifically what would happen
if I looked at my own reflection. Hadn't I thought, all those
weeks ago, that the snakes had warned me away from the
water because even I would not go unaffected by the paralyzing power behind my eyes? Rage and shame had filled me all
at once when I figured out the secondary curse of Athena's
wrath, since I would no longer be able to look upon my own
reflection to see the beauty of my face. And yet, I had been
silently relieved to never have to truly see what I looked like.

But now I knew that others could look into my reflection
and be left unharmed.

All at once, I remembered a piece of the Graeae's

prophecy: *He will carry a shield from the goddess of wisdom… the glinting reflection he can use to misdirect your gaze.*

This part of the prophecy had never stuck out to me before, as I had been too overcome with the news of my inescapable beheading to really pick through each fragment. Now, though, now I understood why the snakes were restless.

"The boy can look at my reflection," I said aloud, though only the snakes and the sea and I could hear it, "and live. He will know how to survive me."

Even though I knew the Graeae's prophecy was truthful, in as much as there was no way for me to escape the fate coming for me, I had secretly hoped that this power would surpass all expectations. I had been so frightened by what I had seen myself capable of that I thought such a power would be able to save me, in the end. But this power had a weak spot. And within that weak spot was the path to my own destruction.

The snakes were still frightened of what would happen if I looked at my reflection. If I looked into my own eyes, in the only direct way anyone could see themselves, my reflection would turn me to stone. This was the truth my snakes had tried to hide. This power could kill me just as easily as any of the people I had left stiff and unfeeling in my wake. My reflection, which was harmless to everyone else, could turn this power against me.

The waves had been minimal as the snakes and I struggled with the idea of self-destruction, but they began to turn into swells and my raft swayed as it rolled over the crests and sank into the gullies before rising again. I took ahold of the rudder again to keep it steady. The sky above me was turning dark with both the setting sun and gathering clouds.

From the middle of the raft, I could not peer over the sides to look into the water. But if I leaned over just enough, I would have been able to look down and see the reflection that scared the snakes so terribly. For one horrible moment, I thought about doing just that. Lunging for the water before the snakes could do anything to stop me and meeting my own eyes in the reflection—would it hurt? The people I had turned to stone had always had their last emotion frozen on their faces, mostly terror or confusion, but I did not think they had been in pain. Perhaps the stone would take over too fast for me to feel anything, even if I was prepared for it.

Polli's rigid face would rise up in my memory from time to time. It would bubble to the surface without warning. The first few times, I had been helpless to do anything but curl in on myself and sob over what I had done to my friend. A small, crumbling part of me was glad that Polli never had to see what I had become. That one glance had cut off any reaction she may have had. That glance had taken my only friend from me.

And what had I done since then? I felt like I was stumbling through each day.

Dionysus and Naidah had shown me kindness, but the only ones who really understood me were my snakes. With Dionysus and Naidah, I had to find the words to explain what I felt, but with the snakes, I didn't even need to speak for them to know how I was feeling. It was easy with them.

The only reason I had these snakes was because of this

curse. Should I have felt guilty for loving them, for feeling grateful that they understood me?

I had kept myself away from everyone, even before Athena's curse. I had been building this stone fortress around my heart since I was a child. Would turning myself into stone be any different?

I thought, selfishly, that the final moment before my body turned to rock would feel peaceful.

No!

I jerked back, even though I had not been leaning toward the water, and felt a great dread wash over me. The snakes were despondent, writhing and twisting above my head with distress.

No, the not-voice cried again. *Please!*

"I won't," I gasped, and felt tears spring to my eyes. I released the rudder so I could reach both hands up and wind them into the twirling mass of snakes. They flinched at my touch at first, but then they began to wind themselves greedily around my fingers, my wrists, trying to hold me in place. I shut my eyes and a few tears slipped down my cheeks. "I'm sorry, I'm sorry."

I felt ashamed of myself. This body did not belong to only me, and my life was now undeniably tied to the snakes as they were tied to me. To kill myself meant condemning them, as well.

"Forgive me," I pleaded to them, and they just wound themselves even tighter around my hands, their tongues flicking out to taste my skin and settle themselves with the familiar scent. One of them even opened its mouth and bit the pad of my hand between my first finger and thumb, though its teeth did not puncture my skin. It simply held me in its mouth.

Ours, the not-voice said. It was not a reprimand, but a reminder.

"Yes, yes, I'm sorry, I know," I said wetly, "you and me, it belongs to both of us."

Ours, the not-voice said again with more emphasis, and I understood.

"Yeah, I'm yours," I said, "and you're mine."

These snakes had taken care of me, watched over me, and done everything they could to help me as long as they had been a part of me, and I owed it to them to do the same. I had to love them as they loved me.

I left the raft to roam as the waves and the current saw fit, since the snakes did not release my hands for quite some time after that. When the storm that had been hanging heavily in the clouds finally broke and sent the ocean into a flurry of crashing water, I wrapped my legs around the mast and clung to it as the raft was pummeled by the sea and the sky.

Both the snakes and I were soaked to the bone, and as I shivered, I let the terrible thoughts I had had about looking into my own reflection wash away with the water.

When the sea finally calmed again, it was morning. My snakes had released their grip on me during the night so that I could hold on to the mast with both hands, and I flexed my wrists and fingers to relieve the leftover strain. I was exhausted, but I pulled the rudder straight and angled the sail into the wind to follow the path the snakes laid out in my head.

With a flat, clear sea ahead of us, one of the snakes

spotted the ship while it was still far off. I squinted into the light shining off the surface of the water, but I was not able to make out any distinct features of the ship until it was much closer.

There was nowhere for me to hide, and I was much too tired to try and slip into the water and float beneath the surface until the boat passed.

I thought about just putting my back to the ship until we had passed one another, but then I began to hear the calls from the men on board.

"—see it? Is it the creature they told us about?"

"Look at its head! It's true about the snakes!"

"Someone get the captain!"

Men were lining the railing of the ship, goggling at me from high on the deck. I let my gaze skirt along their chests, frowning.

They knew of me. They recognized my snakes. There were very few people who had seen me and lived to tell others of the monster they had encountered. The most recent one came to mind, along with all of Dionysus's warnings.

I tried to see if these men were wearing the same uniforms as the soldiers I had seen on Dionysus's mountain, to see if these men also belonged to Polydectes. My fears were confirmed in an instant. The crest carved into the leather on every man's shoulder was the same as the ones carved into the armor of the men now frozen, forever, in a stream. A few of them had already pulled out their swords.

"In all the wide world," I cursed, "how did we come to the same patch of ocean?"

Polydectes's men were still muttering to one another as

my raft drifted closer and closer to their ship. I tightened my grip on the rope tied to the sail, intending to pull it and guide my raft away, when another man joined them.

He was different from the others. Younger, for certain, with shoulders like a bull, and his dark hair curled around his temples in a way that was horribly familiar.

"Perseus!" one of the men shouted, and my heart dropped right out of my chest. "It's the monster!"

The boy was searching the water, and when he spotted me on the raft, he froze. When his eyes found the snakes, he spun himself around so fast he stumbled over his own feet.

His men were not so quick to act. I stood from where I had been crouched behind the mast and tilted my face up. If these men belonged to Polydectes, and Dionysus's prediction of the king's reaction to my power was right, then they would have orders to kill me. I had to act first.

The first man began to turn to stone even as the boy, Perseus, called out, "Look away! Don't look at it, fools!"

But the men had either not truly believed what they were seeing, or they were simply too dumbfounded to move away from the railing. I met the eye of each one standing at the edge of the deck with their hands clenched hard around the wooden handrail, where they would be forever frozen. The red flash from the snakes turned to a persistent glow as I went down the line. I did not feel any pain. A few of the sailors managed to avert their eyes before I could get to them, but I counted nearly a dozen statues now lining the edge of the ship.

My raft floated gently on, and soon I was past the ship. I turned to keep facing it even as we drifted apart. The boy touched one of the statues, as if examining it, before he yanked his hand back.

One of the surviving men was shouting, "Captain, the crew, we've lost too many to manage the ship, we need—"

But the rest of his frantic shouts were carried away by the wind.

The boy did not seek me out amidst the waves. He touched a hand to his chest, the same one that he had used to touch the stone arm of his man, and then turned away from the railing. A few steps farther, and I could no longer see him.

I realized that my chest was heaving as I gasped for air, and my heart was pounding so fast I could feel it from the top of my head all the way down to my toes. With a staggering step backward, I leaned against the mast and felt the raft rock underneath my feet.

Perseus. He was the boy from the Graeae's prophecy, and we had nearly been face-to-face. Surely, this had not been the meeting the Graeae predicted? The boy did not have on any armor or hold a shield like the three gray-skinned sisters had described, and yet he was surely the one who they had warned me about.

Was this meant to be where our paths crossed for the first time? I had killed his men without hesitation, because of what a god and three divine beings had foretold for me, and yet, I had not needed to kill them. Not all of them had been brandishing weapons. The men had simply been staring at the monster they feared, and their fear had become a reality.

But it was the fact that they had called me a monster that had spurred me to action, I realized. They saw me as a monster, as Dionysus had said they would, and so I had become one.

My chest was still rising and falling like the ocean during a storm, which was ironic, with the sea now as flat as a tilled field. I touched the skin under my eyes. I had barely noticed the red haze from the snakes. I had been too focused on killing the next man on Perseus's ship that I had not even stopped to consider what happened to the previous one. The sharp prick of pain I used to feel when I used my power was gone. It was like I had pulled out a stinging thorn and removed the pain, but now the blood was flowing freely from the wound.

I remembered what Dionysus had said about his power, which mimicked my own: *There is no escaping yourself.*

A new sob slipped from my throat. I pressed my palm over my mouth as the tears spilled down my cheeks. My snakes tried to rub them away. But even as another choked sound pushed its way up, and as I felt my world crashing down around me, I kept my eyes open. I could not take back what I had done. Even if this should not have been the moment when I crossed paths with Perseus, there was no going back now, and I had given him a reason to seek my head. I had become the monster I had feared I would be.

But even as I realized this, my tears ran dry on my cheeks. I fit my hand over my chest to feel my heart beating beneath the flesh and bone. I was still alive, still breathing. This was not going to be the end that the Graeae had predicted for me.

So long as I was still whole, I could keep going. I reached for the rudder and asked the snakes to show me the path, once again. Rubbing the heel of my palm against my cheeks, I kept a steady hold on the rudder and pointed my raft toward Echidna.

Okay? the snakes asked.

"No," I said, "but that's all right. We've got time."

Barely a mark on the map

ECHIDNA'S ISLAND WAS SMALL, just appearing as a faint bump on the horizon until I was nearly right upon it and the vague silhouettes finally turned into a flat stretch of land with a tightly packed forest at its center. While I was still sailing closer, I felt the raft pass through a patch of dense air, like we had just gone under a waterfall. It was the indescribable curtain of magic that kept mortals away from divine places.

I jumped into the knee-high foamy shoreline and pulled my raft up onto the sand. The trees began just a short stretch up from the shore, but despite being close enough to hear the familiar chatter of birds or small creatures rustling around in the leaves, I could not hear any signs of life coming out of the forest.

The silence amongst the trees grew even more pronounced when I moved from the sea, and the sound of the tide breaking on the sand faded away completely. I treaded carefully, and the snakes were on full alert, the unnatural noiselessness of the forest putting us on edge. My run-in with Perseus had both rattled me and set me at ease. I had made it away from a confrontation with him unscathed, but I doubted I would be so lucky next time. Until that time came, however, my power could protect me from any harm.

Twigs cracking under my feet made me flinch, but nothing came for me from out behind the trees. The snakes urged me forward.

The trees suddenly cleared in the middle of the island to make room for a round glade. Just off-center of the clearing was a small rise, like the giant foot of a titan had caught the edge of the grass and rumpled it, leaving a gaping hollow behind. The cave had a wide mouth and dirt walls leading down under the earth, which was so unlike the dark, rocky cave the Graeae had claimed in Delphi. I knew that this was Echidna's home, because the snakes were telling me so, and because my sibling's presence was everywhere. Echidna had not restricted her living space to the inside of the cave. There was a rough wooden table and a log bench set up for eating meals outdoors, as well as a woven blanket and a pile of pillows resting against the edge of the glade where the shadows of the trees could stretch over them.

I had taken one step into the clearing when I finally heard a noise. I remembered it from my childhood. It was the rhythmic scraping sound of Echidna's tail dragging along the ground.

My sibling emerged from the mouth of the cave carrying a basket of vegetables, and I allowed myself one good look at how her tail shone brilliantly green in the sun, how her dark skin was full of health and luster, and her golden hair was tied up into complex knots on her head, before I closed my eyes.

"Echidna," I said, my voice loud as it filled the silent clearing.

I heard the scraping of her tail cease, and then her intake of breath, and then something heavy hit the grassy floor of the clearing—Echidna's basket.

"Oh," she said, and her voice was moving toward me, "little queen."

In the next moment, her arms were around me. She was warm and familiar and I nearly cried at the feeling of calm that settled over me when she was near, like she had lifted me off the knife's edge of terror I was balancing on and placed me safely on solid ground.

"I wondered if you would come see me," she said, her words muffled as she pressed her face into my shoulder. "I hoped that you would."

I was not surprised when she had not reacted to the snakes, or to the fact that I wouldn't look at her, but I did wonder how she knew what had happened to me. When she finally drew back and I could feel her looking me over, I asked, "How much had you heard?"

"Only rumors," she responded, and I frowned, thinking of what the men had shouted at me from the ship. But she clucked her tongue and smoothed out the wrinkle between my brows with her thumb as she continued, "Rumors from minor gods and deities, who happened to overhear some things from the Graeae, and even more scarcely, a rumor based on what the goddess Athena herself had to say when she explained the curse to the gods on Olympus."

"From Athena," I repeated, stricken. Of course, I knew Athena had placed the blame of Poseidon's transgression on me. She had even told me that this shift in fault was done to prevent any more tension between the gods, but it still rattled me to think that the most divine beings in our world thought of me as some disrespectful mortal who had reaped what she had sowed. I wondered if Dionysus had been there when Athena gave her account and had pretended not to know of my curse when he met me, or if he had been absent from that meeting. I hoped the latter was the truth.

"What do the rumors—what do they say about me?" I asked.

Her thumb now stroked the skin above my brow bone. "Mostly they just talk about your power, how it can topple not only kings but immortals, too."

"And so they fear me," I guessed.

"Many do, yes," Echidna said bluntly, "but I think a fair few of us surmised what had really happened, and so we view your power and your curse slightly differently."

The snakes, silent up until now to let me enjoy my reunion with Echidna, uncoiled from their defensive positions and a few reached out, tongues flicking, to taste Echidna's fingers. The scent of her, which I had been unable to pick out with my mortal nose as a child, was distinct and altogether surprising, because she smelled like me. At least, the snakes showed me how our scents matched in their comparison. Perhaps it was because I, too, now had a part of my body made up of serpentine scales.

Having recognized the scent, the snakes relaxed completely, and one of the more daring ones rubbed its chin over the back of Echidna's hand.

"Hello there," she cooed at it.

And then she must have run her finger down the top of the snake's head because I felt a sensation that I had never experienced before, like a shiver down my back caused by a phantom wind. No one had ever touched my snakes apart from me. And it was different from when the snakes reached out first, because they, too, were taken aback by the feeling of Echidna's gentle touch. Even Naidah had kept her touches reserved to my mortal body. The only contact the snakes and I had were with one another, and the feeling of an outsider treating the snakes so delicately was wonderfully new.

"Come," Echidna beckoned, and she took my hand to pull me forward from where I was rooted on the spot, still processing the feeling of her hands on my snakes. "I want to hear everything."

My eyes still closed, Echidna directed me to the bench and table by her cave's entrance and sat me down before moving away to pick up the vegetables she'd dropped.

"Can you not even look at me with those eyes of yours?" she asked conversationally, setting down the basket on the table with a *thump*.

"I can," I said, "but if I look in your eyes, I will have no control over my power, and so closing my own just makes it easier."

"That doesn't seem fair," she murmured. "You mean, everyone else can look at you, but you can't look at them if you don't want to turn them to stone?"

I nodded.

"That is not fair," she said again, this time with more emphasis. "Here, give me your hands."

I placed them palms up on the table. She set something

firm and round in one hand and something smooth and thin in the other.

"Now open your eyes."

I did. I was holding a small potato that still had dirt clinging to it, and a paring knife.

"Peel it," Echidna commanded. "And I will peel this one," she waved another potato under my face, "and you can look at me whenever you want, but I'll keep my eyes down, okay?"

I studied the vegetable and the knife in my hands. I had not peeled a potato since I had left the temple. I set the edge of the blade to the rough skin and pressed down, turning the potato until a single, long ribbon of skin fell onto the table. The movement was familiar and comforting, just as Echidna's presence was.

"Okay," I said. I waited a moment, and then looked up. Echidna's eyes were almost closed, the lids just slightly parted as she looked down at her own vegetable. Her face was the same as I remembered it.

"Now," she said, reaching for another potato once she had finished peeling the first, "tell me everything. Everything that has happened to you since we parted last."

I picked up another potato, too, and I told her.

The story was long, and I don't think I told it well. I kept getting caught up on small moments. When I got to the part with Poseidon, I had to put the knife down because my hands were trembling so badly. They shook not just from fear, for that memory still sent a shock of alarm that seized my whole body when I thought of it, but also anger. I was angry thinking back to how helpless I had been, how powerless I had allowed myself to be even while I fooled myself into thinking my beauty gave me power. While I had been able to use my looks to get what I wanted at the time, I had become blind to the fact that my vanity would not protect me from everything.

When I was silent for a good handful of minutes, Echidna reached across the table and placed her steady fingers over my shaking ones.

"It's not all right, what he did to you," she said. "But that does not mean you cannot move past it. You have the strength to overcome this."

I felt tears prick my eyes at her affirmative words and her voice, so full of kind determination, and I tried to blink them away. I had been waiting to hear something like this, I realized. To hear someone say that what Poseidon had done had been wrong. And to hear that the way it affected me would not last forever. Hearing it confirmed by Echidna, someone who had known me before my transformation, and now after, unlocked that part of me that had been holding back.

Flipping my hand over so that my palm was face up, I squeezed Echidna's hand.

"Thank you," I said.

She gave my hand a reassuring squeeze in return, and then pointed at the basket of potatoes with her knife.

"Keep going," she said.

I kept peeling, and I kept talking.

Echidna was quiet throughout the whole story, never interrupting to ask questions or to comment on the things I had done. I had expected her to say something about when Athena had first placed the curse on me, or perhaps when I had explained how I had accidentally turned all those people in the forest into statues in the early days of my journey. Or when I had done it again on purpose.

She was even quiet when I told her about the Graeae's prophecy, though I saw her nod like she had been waiting for it.

The only noise she made was a small laugh when I had talked about meeting Dionysus for the first time.

I finished by telling her about how Naidah had helped me face the smell of the ocean and then gave me a raft to sail on. I did not tell her about the kiss, though I wasn't sure why. That just felt like something that I wanted to keep for myself.

"And I saw him, on the ocean."

"Who?" Echidna asked, scraping a few brown spots off the potato she had just finished peeling.

"Perseus."

Echidna paused and set down her knife.

"The boy from the prophecy?"

I nodded, sure she could see the movement even if she wasn't looking right at me. Although I had finally released the torrent of emotions and memories that I had been struggling to dam up in my chest by telling Echidna everything that had happened, I felt like the weight of those events had only grown heavier.

What did it mean? Why had I seen Perseus before we were fated to meet?

Echidna was tapping the rough top of the table, the soft points of her nails finding small seams in the wood with a gentle *tak, tak, tak.*

"And the creepy one-eyed triplets," she asked, and I couldn't help but smile at her nickname for the Graeae, "they didn't say anything about this in the prophecy when they told it to you?"

"No," I said. "Just that when he found me on the island, he would, you know," I scraped off a large chunk of peel from a potato, "cut off my head."

Echidna made a clicking noise in the back of her throat and sighed.

"They have never been all that helpful, those three," she said. "Well, let's see. You said you saw Perseus already, and you did not get your head cut off, obviously, and he's still alive?" The last part was phrased as a question, so I nodded. She went on, "Then your fated encounter is still waiting for you somewhere in the future."

"But why did I see him now? I had imagined that our paths would not cross until the prophecy came true, and now I feel like," I blinked down at my lap, searching for the words, "like something should have happened."

"Did something happen?"

"I—" I started, and stopped, feeling the heat rise up my neck as I thought about what I had done to the men on the ship. I wasn't sure if I was more ashamed of what I had done or worried about what Echidna might think of me if I told her. "Some of his sailors saw me, and saw who I was. I—I met their gaze and they were petrified. I could have looked away, but I did not."

"Hmm. And Perseus?" Echidna didn't sound upset that I had used my power.

"He looked away."

"Well, that was either very smart of him," she summarized, "or very cowardly. He'll know what you can do now,

269

anyway. Perhaps the Fates designed this meeting so that the boy would have reason to come after you?"

I dug the tip of my knife into the soft white meat of the potato I had finished peeling, drilling a small hole into its side. Echidna was making sense, but that didn't make me feel any better. If what she said was true, then my actions were the reason the Graeae's prophecy would come true. It was because I had struck first, I had killed Perseus's men, that Perseus himself would come after me, sword drawn.

When I explained this to Echidna, her voice became gentle. "No, Medusa. It will not be your fault. You have seen how fate and prophecies work their way into the minds of mortals and immortals alike. Even Athena was trying to avoid a fated prophecy of a godly war when she wrongly blamed you for that stinking sea god's despicable actions. If this boy does come for your head with, what did you say? A shield to divert your eyes? Then it will have been his choice to do so, his choice to attack a woman who has only ever tried to defend herself."

When Echidna called me a *woman*, I froze. I set down the mutilated potato and closed my eyes to lean my head back.

"It's been a while since anyone has called me that," I said. "A woman. I've started to expect *monster*."

"You can be both," Echidna told me. "A monstrous woman is not a terrible thing to be."

I tilted my face down and peeked one eye open to look at her. Echidna was smiling down at the table, putting the peeled potatoes back in the basket and sweeping the skins off to one side. She rose on her long, muscled tail and brushed off her hands.

She was wearing one of the cropped tunics I knew she favored, and it revealed the strip of brown skin and her belly button, which sat right above the place where her human body became scales. Even when I was a child, she had always proudly displayed this part of her body. Where mortal and monster met.

I knew, then, why I had wanted to come see Echidna. Why she had been the one I thought of when Dionysus had asked where I would go. She was the only one who could possibly understand what I had been through, and what I was going through now.

"Being a monster," she went on, "does not stop you from being a woman. In fact, I think an essential part of being a woman is finding that part of you that others would see as monstrous; finding it and nurturing it so that it does not overtake who you are. If you ignore it or try to hide it, that is when other people will turn it against you."

She reached out and gripped my chin in her hands, forcing me to look up and face her head on even as her eyes were closed. There was a fierce grin stretching across her lips. In that moment, I knew I had made the right choice to come see Echidna. My snakes stretched to brush themselves against the back of Echidna's hand. She told me, "You be who you are, Medusa. Love the monster within, and it will love you right back."

I had no words to say in response, so I just nodded. When she released me, she patted me once on the cheek.

Echidna moved to stoke a fire in a rock-lined pit just

behind the wooden table with a large pot of water simmering atop it. She told me to cut the potatoes we'd peeled into bite-sized pieces as she worked on the fire. The island wind wove through the branches of the trees around us, the limbs clicking and clacking together.

"Why are there no animals on your island?" I asked her.

Our conversation had mostly stalled after I had found myself at a loss for words, and my voice was scratchy.

"Oh," she said, waving a hand at the earthy cave entrance, "because of the noise."

I stared at the back of her head. Every pop and crackle from the fire was amplified by the silent forest around us. I thought I could hear a shell being dropped in the ocean from the far side of the island if I listened hard enough.

"What noise?"

"Of course, you wouldn't know, would you," she said with a laugh as she stirred some of my potatoes into the pot. "While you were being cursed and receiving prophecies of your death," I frowned at the callous summary of what I had been through, even if it was true, but she continued on, "I gave birth to my first child."

"You have a kid?" I tried to remember if she had mentioned wanting children before, or if she had ever mentioned children at all.

"Mm-hmm," she hummed. "You'll meet him soon. He went down for a nap right before you got here. It won't be so quiet anymore when he wakes up."

I cut another potato in half and peered suspiciously into the cave mouth.

"Does your husband live here, too?"

Echidna's laugh was bright and clipped. "Of course not. I haven't seen him in ages. I expect he'll come around again sometime in the next century or so, and maybe I'll let him stay here."

She flicked her fingers at me over her shoulder and I could see the mischievous grin curling up the corner of her mouth.

"I may want another kid someday."

I wanted to ask whether she got lonely on this island, with only her child to keep her company, but then a loud noise echoed up from the inside of the cave. It sounded like a thunderclap muffled by a blanket. The sound of something heavy crashing into sturdy furniture followed.

"Ah," Echidna said, putting down the giant spoon she had been using to stir the pot, "he's awake."

I heard a clamor of footsteps scrabbling up out of the cave. While one part of me knew that I should look away in case Echidna's kid couldn't stop himself from looking in my eyes, I desperately wanted to know what the off-spring of my snakelike sibling and her husband would look like.

When Echidna's son bounded out of the cave, I nearly fell off the bench.

A three-headed dog with thick, dark fur and paws the size of dinner plates tripped over his own feet as he raced out of the cave. Each head was looking a different direction, tongues lolling out. I gaped as the dog barked at Echidna, struggled to his feet, and then promptly tripped over him-self again because one of the heads had turned sharply in my direction. He barked again, a great booming noise that would have sent all the birds in the trees streaking into the air, if there had been any left.

I avoided the dog's eyes. There was so much to look at that it wasn't very difficult. Now that he was closer, I could see that the dog had the soft, downy fur of a puppy still growing into its coat. The place where the three heads joined at the neck had rolls of skin that stretched with his movements. His long tail thumped on the ground, kicking up small clouds of dust and bits of grass.

"His name is Cerberus," Echidna said.

"Your son is a dog," I said blankly.

"Yes."

"How—" I started, and then tried to think of a way to phrase the question I wanted to ask without offending her. Eventually I gave up, just letting the single word stand for itself. The snakes were flickering their tongues at Cerberus, and the scent that they caught rolling off him was distinctly similar to Echidna's, though it was also heavily dampened by the smell of dog hair.

"I wasn't sure what to think either," Echidna told me. "When he was born, I mean. Typhon had been gone for a while already, and it was just me and a minor deity that Eileithyia had sent to help me through the birth, and I'm sure that nymph was scared half to death when those three heads popped out. I thought some god or goddess was playing a trick on me, or that the pain of giving birth to him was making me hallucinate." She held her hand out, and Cerberus scrambled to run to her, tripping again, and all three heads tried to snuffle their way into her palm. Echidna cupped each of them in turn, rubbing them between their eyebrows.

"But then he started crying, as all children do when they are born, and I knew he was mine. I knew he was my son."

I watched as Echidna caressed Cerberus's many heads, his tail whipping back and forth so fast that he smacked himself in the side of the far left and right faces a couple of times.

"Why is he so...unlike you?"

"I do not mind that he is not like me," Echidna said, which isn't really what I had meant, but she kept going. "Mothers should not expect their children to be exactly like their parents. Rather, they should fear raising a child who is exactly like them, for there will be no room for that child to grow."

She rubbed down Cerberus's side, finding a spot to scratch that made Cerberus flop to the ground, belly up with his feet pawing the air for more. He was just a child, enjoying his mother's affection.

I knew I was not what my parents had expected me to be. They had not known what to do with me when I was a simple mortal girl, and now, I was sure they would not treat me as kindly as Echidna was. But I had become more than what they thought I could be, in the end.

"He's beautiful," I told her. And he was, because he was full of happiness, and I could see that the love Echidna had for him was making him into a fine dog.

"That he is," Echidna agreed. She gave Cerberus one final pat, and when she took her hand away he sat frozen on his back for a moment before scrambling back to his feet and shaking off. Tail still wagging, he gave Echidna's hand a lick with one head before trotting off into the forest. I saw him sniffing at the bases of trees, and I thought that he may have been looking for a mouse or creature to chase that had not yet been able to flee the island.

Cerberus must have found something, because all six of his folded ears pricked up, and with a cacophony of barks, he bounded off farther into the woods.

Echidna had already turned back to the giant pot of soup and was stirring in more vegetables.

"You said you may want more children, in the future," I said. "Do you think they will all be like him?"

"I think they will all be what they're meant to be," she answered. "Whether they look like what some people would call monsters or not, they will all be my children."

A smile found its way to my lips before I knew it.

"It suits you," I told her, and Echidna turned slightly so that I could see her face. "Echidna, mother of monsters."

Echidna smiled, all teeth.

I SPENT THE NIGHT sleeping on the floor of Echidna's cave on a pile of soft, woven blankets. Echidna had tried to get me to take her bed, which was a larger pile of blankets on a feather mattress with several squashy pillows, but I refused. When she had tried to push me onto the bed to make me take it, I spun out from her grip and stole a few blankets from the bed before sitting down defiantly against the cave wall and curling up.

"Nope," I told her. "Good night."

She threw one of the pillows at me, spitefully. "Good night, little queen."

I took the pillow and shuffled into a more comfortable position. The scent from Echidna's bedding was sooth-ing, and the floor of the cave was much softer than most of the forest floors I had slept on during my journey, and the gentle curves of the cave walls were not constricting like the stone walls of the Graeae's home. In the depths of Echidna's cave, I felt like I was being protected by a moth-er's embrace.

Cerberus was sniffing around the bottom of the bed with his heads and chest low to the ground and wagging tail held up high. Earlier, he had returned from his romp in the woods when Echidna had begun to pour out bowls of stew. Cerberus had scarfed up his bowl just as soon as Echidna had set it down for him. She put a bowl in front of me too, and I ate it, even though I knew I didn't need to, and I didn't think she needed to either, but it was nice to share the meal we had made together.

Cerberus finally gave up on whatever he was smelling at the base of Echidna's bed and jumped up onto the blan-kets to throw himself down next to Echidna. After she blew out the candle and plunged the room into darkness, she drew her long tail up onto the bed and curved it around her son.

I knew that my mother had never held me, or my sisters, like Echidna held Cerberus now. I wondered what it would feel like to be held close to another being as I slept.

My snakes arranged themselves around the pillow as I laid my head down, a few of them brushing over my face.

I knew they could feel the longing in me, but there was really nothing they could do. With the way I was, I doubted

I would ever be able to sleep so closely with someone else for fear of what would happen should I forget the danger, even for a moment, the following morning.

ON MY FIRST FULL day at the island, Echidna taught me how to fish. This was a skill I had never had to or thought to learn, but as she placed my hands on the simple rod and showed me how to draw back and throw the line, I was surprised at the pleasure I found in focusing on the task. The ocean surrounding the island was bright blue and winked like a precious stone. I could feel the heat of the sun reflecting off its surface and warming my face.

The snakes, ever wary, even when my own defenses were dropped, reminded me not to look at my reflection.

The first fish I caught was small and silver, wiggling valiantly against the line as I tugged it in. I trapped it against the sand with one hand. Its gills fluttered against my palm, and for one second, I met its wide, pale, unblinking eye.

The fish froze immediately. Its silver body turned dull as it transformed into stone.

I stared at the fish. Its body was curved stiffly up around my palm, and I quickly drew my hand back. The sharp movement sent me rocking back from my crouched position and I landed heavily in the sand with a small sound of surprise.

"What is it?" Echidna called out, and I heard the slow rhythmic slide of her tail on the sand.

I put my hands over my face as she drew up next to me. She had to have seen the fish, but she didn't say anything for a while. I heard her move closer to where the little fish rock lay in the sand.

"Well, we certainly can't eat this," she said finally, "but I think it will look nice as a decoration."

Lifting my head from my hands, I looked up at her. She was holding the petrified fish in her hands, turning it this way and that so she could see it from all sides, and I couldn't help the laugh that bubbled up out of my throat. She grinned, too.

She set the fish statue down next to the basket we were meant to be filling with our catch for dinner.

"How about you reel the fish in, and then I put them in the basket," Echidna offered.

I nodded, pressing the backs of my hands into my eyes for one moment before getting back to my feet.

The next fish I brought in was bigger, and it made it all the way to the basket without being turned to stone.

On another day, Cerberus sniffed around my feet one morning after breakfast before taking the hem of my dress in his slobbery mouth and tugging at it.

"Hey," I said, trying to gently pry his teeth open. "This was a gift."

"He wants you to follow him," Echidna told me from where she was sitting in the shade of the tree by the edge of her clearing, where the blankets and pillows sat in a pile. She was weaving something out of thin strips of bark.

"Oh," I said. I stood, and Cerberus immediately let go of my dress and bounded into the forest. I followed him.

Sometimes it was hard to keep my gaze away from all three sets of Cerberus's dark eyes, but other times he was much too busy trying to smell every leaf or dig through a patch of dirt or bark at a twig that twitched to even spare one pair of eyes to look at me. When I had to look at him, I kept my focus on his ears or his tail. One of the ears on the left head was torn and healed, like one of the other heads had bitten a chunk out of it when he was younger.

That morning Cerberus led me on a long walk through the forest, often circling back on the trail we'd already passed over while he followed a smell. Eventually, we came to a far side of the island where there was a low, rocky cliff that dropped off into the sea. The cliff was only about as tall as I was, but the sea bashed against it and sent up a fine salt spray as the tide moved in and out.

Cerberus barked at the water and then turned to me, taking the hem of my dress in his mouth again for one moment before nosing me into the position he wanted me to stand in. When I was in the right place, which was apparently close to the tree line, according to him, he scrambled back toward the flat cliff. His heads snapped at each other playfully.

Then Cerberus shook himself, ears flapping, and stood up tall. His heads went as still as I had ever seen them. With a great sense of purpose, Cerberus picked up one large paw and began to do a sort of march from one side of the low cliff to the other before making an about-face and marching back. When he had completed this pass a few times, he turned toward the ocean, his ears and eyes all pointing outward and his tail held high. Only his wet noses were twitching.

He barked once, and then turned back to me.

I stared at the torn ear.

"Are you…guarding the island?"

He barked again and bounced toward me, his tail thrashing madly.

"You're a very good guard dog," I told him.

I thought he might vibrate out of his body from excitement.

"Did Echidna ask you to do this?" I asked him, as Cerberus darted back and forth between me and his cliff. Even as I asked it, however, I knew what the answer would be.

Echidna wouldn't have asked her own son to guard the island, especially seeing as he was essentially still just a kid, and this place was only discoverable by other immortals. But Cerberus seemed so happy to show off his little prancing march from one side of the cliff to the other. He growled at the crashing waves that threw water high up over the side of the island.

Cerberus paced a bit more, checking in on me every now and then to make sure I was still watching him, and then eventually he decided that he had guarded the island enough for one day. He shook off the salt water that had sprayed him and I jumped back to avoid being dripped on.

It was late when we returned to the clearing in the middle of the island. Cerberus immediately flopped down next to Echidna on the blanket under the trees and fell asleep, one head resting on her tail. She stroked him between his eyebrows.

"How about I make dinner tonight," I offered as I watched them.

Echidna didn't look up from her son, but I heard the smile in her voice. "That would be wonderful. Though if you're only offering because you're worried that if I stand up

I'll disturb him, don't be. This boy could sleep through a hurricane. You've heard how he snores."

I laughed, and then began to put together dinner anyway.

AND SO WEEKS WENT by. Echidna did not ask me why I stayed, or what I was going to do next. I spent many days on the edge of her island high up on the beach, my back to a tree and the sea stretching out in front of me.

My snakes were content to be wherever I was. I knew this, but I could feel that they were also wondering where we were meant to go from here. I had no answer for them, and instead we spent quiet afternoons watching the waves try to climb up the sand.

Not happy, the not-voice spoke up suddenly late one afternoon, when the sun was finally sinking below the horizon and I started thinking I should head back to Echidna's cave before it got too dark.

"What?"

Not happy.

"You're not happy? Why?"

No, the not-voice said, *not just me. We.*

I closed my eyes. "I feel like I should be. Happy, that is. Here, with Echidna, I feel like I should be happy, and I think I could be. But—"

But, the not-voice agreed. *We know why.*

"Can't we just stay here?" It would be so easy, I thought. To simply stay hidden away on Echidna's island, with

Cerberus guarding just one side and Echidna humming quietly as she weaved wonders out of strips of bark and made magic of potatoes, to hide in my bed in Echidna's cave that had begun accumulating more and more blankets as the weather got colder. I had caught Cerberus, one night, dragging a large blanket from his and Echidna's bed over to my pile.

I knew what waited for me once I left this place. Passing Perseus on my way here had been no coincidence, and instead it felt as though that moment that our paths finally crossed had locked our fates into place.

But if I stayed here, if I did not go to the island that was meant to be a home for my sisters and I, then perhaps I could avoid that fate for as long as time would allow. I was immortal now, after all. Perseus may have been the son of a god, but he was still flesh and blood, and he would die someday. Could I wait out his life span here on Echidna's island?

Fate had a patience as wide as the horizon, but I knew I would come to the edge of it someday.

IT WAS MORNING ON the island, Cerberus was sleeping late, and Echidna and I were at her wooden table. I was carving a snake out of a piece of driftwood, just to have something to do with my hands. As the diamond head took shape, my snakes began to eye it curiously.

But then there was a noise in the forest. This was

surprising, first because there were no noises in the forest, second because it sounded like a voice, and third, because it sounded like a voice I recognized.

"Hello? Is anyone actually on this miserable little spit of land?"

"Stheno, don't be rude," a second voice responded, and while I knew that voice too, there was a force behind it that was new.

"Hello?" the first voice called out again, the last vowel dragging out nice and long in the quiet of the morning.

"Is this real?" I whispered to Echidna.

"They're too loud for it not to be," she responded.

I closed my eyes. I had not seen my sisters since we had parted in Athens. The last they had seen of me, I had been a mortal girl desperately trying to find a place where she fit in. That girl I had been felt like a distant memory. But for Stheno and Euryale, she was the only sister they'd ever known. I didn't know how they would react when they saw what I'd become.

Two sets of footsteps approached us, loudly, through the forest, and I heard them stop as they came to the clearing. They came in right behind me. I felt my snakes turn to look.

"Oh my," Euryale said, and my sister sounded the same as she had when I'd last talked to her, what felt like years and years ago.

"It's true then," Stheno snapped. She sounded the same, too.

"Hello, Gorgons," Echidna called over my shoulder. She reached across the table, out of my sister's sight, and laid her hand over mine. Grounding me.

The snakes were calm, belying the rapid beat of my heart. There was so much I wanted to say, but instead I asked, "How are you here?"

"We've been looking for you," Euryale said, and I thought that I must have been a fool to ever believe I could outlast the Fates.

Gorgons

As it turns out, my sisters had been looking for me for quite some time.

"We went to that wine god's mountain," Stheno said, her scathing tone very telling of what she thought of Dionysus's home and the people who stayed with him.

My sisters sat on one side of the table, while Echidna and I sat on the other. I kept my gaze trained down, still fiddling with the wooden snake I had carved. I had not looked at my sisters yet. While they did not seem so surprised at my appearance, I did not know how much they knew about the power I had and how much caution they would spare me. It was easier for me to look away.

"There were many mortals there," Euryale added. "They seemed to be having fun."

"That wasn't fun, that was raving," Stheno shot back.

"Either way, they enjoyed it. Dionysus was nice," Euryale concluded.

I asked, "You spoke to him?"

Stheno made a noise that signaled a snarky remark, but Euryale cut her off.

"Yes! That was why we traveled there, to speak with him. We had heard that you were staying with him from a water naiad or something, I wasn't quite sure what she was, I should have asked." Euryale softly drummed on the table with both hands. "Oh well. Anyway, she told us that word had spread through her kind that you were staying with Dionysus. We had been looking for you for a bit by then, but this was the first actual word we ever got of your whereabouts, so we were really relieved to finally have a direction." Euryale inhaled sharply, and then kept going. "So, the naiad told us how to get there, but once we'd arrived you'd already gone. Dionysus, though, he was very kind. We told him we were your sisters and asked if he knew where you'd gone, and it took him a bit of time to get to the point." I smiled as Euryale went on, both at the memory of how Dionysus could get into a ramble and how Euryale seemed to be doing the same now. "But he finally told us that you had set out to find Echidna. Then of course, we had to find out where Echidna was, and that took some more time, though luckily the Graeae lived pretty close to Dionysus, did you know that?"

She waited for a response, so I nodded my head, just once. I was a bit shocked at the sheer volume of words tumbling out of Euryale's mouth. She had been happy enough to let Stheno speak for her when we were younger, and I wondered what had changed in the time we had been apart that had helped her find her voice.

Euryale continued, "Yeah, they live very close to his

mountain, so we went and saw them and they lived in this deep dark cave and—"

"They told us you had another prophecy," Stheno cut in. My snakes, who were busy sifting between my old memories of Stheno and evaluating the real thing before them, tensed and curled up protectively at her tone. I didn't stop them.

"And they told us where Echidna lived," Euryale finished quickly. My snakes didn't seem to mind her much at all.

"Is that why you came?" I asked, my fingers tightening on the diamond-shaped head of the wooden snake. "Because of the prophecy?"

"No," Stheno said, "we were looking for you before we ever heard of it. Weren't you listening? We had made up our minds to come find you, even before we heard the rumors about your...change." Stheno said the last word carefully, like it was a fragile thing. "But it's true then. The prophecy."

My snakes hissed, and this time I did shush them. I closed my fist around the wooden snake and closed my eyes. "How much did the crones tell you?"

My sisters were quiet for a moment, and it felt like one of the silent stretches from my childhood where they would share a knowing glance, conveying words to each other I would never hear or understand. Then, Euryale spoke.

"The Graeae told us that we would be together again. Us, the Gorgons. And that we would live together like we did when we were younger. But they also said that once that happened, someone would come for you. To—" She dropped off.

Stheno picked up the thread of her point, blunt as ever. "To kill you."

Echidna, who had been listening silently the whole time,

finally spoke up. "And so you both decided it was right to come here and find her? To set that prophecy into motion?"

"It has been in motion," Stheno shot back, though I could hear her getting defensive. "We did not think our actions would influence it either way."

"All actions have their influences," Echidna said, "whether you see it or not."

Stheno began to argue back with quick, biting words, but Echidna was not thrown off by her callousness. I was glad that Echidna had asked the question that had been on my mind. The wooden snake was pressing indents into my palm with how tightly I was gripping it, and I forced myself to take slow, deep breaths, until I felt that I could keep my voice level.

"He will only come once I am content," I said, and Stheno and Echidna fell silent. "The boy will come to kill me at the home we make for ourselves when I am at peace with what my life has become."

There were no birds or animals on the island to make soft noises to disrupt the silence that laid thickly over the clearing. My snakes were torn in their emotions, half of them wanting to keep a wary eye on Stheno and Euryale, and half of them fretting over me as I considered my fated demise. I propped my elbow on the table and leaned my cheek on my empty fist. My head felt so heavy.

"We came here because we wanted to ask you a question," Euryale said. With a slight scraping sound, she reached across the table and laid her hand over my fist clutching the wooden snake. Her hand was warm. I could not remember either of my sisters ever touching me with purpose; we had brushed arms when I stood between them and their shoulders would knock into mine when they pushed past me to dart away and play a game I was not invited to join, but this was the first time Euryale had held my hand.

"What?" I asked softly, eyes still closed.

"Do you want to come with us?"

I lifted my cheek off my fist. "Come with you where?"

"To the island, or whatever place, wherever we are meant to find a new home," Euryale said, and there were conflicting notes in her voice I had trouble picking out. She sounded like she regretted asking the question even as the words came out, but she also sounded as though she could not wait for the answer. "Do you want to be together again?"

"Close your eyes," Echidna said, and I was about to tell her they were already closed when she specified, "Both of you."

Stheno sent out a sharp burst of air from her nose, but Euryale was quiet.

Echidna tapped me on the arm a moment later. "Okay, Medusa. You can look."

I hesitated.

"Don't open your eyes," I warned my sisters. "I cannot control it once you've seen."

Stheno and Euryale both made noises of agreement, and I opened my eyes, looking down at the table at first before slowly raising my gaze to look at my sisters for the first time in years.

They were immortal, and so very little had changed about their appearance. Stheno was still a savage beauty, all straight angles and sharp lines, and Euryale had soft, full cheeks and our mother's finely shaped mouth. Stheno's hair was pulled back from her face and braided into a knot at the back of her head. Euryale's hair hung freely down her shoulders like it had when we were girls.

Both of their eyes were shut, but Euryale had her eyelids pressed down so tightly that the skin around the corners of her eyes crinkled and folded. I thought she looked a bit like a child thinking it could hide from danger just by not allowing themselves to see it. At least she was listening to me. Stheno's eyes were shut, but her brow had a wrinkle in it like she was focusing hard on something. I thought she was likely to open her eyes if I made one wrong move.

Seeing the two of them together, though, shoulder to shoulder like they had always been in my childhood, sent a wave of nostalgia over me that I was not prepared for. I remembered how it felt when I had stood between them. How we had formed a wall of defense to protect ourselves from the Graeae. How I had wanted so desperately to feel like I had belonged with them, even for a moment.

And now they were here asking me to do just that. They had been following me for what sounded like months, but even after making the trip here and finally finding me, they were leaving the choice up to me. They wouldn't force me to join them. But they were letting me know that the space between them was available to me once again.

"You would have me go with you," I said, watching their faces. "Why?"

Stheno's brows drew together in a hard line, and I braced for the biting answer, but Euryale spoke first. "We want you to know that you are still a part of this, of us, the Gorgons.

We can't be the Gorgons without you. And we know that something awful is waiting for you down the path that we're offering, but it felt wrong not to give you the choice, to let you know that you don't have to be alone in this." She fidgeted in her seat. "You should have never been alone."

Euryale's face was still the open book it had always been, and so I could tell that she was being sincere. Stheno, too, could not hide what she was feeling, especially since she seemed to be struggling with her thoughts.

Stheno said, "I may not be able to understand what you've gone through, or what you've become, but that is no fault of yours. Euryale has proven to me," she tilted her head toward her sister, "that we are not as different as I made myself believe."

"Proven?" I asked, looking to Euryale's pinched face.

"I have a scream," Euryale blurted out. "I mean, I can scream. But it's not a normal scream. I can make this sound that would really hurt anyone who hears it. Not that I've done that, only by accident, one time, and I felt so terrible afterward, and I really wanted to tell you about it, Medusa, once I heard your first prophecy! But by then, you had already pulled away from us." Her voice shook. "I didn't want you to think I was mocking you. And I didn't want to burden you with my own problems when you had just been shouldered with the Graeae's prophecy."

"Euryale—" I started, but her words were flooding out in a torrent now.

"I didn't tell Stheno either! She only found out recently, when I realized that I could have kept us together if only I had been honest with you. She needed to hear it. But I also needed to say it out loud. I had been denying that part of me for so long, hiding it, because I was so frightened of what you both would think of me."

At this, Stheno groped blindly for Euryale's hand and gripped it.

"I may not have a prophecy," Euryale said, interrupted by a loud sniffle. "But Medusa, you are not alone in this. I, too, am a monster." She felt at her throat. "I can cause destruction, with just my voice. You wield it with your eyes."

I had always thought, even when they despised me, that Euryale was the kindest amongst us. Knowing about her power did not change that. It was just another piece of her.

"And Stheno," I prompted, cautiously.

"Has nothing," Stheno said flatly. "Except for you and her."

Echidna leaned forward, head cocked. She watched Stheno for a long moment, long enough that I reached out and touched her on the arm, a silent question. Waving me off, she sat back again.

"We have our differences, but we are still the Gorgons," Stheno went on. "And now that you've become someone worthy of a legend, I dare say you will defy everything that our mother and father thought about you. You will be remembered."

Echidna finally spoke up. "While I am in full support of you three finding some common ground, it sounds as though you only came to Medusa now because of the second prophecy. Sisters you may be, but the Gorgons are fated to go down in legacy thanks to Medusa. Have you only come here to be in her shadow?"

"No," Euryale and Stheno said together.

"Then why?" I asked again. Euryale's power did not come with a visible marking, as mine had. She could have kept it concealed to everyone except Stheno, and no one would have called her a monster.

"It's..." Euryale said, fiddling with something in her lap as she worked out the words. I saw a flash of white, like a shell. "It's like everyone knows who you are now, Medusa, both the mortals and immortals alike, and they've all got these opinions about you based on the stories that get passed around. And I know we haven't seen you for years, but those stories, at least most of them, didn't sound like you at all. I remember from when we were girls. We didn't...well, we treated you really bad, to be honest." I snorted as Stheno made a noise of dissent and Euryale slapped at her arm. "Quiet, Stheno, you know we did. You even admitted it, remember? We treated you terribly, Medusa, even though you were our sister, but then when we needed you, you were always there. You would protect us, despite how awful we were. And so those stories that paint you as some terrible monster who attacks for no reason, I just don't believe them. We don't believe them."

She paused for a moment, and then elbowed Stheno in the side. My sister winced and frowned, but agreed, "We don't believe them."

"You don't think I'm a monster?" I asked. Echidna stirred next to me, but I held up my hand so that she'd stay quiet.

"We think that whatever you've done, you've done to protect yourself," Stheno said firmly. "We think that it was time for us to come and tell you that not everyone is against you. We think that whatever kind of legend you become in our history," she tilted her head up, eyes still closed, but I could imagine the sharp glint in them all the same, "we want to be on the right side of it. On your side."

My snakes, who had hissed every time Stheno had spoken thus far, were silent as they stared at my sister. One of them flicked their tongue at her, tasting for a lie.

"We don't think you're the monster that the mortal men make you out to be," Euryale said softly.

I felt my eyes prickle, and it wasn't because of my power. My sisters and I had been separated for a long time, and they could have easily believed any of the stories they had heard about me, and yet they had chosen to come to me anyway and ignore the words of mortals. Perhaps it was because they were immortals who distrusted mortals inherently—but they had come despite the word of a god, too.

"I have accepted that others will think of me as a monster," I told them. "And I've also accepted that I am monstrous because of my actions, but I intend to embrace that title and not let it tear me apart. I am fine with being monstrous," I said, and it was the truth. "Let others fear me for what I have done, because those who would fear me for protecting myself and those that I love deserve to hold that terror in their hearts."

"History will not remember you that way," Stheno told me.

"That is fine. You have shown me that there are those who will see beyond the legend, beyond the stories of mortal men, to see who I actually am," I said. "Both of you, and Echidna as well, have proven that my monstrosity is not something that will set everyone against me. You see me."

Euryale smiled, eyes still closed, and said, "Well, sort of."

"Right," I said slowly. I made a decision and stood. The three women startled at my sudden movement, but they all kept their eyes off me. I stepped around the table, and then remembered the wooden snake I was still clutching in my hand and turned back to carefully uncurl my fingers and place it on the table next to Echidna's weaving. The wood made a soft *clack* as I set it down. I headed toward the forest, calling over my shoulder, "You can open your eyes. I want you to follow me."

There was the slight scraping noise of Echidna's tail on the ground as she did as I asked, though I could tell that my sisters were slower to get to their feet. Stheno said something quick and fast under her breath to Euryale. Euryale replied, louder, "Of course she wouldn't. Don't be mean."

"I won't petrify you now, Stheno," I said clearly, speaking to the trees but knowing that my sisters could hear. "I want to show you the same amount of trust that you have shown me."

Another scrape, the log bench being shoved back from the table, and some quick footsteps hurried after Echidna. I moved forward, and the three women followed me.

There was a small pool of fresh water on the island. Cerberus had shown it to me once during one of our long walks, though he had raced toward it and then jumped in with a great splash when we were near enough. I led Echidna and my sisters there. Echidna may have known where I was going, but she did not say anything.

A light breeze ruffled the leaves in the trees, shaking a few of them from the thin twigs at the edge of the branches.

Those leaves fluttered to the ground, adding to the carpet of foliage.

The pool was still when I finally came upon it, and I made sure to skirt around it with enough room to avoid my reflection.

"Come to the edge," I told them, "and look into the water, please." I kept my gaze down on the forest floor as I turned on the opposite side of the pool to face them.

"What is this?" Stheno asked.

"It is a pool of water," Echidna said dryly. "Surely you have come across them before, Stheno." She was already perched at the water's edge.

Euryale giggled as she stepped up beside Echidna. Stheno muttered something under her breath and inched forward.

"I have found," I explained, "that I can look upon others, while they look upon me, through the reflection of a surface and not harm them. There was someone I trusted, and I saw her reflection by accident, but she did not turn to stone." I wanted them to understand that I did not want to hurt them.

"She saw your eyes?" Echidna asked.

I nodded, and then answered when I realized she wouldn't be able to see me yet. "She told me they were green."

Stheno finally stepped all the way up to the pool's edge.

I took a careful step forward, my eyes still down. A leaf landed on the surface of the still pool, the small ripples caused by its landing ruining the flat effect.

"Please, look only at the water. That is the only way I know the power will not work," I warned them.

Euryale said soothingly, "Okay, Medusa. We trust you."

Echidna agreed. "Obviously."

Stheno said, "Show us."

I stepped up to the water's edge and raised my eyes, skipping over my own reflection to see the images of the three women before me flipped upside down. The faint ripples from the leaf faded away slowly and the smooth surface of the pool returned.

Their faces were distorted slightly in the water's reflection, though I could still clearly see their expressions as they met my eyes for the first time. I looked at Echidna's image first, as I had been waiting to meet her gaze the longest, ever since I had arrived on this island. But I had been too scared to try and test the reflections again after Naidah. It was Stheno and Euryale's confidence in me that had moved me to share this with them, to trust them with this one weak point of my power.

Echidna was smiling at me. I thought that perhaps her eyes were wet with tears, but it was hard to be sure through the reflected double.

"Hello, little queen," she said.

I smiled back at her and my snakes curled lazily around my face, their attention flickering between the three women and their duplicates in the pool.

I looked to Euryale next. Her eyes were wide as saucers, and she had her hands clasped in front of her chest.

She said, "Your eyes match your snakes!"

"So I've been told." I laughed as my snakes wiggled with joy. They liked that we matched.

Stheno's eyes were slits as she peered at my reflection. I waited for her to look her fill of my face. She opened her eyes bit by bit, until she was able to look me over fully, and then she crossed her arms.

She asked, "Why does it not work like this?"

"I'm not sure," I said, looking between all three of them. "I discovered it by accident. I wasn't sure if it happened because I wished it to or if it was because of a loophole in this power that I didn't know existed. I can't..." I had never told anyone of how the snakes spoke to me, how they warned me away from my own reflection, and I wanted to keep their counsel to myself. "I just know that I cannot look at my own reflection. If I do, my power will turn itself against me."

"You mean, if you look at yourself, you'll be turned to stone?" Euryale asked, shocked.

I nodded.

"There really is no way to control it, then," Echidna said. Although she did not sound surprised, I could tell that she, like I once had, was hoping that there was a way for me to take full control of this power. But the truth was not as kind as that hope.

I found that the lack of control no longer frightened me, however. As long as I knew the truth of my power, like I knew the truth of my monstrosity, I would not let it overcome me. In this way, I did have control over the power inside me.

"It is all right," I told them. I met each of their gazes. "I have come this far. And I have been able to see you all again, despite what has happened to me. I would deserve your pity only when I let the curse drive me to hide out of fear."

"Was that not what you were doing here, on this spit of land?" Stheno asked. Euryale elbowed her again, but my sister simply stared down at our crossed reflections.

"Perhaps at first," I admitted. "But I was not ashamed of what this power could do, or what I could do with it. You know of the prophecy." My sisters nodded. "I did think about how long I would be able to stretch out the timeline of my fate here with Echidna. I thought, Perseus is only mortal, while I am mortal no longer. I thought, perhaps he will die before he gets the chance to find me. I thought, how far can I test fate?"

I reached up with one hand and let the snakes twine themselves through my fingers, circling around my wrist like thick bracelets.

"And you have brought my answer to me, Stheno, Euryale. The Fates will grant me no more time. So, my choices are this," I said. "Either I run now, and live the rest of my days in fear of the end that has been promised to me, in fear of happiness, or I go with you and seek out that happiness myself and greet my demise face on. I believe there is only one way where I will have control." My snakes tightened their grip on me, imperceptibly, but I curled my fingers around them in return. "I will go with you, sisters. I want to be happy. Let us find our new home together."

BEFORE MY SISTERS AND I left the island, Echidna and I brought Stheno and Euryale back to the clearing to meet Cerberus. My sisters obviously didn't know what to expect when Echidna told them that they should meet her son, just as I had when I first arrived, and I grinned to myself as I led the way back to the clearing.

Right as we stepped through the trees and into the grass, Echidna whistled.

The telltale crashing and thumping of Cerberus waking up echoed up through the cave opening, and Euryale jumped. Stheno was watching the cave warily, but her hand was braced on Euryale's arm.

After a few more moments of Cerberus knocking into Echidna's sparse furniture in his sleepy daze, I could hear his heavy footsteps scrabbling up to the cave entrance. I smiled as he tumbled out into the clearing with a symphony of barks to greet the strangers at his doorstep.

Stheno's incredulous noise was covered up by Euryale squealing, "A puppy!"

Cerberus angled his three heads toward my sisters and bounded over to them. Euryale knelt down to greet him, but Stheno just eyed him, her shoulders tight and her hands clutched up high to her chest. Cerberus didn't seem to notice her, too preoccupied with trying to get all three of his tongues to lick a part of Euryale's face or arms or neck all at once. She giggled as he pushed up into her space.

"Oh, Echidna," she crowed. "He's beautiful!"

"Indeed he is," Echidna agreed. She flicked Stheno a glance but didn't say anything as she slid past my sisters to sit at the table once more.

"What is its—his—name?" Stheno asked.

"Cerberus," I answered.

The corner of Stheno's mouth twitched, and she peered

down at the three-headed dog with a sharp eye. She seemed to be looking for something.

"Cerberus," she repeated slowly, and then, "But he doesn't have any spots?" She sounded almost accusatory.

Echidna, who had picked up the weaving she had been working on before my sisters had arrived, looked up from the table. She stared at Stheno. Then, without warning, she threw back her head and burst into laughter.

I blinked, looking between Stheno, Echidna, and Cerberus, who had turned one head to *woof* lovingly at his mother as she laughed. In our language, Cerberus's name was quite close to our word *kerberos*, which meant "spotted." Stheno was right, however, as Cerberus's thick fur was an unbroken dark brown all the way from the tips of his six ears to his toes.

Echidna's laughter faded, though she was still chuckling when she said, "I was wondering when his name was going to come back and haunt me. He was born with spots around his middle, but they faded after a month or so."

"How old is he now?" Stheno asked.

"It'll be six months the next full moon," Echidna said idly.

"This dog is only *six months old*?"

I could understand Stheno's confusion, since the top of Cerberus's heads already came up to my hips. Cerberus acted like a puppy, tripping over paws that were still too big for him and jumping on every new smell or sound, but he was already the size of many full-grown dogs I'd seen. If the width of his feet were any indication, I thought that Cerberus could easily pass me in height by the time he was one year old.

302

"How big do you think he's going to be?" Euryale asked, her voice full of wonder as she scratched under Cerberus's middle chin, while the other two heads tried to shove their way in to steal the attention. Euryale brought the other hand up to appease one of them. The head that was left out nipped at the middle one's ears.

"No idea," Echidna answered. "I suppose that's up to him."

"He likes being a guard dog," I said. I kept my eyes on Cerberus's tail thwacking on the ground. "If he has his way, I'll bet he grows up as tall as the trees around us."

Despite what I had just said, Cerberus rolled over onto his back to allow Euryale to scratch his tummy, looking the opposite of a fearsome guard dog. All three of his tongues lolled out of his mouths as she obliged him. He went half mad with happiness as she found just the right spot on his stomach and his back leg began to twitch uncontrollably.

"Guard dog," Stheno repeated flatly.

"Guard dog," Echidna echoed. "Well, I suppose he'd be good for it. It'd be hard to get past all those eyes."

"He has been practicing already," I told her.

"Who's gonna be the best guard dog?" Euryale cooed. "Who's gonna be the best boy? You are!"

Cerberus wiggled with happiness.

"What will he guard?" Stheno asked over the noise of Cerberus's tail thumping on the grass.

"Something important, I'm sure," I said. "But for now, I think he's happy just guarding his home."

Cerberus remained on his back as Euryale scratched up and down his stomach, searching for places that made his legs twitch. When she finally leaned back, he remained in his belly-up position for a moment, frozen, waiting to see if she would come back. Then he scrambled over to his feet and bounded toward Echidna.

Echidna leaned down to cup the middle head's chin. He licked her nose.

"Well," she said, and even though she was looking at her son, she was speaking to me, "if you're going to be leaving us soon, we'd better give you a good farewell dinner."

I smiled a little morosely. "If you must."

Echidna kissed each of Cerberus's heads between the ears and stood from the table. She began to gather ingredients from her stock near the cave and asked Euryale and Stheno to help prepare the soup. My sisters went, a bit apprehensively. I wondered when the last time either of them had eaten something. I knew that they had never cooked anything in the time we were together, though I hoped this was not their first attempt at it.

Echidna didn't seem to mind or didn't notice their slow movements as they copied everything she did, peeking over each other's shoulders.

Once my sisters were staring intently into the large pot Echidna had simmering over the fire, trading off who got to stir the stew with the large serving spoon, Echidna came over to the table where I was sitting and scratching Cerberus behind an ear. She set a bowl in front of me and pointed at it.

"Mix it."

I mixed. The bowl held a loose, sweet-smelling dough that began to thicken as I folded it with my spoon. Echidna checked in on the dough every once in a while, and then when she saw the consistency she wanted, she brought me a pan and told me to measure out equal portions into the size of my fist. She gave me some flour to dust on my hands.

The dough was sticky and hard to work with, but I got six fist-sized portions laid out on the pan and let Cerberus lick the doughy residue from my fingers.

"Medusa," Echidna said quietly, when she returned to the table. "I feel that I must ask, because you will not. Why could this not be the island you find your happiness on?"

I stared at the bits of flour and dough clinging stubbornly to my hands, rolling them between my fingers so they would flake off.

"I think," I said, "I could make myself very happy here. With you. But that would mean that Perseus would come here, to your home, to seek me out. I would not be able to live with myself, in this life or the next, if he harmed you or Cerberus to get to me. And I think that concern," I explained, "is why I would never be fully content. I need to be sure that you can keep living in peace. I need to know that at least one life is not ruined because of me."

Echidna laid her hand on my arm, squeezing gently.

"Okay," she said. "I wish it could be different, but okay. Just know," and she tightened her grip on my arm, "my life is better, because you were in it. All that you are, all your monstrosity, has only made me love you more."

I covered her hand with mine, smearing flour over her skin as I gripped her back.

"Thank you."

Echidna let go of me after a moment and took the pan of dough I had been working on back to the fire where she began to lay the dough out on the flat rock she often used to bake thin breads. Cerberus, seeming to sense the somber mood that had settled over me, put his heads in my lap. I stroked him behind the ears.

While the buns cooked slowly, as there were only embers simmering beneath the flat cooking rock, Echidna ladled out large bowls of stew for me, my sisters, and Cerberus. I ate unhurriedly, as I always did, watching as my sisters took small sips of the broth. Euryale's eyes widened after the first spoonful, and she quickly moved on to bigger bites of stew. Stheno ate as I did.

With the sun setting much earlier in the day this late in the year, we were dining early in the evening. The glade was still lit with weak sunlight. The treetops shivered in the sea breeze, and I thought about how difficult it would be to leave this place.

But then Euryale asked if food had always tasted this good, and Stheno said certainly not, and Euryale turned to me, eyes focused on a point somewhere near my collarbone, to ask what kinds of foods I liked.

"I don't really need to eat anymore, like both of you," I said, "but Echidna's cooking is the best I've ever had, for sure."

After we had finished the stew, Cerberus licking all our bowls clean, Echidna took the cakes off the embers. She placed them back on the floured tray and brought it to the table along with a stoppered jug and a small pot. Cerberus hounded her tail the entire way from the fire to the table.

"No," she laughed, holding the tray high up so that

Cerberus could not topple it, "not yet, you know better. They're not done."

She placed the tray in the middle of the table and took the cork out of the jug. The sweet smell of honey spilled out, and my snakes flicked their tongues in the air appreciatively. Echidna smiled at them as she poured generous amounts of golden honey over each cake until it dripped down the sides. Then she took up the pot and sprinkled a sweet, sugary crumble over the lot of it.

"There," Echidna said with a satisfied smile, setting down the pot. "Honey cakes. They're Cerberus's favorite."

Cerberus had all three of his noses snuffling at the edge of the table. Before he could jump up and snatch up every cake from the tray, I peeled a sticky cake off the table and pulled it into three parts. Cerberus followed the smell of the hot cake and honey, and I laughed as I dropped a piece into each of his mouths. He drooled onto the ground as he snapped them up.

Stheno made a noise of disgust, but Euryale covered it up with another crow of delight.

I took another cake for myself, my fingers already sticky with honey and coated in the crumbly topping. The cake was sweet and still warm on my tongue. Euryale made another noise as she bit into her own cake, and she tried to say "it's so good" with her mouth still full, so the words came out in more of a muffled jumble.

"Thank you," Echidna said, understanding what she meant.

Stheno seemed to enjoy the cake too, since she took

larger bites of it than she had with the stew, and her cake disappeared around the same time as everyone else's. I let Cerberus lick my hands clean when I was done. When he had licked every drop of honey off my fingers, he began to sniff around the edge of the table again. Echidna quickly lifted the tray and clicked her tongue at him.

"Nope! No more, I don't want you to get sick," she said as she took the cakes away and transferred them into a covered basket. "You'd eat until you passed out if you could."

Cerberus trailed behind her as she put the cakes away, his tail hanging down, but his ears were still cocked in the half hope of begging off just one more. Echidna didn't fall for it.

Later, my sisters, Echidna, and I sat sprawled on the grass near the tree line. I lay flat on my back, looking up at the stars as they blinked into existence in the steadily darkening sky. Echidna was teaching Euryale how to weave a simple basket. Stheno sat with her legs tucked up underneath her, her gaze switching between Echidna's and Euryale's hands and the surrounding forest.

"No one is out there," I said quietly the next time I caught her scanning the trees.

She stiffened and said, "I know that."

"Then what are you looking for?"

"I'm not looking for anything," she said, even as her eyes flicked back to the woods. I stayed silent, and she sighed sharply. "Aren't you at least a little bit worried about someone being out there? Or at least worried about what might be coming for you?"

I dug my fingers into the grass. I wondered if Stheno was

worried about her safety in proximity to me, but then, she and Euryale had said that they had heard how the mortals feared me, and they knew how that fear could turn to violence. And they had still come. Stheno's concern was for my well-being.

I said, "Whatever is out there waiting for me, I know that it will not come here. There is no use worrying about it."

Still lying flat on my back, I released my grip on the grass and slid my hand over the ground, palm up. I let it rest a few spaces away from Stheno's foot. She took a moment before placing her hand over mine.

"And when we leave here?" she whispered.

I curled my fingers around hers and held on tight until she gripped me back.

"Then we will face what fate sets in our path with our heads held high, and our eyes open."

The Graeae

THE GRAEAE DID NOT get visitors often. In their younger days, they had traveled the country revealing prophecies to their unlucky subjects. Due to the distressing and grim nature of the prophecies that the Graeae were able to produce, legend of the three sisters had spread and most mortals feared receiving any fortune that came from them. Once they had begun squatting in the dim cave in the recesses of Delphi's cliffs, however, the Graeae saw fewer and fewer mortals.

This did not bother them too much, since they did not like mortals. However, the prophecies did not cease, and the three sisters' minds were cluttered and cramped with all the untold fortunes that their gods-blessed eye revealed.

"On a day when the sun touches the moon," Pemphredo muttered to her sisters, "he will crack his leg on the northern rocks."

"Who will?" Enyo asked.

"A boy," Deino said.

"Which boy?"

Pemphredo covered the eye with one wrinkled hand. "Don't know."

Deino said, "Who cares."

"The boy will," Enyo said.

"Hello?" called a male voice from the mouth of the cave.

The Graeae stiffened in their crouched positions around the dim fire. Pemphredo uncovered her eye and snatched the tooth from Enyo's mouth. Her sister hissed gummily at her, but then fell silent at the sound of footsteps.

"Who approaches the Graeae sisters three?" Pemphredo rasped.

"My name is Perseus."

A boy still a few months from becoming a man stepped into the faint light of the fire in front of the Graeae. He was handsome, the Graeae thought, in the way that mortal men could only achieve if they had divine blood in their veins. His face showed that he knew this.

Then the Graeae remembered.

"A boy," Pemphredo said, "who seeks a monster's head."

"Yes," Perseus said.

"How did you find us?" Pemphredo asked, her sisters whispering to each other uneasily.

The boy peered at them over the fire, and his lip curled as he took in their gray skin, their thin, patchy hair, and their five black empty eye sockets.

"An old woman told me," he said. "She showed me the way."

"Old woman," Pemphredo repeated. "What old woman? There are no women here who would be able to pass through the wall."

"I did not ask her name. She carried a wooden staff. She was blind."

A blind woman with a staff, the Graeae thought, should have been the last to know where the Graeae's cave was.

"She told me you could tell me where to find the monster I seek."

The Graeae remembered a prophecy that had crashed through them like a tidal wave. The subject had sought them out. This was already uncommon for the Graeae, more so that the subject had already received a prophecy from the Graeae in her youth and had received yet another. Then again, the being who came to the Graeae seeking her prophecy was very different from the girl they had scorned in childhood.

"We may know the information you seek," Pemphredo muttered. She touched her fingers to the skin under the eye.

The Graeae had heard Medusa's scream once she fled their cave, the day she had received her second prophecy. It had been the scream of a woman broken down to the roots and ripped from the soil, the scream of one who had nothing to hold her down. The Graeae had flinched as it echoed through their cave. They did not feel guilty about what they had told Medusa about her future. She had asked, after all. But that scream had haunted the Graeae's ears for many days to come.

The Graeae had wondered what had become of Medusa after that. Surely one who had been able to let out a scream like that was not going to find her happiness any time soon.

Now the Graeae wondered how close to the end of their

second prophecy Medusa had come. Had Medusa found happiness? Was that why the boy finally sought her?

The Graeae thought, *Could we give her more time?*

Perseus was not patient.

"Give me the answers I seek," he demanded.

Pemphredo asked, "Why?"

Calm as a lion during a hunt, Perseus leaped over the low fire, caught ahold of Pemphredo's ear, and dug his fingers into her eye socket. He pulled the eye out and held it high above his head.

"Tell me!" he shouted at them.

The Graeae screamed. Pemphredo whimpered and thrashed under Perseus's grip, but he was stronger than her.

"Give it back! Give it back!" the Graeae screeched.

Perseus stretched the hand holding the eye higher and began to squeeze it. He said, "Not until you tell me where to find the stone-maker! The snake-haired monster! Tell me where to find the Gorgon Medusa!"

Deino scrambled over to Pemphredo and ripped the tooth from her mouth. She shoved it into her own rotting gums.

"Go to the sea," she cried. "Go south, past the waters where a chance meeting has left your men hardened. You will find her with her sisters on an island that has no trees."

Perseus stared at Deino for a moment, Pemphredo's ear still held in his tight grip. Then he nodded. He released Pemphredo and she collapsed onto the ground and scrambled back, away from Perseus and out of the light of the fire.

"Give me something to kill it with," Perseus demanded.

Deino hissed, but shuffled through the shadows behind the sisters and drew out four objects. The first was a pair of sandals with thick, white feathers attached to the sides, fluttering softly as they were lifted.

"The winged sandals of Hermes," Deino explained.

The second object was a gold helmet, with panels that would only cover the top of the head and the eyes.

"Hades's cap of invisibility."

The third object was a sword. It was quite short and curved, like a sickle, and it came in a worn leather sheath. Deino tied the fourth object to it, a dark canvas bag.

"A sword to behead her," Deino said, "and a bag to hold the head."

After raking his gaze over every object, Perseus brought the Graeae's eye down and looked at it, another curl of disgust forming on his handsome mouth. He dropped the eye in front of the sisters. Deino heard the faint thud of the eye hitting the floor, and she darted forward to run her hands along the ground until her fingers bumped into it. She snatched it up and clutched it protectively to her thin chest. Perseus gathered up his new possessions, placing the cap on his head for a moment to watch his body disappear before tying it to his belt along with the sword and the bag. He held the sandals in one hand.

"Leave now, boy," Deino rasped.

Perseus spun on his heel and strode away, his shoulders straight. He wiped off the fingers that had clutched the eye on his pants.

"Bah," Pemphredo spat from the shadows.

As his steps faded, Enyo spoke to her sisters. "They're getting worse."

"Demigods?" Deino asked.

"Men."

They resettled around the fire, withered shoulders huddled close together. Pemphredo rubbed her spindly fingers over her mouth.

"I hate to see him succeed," she said.

"More than we would like to see Medusa fall?" Enyo wondered.

For the first time, the Graeae thought about the possibility that one of their prophecies would not come to fruition as they had predicted it. During all their centuries, the sisters had taken what they had foreseen as set in stone. They did not see events in terms of good versus evil, hero versus monster. They were simply outcomes.

For the first time, the Graeae considered the chance that fate had been wrong. But perhaps "wrong" was too decisive—could fate have been misled? The Graeae had seen the gods intervene in the lives of mortals, both those they favored and those they hated, time and time again. This prophecy was weighed down with the touch of a goddess like a sword with a gilded hilt, tilting the balance just a bit too far to be practical.

For the first time, the Graeae wondered if the prophecy they had laid out at Medusa's feet would result in more than just an outcome. They did not want to see the boy-hero triumph. But did they want to see Medusa prevail over this boy, the gods, even fate itself? Out of all the beings that received prophecies from the Graeae, why was their sibling, who had been so unremarkable as a child, in the position to upend everything the Graeae believed in?

Deino lifted her thin hands over the fire.

"Our hand in this is done," she said.

"But the mark remains," Pemphredo added.

Enyo spoke for them all. "We have sent death to the stone-making Gorgon's door. She knows what is coming. Only she has the power to answer the knock, or become death herself."

Sisters three

MY SISTERS HAD TRAVELED to Echidna's island on a boat. It was four times the size of the raft I had used to cross the ocean and carved from a light wood that reflected brightly off the clear ocean surface. The day of our departure from Echidna's was dawning slowly, the early morning sun steadily building in warmth over the sea's horizon.

"Mother made it for us," Euryale told me when she saw me studying the boat.

I blinked, surprised, and scoured the ship again. I had missed the figurehead at the bow of the ship, which was one of the sharp-toothed fish creatures our mother favored, and as I recalled the delicately elaborate style of Ceto's under-water chariot I saw more and more of those elements in the boat's design. The boat was slightly listed on its side, the sails and rigging hanging limp on the mast.

"Did she ask where you were going with it?" I asked, wondering how long ago my sisters had spoken to our mother. I had not heard from her since I was a girl. Since I was mortal.

Stheno said, "No. We just said we needed a way to cross the ocean."

Euryale hummed in agreement. She had the hem of her dress lifted almost to her knees as she dipped her toes in the shallow surf. Stheno was standing higher up on the dry sand next to me. Euryale kicked at the surf and smiled as she spattered drops of water and foam in a small arch over the receding tide.

"Can you sail?" I asked.

"Not really," Euryale said, "but I think Mother must have done something to it, since we just had to think about finding you and the boat sort of steered itself. It will probably work if we ask it to find us a new home, too!"

"It does need one of us to steer," Stheno explained further. "When you hold the helm and think of where you need to go, you'll feel the direction that the ship wants to go in and you have to angle it to set it on the right course."

The ship's innate sense of direction sounded similar to my snakes' ability to guide me wherever I wanted to go.

Not same, the not-voice said, almost snottily. *We have minds, we use our senses. Not just a piece of wood.*

A few of the snakes flicked their tongues out pointedly, and I smiled and let out a soft snort of amusement.

"What?" Stheno asked.

"Nothing," I said. "It's just that I find it amusing that our mother could bring us together again, after all this time."

"Oh yeah," Euryale exclaimed, looking up from the surf to look between Stheno and me and the ship. "I guess Mother is the reason we're all together again." She turned to stare out at the ocean and cupped one hand around her mouth, causing a part of her hem to drop into the water, though she didn't seem to notice, and shouted, "Thank you, Mother!"

"I told you to stop doing that," Stheno sighed. "She can't hear you."

"Sure she can," Euryale said confidently, picking her hem back up and turning to climb up the sand. "She's our mother. And she's as much a part of the ocean as the water itself. Anything the ocean hears, she'll hear."

I quickly ran through anything I'd said in the past years near the ocean, wondering what Mother could have overheard. Nothing too pressing came to mind.

The sound of leaves crunching made me turn and look over my shoulder. Echidna appeared between the trees at the edge of the forest where dirt gave way to sand, carrying a small woven basket with a tight lid. Cerberus was snuffling at the base of a tree just a few paces behind her. Echidna had already reached my side by the time he realized she had gone, and he quickly trotted over, heads bobbing.

I desperately wanted to watch him grow up.

"Here," Echidna said, handing me the basket.

It was a little heavy for its size, and the woven bottom was warm to the touch.

"Extra honey cakes," Echidna explained. "I'm sure Cerberus would want you to have them."

Cerberus was in fact sniffing at the basket in my hands with great interest, a bit of drool hanging from the lips of the left head.

"Really," I said skeptically. "He wants me to have them?"

Echidna grinned down at her son.

"As long as he knows he can't have them, he'll be happy to know that they've gone to you."

Now I smiled, and said, "Thank you for your kindness, Cerberus."

Cerberus wagged his tail when I said his name. I closed my eyes so that I could lean down and place a kiss on the short, soft fur of his foreheads. His right head licked my cheek. His left head was sniffing curiously at my snakes, which concerned them greatly.

Big mouth, the not-voice told me urgently, since my eyes were closed but my snakes had their eyes wide open, *large teeth*.

I ignored them. I knew Cerberus would sooner jump into the ocean and leave his mother forever than bite me. A lone snake seemed to agree with me, and it leaned out of the tightly coiled huddle to flick its tongue over one of Cerberus's noses. The taste of him calmed the rest of the snakes, who recognized Echidna in him, and therefore saw a piece of me in the three-headed dog.

"Be good," I told Cerberus. "Be sweet to your mother."

"Not likely," Echidna muttered good-naturedly. She placed a hand on my arm and drew me into a hug. I curled my free hand around her shoulders and squeezed tightly. A few of her golden curls tickled my nose and some of my snakes got tangled in the strands since our heads were so close together, but I just pushed my nose into her shoulder.

I tried not to think about the fact that this would be the last time I saw Echidna. The thought was too distressing, and it made me want to march right back into the forest and hide in Echidna's glade forever.

But then I reminded myself that if I did not leave, the fate intended for me might come here and wreak havoc on anyone in its path. I couldn't subject Echidna to that, nor Cerberus. They did not deserve to bear the fate that was meant for me. I told myself that after all the kindness and understanding Echidna had showed me, this was the best way for me to return the favor. They would be safe here, together, once I was gone.

"I'll miss you, little queen," Echidna said, the words muffled against my shoulder.

I squeezed my eyes shut tighter as I felt the heated threat of tears.

"Thank you," I told her. "For everything."

She tightened her grip around my ribs for just a moment. Then said, "I've done nothing that you did not already deserve."

"Still," I pressed, "thank you."

She laughed wetly, and I knew if I saw her crying, I would not be able to hold back my own tears. "You're welcome, then," Echidna relented.

We held on to each other for a few moments more. I was reluctant to draw away. Echidna waited for me to loosen my hold before she leaned back.

She reached up and ran her fingertips down over my brows and closed eyelids.

"Do not let your future be as terrible as others would make it out to be," she said. "You have the power to make your life what you wish of it."

"I will do what I must," I replied.

She took ahold of my free hand and placed my fingertips

to her own brow, and I mimicked what she had done to me, lightly dragging my hand down over her now closed eyelids. Since I was sure she was not looking, I opened my eyes to get one last look at Echidna.

She was smiling as a few tears tracked down over her left cheek. I wanted to commit her kind face, her freely wild hair, golden and shivering in the breeze, and her smile to my memory.

"Farewell," I told her, and stepped back. I turned before she could open her eyes again.

Euryale and Stheno had slipped onto the boat while we said our goodbyes, and Euryale waved to Echidna and Cerberus as I climbed aboard.

Stheno was at the helm. She looked over her shoulder to where Echidna must have stood on the beach and nodded. I looked straight ahead at the ocean before us. When Stheno turned back around, she took ahold of the helm with both hands and closed her eyes. I could see her lips moving soundlessly. Then, the boat gave a small lurch as the sail unfurled and the rigging creaked under the force of a sudden wind. The hull of the boat scraped noisily over the sandy shallows, but then we were free and clear, and the boat began to pick up speed. We were headed south, from what I could tell.

When we were far enough away, I went to the railing and looked back. I could just see the faint figure of Echidna, and the smaller figure of Cerberus sitting next to her on the sand. I raised one arm to them, clutching the still warm basket of honey cakes close to my chest. Echidna raised her arm in return, and even though we would not be able to make out each other's faces, I thought perhaps we both had twin tears slipping down over our cheeks.

WE SAILED FOR A week. Each of us would trade off who stood at the helm for a few hours every day so the others could rest, though I didn't sleep when I was away from the helm. I spent most of my time watching the horizon. When the endless quiet became too much to handle, I asked what Euryale and Stheno thought of when they guided the ship.

"A new home like the one we had as girls," Euryale said happily.

"Someplace safe from mortals," Stheno said. "Somewhere any mortal would fear to go."

"What about you?" Euryale asked me, when I took over the helm for her.

I gripped two rungs of the helm and looked at the flat stretch of ocean before us. "A place to be content."

The ship seemed intent on taking all our requests into account, adding slight course corrections whenever one sister traded out for another. I thought perhaps the ship would never find such a place that would suit all three of us, and we would be trapped on a boat seeking out a land that did not exist until my time ran out.

WHEN THE SUN WAS high above the boat on the seventh day of sailing, my snakes tugged my head in one direction.

Look, the not-voice said excitedly, *land.*

I looked. There was a small rise on the flat blue water, clear and distinct against the horizon.

I called to Stheno, who stood behind the helm. "Land! To the east!"

While Euryale ran to lean over the railing next to me, Stheno dutifully began to turn the helm and adjusted course so that we were heading straight for the island. Euryale was shading her eyes against the bright midday sun and squinting as it reflected off the water.

"It looks kinda flat," she said. She leaned farther over the rail as if that would give her a better view. "Are you sure it's an island?"

"No," I said. "But it's the first thing we've seen since we left Echidna's home."

After a week on the boat with only the ocean and my sisters for company, I needed to get to land where we would not be on top of each other all the time. I missed the solitude of Echidna's forest. Even if this stretch of land was just a place to rest, I was eager to get to it.

With the slight touch of Stheno's hands, the boat and the unwavering wind in the sails brought us steadily closer to the island. As we neared, the flat shape of it broke up into uneven rises and valleys. Compared to the blue of the sky and sea around it, the land stood out starkly like a bright copper shield.

We were still about a hundred feet away when I felt the boat slide through a stiff curtain of air. Unlike the invisible walls around the Graeae's cave or Echidna's home, which were thin as a breath, this barrier seemed to stretch on for

a handful of moments. I could feel my lungs tighten, pro-
testing the pressure bearing down on us. But then we were
through. I glanced behind us, but there was nothing to see.

When we were close enough to actually make out the
landscape, however, Stheno was frowning.

"There are no trees," she said.

"Just like home!" Euryale said.

"Home had trees," Stheno shot back.

"Only little ones."

"They were still trees. This island is simply a rock come
too far above the water."

"You haven't even set foot on it yet, Stheno," Euryale
whined. "At least give it a chance."

The boat was close enough to the shore that I could see
the sand beneath the boat. I jumped over the railing, the
bottom half of my dress instantly soaked and clinging to my
calves like seaweed, and made my way to shore as my sisters
continued to bicker back and forth.

Stheno was right. There were no trees on this island, it
was mostly rock and sand, but there were signs of life. Small,
leafy bushes dotted the land higher up the shore, and I recognized a few of the hardy weeds that grew at the bases of large
rocks. Beyond the beach was a great tumble of huge boulders
that towered over me and offered many nooks and crannies
for anything to hide in. I could not see to the other side of
the island from where our boat had landed, and the shore
stretched in a wide curve on either side.

When I stepped out of the surf, I paused to wring out the
water from my hem before continuing up the shore toward
the boulders. Many of the huge stones were varying shades

of dusty orange, like that of unvarnished clay, and they were leaning on one another, forming tight passageways between them. I walked a ways into one of the paths to see how deep it went, and shortly turned back after following a complicated series of right and left turns. I had to duck a few times under a low-lying boulder that blocked my path.

Stheno and Euryale had just made it to the shore when I reappeared. The boat wasn't tied down, but it stayed in the spot my sisters had left it in.

"Well?" Euryale called to me. Stheno was watching a point just over my shoulder.

"Have a look for yourselves," I returned. "But I think it's perfect."

Stheno and Euryale spent quite a bit of time exploring the twisting paths and dead ends created by the pile of boulders. I continued to wander through the paths as well, but I did not come across them. After a few nervous calls from Euryale, however, I realized they had both become lost in the maze. The only reason I was not lost was because my snakes could tell me which way I had been and which way to go.

"This way," I called to Euryale as I stepped around a rock about two heads taller than me. I suddenly found myself in a wide-open space inside the maze. "Follow my voice, if you can."

The open space was made up of a large circle of smooth ground that was surrounded by the towering boulders, except for the narrow entrance. There was a gigantic rock on the side opposite the entrance that was nearly twice my height.

The floor was clear beyond a few stubborn weeds and plants sprouting out from the dry dirt.

Stheno, who sounded much closer than Euryale, called out, "Medusa?"

"This way!" I shouted through the opening in the boulders, hoping that they could follow my voice better.

While I waited for my sisters to find their way through the maze, I paced a slow circle around the cleared space to check for any other openings. While I found no other entrances, I did discover a tumble of smaller rocks piled up next to the largest boulder that were spaced just close enough to serve as steps in a natural, crude ladder. Grit and sand coated my hands as I climbed it.

When my head breached over the top of the wall, I inhaled sharply.

The view from over the edge of the boulders reminded me of the view from my window in the white house on the lonely beach. The clear sand reaching toward an endlessly blue ocean and sky. I instantly remembered how I had sat at that window alone while my sisters were elsewhere without me, and I would wonder about what else existed out beyond our little horizon, what else existed for a little mortal girl who felt as though she would never find her place in the world.

Waves surged and broke against the sand below, and I thought about how that little girl had found what existed beyond a lonely beach. How the world she had discovered had changed her forever. But even though that little girl could have never anticipated what was to come, I knew I would not have changed what I had gone through.

The path of that little girl had Polli and the priestesses at Athena's temple, Dionysus and his clearing on Mount Parnassus, and Naidah. Echidna and Cerberus. They were worth all the moments I would have liked to forget.

We, said the not-voice.

"Right," I said softly. My memories also belonged to the snakes. They loved Echidna just as I did, and they missed Dionysus, too. I could not even remember what it was like to live without my snakes. I did not think I could, if given the choice. They were as much a part of me as the beat of my heart.

Everything I had been through had brought them to me. And now, it had brought my sisters back to me as well. Not only were we together once again, the Gorgons three, but we had discovered an island of our own, with a lonely beach and a new horizon.

I heard the faint scuffing of the sole of a worn sandal on soil from behind me.

"Hmm," Stheno hummed, considering.

"Hidden enough for you?" I asked, still looking out at the ocean. The sun was just beginning to dip lower in the sky, and it made the far-away waves sparkle as light reflected off their crests.

"Actually," she said slowly as she copied my earlier movements and paced around the circle of boulders, "yes."

"And Euryale?"

Faster footsteps than Stheno's echoed through the rocks, and then Euryale's quick breaths filled the circle's entrance.

"This," she said between gasps, "is the *best* place we could have found!"

"You like it?" Stheno sounded doubtful, and I wondered if it was because she was surprised by Euryale's support or just wanted to argue about it a little more.

"Of course I do!"

I turned to lean against the edge of the boulders and looked down into the open space. Euryale was bouncing on her toes in the middle of the clearing, her eyes darting around in every direction, skipping over me, and there was a grin stretching across her face.

"It's a lot like home," she said. "At least, it reminds me a lot of home. Something about the quiet in the rocks, you know like when you're lost in there, and you can just hear the waves down on the beach? That's what it sounded like in my room at home. And the way the rocks make a huge maze all over the island is perfect for what you wanted, right, Stheno? I had such a hard time finding my way here. I only got through because I could hear you guys. I bet if we were really quiet, no one would be able to find their way here. Or we could get another boulder to move in front of the entrance!"

Her chest was still heaving as she spoke. When she took a deeper breath as she paused, she shut her eyes and tilted her face up to me. From this angle, I could see the clear outline of her face, just like our mother's, her hair tumbling back over her shoulders in a thick, dark curtain.

"Don't you feel it, Medusa? I think we all do. This is the place we're meant to be. And the boat would have known where to take us, even if it took a lot longer than we expected, but since it brought us here it had to know that this was the place. So," she took another deep breath, "do you feel it?"

"Yes," I said simply. "Here, switch with me."

I climbed back down the natural ladder and then dusted off my palms when my feet were flat on the ground. I pointed to the places that Euryale should put her hands to climb.

"Go and see," I told her.

When she reached the top, she had nearly the same reaction as I had.

"It looks just like home! The view from my bedroom window looked just like this!"

"That's what I thought, too," I said.

"Stheno," Euryale shouted as she scrambled back down the rocks, "come see!"

Stheno refused to go near the rock ladder at first, but Euryale wouldn't relent until she had climbed up the rocks to see the view over the top. When she finally gave in, Stheno agreed that it did look just like home, though her reaction was muted.

"So," Euryale said slowly once Stheno came back down. "Are we staying?"

With the faint sound of the waves crashing beyond the stones, my sisters both looked to me. I closed my eyes briefly and asked my snakes what they thought. After all, the prophecy that had predicted my end would result in their demise, too.

We like rocks, said the not-voice, *good place for snakes. Many places to hide.*

Many places to find peace, I clarified.

That too, the not-voice allowed.

I said to my sisters, "We'll stay here."

Athena

ATHENA DISLIKED TRAVELING AS a bird. At the moment, she was primarily bothered because she could not even travel in her preferred owl form this far out in the ocean. As a god, she did not have to take a corporeal form to travel long distances, of course, but traveling as a large seabird allowed her to watch the boy-hero from above without him noticing.

She had known of Perseus's existence for quite some time, as a bastard half-mortal son of Zeus, but she had not bothered to learn much about him until word had spread of what the three Graeae hags had prophesized for him. When the gods had first discovered the fate laid out before the snake-haired Gorgon's feet, Athena had seen the gleam of recognition that came to Poseidon's eye. She had spoken up before he had even opened his mouth.

"Father," she had said to Zeus, "let me help the boy. As one child of Zeus to another, I believe I will serve as the greatest ally to him."

Poseidon had turned to look at Athena with narrow eyes from the opposite side of Zeus's throne, but she ignored him.

Medusa's life had nothing to do with Poseidon anymore. Athena intended to keep it that way.

She pressed on, addressing Zeus, "I am also the one who created the snake-haired Gorgon. Let me finish what I have begun with Medusa."

Athena did not appreciate feeling like she was a spoke in the wheel of fate. Hearing the Graeae's prophecy had set her on edge. She had not transformed Medusa for her to be the monster in this boy's story, but she could not let him face her alone.

She was the goddess of strategy. She was worshipped by mortals to ensure success in battle, against humans and monsters alike. This boy already had the attention of gods and kings and she couldn't just ignore him. Whether or not he could succeed without her did not matter. All that mattered was that her name stayed on mortal lips, and since rumors of Medusa were spreading across the land like a creeping vine, Athena needed to keep herself tethered to the Gorgon's story.

Zeus eventually agreed to Athena's request to oversee Perseus, after a great deal of contemplation and beard-stroking, as he surely thought about every other place he'd rather be than discussing the fate of a minor divinity.

"Brother," Poseidon cut in. "I could—"

"The task falls to me, Uncle," Athena said, standing and donning her plumed helmet. A tiny, curling flame of victory sheltered in her chest. She'd disappeared from the great hall of Olympus in an instant, before Poseidon could get another word in.

Now, however, Athena studied the situation she had inserted herself into. The boy was sailing for the island that Athena knew Medusa to be on, as she had been tracking the Gorgon ever since she'd left the temple in Athens. From what Athena could see with her sharp bird eyes, Perseus had no weapons other than a short, curved sword on his hip. The boat he was sailing was small, able to be controlled by one person, and it appeared as though he was traveling alone.

Athena tilted her wings and dropped several lengths in the air. A little closer to Perseus now, she could see the crease in his brow as he searched the sea before him. He was squinting against the sun and had a white-knuckled grip on the helm. She dropped a bit more and saw that his lips were moving.

"Gods above, hear me now," he prayed. "Help me to slay this monster, which was tasked to me to prove my worthiness."

That's not really why, Athena thought, remembering the king on the tiny rock that was trying to get under the skirts of this boy's mother.

Perseus went on, "I will show how much of a man I've become. I ask for your assistance."

It wasn't the most impressive invocation she'd ever heard, but it would do.

Athena dropped down to the boat. She landed gracefully with a single flap of her wide wings and set her claws on the grainy wood. The moment her feet touched the deck, Athena transformed.

Perseus was gaping at her from behind the helm. The look on his face was one Athena was familiar with amongst mortals, and she allowed him a few seconds to take her in.

"Perseus," she said, "son of Zeus and Danae. I have heard your call."

Perseus squinted at her. "Why did my father not come?"

"Zeus has left the task of aiding you in your quest to me."

"But why could he not come himself?" Perseus said, his tone just on the edge of whining. Athena stared at him.

"Zeus is not involved with your fate," she said bluntly, "or the Gorgon Medusa's. I have been a part of this story since the beginning. I will help you end it."

To prove her point, Athena transformed again to become an old, wrinkled woman with a large staff, her gray eyes clouded with sightlessness. Once again, Perseus's face adopted the expression of one who had been slapped upside the head.

"The old woman!" Perseus gasped. "You helped me find the Graeae."

Athena turned back into her goddess form.

"Yes," she said. She waited for Perseus to display his gratitude for her divine intervention, but the boy simply stared at her with his jaw hanging loose like a wide-mouthed fish. Athena cleared her throat.

Perseus started, and bowed his head the slightest amount. "I thank you, goddess, for assisting me on my quest."

Athena suppressed the mortal reaction to roll her eyes. The children of gods, and especially the children of Zeus, were never as devoted to the divine customs that were expected from mortals, unless they were paying tribute to their parent.

"I will aid you once more," Athena pushed on. She reached over her shoulder and pulled off the shield that was strapped between her shoulders. Perseus came around the helm and knelt before her.

"This shield will serve to protect you, but it may also be your greatest weapon," Athena explained. Perseus, who had been eyeing the massive sword at Athena's hip with great interest, looked up with a furrowed brow.

"How can a shield be a weapon?"

"You know of the power behind Medusa's eyes?" Athena asked.

Perseus nodded. "The monster can petrify anyone it sets its gaze on."

"This shield," Athena explained, the corner of her lips tight, "will allow you to misdirect her gaze. You may look upon her reflection and fear no harm."

She held out the shield and Perseus took it with both hands, looking at his own reflection in the shield's smooth, polished surface. The shield was one from her temple in Athens, presented to Athena as a tribute from a soldier.

"Do you have the gifts of the Graeae?" Athena asked. *Gifts* was a generous term for what Perseus had forcibly taken, according to the report from the three sisters.

Perseus unsheathed the sword from his belt and held it aloft for Athena to see.

"And?" she demanded.

"Uh," Perseus mumbled, and he stood to go dig through a bag behind the boat's helm. He returned and knelt in front of Athena again, this time with his arms full of the golden cap, the winged shoes, and a plain, dark canvas bag.

"Very good," Athena said. "These gifts will allow you to

approach Medusa unscathed. Do not be foolish. Use every item that you have been blessed with."

She reached out and touched the tip of the curved sword so that the sharp point pressed lightly into the soft skin of her finger.

"When you find her," Athena said slowly, so that Perseus would be forced to hang on every word she spoke, "remove her head. But be warned, the power to petrify will remain functional even after the head is separated from the body. Place her head in the bag and bring it to me."

Perseus looked up and spoke, his tone indignant. "I need to bring it to Seriphos, to show it to the king. It is to be his wedding present."

Athena stared at the boy coolly. She knew, of course, why the boy needed Medusa's head. How he would show her off like a war prize, trailing blood and gore behind him like a vile trail of bread crumbs.

Perseus shifted in his kneeling position, unsettled by the silent gaze of the goddess.

"I need it to save my mother," he tried. "The head. I have to deliver it to the king to free my mother."

The boy was no hardened warrior. His intent was clear on his face, despite his vague words. Perseus's brow was set in a hard line as he spoke of his mother, and Athena figured that he was not intending on simply delivering Medusa's head to the king. With all that power in his hand, the temptation to use it would be overwhelming.

Athena could see the simple, brutish plan forming in the boy's mind. He would bring back the head under the facade of a wedding gift, and then use it on the king. He believed that with the king out of the way, he and his mother would be free of mortal rule. But there were always more kings.

"Very well," Athena said. "Once you have shown the king of Seriphos that you have kept your word and slayed Medusa, *then* you will deliver her head to me. Do you understand?"

Perseus nodded, tight lipped. "Yes, goddess."

"Then, I will see you at the end," Athena said. She stepped back, and when the sun glinted off her helmet and the light hit Perseus's eyes so that he was blinded by the sudden brightness, she transformed back into the wide-winged seabird. She knew Perseus was watching as she climbed into the sky.

Rising on the buffeting sea gales, Athena peered over the horizon to where she knew Medusa's island was hiding just out of sight. She looked back down at the boat and saw that Perseus was slightly off course. With a powerful beat of her wings, she sent a forceful wind to turn the unwatched helm a few notches. When the boat jerked back onto the correct course, Perseus stumbled, and he cursed as the helmet of invisibility tumbled out of his arms and clanged on the deck.

In her bird form, Athena could not sigh out her annoyance, but she let out a sharp, grating noise from her beak and angled away. Divine intervention could only do so much. She would return to Olympus and wait for the mortals to finish the work she had begun.

A flash of green as dusk fades

WE GREW BORED OF the few amusements the island had
to offer somewhere around the third day. As we were not
occupied with catching fish or making food to eat like I had
been on Echidna's island, the hours of the day stretched
out long and empty. I circled the entire island in only half
a day. Euryale joined me when I went again the following
morning. Stheno asked what else existed on the island when
we returned and decided she did not need to see it after we
told her.

I asked them what they had done all those years without me.

"Not much, really," Euryale had answered. She was
scratching out a picture in the sand as we sat along the shore
near the entrance to the boulder maze. I thought it might
have been a tree. "We traveled to a few more cities after we
left Athens, but none of them were very large. We settled in
one with a temple that offered us shelter and took care of
us. Once we were there, though, we scarcely did anything

different from what we had been doing at home. We were unsure of ourselves without you."

"You were?" I asked, surprised.

Euryale shrugged. "You were mortal then, and in the mortal world you had been the one who fit in. Without you, we were just two divinities who could barely find our way through the streets."

"We asked Mother for guidance," Stheno said. She sat in the sand next to Euryale and began to add short divots in the sand to make leaves for Euryale's tree. "She told us to do what we wished. We did not have to stay in mortal cities if we did not want to."

I remembered the words scratched into the shell that Mother had sent to us when we had lived in the white house on the beach. They had been so specific about finding a mortal city. But if my sisters had not pursued those orders when I was gone, had Mother meant for that message to apply to just me?

"We visited Ladon," Euryale said, "in the Hesperides' garden. Remember how Father gave him the task of guarding them?"

I nodded. I had not seen my multifaced and hundred-eyed sibling in many years, but I did remember the small kindnesses he had afforded my sisters and I when we were younger.

Euryale went on, "Well, he's doing well. At least, he seemed to be doing well. I think he was a bit bored since no one has come to attack the garden since he was posted there. Though, I told him I thought the reason no one was coming was probably because all the mortals knew he was there." Euryale scratched at the side of her nose, leaving a few bits of sand stuck to her face. "No regular mortal was about to try and steal from a garden that's guarded by a dragon with eyes in the back of his head. Literally."

I smiled down at Euryale's picture in the sand. "You're probably right."

"Yeah, well." Euryale started to draw a little snake curling through the branches of the tree. "I hope he stays bored. I don't want any hero going in and—" She cut off abruptly.

Going in and cutting off his head, I thought, finishing her sentence for her.

"There is nothing we can do to stop it, if that is what his destiny is," Stheno said. She finished with the leaves on the sand tree and stood up, brushing sand from her skirt. When she disappeared into the entrance of the boulder maze, Euryale sighed and leaned back from her picture.

"Sorry," she said.

"What for?"

"Just…" She blinked quickly and turned her eyes up to the pale blue sky. There were no clouds. "We don't want to make this worse. We talked about this before we set out to find you. There isn't much that we can actually do, right, but we don't want our presence to make this harder for you. That was never our intention." She scrubbed the back of her hand over one eye and knocked away the sand that had been stuck there. "Stheno has always been so blunt and careless with people's feelings. You know that she cares about you, though, right? We both do."

I looked at her. With her eyes focused elsewhere, I

studied the faint lines that appeared around her mouth when it drew tight, how her freckles stood out against her flushed cheeks. I looked for any resemblance between us. Though I had not seen my own face since I had been transformed, I thought that our noses were the same, as well as the wrinkle that formed between our brows when we were concentrating.

"I know," I said quietly. I reached forward and took her hand to keep her from scrubbing at her eye anymore. Her fingers curled around mine. "You will not make it worse. If I had to choose between facing this alone and facing this with you and Stheno," I squeezed her hand tightly, "I would always choose to face it with you."

"I'm glad," she said wetly. "No one should be alone."

"I'm never alone anymore," I told her.

"Because of us?"

"And them."

I waited for her to look over to see that I was holding my other hand up so my snakes could twine through my fingers. While I was not looking at her, my snakes watched Euryale. A few of them flickered their tongues at her.

"Do they talk to you?" she asked.

"When they want to," I admitted.

"What do they say?"

My snakes were now switching their focus between Euryale and me. The ones twined through my fingers turned their heads to gaze back at me, pulling their bodies taut against my head. I brought my hand closer to my face to lessen the strain on my scalp.

I knew my snakes didn't want me to tell Euryale what we spoke about together. Many of the things we talked about would not be easily understood by another person, even for Euryale, who had a power of her own. She may have been able to see through the mortal facade and appreciate the monstrosity within me for what it was, but that did not mean she would understand everything.

Also, the not-voice added snidely, *not her business.*

Be nice, I chided them silently. One of the snakes pointedly flicked a tongue at me.

"Sometimes I ask them questions," I said eventually. "And they give me answers if they can help. Mostly it's just like I'm talking to myself."

The snakes wound through my fingers tightened their hold for a moment before drawing away.

"They're also very useful for navigation," I said.

A snake nipped at my thumb.

But Euryale just smiled at them.

"Sounds nice," she said, "to have someone to rely on, and they're with you all the time."

"You and Stheno are together all the time."

"Not like that, though. You and your snakes are special."

"That's one word for it, I suppose," I said, looking out at the water. The ocean lapped softly at the sand below our feet. I wondered if our mother was listening to her daughters talk.

WHILE WE HAD NOTHING to do on the island, I did not find that I was bothered by the boredom. I had found the eye of the storm, and everything was calm, even though I knew another torrent was yet to come.

In the evenings, Stheno, Euryale, and I would return to the encircled space inside the boulder maze. Euryale had begun plucking a few of the weedy flowers on the island and would line them up on a natural shelf on the side of one of the huge rocks inside of the clearing. At first, I thought she was simply trying to decorate the rather barren space we now occupied, but after a few nights I realized that she would only bring back one flower every day. She was using the flower buds as a tally of each day we spent on the island.

On the day that Euryale placed the thirtieth flower at the end of the line, I sat on the pile of blankets we had taken from Stheno and Euryale's boat to make the ground more comfortable to sleep on. I watched as Euryale ran her finger over one of the thin, white petals of the flower. It was so delicate. In a few days, it would become brittle and would disintegrate if we tried to touch it.

When I was certain that Euryale and Stheno were asleep, I slipped out between the boulders and made my way to the shore.

The moon was a pieced-together sliver, sliding in and out of sight between the clouds that had gathered in the afternoon. The sharp, musky smell of a sea storm rolled over me. My snakes swayed sleepily around my head.

There was no danger on the island, but they were exhausting themselves by fretting over what was coming. I had tried to reason with them, telling them that worrying was only making the inevitable seem worse, but they had scarcely been able to listen. The threat was approaching and there was nothing they could do.

I watched the waves wash over the sand. Thousands

of grains resettled under my feet as the water carved out divots around my heels and toes, making new formations with every pull of the tide.

Was I just meant to wait here? I had come to the island with my sisters, I had resolved myself to find a happiness that would bring about the end to this cursed prophecy, and yet the days dragged on. Moments would pass when I would remember what it felt like to use my power willingly. How I had finally felt at ease in this body.

Did I really have to succumb to the boy? I had the strength to turn the prophecy on its head. A few snakes twitched at the thought.

I had meant what I said to Stheno and Euryale. I wanted to end this on my terms, and I did not want anyone else I loved to get hurt. A snake rubbed its stiff nose against my temple. I leaned into the feeling.

"I can't stand this limbo," I said. A gentle hiss of agreement from the snakes mimicked the rasp of the waves.

We wait, the not-voice said, *stuck in a trap we made.*

"But are we the prey, or the hunter?"

Neither my snakes nor I had the answer. A month had already passed, and there was no sign of the boy on the horizon.

Stheno and Euryale were unsure what to do around me. They were determined to support my decision, but they would also whisper in each other's ears and grow abruptly silent when I'd get close. It reminded me of our childhood. I knew their feelings about me had changed, but their unity was built on decades of trust. I knew my snakes better than I knew Euryale and Stheno.

I struggled to understand why my sisters had stayed with me. What had they expected would come of our being reunited? What had our mother wanted for us, after all those times she stressed the importance of our triplicate? We shared no power. We weren't like the Graeae.

Would Stheno and Euryale be disappointed when it was over? When I was gone, would they resent that I had left them nothing but legends of a monstrous sister?

"And I was supposed to be happy here," I muttered. "As if I could tame my thoughts long enough to be happy for even a moment."

Another wave tugged at my feet, and I pulled my heels out of the shallow holes that had formed in the sand. I waded deeper into the surf. My snakes curled up high around my ears, but I stopped when the water was hip high so that my hands could skim over the surface.

Unbidden, my snakes tugged at a memory. I had been sitting in a stream, the water curling around my hips. I had been alone until I wasn't. I had been anxious, and then I wasn't.

I had a kiss like the dawn, as sure and as sweet as each new day.

In that instant, I had been happy.

I laughed as my snakes nudged that memory at me. "I'm afraid that isn't an option here."

But even as I spoke, I let my gaze go unfocused over the messy line of the horizon. Somewhere between the dark line of the sea and sky, the mainland rested unseen. I felt the water rise to meet my fingertips, and I flexed my hand.

"A stream or river," I said, remembering what Naidah had told me. "Or even the wide ocean."

I broke the surface with my palm, my fingers curling in the cool tide.

"If anyone can hear me," I spoke quietly, "I need to speak to one of your sisters. Her name is Naidah."

A single ripple spread from the point where my wrist met the water. Working against the waves, it dissolved into the tide.

I waited. I knew that there was a chance no one was listening. There was also the chance that the wrong person was listening, and I had left a trail of bread crumbs right to my door. But I found that I didn't care.

The rippling water glowed silver under streaks of moonlight. My legs were cold and stiff in the chilled surf, but I kept my hand steady.

After a few long minutes where the moon faded in and out of the clouds, a head appeared in the water before me. Only the dark outline was visible in the light.

I flipped my hand to offer my palm. "Hello."

The figure drew closer, rivulets of water flowing from long dark hair as her shoulders rose above the waves.

"You know," Naidah said, "freshwater naiads are not fans of the ocean. The salt water is too rough on our skin."

I grinned, letting my gaze glance off her collarbone. "Then I feel very lucky that you came to meet me anyway."

My snakes were curling and uncurling their bodies, their excitement giving away my own emotions as Naidah came to stand right in front of me. Her dress clung to her ribs, the

flare of her hips, the soaked fabric curving into the minute
divot of her belly button.

She slid her hand into mine. "I worried that I would
never see you again," she admonished.

"I thought you wouldn't," I admitted. "I thought that
moment was going to be the last I ever saw you."

She brought her hand up to my face, thumb to my cheek.

"It didn't work," she said quietly, like a secret.

"Yes," I said. "I didn't know, but the power won't trigger
through a reflection. I only found out after you saw me." A
trembling smile tugged at my mouth. "I'm very, very glad
that it didn't work. I'm so glad that you are still here." I tightened my grip on her hand, my fingers brushing her wrist to
feel her pulse beneath the thin skin.

"So am I," she said, gripping my hand right back. With
her other, she tugged my face forward. I let my eyes slide fully
closed and fell into the shape of her mouth on mine. She
still tasted of fresh water, despite her complaints about the
sea, and I gripped her waist to steady my feet in the waves. I
gasped a breath and felt her grin against my lips. Her nose,
with a drop of water still clinging to the tip, slid against my
skin as she deepened the kiss.

The relief I felt was akin to the first drink of water after
days of wandering, dry-mouthed, through an arid wilderness,
and I was helpless to do anything but scoop handful after
handful of cold water to my mouth.

When I tried to pull back for another breath, she took my
lower lip between her teeth. It wrenched a sound out of me
that startled both her and me, but while I froze, she laughed

softly, kissing the curve of my lip, the corner of my mouth. I was breathing hard. Her lips drifted to my jaw, finding the hard edge before ducking down to my throat.

Her warm breath on my skin made my fingers tighten on her waist. I felt her teeth graze the point where my pulse was fluttering wildly, and another sound flew from my mouth.

"If I didn't know any better," I panted, "I would think Dionysus was somewhere nearby, making my head spin."

Naidah's lips twisted into a smile against my skin. "Just me," she said. "But I can do much more than him."

She took a step forward and I swayed with the movement until I was forced to take a step back. She walked us out of the pull of the tide, leading me blindly up the beach until the water barely came up to our ankles as it rose and fell. With both hands, she pushed down on my shoulders until I collapsed on the sand. I braced my hands behind me to keep myself from falling flat on my back as she followed me down. Naidah's thighs parted around my hips, knees digging into the wet sand, and she slid her hands from my shoulder to my neck. She cupped the back of my neck with her fingers, thumb pressing against the spot where she had put her mouth.

Tilting my head, she brought her lips back to mine.

I dug my fingers into the grit of the sand, needing to cling to something. The sound of the waves was drowned out by my rapid heartbeat, which I could feel like a drum in my head. I was desperate to breathe but could think of nothing worse than asking Naidah to stop.

Luckily, after a few more breathless moments where I

thought I might've gone mad at the feeling of Naidah's hips pressed against my stomach, Naidah pulled back.

"By the way," she asked, "what is this place?"

"My sisters and I found it. It's really nothing more than a deserted island," I panted.

Naidah glanced around the dark beach and the shadowed rock formations in the distance. "Well, it's not really deserted anymore. You staying in there?" She motioned toward the boulders.

I nodded. I watched her take in the simple landscape, marveling that she had come when I called. A part of me hadn't expected her to answer.

"So," she said slowly, "what now? What are you doing here?"

I rolled my tender lips between my teeth. Dionysus hadn't shared his concerns about me with Naidah, it seemed, and I wasn't sure how to explain that I had come to this island expecting that I wouldn't live to leave it. I didn't want to dampen a single moment with her.

I said, "I'm trying to be happy."

She looked down at me, and I made my eyes settle on her collarbones. My wrists were starting to ache.

"How?"

"How what?" I asked, trailing my gaze down the line of her breast, the dip of her waist.

"How are you trying to be happy?" she pressed.

A few tumbling waves crashed against the sand before I answered her. My snakes, soothed and content by the presence of someone we trusted, gave me a few half-hearted nudges. I wasn't sure what they wanted.

"I've been trying to live like I wish I could have, with my sisters," I attempted to explain. "When we were young, we didn't get along. I've changed, but so have they, and we're trying to make the best of it."

Naidah shifted back. "That's it?"

The small bones of my wrists were crying out, so I dropped to my elbows. I could feel the wet sand against my back, the grit and chill a stark contrast to the feeling of Naidah above me.

"I'm not sure what else I'm meant to be doing, if I'm honest," I told her. "I've accepted that this is how I will always be, and I've accepted that this power is my curse and my responsibility to use."

Naidah hummed. "It sounds like you've found a peace with yourself, despite all odds. I'm happy for you."

She brushed the rise of my cheek with a thumb. I leaned into the touch.

"It's not enough, though," she guessed.

"I thought it would be, but you're right," I said lowly. "For some reason I'm still not happy."

"Could it be because of your sisters?"

I tensed, reflexively. "They haven't done anything to make me unhappy—"

Naidah curled her fingers loosely beneath my chin. "No, that's not what I meant. Could it be that you feel like something is missing, relating to your sisters? Why do they need to be here for you to be happy?"

When Stheno and Euryale had crashed loudly through Echidna's woods, I had felt my heart clench. I had mostly attributed the feeling to nerves, but I couldn't ignore the small part of me that was glad to see my sisters again. Even after I had gone through such a transformation and barely resembled the little mortal girl they had known, I could still have a place amongst them. The Gorgons could be together again.

But now, I had brought about the end of the Gorgons. The boy would come for my head and three sisters would become two. How could I ask my sisters to come with me, to try and mend the bonds with hasty patch jobs and looming prophecies, just to tear us apart again? Where would that leave them?

"I need to know," I said, "that they'll be all right. When we are not together, I need to know that they will be able to keep going."

"Who says they can't do that already?" Naidah asked.

I let my head drop back between my shoulders, neck extended and eyes closed. "Ever since we were little, our family has been telling us that we are stronger together. We're at our strongest when all three of us are together. But a time will come when I can no longer be with them, because of what I've become."

"What happens when the three of you are together?"

I opened my eyes. Between the breaks in the storm-laden clouds, the tiny specks of stars shone through the gloom.

"You know, I'm not really sure. When we were young, we banded together when we had to because it was easier to defend ourselves against our siblings as a united front. Nothing special ever happened. They are immortal, but that is the extent of it. Now that I'm like this…" I trailed off. Euryale's power was another thread I could cling to, tying me to my sisters' lives, but I wasn't certain how binding that thread could be.

What had our mother expected when she told us we were stronger together? We weren't like the Graeae. Even now that we had found each other again, all we had done was find a place to be together.

Naidah sucked in a deep breath. Then, to my dismay, she rolled off my hips and sprawled in the sand next to me with her head resting on my stomach. I made an annoyed noise, and she chuckled, patting my hand.

"I don't always get along with my sisters," she said frankly. "I have a lot of them, maybe too many, and we're always getting into fights or taking sides. It really can't be helped. It's just the way we are. But no matter what, we will always come to the aid of a sister who needs us. We could have gone decades without speaking, but if one of my sisters needs me, I'll be there for her. Just as sure as a river will run to the ocean.

"I don't know everything about you and your sisters, but if they're anything like mine, they've come to be with you because they wanted to. Even if the three of you together don't have a specific strength that only triggers when you're together, the fact that they are here with you speaks to your bond. Not even time could wear it away."

"But," I muttered, "when they can't come with me, and I can't go to them, what then?"

"They managed to find you this time, right? They're not as helpless as you seem to think they are."

"I don't think they're helpless." I took a deep breath to feel Naidah's head rise and fall with my lungs. "I don't want them to be tethered to me and this power. I have already seen that death follows wherever I go."

"You think they're trading their safety to be with you?" Naidah sounded skeptical. "Couldn't they just be here because you need them to be?"

My sisters had come to find me, I reminded myself. They had been the ones to seek me out. And when they had found me again, they only spoke of making amends for our past. Had they really achieved all they wanted in finding me again?

"You know what," Naidah said, taking up my hand to toy with my fingers, "I think you should be talking with your sisters about this, instead of me."

I laughed, once again startled out of a whirlpool of thoughts by Naidah's determined straightforwardness.

"You're right," I said. "About many things."

Naidah intertwined our fingers and shifted her head to look up at my chin. "I just want you to only have me in your thoughts right now. I'm being selfish."

I tugged at her hand.

"Then come let me be selfish too."

The last thing I saw before closing my eyes as she rose over me was the glint of moonlight on her dark hair, and then I let her make me forget everything but the feeling of her skin on mine.

After, she lay beside me again. Her head was tucked into the space between my neck and my jaw. We watched the moon make her slow progression across the inky sky. I felt sated, and calm, and I could have drifted off into sleep between one blink and the next, but Naidah suddenly sat up.

"The moon's wrong."

"What?" I asked, struggling to sit up. The moon looked fine to me.

"Yesterday, I remember seeing the waxing moon from Dionysus's mountain. The sky was clear, as it is now." She pointed to the heavens, as if to touch the crescent of light with her fingertip. "But this moon is waning. It's nearly gone."

She was right. The sliver of moonlight was curling away, at the end of its cycle. But how could there be two drastically different moons, just a day apart? I thought back on the previous nights, but I knew that the progress of the moon had been normal. Blinking away the haziness of the stars, I peered up at the sky. I could see no explanation.

Not seeing, the not-voice told me, *does not always mean not there.*

My gaze dropped to the horizon, where somewhere between this island and the rest of the world was a thick curtain of magic. The day we arrived here, it had felt like we pushed through a thick hedge. I hadn't thought much of it then. But if Naidah was right, and she had come from a day where the moon was just starting to grow, then there had to be more to that curtain of magic than I originally thought.

"I think," I said to Naidah, "that this island does not experience time like the rest of the world. Did you go through the barrier when you came here?" She nodded. "It was so strong, and we haven't gone outside the barrier since we first arrived. My sisters and I have been here a month already."

Naidah shifted, the sand crunching under her. "I saw you last about a month ago."

I shook my head, searching for her hand in the sand. "I

went to Echidna's before I came here. I was there for over a month, too. When we left, the moon was waxing. It's been two months since I've seen you, Naidah." I repeated, "For me, it's been two months."

Naidah laced her fingers through mine. "You've found an island that has unhitched itself from time," she marveled.

We didn't have much to say after that. Naidah held on to my hand as I searched for the faint line of the horizon, knowing I wouldn't be able to see the invisible curtain that separated this island from the rest of the world.

NAIDAH LEFT QUIETLY THE next morning, before the clouds released the storm onto the sea. She left a kiss on my temple while I was still half asleep, and the faint memory of her whispering in my ear. I woke up fully when the first fat drops of rain broke free of the sky.

I got up and stood in the early bluster of the storm, reeling with the revelations from the evening and grasping for the words Naidah had left with me. I wanted to remember what she had told me about her sisters.

She said that a lone stone cannot withstand a raging river, the not-voice told me, *but enough stones can make an island in the rapids.*

I held my hand up to my temple, letting my snakes wind in and out of my fingers and around my palm. As the rain grew heavier, they began to tug at me, urging me back toward the shelter of the boulder maze. After another moment, I relented.

Naidah had left, plucking the dread of having to tell her that I wouldn't see her again out from my hands, but turning my back on the water felt like a goodbye.

THAT STORM REVEALED THAT we were not as settled into our life on the island as we thought. The enclosed area we had chosen to shelter in, while fortified by solid walls of rock, had no roof and the floor quickly became unsuitable for sleeping. By the time I had returned from the beach, my sisters were awake and damp.

Stheno had wedged herself beneath an overhanging boulder to avoid the rain, but Euryale quickly pulled her out to help scavenge the island for driftwood.

"We need a roof! And maybe a bed that isn't on the floor," Euryale declared.

I went with them as Euryale led us to the side of the island where the current had washed the largest pieces of driftwood ashore. While my days of being a priestess were behind me, my limbs remembered the hard labor of caring for the temple grounds. I picked my way across the rain-washed beach and found a piece of wood that looked long enough.

As I worked, my mind wandered. If I had not asked for Naidah to come, would I have noticed that the island was not attached to the wheel of time that churned on beyond the curtain? What had been a month here seemed to only be a day or so on the other side. Would Euryale and Stheno notice, if I didn't tell them?

My dress had already been soaked by the ocean, but I carefully wrung out the added rain before tying the hem up above my knees. As I tied off the knot, I smiled at the memory of the first time I had met Naidah in Dionysus's meadow. Her dress had been tied up as she danced.

Euryale grunted behind me. She had tried to lift a piece of driftwood that was nearly a whole tree trunk, but barely got it a few inches off the ground before she let it slip from her fingers.

"This," she said with a gasp, "may be more difficult than I thought."

I smothered a smile. "Start with something smaller, perhaps," I suggested. "You and Stheno can split the weight."

I picked up one end of the piece I had chosen and hefted it onto my shoulder. It was heavy, weighed down by rain and wet sand, but I managed to start dragging it up the beach. My snakes, displeased with the constant barrage of raindrops, were fluttering in the corner of my eye.

Calm down, I told them, *you'll just make this take even longer.*

They pulled back with a vexed hiss.

Stheno was studying me as I passed her. I kept my gaze down, watching where I put my feet so that I wouldn't trip.

I paused when I reached the start of the maze and checked behind me. Stheno and Euryale had lifted a log between them, balanced on their shoulders. Stheno was in the front, guiding them up the beach and calling back to Euryale when she stumbled. Euryale was grinning.

It took us multiple trips and left blisters on our palms and aches in our backs, but we managed to cover our rocky shelter with driftwood. Lifting the logs into place required all three of us. Euryale urged us not to rest.

"If we stop before it's done," she panted, shifting her grip on the wood as we lifted it into position, "I'll never want to move again."

We finished the roof. With the extra driftwood, we fashioned a large, low bed frame that could fit all three of us. Euryale ran out to the boat and returned dragging a huge sail. An extra, she claimed, which she folded and stuffed into the bed frame as a makeshift mattress. Stheno retrieved the blankets from where she had shoved them under a rock to keep them dry. Once the bed was made, however, we realized that we were soaked to the bone and couldn't bear to ruin the dry blankets.

Euryale simply collapsed onto the floor to lean against the bed frame. Stheno wrung out her dress before copying her. I figured this was the first time they had ever done any hard labor, and they reminded me of how I had been in my first few weeks at Athena's temple, exhausted by endless hours of chores and desperate to fall into bed at the end of the day.

I stood right beneath the edge of the roof, letting my snakes stay out of the rain but still close enough to the open sky to feel the drops hit the ground in front of me. Hugging my arms to my stomach, I watched the bruised clouds roll tumultuously across the sky. Naidah's advice from the night before nudged at me.

"I know," I said, speaking just loud enough to be heard over the rain, "that this is probably not what you were expecting when you came to find me. This isn't what you're used to."

"It doesn't matter what we were used to." Euryale spoke as if I had said something absurd.

"It does," I quickly replied. "To me, it does. You came here for me, and it is because of me that you have to put up with all of this." I waved a hand at our surroundings.

My sisters shuffled in their seats, and I could imagine the look they would share that could convey more than a handful of words.

"Are you not also putting up with it?" Stheno asked pointedly.

"This is far from the worst thing I've had to put up with. But you two—"

"If what you're trying to say is that we're better than you in some way," Euryale interrupted, her tone as sharp as I'd ever heard it, "then I need to tell you that's absolute bullshit."

I almost jerked around in surprise. Euryale never swore.

"Listen," she continued. "We're your sisters. I know that we're trying to build a bridge on a foundation that we ruined ourselves, but I need you to get it through that thick skull that we are not here against our will. We didn't think this would be easy. We just knew that it was the right thing to do."

Fixing my eyes on a small, scraggly white flower that had grown out from under the edge of a boulder and was struggling under the rainfall, I tightened my grip on my elbows.

"I have nothing to give you in return."

"Who said we wanted anything from you?" Stheno said, her voice sharp. She had risen to her feet and joined me by the edge of the roof. "Euryale has a power that would be feared, too. She's safer here than in any of those mortal cities, and she doesn't have to worry about hurting anyone."

I glanced back at Euryale, who was smiling softly at Stheno. She nodded. "We didn't come here to take anything from you, Medusa. We wanted to do the opposite, to give you whatever you needed, for however long we could."

The rain pattered against the boulders. I flicked my gaze over the speckled ocean and revealed, "Then you may be here for a lot longer than you anticipated." I told them what I'd discovered about the island and its path through time, mentioning Naidah just briefly as the catalyst for the discovery. Stheno's questioning look burned on the side of my face when I talked about the water nymph, but she didn't press further.

"So we could be on the island for months before anyone finds us? And it would only have been a few days on the other side?" Euryale wondered. She was being vague, but I knew she was thinking of Perseus.

"Perhaps longer for us," Stheno said. "We don't know what the rules are."

"Well," Euryale said cheerfully, bouncing up to join Stheno and me, "that gives us plenty of time!"

"For what?"

My lips pulled up at the corners. "Who knows, Stheno. Maybe in all that time, you'll get a power, too."

Stheno's sharp glare returned to me, but I was carefully looking down at the beach.

Euryale gasped, "Oh, Stheno, wouldn't that be great! All three of us! Mother always said that we would be stronger together. Maybe your power will come soon, now that we're all together again."

"Mother always had half a lie in her mouth," Stheno muttered.

"How do you mean?" Euryale frowned.

Stheno lifted a bony shoulder, brushing against me. "Just, take whatever Mother says with a grain of salt."

"Well, Mother helped us get here. So you can't be too hard on her," Euryale decided.

She was right, I realized. I hadn't seen my mother in years, and she hadn't seen me since my transformation, and yet she had delivered to me the few things I wanted as I felt my second prophecy looming on the horizon. She had given me my sisters, and she had given me more time.

I WAS LUCKY TO have Euryale and Stheno with me, as they had been immortal all their lives, and well versed in passing endless days doing little to nothing at all. We spent long hours working on our home, adding things like chairs we crafted out of driftwood, and a big flat boulder we had to roll in on its side for a table.

Stheno took up weaving, using the thin but plentiful grass that sprouted up through the rocks, though her first few projects she tore up before she even finished them. Euryale had pried a lopsided basket out of Stheno's mutinous fingers before she could rip it up and placed it on our table, filling it with shells and interesting stones she had collected from around the island.

We didn't eat often, but when Euryale decided to learn

to fish, Stheno and I dutifully picked at the fire-roasted meals she put together for us, served on Stheno's sturdiest weaved plates.

Sometimes I left the boulder maze and would wander the island for a few days, sitting at the edge of the surf on the opposite shore and talking to my snakes. Euryale and Stheno didn't seek me out during these times. I was grateful for the space.

My snakes and I would talk about our past, and the decisions we'd made. We argued about choosing to come here with my sisters, since the snakes saw it as giving in to the prophecy, while I reasoned that the island was granting us more time than we would have ever had on the other side of the invisible curtain. Had we stayed out there, on Echidna's island or even back on the mainland, Perseus could have found us by now. I knew he was looking. It was only the island's twisting path through time that had allowed us to avoid him.

There were days where we wouldn't speak. The snakes and I would simply sit, in silence, letting the sound of the waves and the wind wash over us.

Contrary to Euryale's hope, Stheno did not develop any powers. Since both Euryale's and my powers could kill, however, it didn't seem like she was trying too hard to figure out if one was hibernating within her.

"Maybe you're the lucky one," I told her one night as we lay in bed. We were shuffled in tight, Stheno between Euryale and me.

"The lucky sister with no powers?" she scoffed.

"Yes," I replied, and she must have heard the honesty

in my answer, because she took one of my fingers between hers and squeezed it. I knew that Stheno, who had always been the strongest, the pseudo leader of our triplicate, was unmoored by the fact that Euryale and I shared something she did not.

"I think," she said slowly, and I turned my head toward her, "if given the choice between no power and a long, endless life amongst mortals, or a shorter, turbulent life with powers, I would choose the power."

"Are those the only two choices?" I whispered.

Next to Stheno, Euryale sniffled in her sleep. Euryale had a power, like me, but she had no prophecy linking that power to her death. She could have a long, endless life ahead of her, even with death harboring in her throat.

Stheno pinched my finger again. She had no answer for me.

IF NOT FOR THE rising and falling of the sun, for the lazy changes in weather we could see coming from miles away, the days would have passed like one big mirage. Euryale stopped keeping track with her flowers. She had accumulated a small mountain of them on the shelf, but the oldest petals crumbled away or were flattened under the weight of all the others.

In some ways, I felt as if this time I had with Euryale and Stheno was making up for a childhood spent at arm's length. Compared to the sharp, biting scuffles we had had as children, any argument we had on the island felt dulled.

When Stheno and Euryale had a spat about Stheno's lack of power that led to them not talking for three days, they still shared the bed with me, both of them turned on the opposite shoulder on either side. I attempted to serve as mediator one time, but Stheno snapped, "Just let me be upset about it."

"Fine," I responded. "But if you're both still acting like children tomorrow you can sleep outside."

That evening, Euryale made dinner. When we sat down at our table, Stheno passed Euryale her favorite plate without saying anything.

"Thanks," Euryale murmured. Stheno made a small noise in return, and just like that, they were past it.

On sunny days, the sea turned turquoise and glinted at us like a clever friend. We were helpless to do anything but run across the sand and dive in. With my sisters at my side, the salty ocean only brought memories of when I was a child, finding solace in the windswept brine and tide. Any thoughts of Poseidon had been washed away. I swam with my eyes shut, pulling myself along with long strokes against the waves and letting my snakes tell me where to go. They didn't love my swims, but they could feel the way it settled my heart.

If I bumped into Euryale or Stheno in the water, we would link our fingers and float on our backs, just two sea creatures bobbing on the rolling waves. Sometimes Euryale would tap her fingers against the surface of the water and tell me, "I'm saying hello to Mother."

When the sun passed its arch in the sky, we would pull ourselves to the shore and retrieve our clothes. Euryale had carefully torn the bottom of her dress so that the hem rested at the middle of her thigh, using the excess fabric for fishing nets and thread. When she pulled her dress over her head, it clung to her still wet skin.

"At least wait till you dry off," Stheno admonished, one foot still in the tide as she squeezed salt water out of her long hair. Euryale waved her off, kicking up sand as she climbed up the beach toward the boulders.

I waited with Stheno. My snakes were hanging loose over my shoulders, letting the sun burn off the last few drops of water.

"Oh, for the love of," Stheno cursed. She was struggling with her hair, fingers caught in the dark tangles. "I never knew it could be such a hassle to take care of."

I pulled on my own dress. "Do you want to cut it?"

Stheno paused her finger combing. Her hair, now that she rarely had it up in her severe bun or ponytail, was almost brushing her waist. Pulling the strands over one shoulder, she held the damp mess in her hand and examined it.

"Actually," she said, "yes."

When we told Euryale, she screeched.

"We'll be different!"

"What are you talking about?" Stheno said, dragging one of our chairs outside. I dug through the kitchen tools we had made until I found the sharp knife, the blade a finely honed shard of rock with a wooden handle that Euryale had whittled flowers onto. "We've always looked different, Euryale."

"But we've both always had long hair," she complained, following us out. Hers was in a still-damp braid hanging thick and long down her back. "Now we'll be really different."

Stheno set up the chair just outside the boulders and

sat down. Pushing all of her hair behind her shoulders, she glanced back at us. "Who's going to cut it?"

I was holding the knife, but I glanced at Euryale. Her throat bobbed. She whispered, "Have you ever cut hair?"

"No."

"Me neither."

Stheno barked, "Would one of you just do it."

I picked up Euryale's hand and pressed the handle of the knife into it.

"Oh, but—" she started.

"You can do it," I told her. "We trust you."

Euryale's fingers closed around the handle. She sucked in a breath through her nose, her chest puffing out, and marched over to Stheno's chair. Grasping a handful of hair by Stheno's right ear, Euryale pressed the blade against the strands. The hair sheared off easily. The long strands dropped to the ground, curling around Stheno's feet.

"Wait," Stheno shouted when Euryale made to grasp another section. "How much did you cut off?"

Euryale froze. "I— Well."

Stheno felt at the chopped strands, and twisted in her seat, narrowly missing the knife Euryale was still holding near her neck. Euryale flinched back and threw her hands up.

"How much!"

"You didn't say how short!" Euryale yelled back, frantic. "I just cut what I thought was a good amount!"

"A good amount," Stheno shrieked. "I've less hair than our father!"

Euryale blustered again, gripping the knife like a thief caught red-handed.

I had been watching, mouth slightly agape, ever since Euryale brought the knife to Stheno's hair. But suddenly, a laugh bubbled up in my chest. I snorted, covering my mouth with the back of my wrist, but it was no use. A full laugh burst out. I gripped my side as I felt a stitch pulling at me, my eyes squeezed closed against tears.

Euryale and Stheno stopped shouting at each other. Stheno had Euryale's wrist in her hand, holding the knife hostage. They were staring at me.

The laughs wheezed out of me, and my snakes were baffled. They flicked their tongues against my cheeks, which were beginning to hurt from smiling.

"I just," I gasped, and trailed off in giggles again. I took a breath. "You're so ridiculous. I love you both so much."

Now they were watching me with open mouths. Euryale broke first, a wide grin stretching across her face as she joined in my laughter. Stheno, still aghast, glanced between us.

"My hair!" she cried, and that sent both Euryale and I into another wave of laughter. Eventually, Stheno released Euryale's wrist and collapsed back into her chair. She rolled her eyes, but she was smiling. "You may as well cut off the rest, then, you wretched sister."

Euryale giggled, wiping her eyes with the backs of her wrists. She took a few steadying breaths, a couple of laughs slipping out even as she did so, and gathered up another handful of hair.

I braced my hands on my hips and leaned against a boulder. My lips seemed to be stuck in a grin.

"Us, too," Stheno called after a couple more chunks of her hair had fluttered to the ground. "We love you, too."

Euryale said, "Of course we do."

A warmth bloomed in my chest, and I pressed my hand against it like I had with the stitch in my side. I felt as if I didn't hold myself down, I would burn up with the feeling.

I DON'T KNOW WHAT I expected it to feel like. Perhaps I thought it would have been more obvious, as if one morning I got out of bed and it was painted across every surface of our home. Or maybe I was anticipating the fallout, readying for the steep drop once I crested the peak.

In the end, I didn't see it coming. I had to be warned.

I had been away from the boulder maze for a day or two, wandering the island. My feet cut divots in the wet sand as I trailed along the shore, before they were washed away in the reaching tide.

"Medusa," a voice called.

I turned. A dark head broke the surface of the water, her hair plastered black against her cheeks. Naidah.

My snakes perked up, and I with them, but when Naidah drew closer my excitement dimmed. Naidah wasn't meeting my gaze, which wasn't unusual, but there was a pinched look on her face. She moved slowly, as if not to frighten a wild animal.

"Naidah," I called, stepping farther into the surf. "What are you doing here?"

"Dionysus asked me…" she started, and then stopped. "I asked if I could tell you myself. He was just going to send a message through the wind or something," she said quickly, like she couldn't get the words out fast enough.

"Tell me what?"

Naidah bit her lip, her eyes flitting between the waves, the sky, the beach behind me. Salt water dripped from her chin. "Dionysus overheard from Athena"—her voice shook— "that your time is up."

The tide pulled at my calves. The hem of my dress was soaked, but if a hurricane had blown over the island in that moment, ripping up the life I'd tentatively given myself, I wouldn't have noticed.

Naidah was still talking. "He wanted to warn you; he thought you should at least have some time." She moved closer, staying low in the water, and reached out to brush her fingers against my ankle. "Medusa?"

Time, I thought. Had that really been all I wanted? More time? Time to spend with my sisters, to see that they would be okay without me. Time to talk to my snakes, to feel that we finally understood each other. Time to breathe the first breath after a sunrise, the air painted pink and gold and orange, over and over and over. I was no longer mortal, and yet time was still my greatest lack.

"Medusa," Naidah whispered, "I don't know what your prophecy is, only what Dionysus has told me, but he made it sound like I'd never see you again."

My snakes were curled in close to my head. They brushed their scaled cheeks against my temples.

How long had my sisters and I been here? A year, at least. I had been given another year, but that was all my mother's island could afford me. Fate, like time, could chip away at any defense. But this stolen year belonged to me. Beyond every circumstance, every chance that brought my sisters and me here, I had made the island feel like home. I had made my sisters feel like family. I had found peace in this body.

Steadily, I knelt down in the water. I found Naidah's fingers on my ankle and slid them between my own. Keeping my open gaze on the horizon, I lifted her palm to my lips.

"You won't see me again," I told her. I pressed her palm to my cheek, her skin warm despite the chill of the ocean. "I'm sorry."

Naidah's fingertips flexed against my jaw, and then she brought her other hand up to take hold of my face, pulling me down into a kiss. Her eyes were squeezed shut, and I couldn't tell if it was the sea or tears dripping down her cheeks. We overbalanced, tipping into the shallow waves. I put a hand on her waist for balance, the other buried in the sand.

"Don't be sorry," she told me, breaking away to pepper kisses across my nose, my cheeks. A snake licked her in return. "I'm so glad to have met you, my Medusa."

I smoothed her hair behind her ear. "And I you, my Naidah."

There weren't tears on her face. It was just water. I was glad, as I couldn't stand the thought of her crying over me. Water naiads could be as loose and free flowing as the rivers they inhabited, their emotions lasting only a day or two before they were lost in the flood. I was lucky to have had Naidah come back to me. But I was also glad that she had the chance to be swept away, once it was over. Naidah slid her hands around my neck and hugged me close.

"Thank you for coming," I said. "And Dionysus, too, tell him thank you. And that his friend misses him."

Naidah squeezed me tightly, once, and then slipped away. I stood, water streaming off me, and watched as Naidah backed away into the surf. I thought of trying to find her gaze in the reflection of the water, but thought I would be too tempted to lift my eyes and see the real thing.

"I'll remember you," Naidah promised. "In every green, in every sunrise."

Only when her head disappeared beneath the waves did I finally let myself cry.

An open hand, held out for the taking

IT WAS A WARM evening when I returned to the boulder maze. I sat on the blankets of our bed. This evening felt no different from all the rest, except for the weight of the knowledge that I only had a few evenings like this left.

"Euryale," I said. "Stheno."

Stheno was sitting near the entrance. She looked over at me when I spoke, her short hair brushing across her jaw.

"I need to ask something from both of you," I said. "For when the boy comes."

Euryale paused from whittling at a bit of driftwood and didn't look at me. We had talked about him a few times since we came to the island, and I made sure to keep my voice steady and not reveal that this time was different.

Stheno said, "What is it?"

I closed my eyes and patted the blanket next to me. After a few moments, I felt both of my sisters settle into the spaces beside me, and my snakes met their eyes since I could not.

"When the boy comes, he will come for me. Only for me," I started. "You are not meant to be a part of my prophecy beyond being by my side, and I do not want you to meet my same fate. My actions are mine to bear."

I took a breath and listened for the tumble of the ocean on the shore just beyond our rocky labyrinth. The sound reminded me of the white house on the lonely beach and, more recently, of Echidna's island, when Cerberus showed me the piece of his home he guarded so fiercely.

"When he comes," I said, "he will come to kill me."

Euryale made a small noise, but then she was quiet. My snakes told me Stheno had reached over and laid her hand over Euryale's arm. I was glad. I didn't think I could finish if she interrupted me.

"I know he will kill me. I have…" I tried to find the words to explain that I had realized my own death was approaching and would not try to stop it. "I have known for a long time now, how I was meant to end. There is nothing I would change about my life."

"Medusa," Euryale said.

I kept talking. "When he comes, do not try to stop him. I don't want you to try and intervene. I don't want him to hurt you, too. As long as he gets what he came for, I think he will leave both of you alone."

"You're not going to fight?" This time it was Stheno who had spoken, and Euryale did not try to quiet her. "You said that you would face this with your eyes open. Before we left Echidna's island, you *said—*"

"I did," I admitted. "But I've thought about it, during our journey here and after, and the way I see it, the Fates have given me two choices. Either I fight, and act like the monster that the mortals want me to be by taking this boy's life,

373

or I let him kill me. No, listen," I said, as Stheno tried to speak again. "I have killed his men. They may have meant me harm, but none of them actually raised a hand against me, and yet I killed them anyway. I do not want this to happen again."

"But you didn't mean it!" Euryale burst out. "All you've done is protect yourself!"

"Have I?" I asked, tilting my head. My snakes swayed with the motion.

"Yes," Stheno said, her tone leaving no room for argument. "And you would be protecting yourself again if you stopped this boy from *beheading you.*"

"The Graeae have predicted this end for me," I said, trying to keep my voice even. "If I try to avoid this now, it could be even more painful when it finally does come for me, whether it is at the point of this boy's sword, or something worse. I will not be made a monster because of the decisions I have made up until now, but should I choose to end that boy's life, I only see destruction down the rest of that path. Who else could I hurt? What if it's one of you?"

Stheno and Euryale had nothing to say to that.

"I will not let myself become the monster the mortals want me to be," I said. "Both of you said that you came to find me because you wanted to be on the right side of my legend," I reminded them, reaching out with both hands to place my palms on their knees. "I want to be on the right side of it, too. This is my choice. That is what makes me different from the monster they want me to be. I chose this, and they cannot take that from me. My monstrosity was for myself, and for the people I cared about. These men will not be the ones to transform it into something terrible."

"What of the others?" Stheno said quietly. "The ones after, who do not listen to your side of the legend."

I gave her a small smile. "The others do not matter to me. You, and Euryale. Echidna. Even Dionysus." And Naidah, I thought, but didn't say. She was just for me. "The people who know, and the people who see me and recognize a part of themselves, those are the people who matter. I am trusting you to carry my legend for me. You must keep the Gorgons alive."

I felt Euryale shift underneath my palm, and my hand slid from her knee as she knelt and then shuffled forward. The soft scratch of her movement against the sand was loud in the midst of our quiet. She put her arms around my shoulders.

My snakes were looking at her. I asked them to let her do what she wished, and they moved out of the way as Euryale set her head down in the curve between my neck and shoulder.

Stheno did not move closer, but she matched my posture and put her own hand on my knee.

"If I could control my power," Euryale said quietly, "if I could be certain it would only hurt him—"

I stopped her, softly. "But you can't be certain. You can't risk hurting Stheno, too. You have to let me go."

Euryale sighed. Stheno was watching me closely.

"We will do our best to make sure you are remembered," Stheno said evenly, "as you should be. As you truly are."

I nodded, just once. One of my snakes flickered its tongue out to brush over Euryale's cheek, and the salt they tasted there from her tears flooded my senses. I pressed my lips together for a moment, and then took a deep breath. I let it out in the rhythm of the waves crashing on the shore: a long, tumbling exhale.

"Thank you," I said.

Stheno

NIGHTS ON THE ROCKY island were still. The wind glanced off the tops of the boulders and left the three Gorgons unruffled at the base of the stones. The crash of the waves on the sand was the only sound. Stheno had learned this after many evenings spent awake, listening for the creak of a boat coming to shore, for the step of a foot within the rocky maze, for the breath of a hunter.

The night he came, she heard none of these things. Instead, she did hear a rustle, like a bird struggling against a strong breeze.

Stheno was lying next to her sisters on their bed, curled on her side facing Medusa, who was in the middle, with Euryale mirroring Stheno's position on Medusa's other side. All three of them rarely slept at once. One of them was always awake. Stheno thought she was the only one who heard the rustling, like wings struggling to support the weight they bore. Medusa's eyes were closed, when Stheno spared a glance toward her sister. Medusa was lying propped up against a pillow, her head high, her snakes curled sleepily around her ears and

drooping to her shoulders. One of them noticed Stheno looking and flicked its tongue out lazily at her.

The sound of wings grew louder. Stheno thought she
should sit up and go searching for the source of the noise.

Right as she shifted to lift her head, Medusa spoke.

"Pretend to be asleep," she said, and her voice was unwavering, and it seized Stheno's limbs like Medusa had reached
in and took hold of her from the inside. Stheno struggled
against the command, but she could not move. Her mind
raced and she expected her breathing to pick up with how
fast her heart was beating, but the rise and fall of her chest
was as even as if she were actually sleeping.

Medusa spoke again, in a soft voice that flooded Stheno
like a poison. "Keep your eyes closed until it is over. Don't
fight him." She sounded so calm, but Stheno searched for
the desperate note in her tone. Medusa told her, *"Don't fight
him. I love you both too much to lose you to this, too."*

And Stheno had no choice but to obey. It was like Medusa's words were an instinct she could not ignore. The only
other time Stheno had experienced something like this was
when she had watched a god give a command to a group of
mortals. It had been Dionysus, when she and Euryale had
gone to ask where Medusa was, and the way he spoke gave
the mortals no choice but to obey. The way Medusa was
speaking was like that of a god.

Stheno tried to make sense of how this was possible, but
then she heard another noise, a soft thud, like a heavy weight
being set on the ground. Her eyes were searching wildly
behind her eyelids, but all she saw was black. Then she heard
someone take a step toward them.

A frayed thread has no end

I HAD NOT SLEPT since Naidah came to the island for the last time. I closed my eyes, like Stheno and Euryale did, but I was too wary of myself to sleep. So I was awake when Stheno and I heard the sound of wings approaching the spot where we lay. I knew that Stheno was awake because my snakes told me she was watching me, and I felt her breathing change when the sound of strained, fluttering feathers entered our circle of boulders. I knew Stheno was going to try and get up, to see what it was.

I couldn't let her move. I knew if she tried to fight, she would be hurt, because of me. When I spoke, I spoke with all the desperation of a girl trying to save the remnants of her family. I spoke with the conviction that Stheno and Euryale would not die for their involvement in my prophecy.

I spoke, and they had to listen. Euryale was actually asleep when the boy approached, but she woke up when my words took over her body. She and Stheno would not be able to disobey.

When there was a soft thud near the entrance to the

boulder circle, my snakes stirred. I asked them to tell me what they saw.

Nothing, the not-voice said. But I could tell they were confused. They saw nothing standing above us in the circle. But they could *smell* metal, and leather, and sweat. They could smell that there was someone standing above us.

Another trick of the gods, I thought. Even if I had chosen to face this boy, Perseus, I would not be able to see him. Someone had been very thorough to ensure that this boy fulfilled the prophecy laid out before us.

I heard the step he took. I heard how he hesitated when he was within reach. My snakes flicked their tongues to taste the metal of a sword moving through the air.

In the final moments, my snakes asked me to move. They asked me to open my eyes and fight back against the enemy I would not be able to see. They drew on a deep, desperate emotion I had buried beneath my determination as a final plea. But even as they asked, they curled closer to me. They knew, just as I did, that we had made our choice.

The not-voice said, *We. Now, and forever.*

Perseus's blade found my neck, and I opened my eyes.

Beyond the horizon

I OPENED MY EYES, but I was not in my body. I did not understand why I could still see, why I was not sent to the Underworld. How was I still here, in this world?

I could see myself, my head and my body separated. I could see Stheno and Euryale, lying still beside me. I was no longer constricted to just what was in front of my eyes; I could see everything laid out before me as if I were standing just over Perseus's shoulder.

Perseus, still invisible, though I could see him now like I was peering through a watery reflection, watched my head roll away from my body. He lowered the shield he had braced against his chest, and I recognized it. I had seen the smooth silver of that shield face in Athena's temple. A sharp lance of anger cut through me, though I had no body through which to feel it.

As my head rolled toward Perseus's feet, the snakes dragging limply behind it, two forms appeared out of my body's severed neck. The first trampled his way out, hooves first; he was a gigantic snow-white horse with huge, pearly wings.

The winged horse snorted and stamped the ground with his enormous hooves once he was free, whinnying loudly. Flecks of my blood dripped from his flanks like bright red flower petals.

I knew who he was the moment I saw him. Ever since that terrible night at the temple, I had never laid a hand to my stomach feeling for an intrusion. Rather, I had felt something at the back of my mind, beyond my snakes and me, waiting quietly. It had been easy to ignore, but now there was nothing holding it back.

The winged stallion's name was Pegasus, and with his creation, I felt the last piece of Poseidon being pried from my body. Athena had told me I would not bear his children, and while I had not born the weight of them in my belly, my death purged the god from my body. I was finally free of him.

Another being began to appear from my neck. The crouched figure began to unfurl, stained in red blood, with a golden sword already clutched in his square hands. He rose higher and higher above my body, above Perseus. He was a giant. The fine features of his face were not distorted by his size, and when he blinked his eyes open, they were a bright, clear green. He lifted the golden sword and studied the hilt, perfectly fitted to his grip. His name was Chrysaor: *He of the golden sword.*

Pegasus and Chrysaor looked at each other. They could not see Perseus, I realized. He was still invisible. The winged horse stamped the ground once more, his hoof scraping on the rock, before spreading his wings and beating them, once, twice, flicking drops of blood in every direction. Chrysaor pushed his hair back, slick with blood, and climbed onto Pegasus's broad back.

The winged horse did not immediately fly away, however. Pegasus turned and bent his neck to run his nose over the line of my arm, which was lying limp across my stomach. Chrysaor watched steadily, his eyes sliding over Euryale and Stheno, who were still lying as if they were sleeping. A few drops of blood stained their dresses.

When my body did not move, Pegasus tossed his head and neighed, once, and I thought it could be a longing cry for his mother. Then he leaped into the air, his wingbeats sending a hurricane of wind over the rocky island. Pegasus's powerful wings carried Chrysaor and himself high above the island breathlessly fast, and in just a few moments they were too far away to see.

Perseus had stood silently while my two children appeared and then departed.

Now that they were gone, he finally lowered his sword. When he looked down, Stheno and Euryale had their eyes open. He pointed the tip of his sword at them, even though they could not see him, and shuffled over to where my head had fallen after he had separated it from my neck.

He knelt to pick it up, not taking his eyes off my sisters. My snakes were limp around my face, lying flat like grass trampled underfoot. Perseus grabbed a handful of the snakes near the crown of my head and lifted it, holding it at arm's length. A grimace pinched his face.

When my head was lifted from the ground, Stheno and Euryale's eyes snapped to it.

"Give her back," Stheno demanded. She struggled to

her feet, the remnants of my command weighing down her limbs.

Perseus straightened up. The pale light of the moon illuminated the helmet he wore, glinting coolly off the metal, though I knew only I could see it. His sandals were strapped halfway up his calf, and I finally found the source of the feathery noise that had alerted me and Stheno; fluttering on either side of his sandals were thin, gray and white wings. The wings looked a little ragged and tired, like they had been carrying him a long way.

Perseus still held his sword in the hand that was not clutching my head. It curved wickedly, like a scythe, and a few drops of blood clung to the tip.

When Stheno finally gained her feet by propping herself up against a boulder, Perseus took a step back. The wings on his feet fluttered.

Stheno was looking at my head. I silently urged her to avoid my eyes. A cruel expression twisted her face, torn between grief and rage, and it hurt my heart to see it even though my heart was no longer beating. Stheno took a stumbling step forward as Euryale also began to stir.

Perseus sheathed his sword to free one hand so that he could untie a plain cloth bag at his belt. Keeping his eyes carefully averted away from my face, he shook out the bag and maneuvered my head into it, releasing the snakes so that he could tie the top end closed. He wiped the hand that had been touching the snakes on the outside of the bag. Then he reattached the bag to his belt, the weight of my head knocking against his hip like a purse heavy with coin.

Euryale was now almost to her feet, her mouth opening and closing like a fish out of water, desperate for a breath. When Stheno took another step forward, calling out my name, Perseus curled an invisible lip at them and tapped his heels on the ground. The winged sandals immediately began to struggle and flutter their wings, lifting the boy off the ground.

"Give her back!" Stheno cried again. She reached out for the space that Perseus had just been, but her grasping hands could only clutch at empty air.

"The monster is slain," Perseus told her, an invisible, mocking voice, sharpened by cruelty and pride. "It will torment mortal men no longer."

When he spoke, Stheno's head jerked up to look in the direction of his voice. "Liar!" she cried. "The monster lives on, and he has killed my sister!"

But it seemed that Perseus had spoken all that he desired, because he tilted his body and the wings carried him away from the boulders' clearing.

Even though my head was stuffed in a bag, I could still see everything that was going on. Beyond that, I could see more than I could before. I could follow Perseus as he returned to his boat, anchored far away from shore, but I could also stay with my sisters and watch over them as they fought against the lingering remains of my spell and stumbled through the boulder maze. They were yelling, a mixture of my name and wordless cries tearing out of their throats and echoing eerily against the boulders.

Stheno burst onto the beach and instantly spotted the small, dark outline of Perseus's boat on the water. She made

to charge across the sand and launch our own little boat into
the sea to sail after him, but before she had made it another
few steps, Euryale caught her arm. Stheno spun around to
face her, and I could see a harsh word on her lips, but her
breath caught when she saw the tears tracking silently down
Euryale's face.

Euryale spoke quietly. "We can't leave her here. She
can't be alone."

She meant my body. Stheno struggled with this, looking once between Perseus's boat, which now had its sails
unfurled and was starting to move away from the island, and
back to her remaining sister.

"She didn't want us to fight him," Euryale pushed, tightening her grip on Stheno's arm.

"She didn't want us to *stop* him," Stheno spat back. "And
she made sure we could not."

Perseus was getting farther and farther away as they
stood, trapped, on the beach.

"We will find him," Euryale said. "Later."

"I didn't want him," Stheno whispered. "I just wanted to
get her back."

"She knew what she was doing when she told us not to
move. She must have known that he would take her—her
head, after he cut it off. Perhaps this is another piece of the
prophecy that we simply can't change."

Stheno closed her eyes with a rough sigh. As her body
relaxed, Euryale loosened her grip on her arm and slid her
hand into Stheno's instead.

Euryale went on, "We have to do what she said. This is
the best way to make sure we never lose her again."

"We've lost her already," Stheno said, but Euryale was shaking her head.

"No, we lost her once before, when we left her in Athens. We didn't try to understand her as she was then. But we changed. We sought her out so that she would not be alone anymore, and she came back to us. Just now," Euryale said, through a sniffle, "a part of her was taken. But she is not lost to us. She showed us who she was, and how she wanted to be remembered. Right? It's up to us now to make sure she is not lost in the tidal wave of those mortals' fear." Euryale squeezed Stheno's hand. "We have to protect her now. We will use our power to protect others like her."

It was still dark on the island, with only the faint moon illuminating the beach. Stheno opened her eyes and looked out to where Perseus's ship was just a speck on the inky horizon.

"You're right," she told Euryale. "But I wish it had never come to this, in the first place."

Euryale finally looked away from her sister to stare out at the ship that was taking my head away from them. Even as the tears continued to drip down the line of her cheeks and drop into the damp sand, Euryale kept her head held high.

"Wishes are for stars, and mortals too afraid to take their lives in their own hands," she said. "Medusa needs us to think of the future, not dwell on what has been. And I'm sure she'll watch over us, in her own way." Euryale tilted her head up, as if she could see me, hovering over them like a phantom bird. "She always did."

My sisters returned to the boulder maze, and I tore my attention away from them to focus on Perseus. I trusted

Stheno and Euryale to take care of themselves, and to take care of my body. Perseus, on the other hand, warranted my gaze. I needed to see what his plan was for my head.

The sack that held me was still attached to the belt at his hip as he sailed away from the island, heading north. He had removed the helmet at one point and was scrubbing a hand through his flattened hair. His face was so young. Although, he could not have been much younger than I had been. Perhaps he simply seemed young, in the face of everything I had gone through.

Danae

HER SON STOOD IN the dim hall as if there was never a doubt he would be back again. The oil lamps were just barely lit, and Danae studied Perseus as he stood in the center, close to a raised throne dais, with a sunburned woman behind him, peering around in the dark spaces around the hall. The woman looked exhausted, barely more than a girl, and the way she stuck close to her son's side worried Danae.

On top of the dais, Polydectes's crown was pressing heavily into his brow. Danae knew that he had hoped the monster would kill Perseus, and wondered what the king would do now that her son had returned. A heavy bag with a large, wine-red stain hung at Perseus's hip. Danae couldn't make herself look away from it.

"King Polydectes," Perseus said, his voice ringing out too loudly against the stone of the hall. "I have brought what you asked. Though, I will only give it to you once you release my mother from your rule so that she and I may leave this kingdom."

"Show me its head, first," Polydectes said. A deep wrinkle

was cutting into his forehead, and he clutched at both arms of his throne with bony hands.

"But—" Danae started, her heart jumping in her chest, but the king silenced her. She clenched her teeth. Polydectes had changed in the last few weeks, falling easily into rages and flights of madness that Danae had never seen before. He wasn't in his right mind. His failed plan to kill her son seemed to be the tipping point.

Perseus obeyed him, trying unsuccessfully to conceal his smile. He untied the bag from his belt and opened it, keeping his gaze averted as he felt for the snakes and gripped them, right above the crown. He began to lift the head out when the king spoke, sharply.

"Cover its eyes, you fool boy!"

Perseus's jaw clicked in annoyance, but he did as commanded, using his other hand and feeling over the monster's face before he laid it over the eyes. The canvas bag dropped away, and Polydectes stared at the head. Danae couldn't help but stare, as well. Snakes hung around her face, limp as seaweed out of water, though still a bright, shining green. The skin had gone pale, and the neck ended in a ragged, blood-stained line.

"How did you kill it?" the king asked.

"I had help," Perseus said, "from the gods."

Danae knew this was true. Her son couldn't have accomplished this without help. Someone had listened to her pleas. The shield across Perseus's back, the winged sandals on his feet, and gleaming helmet strapped to his belt were all divine gifts.

"You?" the king said, his tone threatening to spill into anger. "Why would the gods help you?"

Perseus glared up at Polydectes. "I am the son of a god. This task that was set upon me was approved and aided by divine intervention, and it is because of them that I accomplished killing the monster. I did not do this for you, old man," Perseus said, and his eyes glinted with malice and pride. "Nor will I ever do anything for a mortal king ever again."

Danae guessed what her son was about to do, and turned her face at the last second as he took his hand from the eyes and lifted the monster's head before the king's face.

Polydectes's furious gaze was intent on the boy, open-mouthed at Perseus's blatant disrespect, and he did not have time to look away.

When it was over, the king was frozen, forever clutching at the arms of his throne. After he had scooped up the bag and put the head away, Perseus called to Danae.

"We're leaving."

Danae turned, slowly, to look at the king, now a statue. The marriage she had hoped for was gone. Her small, dark, comfortable life in this palace was over. She looked to her son.

"Where will we go?" she asked, as she stood and gathered her skirts. Her delicate eyebrows were pinched together as she approached, and the irritation in her voice was plain. "He had given us protection all these years. Who else would give us that?"

"It does not matter," he said. And he turned and left the hall, shoving the last few snakes back into the bag as he went.

Danae looked to the woman behind Perseus.

"Who are you?"

The woman eyed Danae, the bridge of her nose and cheeks red with sun exposure and face drawn by dehydration. "Andromeda. Perseus rescued me from a giant sea serpent and the man who held me captive, by using that head."

Danae tilted her head toward her son's retreating back. "My son has saved you?"

Andromeda nodded, and said, "He told me we would be married."

With a quick look to the ceiling and a deep breath, she said, "My name is Danae. I am his mother. He says many things, and I am sure he means most of them, but be careful, girl. I do not think he will ever be satisfied with the trappings of a mortal life."

Andromeda shifted from one foot to the other, barefoot on the marble floor.

"He slayed the monster," she said. "The snake-haired beast. As he said he would."

"Had you heard of the Gorgon Medusa before?" Danae asked, using the name she had heard whispered on the lips of servants and gods alike.

Andromeda shook her head.

"She was a monster, in the mortal sense of the word," Danae said, "and Perseus was ordered to kill her and bring her head to the king. But this is not the first time he has used her power to defeat an enemy, is it?"

"No."

Danae nodded.

"He may do as he says he will do," she said, beckoning for Andromeda to follow her as she followed Perseus's path out of the hall, "but it is his selfish actions that truly speak to who he is. Be wary of his hot head. You may be caught in the crossfire of his recklessness one day, too."

The two women walked slowly to join Perseus at his boat. They were both quiet, and thinking hard, and their eyes would flick to the bag at Perseus's waist so many times that the string should have snapped from the weight of it.

Cut off a snake's head and the fangs still drip venom

I WAS PULLED FROM a deathlike sleep when I heard a familiar voice.

Like a sword drawn from a sheath. Like the crash of steel against armor. Like a rough, stormy night when only the sudden flashes of lightning will show you the way.

Athena said, "You have succeeded."

Perseus said, "Yes, goddess. I thank you, and the other gods, who helped me defeat this monster. I have come to return what I borrowed."

It was night, but I knew where we were. This marble hall lit with blazing torches had been my home long enough for me to recognize it in just a few moments. Athena's temple had not changed at all since I had left.

Athena stood before her great altar on the raised dais, and Perseus was perched on one knee before her, shoulders tense.

Perseus laid out the helmet of invisibility, the winged sandals, and the curved sword on the lowest step of the altar. He unhooked the shining, reflective shield from his back and held it up with both hands.

"I thank you for your kindness, Athena, and for this shield. But I did not need it, in the end," Perseus said, his eyes downcast.

Athena looked down at him. A peculiar expression crossed her face from under the shadow of her plumed helmet.

"You did not use my shield?"

"No, goddess. I was able to slay the monster while it slept."

"A coward's way out," Athena accused him. Perseus's head snapped up, a retort ready on his tongue, but Athena continued in her booming voice. "You are a boy sent to do the will of the gods. Only because of their intervention, because of my intervention, were you successful. I knew that men even lesser than you would need to see her slain by mortal hands."

"My father is king of the gods," Perseus started, ego bruised.

"And yet your arrogance and fear reek of mortality." Athena clasped her hands in front of her like a demure maiden, even as her words cut Perseus to his core. "You simply played into the hands of a prophecy where you were no more than a means to an end. The prophecy was not about you. It was always about Medusa, and she was not afraid to meet the end the Fates had predicted for her. If she had been awake," Athena eyed Perseus with her critical, all-seeing gaze, "she could have killed you in a moment."

Perseus stood. He still clutched the shield, and he had good enough sense not to toss it directly at Athena's divine head, though I could tell he wanted to. With his pride smarted, Perseus set down the shield above the other gifts and reached for his belt. He untied the cloth sack containing my head.

Perseus was not so careful with me as he had been with his other gifts. He tossed my head up to Athena, the stained cloth rippling as it moved through the air. All three of us watched its trajectory toward the floor near Athena's feet, but at the last moment the goddess reached out and caught it with one hand, the sack just a finger's length from hitting the floor.

"Careful, boy," she warned, all sharp edges. "I can make heroes, but I can unmake them just as easily."

Perseus bowed in stilted deference. Athena had made him a hero in the eyes of the mortals, but he was still barely more than a child.

"May I have leave to go, goddess of wisdom?" he asked.

Athena stared at him with cold gray eyes, making him wait in uncomfortable silence that was only momentarily soothed by the sound of wind rushing across the marble. I wondered if she was weighing the costs of another godly war that would certainly arise if she struck him. Then the goddess jerked her head, once.

"Go. But be wary, son of Zeus. Not all gods are as forgiving as I."

Perseus spun on his heel and strode quickly out of the temple. I watched him leave, studying the slightly hunched line of his shoulders, and how the pale, fading light of the moon drew the life from his face. His brows were pinched together. He looked like a young boy on the precipice of a tantrum. When he passed through the entrance to the temple, I stopped following and let him walk out alone, and Perseus hurried down the steps and across the wide courtyard of the Acropolis toward two figures waiting by the path that would lead them back down into Athens. Danae and Andromeda. They watched Perseus as he approached.

When the boy passed them, Andromeda turned and followed him down the hill, but Danae stayed still. She was watching the temple. It felt as though she was looking straight at me.

For a few moments, we were both motionless. Then her head tilted down, like an apology. Danae held that pose until Perseus called out to her. Then she, too, turned and left.

The torches lighting the streets of Athens flickered like stars reflected on the inky black ocean. I studied the familiar outline of the rooftops, occasionally interrupted by a tall, spindly cypress tree. The city, like the temple, had scarcely changed. Of course, I could not expect Athens to have experienced as much change as I had, or else there would have been nothing left.

I turned back to Athena when I heard the *clink* of the shield being lifted off the ground. The goddess was holding the knotted end of the cloth sack in one hand, and held up the shield Perseus had left with the other. Her shield. She studied the smooth, reflective outer shell, and then turned toward her marble altar. I moved closer to see what she was doing.

She set both the shield and the sack on the marble. With an absent-minded wave of her hand, the other gifts that

Perseus had returned disappeared from the bottom step, probably sent back to their owners.

Athena picked apart the knot that kept the sack closed with clever fingers and reached into the bag. She felt around for a moment, checking that my eyes were closed.

I expected her to grip my snakes to lift my head like she was tearing a root from the soil, as Perseus had done every time he had lifted me out of the bag, and then held me at arm's length like I was a wasp nest about to burst open.

But she did not act as Perseus had. Athena used both hands to reach into the bag and lifted my head out by cradling my jaw in her palms. The bag slid away from my snakes as they hung limply behind my neck. Athena was holding me like I was a soft-fleshed fruit, easily bruised, and precious. She swiped her thumb over the thin skin underneath my eye.

"I am sorry, Medusa," said Athena.

I gaped at her. These were words I had never expected to hear from Athena's mouth. And while she was many things, a goddess, a warrior, Athena was not a liar. Of course, she had only plucked up the nerve to admit this to my decapitated head, which felt like the easy way out, but I could see that she truly meant it.

But then, "Medusa, I know you can hear me. You are still attached to this world, are you not?"

If my consciousness had still been attached to my head, my jaw would have dropped to the floor. I moved in closer, trying to get a clear view of Athena's face. She was studying me as she would study a complex war map. Then she looked up. Right at me, hovering just above my own head. Our eyes met.

Athena smiled.

"There you are."

"You can see me?" My voice was weak from disuse, as thin and brittle as dried seaweed. "How?"

"I was looking for you," Athena said simply. "As a goddess, I can see many things that mortals cannot, but very often, one can see whatever they wish to see, so long as they are looking for it."

With another tender swipe of her thumb underneath my closed eye, Athena laid my head down carefully on the cold marble of the altar. She adjusted a few of the snakes so that they would not be caught under the weight of my skull. I watched her silently. When she touched my snakes, her fingers just barely brushing their green scales as she nudged them into place, I wished that I could feel them in my hand again. To feel the press of their rounded snouts in my palm. Their little faces were as lifeless as my own, and their glinting black eyes were closed.

I wished they had been able to come with me, after Perseus had taken my head. I felt unbalanced without them.

Athena stepped back from the altar, rising to her full height. She reached up and removed her plumed helmet, the polished metal glinting just like the shield in the moonlight. While any mortal soldier's hair would be plastered to their forehead from sweat and the pressure of the helmet, Athena's dark brown curls were not dented by the shape of the metal. When she ran a long-fingered hand through the strands, they fell into place as if placed there individually, pushed back over her shoulders to keep her face clear of distractions.

Athena set her helmet down on the altar, too, though she placed it far to the edge.

"You," I started, and Athena looked up at me. Though I had no throat, I felt as though there were something caught in it. "You had him bring my head here. Back to you. Why?"

Athena nodded. "I wanted to speak with you, one more time, after it was all over."

"It," I said, "meaning my death."

"Yes."

"Which you had a hand in. Several hands, in fact," I said, and my voice grew stronger the more I spoke. I could feel anger rising in me, and it was almost a relief to know I could still feel as I did when I was alive. The anger that spurred me on was such a mortal feeling, but I let it run its course. "What you did to me, the last time I was here. You cursed me."

The impenetrable wall of Athena's face was as familiar to me as the halls of the temple we were in. I could see the tense line of her jaw, as sharp as a dagger. "I did it to protect you. I gave you an unbeatable power, so that no man would be able to harm you again."

"That is what you told yourself, I'm sure, to rationalize such an act of violence against another woman."

"Violence?" Athena repeated. "I gave you what you wanted. You wished to harm him, as he harmed you, you cannot deny it."

"I was twenty. Barely more than a child, who had no knowledge of the world," I said, exasperated. As the anger in my nonexistent chest threatened to overwhelm me, I felt my grip on this world growing tighter and tighter as I spoke. "I had just been raped by someone I thought I could trust. I felt more helpless than I ever had in my life," I said. "Of course I wanted to fight back. That is what I wanted, but did you ever try to understand what I *needed*?"

Athena opened her mouth, but I kept going. The dam inside me had been smashed open, and everything was flooding out.

"I needed someone to be on my side. But you told me that someone needed to be punished. And you would not punish him, because he was a god, and you did not want to start a war." I let my disbelief saturate each word. "You, goddess of wisdom and battle strategy, did not want to start a war amongst the gods. So you chose to put the blame on me."

"I only meant for it to seem that way," Athena explained, spreading her hands. "The mortals, and the gods, needed to see that someone was punished for the act. But the power I gave you was not meant to be a curse."

"Why did someone need to be punished at all?"

Athena stared at me, her hands lowering. She didn't seem to have an answer, so I gave her one.

"It was to protect your reputation," I spat. "You may tell yourself that what you did was for the good of the gods, or that it was out of some twisted sort of kindness, but you decided that you needed to protect your reputation more than you needed to protect me."

"A slight against a goddess could not go unanswered," Athena stated.

If my snakes were still with me, they would be hissing in frustration. I remembered how Dionysus had acted, the day the hunters came to his clearing, spitting insults and threatening violence. They had labeled him the villain, without even taking a moment to consider what the women had wanted. But Dionysus had not reacted by lashing out against his followers, or even the hunters who had threatened him. Instead, the god had simply allowed the women to seize their fates with their bare hands and do with them what they wished. Dionysus was a god who waved off the opinions of mortal men like buzzing flies. He had been a god who had the lives of his followers cupped in a single hand, and yet he let them chart their own course. Why could Athena not do the same?

I tilted my chin up and asked, "You had to defend your reputation?"

"Yes. As a goddess, I had to show that I would not stand for my temple to be defiled."

"And you did not want someone else's decision to ruin your life?"

"Yes," she exhaled, like I was finally getting it.

"Then why," I asked slowly, "did you allow it to ruin mine?"

Athena blinked. That impenetrable wall flickered, and I remembered the single moment of guilt I had seen flash over her face the last time we were together. Was Athena truly oblivious to the harm she had caused me? Or had she forced herself to ignore it in the sake of self-preservation, so that she would not have to reckon with her role in my torment?

"You made me into what I am today. What I was," I corrected, "before I became this spirit, no more than a ghost. Although, I suppose I am still here because of your hand in my life. Why do you deny that you have caused me such pain?"

"I do not," Athena said, taking a step back from the altar. Her single step echoed loudly against the empty hall. Never, in all the time I had known her, had I seen Athena give up ground. I had shaken her.

I kept pushing. "No? So you admit that you decided that you would allow my attacker to go free, in favor of punishing me for my own rape? You admit that you cursed one of your own priestesses? I was under your care, your protection. And yet you turned on me the moment your own reputation as a goddess was at risk," I said flatly. "Do you deny it?"

Athena's mouth opened, and then closed. The line of her brow folded in.

"I—no, I do not. But I am a goddess, you cannot understand—"

"I was no longer mortal, after you cursed me," I interrupted. "I understand the thoughts of a god well enough. The mortals have expectations of you, right? They will talk of anything they see, or hear about, and spin it into a web of truth and lies until there is no clear way out." Athena nodded, once. I asked, "But why should you care of the opinion of mortal men?"

"Mortals' lives are so short," she said, her hands curling into loose fists at her sides, "but their opinions, their thoughts and fears, what stories they spread between one another, that is what remains after they are gone. What they will say about me." Athena glanced back to the entrance of the hall, where the dark outline of Athens spread out like a great shadow under the temple. "They will need to believe in my reputation, so that they continue believing in me."

I watched her silently for a moment, and then asked her,

"Who amongst the mortals was happy to hear of what happened that night?"

My question quickly brought Athena's attention back to me.

"What do you mean?"

"Of the mortals who heard of my punishment, who heard of how Poseidon had attacked me in your temple, and yet I was the one who bore the deadly gaze and snakes for hair, who amongst those mortals who heard the story was satisfied with that result? Did you notice?"

I let her think about it for a moment. She was looking at my severed head lying on the altar again, her eyes fixed on the space right between my closed eyes.

I asked, "Was it the women? The mothers and wives and young girls who looked up to you as the leader of their city, the goddess who protected them? Were they satisfied? What about the priestesses, here in the temple? Did they feel that just punishment was dealt?"

Now Athena was silent not for lack of answer, but for an unwillingness to speak the words. I knew I was pushing my luck, speaking to a goddess this way, but I figured if she had wanted to speak to me so badly even after my death, she would hear what I had to say first.

I said, "Or was it the men? Did they believe that you made the right choice, sparing Poseidon of any hardship, and pushing all the blame onto me, so that no one even considered to ask if a twenty-year-old girl could refuse an immortal god? Are those mortal men the reason you needed to spare your reputation? You may have proved those men right, but what of your reputation with the women in this city? How did they feel, knowing that not even a goddess could stand against an act of violence from a god?"

"No!" Athena shouted, the word echoing sharply against the marble columns of the hall. Her brow was furrowed, and her chest was rising and falling quickly with fast breaths, and I thought I'd finally pushed too far. But her hands remained loose at her side, not clenched into fists like mine would have been, and I wondered if it was divine control that allowed her to keep her composure. The only other sign my words had finally broken through something inside of her was that the line of her shoulders was slumped, curved like the branch of a tree weighed down too heavily by its leaves.

"I did not do it for them," Athena said. "For the men. I did not do it—I just wanted you to be safe. I tried to give you a power that would ensure your safety."

This time, her voice was unshielded, and she sounded as sincere as she could possibly be. In that moment, Athena reminded me of Dionysus in his meadow on the mountain, far from any mortals, when the god had finally let his defenses drop. Athena had reached that point. She could no longer hide anything from me.

Seeing the sincerity in Athena allowed me to take a breath and release the anger I had been holding on to. I no longer needed it to stay tied to this world. I told Athena, "I learned to use the power for my safety, in time."

"Then," she asked, "it was worth it?"

"Only because I was able to learn to control the power, and control what it would turn me into. You knew how the mortals feared me, you helped Perseus kill me because of those mortals' fear," I said. "Their fear turned me, and my reputation, into a heartless monster. And I would have become what they believed me to be, if I had not found the people I wanted to protect. It was because of the people who believed in me that I was able to see what this power was truly meant for. What I could turn it into, instead of what it could do to me."

I looked down at my own face, at my snakes fanned out around me like a green halo.

I told her, "Perseus killed the Medusa that the mortals were frightened of. He killed the monster they all believed me to be, and he used my power for his own, even though it was that power that made me monstrous in the first place. The mortal perception of Medusa, the one that Perseus took such pride in beheading through cowardly means, she only exists now in the legends the mortals will pass on to their children. But she never truly existed at all. I made sure of it."

The night sky outside the temple began to brighten, ever so faintly, as the first lights of dawn seeped over the horizon. As the inky black turned to bruised purple, and was then threaded through with blue, the shadows around the temple began to dissipate. The light illuminated Athena's face, too, and reflected off the tears that had gathered in the corners of her eyes. Were her tears for me, or for herself? Either way, I knew that I had finally pulled her true emotions to the surface. The Athena who had cursed me would have never let me see her cry.

"My power, and my snakes, became more than just your curse; they became a part of me. I learned to see the truth in myself," I said softly, and tilted my head until Athena looked at me. "Can you say the same?"

"The truth…" Athena trailed off, her gaze sliding away from me to flick over the shield lying next to my head, then over her helmet, the curved metal embossed with artistic depictions of Athena emerging from Zeus's head. In the picture, Athena was stepping out of Zeus's scalp, fully armored and brandishing a spear and the sword that still currently hung at her hip. The image reminded me, vividly, of how Chrysaor had stepped out of my neck.

"The truth of a goddess is muddled in the history humans have weaved for her," Athena said, wiping underneath her eyes with her finger. "I cannot separate what I wish to be the truth, and what the humans in my city will apply to me. But," she continued, looking back at me, "I would make amends for some truths about myself, if I could. And I would start with you, Medusa. If you would let me."

Athena stepped toward the altar once more and ran a finger along the edge of the shield she had placed near my head.

"I did have a hand in your fate. A much larger one than I should have, and by denying the truth of my actions, I have only widened the wound between us. But my intention for having that boy bring you here remains the same. I would offer you a choice, Medusa," the goddess said. "For you have not had nearly enough choices about your own life that you could control.

"You have ties to this world, through your sense of responsibility and love for those you care about, and those ties are what I was able to seize the moment Perseus removed your head. Those connections have kept you tethered to your mortality. Because of this, I could return you to this world, a mortal once again. You would not remember yourself, or any part of this life, but you would be given a second chance."

Athena paused, letting the offer sink in. "Or," she continued, "you can leave all of this behind, and go where the Fates have no power over you."

My own slack face seemed to watch me sightlessly. The eyes were closed, and I marveled at how my eyelids, the thinnest, most vulnerable stretch of skin on my body, could contain such a power. It was as if I had tied a string around the neck of a raging beast, and miraculously the beast had subsided. Now that string was trailing, just waiting for someone to pick it up.

"In either of those options," I said, "I would be abandoning this body, and my snakes, that still hold the power that can ruin mortals and gods alike. You would have me leave that ability in your hands?"

"You know better than any other what it is capable of," Athena reasoned. "Who else should carry it other than the one who brought it into the world?"

"You may have created it," I said tensely, "but I bore it through this world. This face is known as a monster amongst mortals, and it would strike fear into the hearts of all who gaze upon it. You have aided the mortals as they formed this version of me in their living nightmares. But that Medusa is a false one."

The light from the breaking dawn was creeping farther into the hall of the temple, and I watched as it reached for the altar where my head lay. I wondered if the priestesses would wake soon. It had not been so long since I had been one of them myself, but the difference between who I had been in this temple and who I was now was staggering. If any of the priestesses I had known saw what was left of me, I was sure they would have a hard time recognizing the young girl who had once lived amongst them.

Athena was silent, and I could tell from her face that she was thinking through what I had said.

"You are right," she said, finally. "But then what would you have me do, Medusa? What would allow you to release the burden I inflicted, and let you be happy?"

I thought of Echidna, and Cerberus, and sharing a meal we had made together while sitting under the shade of a tree. I thought of Dionysus, his smile loose and easy, as he made a place for me in his home. I thought of Naidah, of her gentle fingers on my lips as she gave my memories back to me. And then I thought of Euryale and Stheno, and wondered what they had done since the night I had been beheaded. I knew they would take care of each other.

And even though it hurt, I thought of Polli. Of how we had kneaded bread together in the kitchen, just a few halls away. Of her laugh as we raced through the streets of Athens. I thought of the friend I had been unable to save.

As the memories flickered by, I was filled with a desperate nostalgia for some of the shortest, calmest moments in my life. I wanted to see the people I had shared them with. I wanted to be able to watch over them and ensure that the happiness they gave to me was returned to them, over and over. And especially during the times that they struggled, and fought, and cried, I wanted to be there for them, as they had been there for me.

The bright light of the sun hit the top of the altar as I realized what I wanted.

"Athena," I said, "I have seen many things in this world. But I have not come close to seeing even a fraction of what is out there beyond these walls, or across the sea. And yet I was happy, because of the people who mattered to me. The people who knew the real Medusa, and who cared about me. She belongs to them." I smiled at that thought. "You gave me immortality when you cursed me, and now just offered to make me mortal again. Can you take me one step further, in the opposite direction? I have lived the life of a being weighed down by power, and I have suffered the consequences because of it, though I never asked for it in the first place. In all your wisdom, goddess, have I earned a place beyond this?"

I tilted my chin down to my own face, and then back up.

"Have I earned a life beyond this death?"

With a few steps, Athena closed the gap to the altar and placed her hands on either side of my face resting on the altar once more. She tilted my head so that the light caught my skin. With the golden light of the rising sun, my skin almost looked alive once again.

"You have," she said, quietly. "You have always been more than what others made you out to be, Medusa. You have earned a place, though you were always worthy of it. With all my power, I will make sure that you will be able to do as you have wished. No longer a mortal, or immortal being, you will live on as a patron goddess of those who believe in monsters, and those who need your protection."

Her next words were stern. "But know this. The mortals you spoke of, who only knew of the Medusa fashioned by fear, will never know of you."

"This is fine with me," I said.

Athena nodded. "And this?" she asked, tapping a finger against my still cheek.

"You will carry it," I decided. "Carve it onto your shield, and let it serve as a reminder that even when mortal men slay their monsters, they must not forget the power that frightened them in the first place. Let this Medusa live on in your shield, as both protection and strength." I raised my brow at the goddess. "Let it also remind you of the weight you must bear. This is not me allowing you to use my power as you please. The power is mine, and it will recognize only those who deserve it."

"I understand," Athena said.

And as the full light of the breaking day flooded the temple, Athena lifted my head and placed it over the shield. There was a flash of red, and I blinked against it, but when I opened my eyes again the shield had been transformed. Protruding from the once flat, curved surface of the shield were the curving lines of my snakes, fanned out like the sun's rays around my own face, which was baring its teeth like a vicious beast. The eyes were open, flat and silver, the power waiting beneath the surface for the moment it would be called forth. I could see that this was the face that would frighten mortals just from the sight of it.

"Are you content?" Athena asked me.

"I am," I said. "I hope you will earn her protection."

Lifting the shield by the edges, Athena found the leather strap on the inside and slung it over her back, a heavy reminder resting between her shoulders.

"And may you guard us all," the goddess of wisdom said. "Farewell, Medusa. Goddess of monstrosity, and protector of those who cannot protect themselves."

She lifted a sword-callused hand and pressed her thumb to my forehead. My eyes widened at her touch, and then I was gone.

As sure as the sun will rise again

THERE WAS SOMETHING TOUCHING my face when I woke. It was soft, but insistent, like the buzzing of a fly in your ear when you sleep. I felt the touch on my cheek, my temple, and it flickered over my skin. The touch drew away, and I heard a hiss.

I opened my eyes.

Gathered around my face, watching me expectantly like they had never left, were my snakes. I cried out, wordlessly, and reached up to cup them in my hands, for I once again had hands to hold them with. They were making excited noises, too, and ran their bodies through my fingers and squeezed me tightly.

"You're back," I said.

We, the not-voice said, *always we.*

Somehow, Athena had returned my snakes to me. I let them nuzzle my fingers as I looked around, trying to make out where I was.

It was bright, like a beach at noon, when the sand was hot and the ocean reflected the white light of the sun back into the sky. But the air here was pleasantly cool. I was sitting on the soft green ground, as if a bed of new grass had sprouted up beneath me. The ground was on a gentle slope, and I was surrounded by willowy trees that rustled and chittered in the breeze. I put my hand to the grass, unsure if anything I was seeing was real.

I was wearing a green, draping dress, tied at my hip and shoulder, revealing the deep, burnished golden skin of my leg through a slit up the side. When the fabric parted, I noticed something glinting against my leg. I lifted my knee, and the skirt of the dress slid away to reveal a delicate, wavy band of gold wrapped around my thigh, hugging my skin as gently as a lover. I looked closer. The band was patterned with the scales of my snakes, delicate marks carving out the rows and rows of scales. At the midpoint of the band, right on top of my thigh, was the thin tail below a narrow snake head, with two pinpricks of green stone for eyes.

The metal was warm when I ran a careful finger along the band. One of my snakes flicked its tongue at me to get my attention, and when I looked the snake stretched up and touched its nose to my forehead. I mimicked the snake, reaching up to feel at the same spot. My fingers met the same metal as the band around my thigh. I was wearing a golden circlet; and if it matched the one on my leg, as I thought it must, Athena had crowned me with a golden snake.

"Hello, Medusa."

I knew that voice, like the warmth in your belly after a drink of wine. I stood and turned. I kept my eyes open. With the power gone from this body, I could finally look at him while he was looking at me.

Dionysus, his boyish curls dappled with grape leaves and curving elegantly around his young face, was smiling at me. He looked me right in the eye, and I could finally see that his eyes were a deep brown, almost black, and they glinted like a star of the night sky. Dionysus opened his arms. Behind him, the peak of the mountain we stood on disappeared into the clouds.

"Welcome to Olympus, little queen."

My snakes curled joyfully around my head as I smiled, laughed, and took a step forward.

ACKNOWLEDGMENTS

MEDUSA'S STORY IS ONE of loneliness, of struggling through the world on her own against all the odds, but it is also a story of finding the people who will take her hand and stand by her side. The process of writing this book felt very similar.

I have to thank my college thesis adviser Kate Bernheimer, who was the first person to read Medusa's story and has been an adamant supporter of her ever since. Those initial meetings in Kate's office where I only had a notebook full of scribbled bullet points and a potential list of source materials are the reason this book exists.

To my agent, Melanie, I am so, so incredibly glad that Medusa and I found our way to you. Thank you for the phone calls that leave me feeling lighter and excited about what I'm writing. And thank you to Oakley, the four-legged witness for many of these calls.

And Kirsiah, my editor, I am equally grateful that I get to

work with you and am so happy to have found an editor that finds all the little bits of myth I put in just for fun. Thank you for giving Medusa another friend, like Dionysus, who only wants the best for her.

Thank you to Winnie Truong and Albert Tang for designing the most beautiful cover, and for bringing Medusa and her snakes to life. I could stare at her all day.

For my friends, my council of women, Ally, Hannah, and Kellene, I could not have made it through this multiyear journey without you, and I'm afraid you're on the hook for every book journey after this one, too. Your words of support and excitement have buoyed me through it all.

And my parents, thank you for supporting me as I pursued this dream, and for pushing me to keep writing. I love you both.

ABOUT THE AUTHOR

NATALY GRUENDER WAS BORN and raised in Arizona and found an escape from the desert heat through her library card. She studied English, creative writing, and classics at the University of Arizona and is a graduate of the Columbia Publishing Course. Giving in to the siren call of New York, Nataly booked it across the country, and when she's not working or writing she likes to pet other people's dogs and spend too much time in used bookstores. She currently lives in Brooklyn, New York.